AT THE TIME, OF COURSE, I HAD NO IDEA OF ITS SIGNIFICANCE

But it looked so out of place in that brightly colored sea of packaged sweets, I couldn't help but notice it—and pick it up.

I flipped the notebook open. It contained perhaps twenty-five blue-ruled pages, each divided into three columns. About half the pages were filled with Ramsey's meticulous hand: the left columns with two or three capital letters, the middle column with dollar amounts ranging from $500.00 to $4000.00, the right column with dates divided by day/month/year. The date of the first entry was October 28 of the previous autumn . . . the last date was the day of Ramsey's murder.

———————— ★ ————————

MADISON AVENUE MURDER

A Forthcoming Worldwide Mystery by
LIZA BENNETT

SEVENTH AVENUE MURDER

MADISON AVENUE MURDER

Liza Bennett

WORLDWIDE®

TORONTO • NEW YORK • LONDON • PARIS
AMSTERDAM • STOCKHOLM • HAMBURG
ATHENS • MILAN • TOKYO • SYDNEY

MADISON AVENUE MURDER

A Worldwide Mystery/February 1989

ISBN 0-373-26016-4

MADISON AVENUE
MURDER

ONE

IT WAS TURNING OUT to be the worst shoot I could remember in my five years at Peabody & Quinlan. And it hadn't even started yet. Already assembled at Tomi Tabor's new lower Fifth Avenue studio were one account supervisor, two account executives, three junior account people, four photography assistants, the stylist and her two assistants, the assistant art director—moi—top brass from Fanpan's Famous Fried Chichen—our newest and one of our biggest accounts—and, of course, Tomi Tabor, the highest paid still-life photographer in Manhattan. We had all been waiting for the past hour for the one person besides me and Tomi who was actually needed there: Ramsey Farnsworth, P&Q's star art director and my boss.

The bagels that the studio had laid out were beginning to harden; the cream cheese to slick over. Tempers were quickly turning as acrid as the coffee in the bank of pots that sat warming along the kitchen counter.

While the stylist fumed and account people paced, I dialed and redialed the switchboard at P&Q's Madison Avenue offices, hoping Ramsey had left a message. In between, I phoned his service, his loft, his summer house, even the men's store where he could frequently be found this time of year being measured for a new summer poplin jacket or some of his favorite combed English cotton button-downs. No luck.

"What's the story, sweetheart?" Victor Bobbin, president of Fanpan, asked, looming over me as I hung up on the start of the recorded message at Ramsey's Fire Island place: "Hi folks, we can't make it to the phone right now, but..."

"It's not like Ramsey to be late," I confessed, looking up at Victor Bobbin. A big beefy man in his early sixties, he monitored the world through a pair of pink-tinted silver-rimmed aviator glasses. His tiny bleached-denim-colored eyes blinked slowly at my response. Seemingly guileless. Perhaps even a bit stupid. The account people tended to treat him as if he were a royal personage in a parliamentary state—well-meaning, but essentially powerless—and turned all their charm on his savvier marketing director.

In the few meetings I'd been allowed to attend with Victor present, I'd watched him carefully. He certainly gave the impression of being slow-witted, easily fooled. And yet in less than fifteen years, this ex-NFL linebacker had fashioned a small truck stop on the outskirts of Macon, Georgia, into the most rapidly expanding fast-food franchise in the country. I'd decided that Victor Bobbin was not at all what he seemed.

I was beginning to think he'd come to the same conclusion about me. He'd almost immediately raised his eyes above my triple-C bustline—where most men assume my talent is hidden—and looked me straight in the eye. He must have liked the slate-gray, no-nonsense look he found there. Victor had asked my opinion more than once during a creative review and seemed satisfied with my monosyllabic responses. I had the feeling he had little patience with the slicked-back M.B.A. jargon the account people dished his way, and that he felt more comfortable with my commonsense approach to things.

"I'm sure Ramsey will be here any minute," I added, trying to sound convincing.

"I hope you're right," Victor drawled, his gaze shifting to the well-lighted set at the far end of the studio. "Or my son's going to work himself into having a full-blown asthma attack." J. J.—John Jacob—Bobbin was the unspoken reason that Victor had decided to turn over his multimillion dollar advertising budget to professionals. We hadn't known it when we—along with a half dozen other major agencies—pitched the account, but J.J. was responsible for the previous Fanpan commercial that featured a plucked chicken chirping blissfully away in what looked to be a roasting pan.

This grisly idea, combined with the terrible production quality of the television commercial, had put Fanpan well on the way to becoming a national laughingstock. I think Victor had chosen P&Q to salvage the situation because we were the only agency not to criticize J.J.'s debacle of a campaign. Whatever Victor's strengths, he had a tremendous parental soft spot for his spoiled, hyperactive, slightly loony thirty-year-old son. J.J. was Bobbin's only child.

"What do *you* know about it?" we heard Victor's precious offspring wheeze at Tomi, our stylist, and the half dozen other people who hovered around the painstakingly arranged still life twenty yards or so down the room. Numerous lights and deflectors, backdrops, stepladders, cameras and director's chairs surrounded a simple dining room table draped with a red-and-white-checkered cloth, where a box of Fanpan's Famous Fried Chicken waited to be photographed.

Neither Victor nor I could make out Tomi's reply, but we both saw J.J. grab the bone-handled serving fork that had been placed beside the filled-to-overflowing take-out bucket and thrust it deep into the heart of the order. The entire table shuddered; steel knives and forks jumped under the impact. A pepper shaker wobbled and fell.

"For chrissakes, J.J.!" cried Tomi Tabor. "We spent half the morning getting that damned poultry stacked just right." Though he was the best still-life photographer in advertising, Tomi was far from the calmest. His breath was usually sweet with the smell of antacid tablets. He tugged at what was left of his hair with the kind of tenacity lawn lovers pull crabgrass. But the fluttery high-pitched nervousness under which he operated helped produce some of the most perfect little cameos of packaged goods in the industry.

"Are you challenging my artistic input, buddy?" J.J. demanded, his wide freckled face flushed to the roots of his cropped fuzzy orange hair. At six foot five, with a clumsy but dangerous strength to his well-filled frame, J.J. was not the sort of person short pencil-thin Tomi would ever tangle with. And yet without Tomi's direction and Ramsey's supervision—where the hell *was* that man?—the Bobbins might as well be back in Macon, shooting their ads with an Instamatic.

"Damn it," I muttered, starting toward the set. I took four or five steps before Victor caught up with me, grabbing my elbow.

"Let me handle this. It's my problem," he said, sighing so deeply that I wondered how many times a day he had to step in on behalf of his son. "You just round up that art director of yours," he added. "And fast."

My boss, Ramsey Farnsworth, relished the role of prima donna. He had about him the air of a man for whom the world would wait—if he so desired it. In fact, I'd never known him to be more than five minutes late for an appointment. Beneath his bonhomie and carefree veneer was a hard-boiled business sense earned through a quarter-century struggle up the spirit-crunching creative ladder of Madison Avenue. In the five years I'd worked for him, I had rarely seen him slip in his ascent.

The past few months, however, he hadn't been himself. Ramsey, who stamped his indelible signature on every design idea that came out of his group, had let me come up with all of the concepts for the Fanpan campaign. And he'd hardly glanced at the finished comps. Ramsey, who prided himself on ten-hour workdays, had begun to come in at noon and vanish from the office at unexpected moments. But worst of all, Ramsey the jovial, Ramsey the fun loving, Ramsey the outrageous, had turned dark, inward, unreadable. The past week had been a particularly bad one for Ramsey's black moods and disappearing acts. Finally last night, as I was leaving—having worked until nine-thirty to get the Fanpan shoot ready—I'd noticed he was in his office and decided to confront him. I found him seated at his enormous antique oak desk, leaning over to get something out of a drawer. He didn't see me come in.

"Ramsey?"

"Yes?" His head shot up, his face red with the rush of blood. The famous bow tie sat slightly askew above the wide, fashionably striped expanse of chest and belly. Though unabashedly overweight, Ramsey's beautiful asparagus-green silk jacket fit with the delicate elegance only a custom tailor could provide. His large round bald head gleamed like a rising harvest moon. He seemed surprised, even shocked to see me there.

"I think everything's set for tomorrow, Ramsey."

"Oh? Um . . . what about tomorrow?"

I was ready to scream, *What the hell do you mean, what about tomorrow? We've only been slaving for a month to get ready for it!* when I noted his hands shaking. Whatever his problem was, my heart went straight out to him.

"The Fanpan shoot," I reminded him gently.

"Yes, of course," he ad-libbed. "So we're all set, are we? Good girl. Wonderful work. See you there, then. Tomi's, isn't it?"

"What's the matter, Ramsey?" I blurted out, my voice cracking under the strain. He had always been so willing to listen to me and ready to help. I owed him so much; and yet it was a debt he made impossible for me to repay. The most giving of men, and the last one to take.

"Nothing. Bit of a cold coming on, perhaps. Haven't felt quite up to par the past week or so. But don't you worry, Peggy dear, I'll be there tomorrow. At the helm.''

Except he wasn't. And it was getting past the point where I could make up any more excuses for his lateness. The shoot would have to be canceled. New arrangements made. The Fanpan account jeopardized before we'd even started. Once again, but without much hope of success, I dialed Ramsey's number.

The wonderful staccato noise that greeted me was more moving than Beethoven's Fifth and the *Messiah* rolled into one. I cupped the receiver to my chest and cried, "I've got a busy signal at his loft! He must be there. I bet he's trying to reach us." I hung up immediately, smiling as Tomi, Victor, J.J. and the rest converged on the reception desk.

In those first few seconds, I felt the weight of the morning lift from my shoulders. I glanced around at the people I worked with—the account group, Tomi, even the Bobbins—and felt a warm wave of affection and hope rush through me. As we waited I let my gaze stray over the sunny jumble of Tomi's huge new studio. Behind the immediate set, which was closed off by plywood dining room walls, were the ruins of other sets, past shoots and the standard props every major studio has on hand: the grand piano, the book-lined den, the chrome-and-rosewood bar, the sleek minimalist bathroom. Here, in bits and pieces, was America's dream house. At that moment, I thought it beautiful. It would be a long time before it looked that way to me again.

"Why hasn't he called?" Tomi demanded when the phone didn't ring after a few minutes. "Try him again."

I dialed. Almost immediately the phone was picked up.

"Ramsey?" I cried.

"No, it's Ted. Who is this? Peg? Oh God, Peg, the worst thing has happened. The worst. It's awful. Oh God."

"What is it?" I demanded, hearing Ramsey's longtime lover, Teddy Maynard, start to sob. "Ted! Tell me what's happened!"

"He's dead! He's been murdered. I'm looking at him now. On the kitchen floor. Oh God, he's been . . . all carved up."

TWO

PEABODY & QUINLAN'S headquarters on Madison Avenue rise fifty-eight stories up in a seamless wall of pressed black granite and plate glass. Old-timers at P&Q claim that cantankerous Peabody built the soulless monolith as a kind of last word on Quinlan, whose taste had been exquisite and who had passed away before construction began. Some even say that Peabody buried his partner beneath the tiles of the men's room on the fortieth floor. But this is all hearsay. Both founding principals are long gone now. And the new breed of corporate M.B.A. admen who have taken over the company have no time for idle reminiscence.

They have their Profit and Loss statements, Travel and Entertainment expenses and competing members of the American Association of Advertising Agencies to worry about. And after Ramsey Farnsworth's murder, they had plenty more on their plates. None of it very tasty.

Though the *New York Times* handled Ramsey's death with aplomb in a glowing obit and a few bland inches on the murder in the Metropolitan Section, the *Daily News* carried the story with a twenty-four-point headline, "Top Art Director Diced in SoHo," on page 3. Peabody & Quinlan's stock dropped four points in one afternoon of trading, and two of P&Q's most important accounts announced agency reviews—the first step toward bolting.

Suddenly doors slammed shut all over the agency. From the senior officers who met in the red-and-beige-toned luxury of the penthouse suite, to the secretaries and assistants who congregated around the banks of Xerox machines—the only subject on the agenda was Ramsey.

Thursday morning, a week to the day of the murder, Fanpan's executive committee met in a closed-door session of its own. Rumors were flying about the Bobbins' reaction to the murder: they were pulling the account immediately; they were putting P&Q on notice; they were sticking by us. But gossip is the stuff of agency life, and as long as the reports remained conflicting, I decided not to take any of it to heart. That particular organ was giving me enough trouble already. Ramsey's death had left a gaping hole right in the middle of it.

He'd been more than my boss. More than my mentor. He had been the life raft that had rescued me from swirling hopelessly in currents that encircled my whirlpool of a mother. He had managed to save me—and still keep us all friends. During the past five years, Ramsey Farnsworth had been the one thing Theodora and I had managed to agree upon; we both adored him.

I remember telling her when I first got the job that I'd never met a more witty, urbane individual. "Wonderful, darling," Theodora had responded, though as usual her mind was on something else. We were standing shoulder to shoulder in the studio she'd rented that summer in Provincetown. The rear of the huge room was filled with the contorted iron works of the previous tenant, a sculptor, and I remember wondering how Theo could concentrate with those hideous encroaching shapes. But then, she rarely noticed her surroundings. Except when they started to hem her in, and then we simply moved on to the next landscape: a town house in London, a villa on the Côte d'Azur, a château near Lucerne. One could live that way when one was Theodora Goodenough, America's most acclaimed abstract expressionist painter. It was a little less easy to handle when one was Theo's daughter.

"He's so willing to teach me, too," I had rushed on, still glowing from my first full week under Ramsey's wing. "He says I have innate talent. *Innate*, Theo, not just acquired." She had sent me to the finest art schools of whatever country we were then in residence: L'École des Beaux Arts in Paris, the Pennsylvania Academy, the Chicago Arts School. I suppose it must have been a disappointment to her when I decided against fine art in favor of graphic design. I'm sure she viewed my work as tame—child's play when compared to hers. Her wild turbulences of symbol and metaphor. The bold clashing horizons of color. Still, she seemed genuinely pleased when I got the job at P&Q.

"Bring the man up with you next weekend," Theo had suggested. Then, to my surprise, she had stopped staring at her room-size canvas and turned her hard gray gaze on me. "My Peg's not in love, is she?"

"No, Mother." I blushed, reverting to a term for her she had long ago encouraged me to drop. "He's almost twice my age."

"Don't let that stop you, dear," Theo had advised kindly. "At your age, it wouldn't hurt to have a man of some experience underfoot. Let me see, when I was twenty-seven, I had a marvelous fling with Picasso. He must have been in his seventies then. I told you about that one, didn't I?"

"Yes, Theo," I had replied quickly, not wanting to hear more. My mother, as most of the educated world knows, is a great believer in free love. She married Rudolph Goodenough, then her dealer, when she became pregnant with me, only to divorce him as soon as she had provided me with a legal surname. Rudi had died before I was old enough to really remember him, but I'd mourned him disproportionately all my life. Or perhaps more to the point, I'd mourned the fact of not having a real father. Theo's endless succession of lovers did not count. Maybe it was that need that drew me so strongly to Ramsey, though nothing Oedipal was involved. I decided to immediately set Theo straight on that score.

"Oh, his age doesn't bother me, either," I replied. "It's the fact he's gay." I made this pronouncement cavalierly, hoping to impress my mother with my sophistication in such matters.

"I see," she said, turning back to her work. "Well, they do make the most marvelous friends."

And, as usual, Theodora was right. Ramsey had been the best friend I'd ever had. He was the first man I ever met who liked Theo, but preferred me. Perhaps because he was something of a star in his own right, he never let Theo's brilliance blind him. They had been friends ever since that first visit to Provincetown, but he saw her faults—especially as they affected me.

"You're a rare hybrid," Ramsey had told me after I'd been working with him for a few months. "You've the makings of a damn good art director, Peggy, and yet you display none of the hysterical traits common to diva designers. Sometimes I fear that you actually like this madhouse."

"I do, Ramsey," I admitted. "It doesn't seem crazy to me." After years of tumbling around in Theo's wake, the frequently pressured pace of the agency seemed almost soothing. The gentle rattle of the morning coffee cart. The metallic purr of the intercom. I cherished all the little routines of office life. They represented the kind of domestic order I'd never known growing up.

And I was ridiculously proud of my position. I took pleasure in doing my own filing. Sizing my own art. I found even the dreariest chores of assistant art directorship rewarding in a way few people could understand. I was earning my keep. I was doing something. I was not just Theodora Goodenough's daughter.

But all this was in jeopardy now. Advertising was like politics. Most cabinets were swept clean with the departing head of state.

"Peg, they want you in the conference room," Ruthie, Ramsey's secretary, announced somberly outside my door. The skin around her eyes and nostrils was chapped from the crying jag she'd been on for the past week.

"Right," I said, getting out of my chair. I'd never been summoned to an executive committee meeting before. And Ruthie's sad sympathetic expression made me wish I wasn't being asked in now. I stared around the cluttered room that had been my refuge for nearly half a decade. Tissue roughs were pinned to the corkboard that covered one wall. Stands of rapidiographs and 4H pencils squatted in a colorful jumble on a low table beside my main drawing board. The finished comp of the take-out bucket of Fanpan chicken we'd never gotten around to shooting decorated the door. I doubted that I would ever see the ad finished now.

The last thing my mind registered as I left the room was the latest issue of *Ad Age* with Ramsey's picture on the front. The photo was of a much younger, slimmer Ramsey. Smiling. A six-point black rule framed it. It was a bad omen, I decided as I started down the corridor. Ramsey was gone. I was going to be next.

THE CONFERENCE ROOM was the one we used for our most important presentations. The carpet was a lush field of burgundy. The walls were a nubbly eggshell-colored fabric on which a tier of award-winning print ads hung in simple Plexiglas frames. Track lighting from the recessed ceiling illuminated the ads with reverent halos. An audio/video console was elegantly hidden behind a sliding wall of lacquered walnut. And a trolley with a silver urn of coffee and a tray of cookies waited at the far end of the room. It would be Damon's coffee and Mrs. Goodie's Cookies, I knew from past experience. Whenever possible, the agency liked to promote the products it represented, even though Damon coffee tasted like pencil grindings.

"Good of you to come at such short notice," one of the three men at the head of the table greeted me in a rich bass tone that perfectly matched the room. "Close the door, please, Peg," he added, and I did.

I knew Phillip Ebert as well as anyone at P&Q did. He was our group president, a man in his early sixties with the rough-hewn handsomeness of Clint Eastwood and the charm and manners of a career diplomat. Rarely without a smile or the right turn of phrase, he always seemed to be delighted to run into me in the corridor or on the elevator. It took me a year or two to realize that he gave everyone this impression. *Madison Avenue* had dubbed him "Mr. Clean," because he'd done so much to successfully promote P&Q as the most conservative and all-American of the big agencies. Ramsey's murder, I guessed, had dealt that image a painful blow.

"You know Mark Rollings, of course," Phillip said, nodding to the man on his left, "and Spencer Guilden."

"Yes," I replied, careful not to meet Spencer's eye.

"Won't you sit down, Peg?" Mark asked, gesturing to one of the burnt-sienna-colored leather chairs that faced the three of them across the conference table. Mark was the account supervisor on Fanpan, a paunchier version of Phillip. Though only in his early forties, he had a slightly embalmed appearance, as if someone had drained away his vital fluids and filled him with quantities of Shiney Brite, the liquid cleanser account he'd managed before Fanpan.

Twenty years of account work had worn away whatever uniqueness his character had once displayed. He had learned to succeed, as so many account people had, by holding no real opinions of his own. He was skilled at sniffing out which way the wind was going to blow, what creative approach a client would like or hate.

I wouldn't have minded so much if my firing squad had been limited to Phillip and Mark, I thought numbly, taking my assigned place. It was adding Spencer to the lineup that made the business so hateful. Though as group V.P. it was natural enough for him to be there. And, of course, the other two didn't know what existed between us.

"Coffee?" Phillip asked. No one else was risking it, so I declined. I kept my gaze glued to Phillip, trying to blinker Spencer out of my line of vision. But I felt him there all the same. How could any full-blooded female not be affected by that ash-blond baby-soft hair, the nose and lips that belonged on a Grecian urn, eyes the shade of blazing aqua found only on Caribbean travel posters? At twenty-nine, Spencer Guilden was the youngest man ever to be named group V.P. at P&Q.

The only thing, in fact, that kept him from absolute perfection was his height. Without his shoes, Spencer was a quarter of an inch shorter than me. As it happened, we frequently had a good deal more off than just shoes when we were alone together. It was against all P&Q personnel guidelines, but Spencer and I had been lovers for more than a year. And secretly engaged for nearly a month. We hadn't even told our parents yet, because if word somehow leaked out around P&Q, one of us would have to go—and neither of us was quite ready.

"I suppose you know what this is about?" Phillip asked kindly.

"Yes, I guess I do," I answered bravely, crunching my hands together under the table.

"Tell us, then," Mark Rollings demanded. I turned to stare at him, my jaw dropping, taken aback by the cruelty of his suggestion. It was like having to explain that I should be taken out and shot. I decided he was sadistic as well as being spineless and that I might as well get the damned business over with. "You've got to let me go," I blurted out. "You've hired a new art director who wants to clean house."

"You see?" Phillip replied, turning to Mark. "She doesn't have anything to do with it."

"I didn't really think she did," Mark answered hurriedly. "But we had every right to make sure," he added sanctimoniously.

"To do?" I asked weakly, my gaze moving from Mark to Phillip and then finally to Spencer. "With what?" Though he hadn't said a word since I'd walked in, Spencer had been sending me strong mental vibes. Warning signs, I thought, our gazes locking. But almost immediately he looked away.

"My dear," Phillip answered, pushing back his chair. He pinched the crease at the knee of one dark blue pin-striped pant leg and crossed it gingerly over the other. "We had a meeting this morning with the owners of Fanpan—Bobbin and his son. I believe you've met them?''

I nodded.

"We're quite concerned about the account, for reasons you can well imagine. The recent publicity has been, to put it mildly, distasteful. The murder, the newspaper reports of Ramsey's, uh, alternate life-style, have seriously damaged our rather clean-cut credibility. Some of our more conservative clients have taken drastic measures. Did you know that Woodles Noodles has decided to go over to NHV&R?''

"No," I answered. The manufacturer of America's number one egg noodle was P&Q's fourth largest account. No one had to tell me what their defection would do to our billings.

"So it's absolutely essential that we keep our existing clients happy," Mark added unnecessarily.

I didn't respond. Let's get to the point, I thought. I'm fired.

"That's why we're forced to take seriously Victor Bobbin's highly unusual request that you be promoted to head art director," Phillip announced, rubbing his forehead wearily.

"Excuse me?"

"You heard correctly, young lady," Mark replied in a tone tinged with equal measures of dislike and envy. "You're being offered the opportunity of a lifetime."

"You want me to take Ramsey's place?" I demanded. It was simply unbelievable. There were lines around the block for that position. Advertising stars with twenty years' experience begging to work at P&Q. Ramsey's job represented one of the few established pinnacles of success on Madison Avenue; something he had struggled his entire career to reach—and retain.

"No, *we* don't want you to," Phillip corrected me. "The client does. And we simply can't afford to put this account in jeopardy right now. So it's yours."

"But . . . what if I can't handle it?" I demanded somewhat wildly. "What if I say no?" They were asking a toddler to take a chance on the high wire.

"That's certainly an option," Spencer stated abruptly. I turned to him, hoping he could offer me some unspoken counsel. But the liquid depths of his eyes were distant and fathomless.

"Sleep on it, Peg," Phillip suggested, sighing as he leaned back and stretched. Obviously he had other problems to address that day. I had become a solution in his mind, though very likely a stopgap one.

"Well . . . okay," I said, rising to go. No one bid me good-bye.

Ramsey had long ago warned me that creative people were as disposable as Kleenex in most companies. Like nomads, they followed the great herds of the major accounts, trekking from one big agency to the next. Fate was handing me a front-runner position, one step ahead of the crush and dust of the stampede. My God, I thought. Ramsey's silent cynical laughter followed me as I started back down the hall.

THREE

"I KNOW because I was *there*, Peg, in the room with them," Spencer said. "All Victor Bobbin wants is someone to baby-sit his moron of a son. Can't you see that? If you would just stand back for half a second and consider your overall career path, you'd see that the job is nothing but a dead end."

Career paths. Advancement strategies. Long-term employment objectives. These terms had a glamour and depth for Spencer they didn't have for me. He had analyzed the Fanpan dilemma, probably even run a few spreadsheets through his IBM, and concluded that I shouldn't accept the offer. I, on the other hand, was overcome by a blind subjective desire—having nothing to do with business, really—to take on the challenge. I felt Ramsey's memory had to be served, and he simply wouldn't have wanted a stranger sitting in his black leather Eames chair.

We had met after work at our usual spot in front of the Quik Copy counter in the Lexington Avenue tunnel leading to Grand Central. It was almost six o'clock. Three hours since I'd met with the executive committee. Less than an hour before I was to meet Spencer's family for the first time. The Guildens.

Yes, *the* Guildens. Mother Miriam, whose eternally tan, gauntly wealthy face can be found at least once a month smiling toothily off the society page behind Pat Buckley or just to the left of Bill Blass. Father Jacob, the Manhattan federal prosecutor who conservatives are hailing as the best thing that's happened to law and order since John Wayne—and who's being cited as a possible mayoral candidate in the next election. Brothers Louis and Martin, senior partners in the Guilden, Guilden & Guilden law firm. Spencer, the youngest, was to have been the fourth Guilden to grace the firm's letterhead. His failure to get into Yale Law was something that his father still hadn't forgiven him for, despite Spencer's M.B.A. from Harvard and V.P. title at P&Q. Parental problems, we'd long ago decided, were one of the many things we shared.

"But you just admitted J.J.'s a little off," I yelled over the rush-hour din as we inched our way into the main terminal. Though it was only the middle of June, already a heat wave had settled over the city—and was refusing to budge. The air was thick with an aroma peculiar to Manhattan summers: a blend of hot dog mustard and exhaust fumes. "Don't you think I can handle him? I've dealt with some winners in my time."

"It's not the same thing when you're in charge, Peg," Spencer replied, biting down on his full lower lip. He'd loosened his crimson Harvard tie, and his hair was falling into damp commas along his neck, yet somehow Spencer still emanated that crisp corporate orderliness that drew me so strongly to him. I loved the laundered smell his monogrammed white buttondowns gave off. The impeccable symmetry of classic blue blazer and spotless summer chinos. "It's easy enough to make nice when you're a cute little assistant," he went on. "But there's nothing like having some authority to make a client's hackles rise."

The heat was dense, acrid with smoke from a nearby track fire. Through the haze the crowd appeared fractionally distorted, as though everyone were clamoring through a mirrored fun house. Suddenly I felt more than just my vision waver. I grabbed Spencer's elbow and let him lead me across the sweltering sea of commuters.

"You don't think I can handle it," I stated flatly when we'd reached the quieter tunnel that led down to the Lexington Avenue IRT.

"That's not true," Spencer protested as we pushed through the turnstiles and rushed down the stairs to catch the departing subway. We stood, panting, face-to-face, kept from falling only by the solid wall of commuters that pressed around us. Spencer put his arms around me and said, "I think you can do anything you put your mind to. The question is, why? You

know damn right well that we're not going to be able to keep
our relationship under wraps much longer. And when word
leaks out, you're going to have to start shopping yourself
around.''

"Why am I the one who has to go?" I demanded petu-
lantly, all the while enjoying the sensation of Spencer's brass
buttons scraping against my breasts every time we swayed toward each other.

"We've gone over all this before, Peg," Spencer replied patiently. "Ebert as much as promised me McMahon's slot when
he takes early retirement next fall. You don't get promoted to
senior V.P. at P&Q every day, Peg," he added proudly.

"Or to head art director," I retorted over the squeal of brakes
as we rolled into the Thirty Fourth Street station.

The Guildens' duplex on Gramercy Park reminded me of an
apartment Theo and I had lived in one August in Paris when
the owner, a famous opera impressario, made her annual pil-
grimage to the Riviera. The high-ceilinged, elaborately corn-
iced rooms were painted shades of cream and ivory. Heavily
framed oils, including one I though might be an original
Gainsborough, decorated the walls. French windows opened
onto the park. Oriental rugs and set pieces from the reigns of
the various Louises were on full display. But beneath the studied effects and obvious luxury, I felt nothing personal or wel-
coming about the place.

"Spencer, at last!" A tall bronzed statue swept toward us
across the living room. As she neared, taut lines around her eyes
and a long emaciated neck gave away her age. Miriam, Spencer's mother, wore a flowery diaphanous gown and the rigid
blond pageboy that seemed to be the signature hairstyle of society matrons everywhere.

"This is Peg, Mother," Spencer announced, and on cue she
hugged me briefly to her, kissing the air next to my cheek. My
nostrils filled with the sweet pure smell of Joy.

"Delighted," she cried, grabbing my hand and leading me
into the room. "Spencer's here with his friend," she announced to the half dozen people who eyed us expectantly from
various lounging positions on the priceless sofas. "Theodora
Goodenough's daughter, you know."

"Hi," I chirped, too brightly, fighting the disappointment I
felt at being introduced—here of all places—as my mother's
daughter. Stupidly, I'd assumed Spencer would have ex-

plained in advance my extreme sensitivity on the subject. But then I realized that he probably had more than enough to explain about me as it was. Even the brief introductions I was given to the two women Spencer's older brothers had married, convinced me that I would never be considered prime Guilden in-law material.

Cecilia, Louis's wife, was reed thin, ash blonde, swathed in an orange-sorbet-tinted Calvin Klein sheath, and the daughter of a microchip mogul. Tracy, introduced to me as Martin's wife, also verged on the anorexic. Her short platinum hair was perfectly coordinated with a blazing white-on-white Perry Ellis halter dress. Her family came from Rhode Island. The way she said it gave me the impression that they owned the state. Both women sported beautiful tans set off by gleaming fortunes in orthodontic work.

I'd inherited Theo's strong horsey teeth with the same gap between the two top front incisors. I also had her wiry combative coal-black hair and blue-white skin, which got painfully blotched at the slightest exposure to sunlight. Where I came by my full-breasted, hausfrau figure, bony Theo could only speculate, since she never took the time to meet my father's relations.

Theo's taste in clothes had always run to the wild primary colors and heavy brocades you saw reflected in her paintings. She loved big chunks of jewelry, bangles and gold earrings the size of bracelets. From earliest childhood, she encouraged me to dress in her image: a wild-haired little gypsy girl in a patchwork dress of silk and velvet.

Though I'd tried during the past few years to shake Theo's influence over me, I still found my style of dress running frighteningly close to her own. The night I met the Guildens, I was wearing my favorite Norma Kamali jungle print, a black-and-bright-gold affair that tended to accentuate my already overly dramatic cleavage. As I wrapped the belt around my waist that morning, I wondered briefly if the dress was quite the right thing to wear when meeting in-laws for the first time. That evening in the Guildens' living room, I knew for certain that it wasn't.

"Hello, hello." Louis Guilden, Spencer's oldest brother, smiled at my bustline. Martin, his eyes flickering behind horn-rimmed glasses, took in my jungly length a bit more subtly.

"Ah, the painter," he pronounced, as if by way of explanation.

"No, my mother's the artist," I replied. "I work at P&Q with Spencer. I'm a designer."

"Of course," Martin sniffed, clearly not seeing much distinction between the two activities. "Well, so nice to meet you."

Jacob Guilden eyed me coldly when Spencer introduced us. He was taller than his sons, gaunt and graying but still aggressively handsome in the Gregory Peck mold. With the deep modulated tones of a public speaker, he announced, "It's getting to be quite a scandal, isn't it?"

"Excuse me?" I demanded, blushing deeply. I wasn't in the least prepared for this frontal attack on my relationship with his son.

"You are the girl who worked for that art director," Jacob demanded. "The recent homicide?"

"Oh, well, yes," I answered, regaining some composure. "His name was Ramsey Farnsworth, and he was—"

"A homosexual, I understand," Louis interrupted.

"Well, actually, I suppose..." I trailed off.

"It's hardly a secret," Spencer answered smoothly. "Farnsworth was gay. What's the big deal?"

"So uninformed, little brother," Louis chided sarcastically. "The gay rights coalition is about ready to storm the mayor's office, demanding the murder investigation get top priority at One Police Plaza. They see it as a case of discrimination. There's even talk about mobilizing other minority groups."

"That's right," Martin put in. "The scuttlebutt we're getting is that city hall is strong-arming the force to come up with some answers. Quick."

"As I said," Jacob reaffirmed, "it's turning out to be quite the little scandal."

"But it's only been a week," I pointed out. "Surely it takes longer than that to solve a murder. Why the pressure?"

"Ah..." Louis murmured, lowering his eyes and clicking the ice cubes around in his white wine spritzer.

"Hmm," Martin said with a sigh, smiling to himself.

"Well," Jacob pronounced, his voice scraping new depths of authority. "It's time for dinner."

I was seated to the right of Miriam, who was at the foot of the table, and next to Martin. Spencer was placed directly across from me, though the forest of candelabras and flowers made him seem miles away. Surprisingly, the discussion of Ramsey's murder continued to dominate the conversation. It was the men who led the discussion. Cecilia and Tracy kept up a low sublevel discourse of their own at the other end of the table. I caught the words *Bloomingdale's* and *bulimia* at one point, but little else. Miriam and I quietly went about the business of dismantling our salmon fillets and Cornish game hens. Miriam also put a good deal of energy into downing quantities of the Pouilly-Fuisse.

"It's just the sort of issue a lot of borderline radical groups can get behind," Louis was telling his father with, what seemed to me, odd enthusiasm. "He clearly had made a success of himself. Apparently, he even made quite considerable contributions to various charities, including the children's fund. Can you imagine? Anyway, what I mean is, here was a working, caring citizen, with one little kink in his character. Does this give the city the right to walk away from the criminal act of his murder?"

"I like it, Lou," Jacob replied, cutting vigorously through the spine of his game hen, "and it has just the undertones we're looking for right now, don't you think? It's generally the incumbent, after all, who gets the credit for supporting gay rights. Hmm, yes, I think we can really use this."

"Excuse me." I turned to Martin. "Do you know what they're talking about? What has this to do with Ramsey's murder?"

"Ramsey?" Martin replied, his owlish eyes widening. "Oh, you mean the victim?"

"Ramsey Farnsworth," I explained. "He was my boss. He was a close friend, as well."

"Let's not get into that now, Peg," Spencer suggested from across the table.

"Why not?" Martin demanded. "Your girlfriend is bound to get involved if all this heats up."

"If all what—" I put my fork down "—heats up?" The neatly browned mound of poultry suddenly seemed an enormous amount of food for a summer dinner.

"Father's hoping to get some mileage out of the murder in his law-and-order crusade," Martin explained. "It could bolster his position with the liberals if he runs for mayor next year."

"If?" I asked, staring down the table at the upright pin-striped senior Guilden. It didn't matter to him who had been killed, I thought grimly, as long as the victim fit the appropriate demo. I thought of Ramsey as I'd last seen him the night before the Fanpan shoot. He'd been flustered. Distracted. It occurred to me for the first time, but with a chilling finality, that Ramsey hadn't simply been murdered. *Someone* had killed him. But who and why were questions that seemed to me to be none of the Guildens' business.

"Okay, *when* he runs," Martin agreed, smiling slyly. "But that's a family secret, understand?"

"Of course," I agreed, my mind on other things. Then it struck me. "If your father is hoping to make an issue of Ramsey's murder not getting solved, then . . . you all hope it won't be."

"I wouldn't go quite that far," Martin responded, taking a sip of wine. "At least not publicly."

"But he was a *friend* of mine!" I cried. Various Guildens stared down the table at me. "I can't believe you'd even imply such a thing. It's just awful."

"No, it's not," Martin objected. "It's just politics."

Later, when Spencer walked me over to Park Avenue to find a taxi, he apologized for the way his father and brothers had acted.

"You understand now what I'm up against?" he demanded. "They're positively ruthless when it comes to this mayoral thing. And because I'm not a part of it, I barely exist for them. You saw how they treated me."

"But you still could have helped me stick up for Ramsey," I retorted. Though we walked arm in arm, we each were nursing different isolated grudges. "They talked about him as if he were a . . . a thing. Not a person. I don't think they even heard me when I said he was a friend."

"Yeah, babe, I'm sorry," Spencer apologized again. "You can't very well pick and choose your family. Not the way you can your lovers."

We stopped in the shadow of a town house, and Spencer drew me to him. We kissed long and searchingly. He is my bulwark, I told myself as we rocked together in the humid darkness. The world is a frightening, unpredictable place. With him I am secure, stable. It's amazing how thoroughly you can fool yourself, just because you like the way somebody kisses.

FOUR

THE STRANGER EMERGED from the shadows of the brownstone as soon as the taxi pulled away. I saw him approaching out of the corner of my eye and started to run up the steps, fumbling through my bag for my keys.

"Hey, lady, wait!" he cried as I slammed the front door behind me. I took the steps two at a time, the three flights up to my floor passing in a blur of fire-engine-red banisters and drab gray walls. Footfalls echoed below. Sweating, breathless, I tore down the long corridor to my front door, besting by at least several seconds the standing Olympic record for the hundred-meter run.

I rattled my keys, jammed one into the lock. Then, without even turning the cylinder, the door swung open and lights I had not left on in the living room flooded the hallway.

I walked in. The place was a shambles. Drawers ripped open. Theo's paintings were torn from the walls. Strangers in dark blue uniforms formed an uncomfortable little clique in the middle of the living room. Millie Cantwell, my neighbor from across the hall, sat perched on the edge of the couch, my cat, Picasso, curled in her lap and a teacup resting on her knee.

"Hello, dear," Millie greeted me cheerily. "I'd get up but dear Picasso has just now drifted off to sleep. It's taken him ages." Most people in our building had decided that Millie was a little batty. She wore the same bright purple hand-knitted beret and yellow "smile" button year-round. But despite her eccentricities, I found Millie one of the few genuinely selfless people I'd ever known. A retired librarian, she devoted her waking hours to drumming up funds for the homeless from various crowded street corners in Midtown. She spent her nights communicating with what she called "the other side." Ouija boards, tarot cards, tea leaves—she dabbled in a bit of everything and was constantly trying to rope me into a séance or palm reading.

"What happened?" I demanded, but I didn't exactly need Millie's psychic powers to figure things out. I'd been lucky in the five years I'd lived in Manhattan. I hadn't been assaulted or mugged. In fact, nobody'd even bothered to pinch my wallet. Until now.

"I heard an almighty racket about an hour ago," Millie explained, gently caressing Picasso's molting forehead. "At first I thought you were tackling your Jane Fonda cassette again—then I heard a slam, crash, bang and footsteps running down the hall. I poked my head out—and saw your door standing open."

"We thought it was a B and E at first," explained a red-headed policeman in the group around Millie. "Just your typical break and enter. Then Millie here explained how you're connected with the Farnsworth case and all, so we—"

"That's enough, Tom." The man who had just followed me up the stairs now slumped against my front doorjamb, breathing raggedly. "You and the boys show Miss Cantwell home. Then wait for me in the squad car until I call you." He stomped into the room, a tall man in a rumpled, cheaply made seersucker suit. He had a long pale face. His dark deep-set eyes were heavy with fatigue. A droplet of sweat hung from his prominent, haphazardly molded nose.

"Yessir," Tom barked, and the men started to make their way through the clutter. "May I help you up, Millie?" Tom asked politely, reaching for the teacup.

"Thank you, dear," Millie agreed, rousing Picasso. My cat stretched, then stalked insolently off her lap and curled up again at the far end of the couch.

"Peggy, when you're through with the detective here," Millie announced nodding at the man who was now wiping at the sweat with the back of his hand, "I want you and Picasso to come spend the night with us."

"Thanks, Millie," I replied. "But you know how Picasso acts with Carlos and Pepe." My tough streetwise stray tended to turn particularly ugly around Millie's fluffy, pampered Persians.

"Better take Miss Cantwell up on her offer," the detective advised. He glanced around the ravaged room. "Your locks are gone. And we'll be poking around here most of the night, anyway."

I followed his gaze. The extent of the damage began to sink in. It was going to take me days, maybe even weeks, to get the place back in order again. I sighed. "Okay, Millie. Thanks. We'll come by later."

The door slammed shut behind them and then fell open again, my locks dangling like pockets turned inside out.

"Detective Dante Cursio," the man introduced himself, holding out a well-worn leather wallet that displayed a badge. "You're quite a sprinter."

"Only when I'm being chased." I confided. "I ran the slowest mile ever recorded in my grade school." I examined his identification with interest.

"Which one?" Cursio asked, flipping the wallet shut and tucking it into the inside pocket of his jacket. I caught a glimpse of leather strap and the dull steel stub of a revolver. I instinctively took a step back.

"Which what?" I asked, watching him ease himself without invitation into my favorite living room chair.

"Grade school," he replied. He patted his breast pocket, then fished out a pen. "The one in Switzerland . . . or Germany?"

"If you know that much about me, you probably already know which one." I sat down on the far edge of the couch, pulling a reluctant Picasso into my arms. During my seventh-grade year, Theo had abruptly moved us from Lausanne to Hamburg, declaring the Alps were making her claustrophobic. It was unnerving to know that a complete stranger had such a fix on my life, but I was determined not to let this show. "Congratulations to your research department," I added brightly.

"Do my own legwork," Cursio replied. "I've been boning up on everyone who worked with Ramsey Farnsworth." He absently patted his breast pocket again, like a reformed smoker who couldn't get over the habit of reaching for his cigarettes. "You got a piece of paper I could use? I keep forgetting to get new batteries for my tape recorder."

"Shouldn't you carry spares or something?" I asked, getting up and carrying Picasso with me to my antique oak rolltop. It was open. The intruder had gone through my bills. My American Express notice had been ripped in half. For some reason this minor bit of vandalism struck me—much more than the larger havoc that surrounded me—as the ultimate assault on my privacy. I leaned against the desk and felt tears burn along my eyelids.

"You okay?" Cursio called from across the room.

"Yeah," I responded. I found a piece of the letterhead Theo had designed for me years ago. It was printed on canary-yellow paper with my name scrawled in her wild free hand across the top in the hottest of pinks.

"An original Goodenough?" Cursio whistled after I'd given it to him. "I suppose this should be framed, not written on."

"I'll give you one as a souvenir," I retorted. It was late. I was tired. I was in no mood to sit around and hero-worship my mother. Especially with someone who probably knew as much about her work as I knew about the New York penal code. That's why I added irritably, "Somehow you don't strike me as a modern art enthusiast."

"M.F.A. from Columbia, sweetheart," Cursio shot back. "Thesis was Rothko's influence on Pollock."

"Oh." Now I was both angry and thoroughly embarrassed. "I'm sorry. That was rude of me."

"Where have you been, Margaret?" Cursio asked, ignoring my apology. He clicked down hard on his ballpoint pen.

"It's Peg," I responded automatically. "At my boyfriend's parents' house for dinner."

"Go right from work?"

I nodded, noting he wasn't writing any of this down.

"Who did you tell you were going to be out tonight?" Cursio demanded.

"Nobody. It's, uh, kind of a secret that we're seeing each other."

"Yeah?" Cursio replied. His tired eyes scanned me but with no more interest than if I had been a subway map. "Care to tell me why?"

"Not really," I retorted, stroking Picasso's badly shedding coat. I didn't like this man's tone. Who was he to take such a superior attitude toward me? And couldn't he at least pretend a small show of concern or compassion? Robberies, rapes, murders—these were clearly routine events for him. It showed in his face and movements that he found my little B and E barely worth noting. If it wasn't for my connection to Ramsey, he probably wouldn't have been there at all. My heart was still kicking around like a hockey puck in the NHL play-offs . . . and Detective Cursio wasn't even bothering to stifle a yawn.

"Okay, okay," he muttered, jotting down something at last. "Let's assume for the moment that your romantic entangle-

ments are incidental to the case. You got any idea why somebody would want to break into a fourth-floor apartment, trash
the place and leave behind a color TV, stereo system, micro-
wave—'' he scanned the living room with a narrowed gaze
''—and maybe a half-million dollars in modern art?''

I stood slowly, letting Picasso slide, still half-asleep, onto the
floor. ''They didn't take anything?'' I asked, for the first time
realizing that, despite the mess, indeed nothing of value seemed
to be missing. I ran into the bedroom. All the drawers in my
antique rosewood dresser were pulled out. The loose limbs of
sweaters, jeans and underwear lay piled in a jumbled heap at
the foot of my brass bed. My hand-tooled walnut jewelry box
stood agape. But not one of the heavy gold chains or chunky
chokers Theo had given me through the years was gone.

''You're right,'' I said, walking back into the living room. I
went through my front closet and the bath before making my
way to the kitchen. Everything had been rifled through, nothing ripped off. Not even the outrageously expensive superde-
luxe Cuisinart Theo had shipped me for my birthday. I had
found its gleaming blades and supersonic velocity too intimi-
dating to tangle with and left it in its original packing box under the sink.

''Peg, somebody was in here tonight looking for something,'' Detective Cursio announced. He leaned against my refrigerator, a tall lean man who looked both physically and
emotionally wrung out. His pasty complexion took on a bluish
sheen under my hundred-watt kitchen light.

''We've established the where. Got any thoughts on the who,
what or why?''

''No,'' I admitted, getting up from my crouch beside the
sink. I didn't have any hundred-dollar bills sewn into my mat-
tress. I had no pitch-encrusted Maltese falcon stashed away.
Whoever had been here had left behind everything of value that
I owned. I watched Detective Cursio try unsuccessfully to stifle another yawn.

''Hey, I'm sorry,'' I added tartly. ''But I'm not harboring
any dark exciting secrets. I'm just your normal boring working girl. I'm not even seeing a shrink. Though, come to think
of it, maybe that's a little abnormal for a New Yorker.''

''Right, Peg,'' he said with a sigh. ''Listen, I know your file,
and in my book Theodora Goodenough's daughter just is not

the girl next door. You want to play games with yourself, fine. But I know the score.''

Once again I felt a rush of anger that he seemed to know so much about me. Then I quickly decided that most of his insights were nothing more than guesswork. He was just doing his job—piecing together evidence, taking long shots. I watched another yawn sweep through him, stretching his mouth wide and tightening his dark smudged eyes.

''Got any coffee?'' he asked, coming out of it. ''Most 'normal' girls do.''

While I poured boiling water through the mocha blend in my Melitta filter, Cursio apologized for his sleepiness.

''I've been working eighteen-hour shifts on the Farnsworth murder.''

''Aren't you wasting your time here, then?'' I asked, giving him a mug full of coffee. He followed me into the living room.

''I don't think so,'' he replied, sinking back down into my favorite chair. ''I'm afraid it's no coincidence that you knew Ramsey—and that someone broke in here. Two other P&Q employees have had break-ins.'' He named a copywriter and a producer, both of whom knew Ramsey well. ''Nothing of value stolen in either case. But plenty of mess. I think somebody's looking for something that had to do with Ramsey. Something that might somehow connect this somebody...to the murder.''

''You mean—'' I sat my coffee down sloppily on the end table and hauled Picasso into my arms ''—it was Ramsey's murderer who...was here?''

''Could be,'' Cursio said, nodding. His eyes had brightened, turning the shiny black of expensive olives. His mood seemed to improve in direct proportion to the amount of danger under discussion. I could feel him tense, come alive. My heart, on the other hand, sank. I felt in turn angry, unbelieving, misused and terrified.

''But why? For what?'' I demanded, my emotional cycle swinging back to anger.

''That's something I'm hoping maybe you can tell me. Something you might know without realizing it—subconsciously. So why don't you just start talking.'' He set his mug down on the floor and fished around for his pen. ''About your job. Ramsey. Everything you can think of. How you met him.

What you thought of him . . . and his friends. Anything. Just talk.''

It was a lot easier than I thought. Ramsey had rarely been out of my mind in the past week. I simply put those memories into words. It was therapeutic, too, I suppose. Cursio said nothing, letting lie the silences that stretched between my words. Though I could feel him listening, measuring what I said—it wasn't an unpleasant sensation. His was a sympathetic ear. I ended up telling him things I hadn't even told Spencer. How I dreamed about the murder at night. How much I missed Ramsey: his footfall in the corridor, his laughter, his voice.

"You planning on staying on at P&Q?" he asked finally, interrupting me. Either he had found what he was seeking or he had given up.

"I . . . don't know," I answered truthfully, thinking for the first time in many hours of my meeting with the executive committee that afternoon. On impulse, I added, "They've offered me Ramsey's job."

"Well, say, congratulations," Cursio replied, sounding genuinely impressed. "I guess that means you're staying."

"Like I said, I don't know," I countered. "It's a big step. A lot of work. I really like what I'm doing now. I feel so secure, so . . ."

"Normal," Cursio finished for me, clicking down on his pen.

"I suppose so," I replied. I didn't like the sound of what he'd made me say. I tried to explain further, "It takes a long time to work up to a position like Ramsey's. Hundreds of really talented people are vying for it. It isn't so easy . . ."

"And you might louse it up, right?" Cursio demanded, smiling at me for the first time that night. It was a slight lopsided grin that flashed briefly in his eyes, as well.

"There's always that possibility," I agreed, laughing. Had he laughed, too? I don't remember. But I'll never forget what he said next.

"Or worse still, you could turn into a big success," he had added, standing. He stretched and the sleeves of his wrinkled jacket slid up, revealing well-muscled, hairy arms. "You could start playing in the big leagues just like your mother. And isn't that what you're really afraid of?"

I was so outraged by what he'd said that I hadn't deigned to respond. I gave him a stiff "good-night," collected Picasso and some overnight things and went across the hall to Millie's. I was so angered by what he'd said that I was short with Millie, got into her spare bedroom quickly and switched off the light. I was so mad that I lay awake in the dark, seething. Where did he come off dispensing quack psychology like that to perfect strangers? Who did he think he was? The bastard, I thought. I was furious. And he was right.

FIVE

MILLIE'S SINGING woke me up the next morning. She was in the shower, which, though situated down the hall from the guest bedroom, acoustically seemed to be just outside the door.

Slowly, I put together why I was waking up in a small dark room papered in green-and-purple paisley and more than faintly scented with cheap incense. The night before came back in uncomfortable little jabs, like a suddenly resurfacing toothache. The memory of Detective Cursio's parting words made me sit up in bed, actually wincing with pain.

"Oh, dear, bad dreams?" Millie stood in the doorway, wrapped in a tartan robe, her little birdlike head turbaned in faded blue terry cloth. Like two slightly unhinged parentheses, her pencil-thin eyebrows arched upward and disappeared beneath the towel. Millie had the bright hopeful smile of the incurable optimist—Little Orphan Annie crossed with a female Gumby—skipping through her social security years with the enthusiasm of a Girl Scout. She beamed at me across the room.

"No, I slept just fine, actually," I replied, stretching beneath the covers. "It's waking up and thinking about what happened to my apartment that's the nightmare."

"Well you know what I always say," Millie responded, "it could have been a whole lot worse. You were a very lucky young lady not to have been home when they broke in, you know."

"'They,' Millie? I thought you said you saw just *one* man running down the hall."

"That's right," Millie agreed. "But before, when I heard that almighty racket, I remember hearing voices—plural. That's why I thought you might be doing that Jane Fonda cassette again. One sounded like a woman."

"Damn." I sighed, throwing off the covers and swinging my legs to the floor. "Somehow that makes it all worse. A woman, I mean. I've been imagining this big dark bad *guy* . . ."

"Well, it's over now, dear," Millie put in soothingly. "And things are starting to look up for you. I've just gone over your chart quite thoroughly. Mercury's on the cusp . . . that nasty business you were having with Sagittarius has faded . . . and then, of course, we've the waxing gibbous moon . . ."

"Great, Millie," I replied, trying to sound enthusiastic. "Now if I could only get the NYPD to let me lease back my apartment."

"Oh, that detective's gone," Millie responded. "He came by here about half an hour ago. Said he's had your front door put to right . . . and he left you this." Millie drew a folded square of my stationery from the pocket of her robe and handed it to me.

"Thanks," I replied, staring down at the little patch of blazing canary yellow. It occurred to me for the first time that I'd allowed a total stranger to pass the night in my apartment. How had he spent the time? Poring over my private letters? Riffling through my underwear drawer? Detective Cursio, I decided, already know a hell of a lot more about me than I would have liked.

"And these, too," Millie added, fishing out a shiny new brass ring from which hung three small keys. I had a single outside lock on my door. I opened up the note. He wrote in neat forward-slanting block capitals.

Ms Goodenough,

 I took the liberty of getting the special unit up here first thing this morning to install some decent locks. I can't believe you've actually lived in this place with one cheap lock and a chain. You now have a new Medico and a Fox police lock, courtesy of my department . . . and I suppose by way of apology. I think maybe I spoke out of turn last night. I tend to do that.

 Please get in touch with me immediately if you think of anything that reflects on the Farnsworth case. Right now we need all the help we can get.

Thanks, Dante Cursio

P.S. You need a new box of Melitta filters.

The apartment was in much the same sorry state as I'd left it—with one noticeable improvement. Detective Cursio, or someone on his staff, had rehung Theo's paintings. Each was carefully, almost meticulously, aligned in its original spot. Though I was touched by this gesture, as well as the rather fatherly business about the locks, I decided it wouldn't absolve Cursio of his rudeness the night before. I had already decided that nothing could.

It wasn't until I started to change and shower that I realized just how violent a cyclone had swept through my tidy little life. My toothpaste water glass had been shattered. Shampoo and conditioner had been squirted into the bathtub, the twin rivulets now coagulated into dull hardened veins.

My closets and drawers had suffered equally. Dresses ripped from hangers, socks and stockings tossed around the room like beanbags. My favorite bathrobe—a faded gold silk komono—crushed into an ugly ball and thrown into a back dusty corner of the closet. But worse than the physical damage was the psychological blow of knowing somebody—or bodies—who meant only harm had done all of this. I picked up a high heel from under the bed and started to put it back in its place on my shoe rack. The thin hard spike made me think of something Cursio had pointed out—that Ramsey's murderer could have been the intruder—and I shuddered, almost dropping the shoe.

I hurried to get dressed after that, not caring about the mess I was leaving behind. Everything that was not in its usual place felt infected, tainted by association with the break-in. It took me fifteen minutes to find things to put on that I was fairly sure hadn't been handled. I was nearly an hour late for work by the time I finally got out the front door. And then it took me another five minutes to figure out which of Cursio's damned keys went into which lock.

"SPENCER GUILDEN'S CALLED *three* times," Ruthie greeted me excitedly. "And Phillip Ebert's office—though not *himself*, mind—twice. Also, Mark Rollings dropped by about half an hour ago to say that the first thing you were to do when you got in was to call *him*. So what will it be?" Ruthie concluded eagerly, picking up the phone to dial.

"How about a cup of coffee?" I asked, trying to sound calm. So much had happened since my meeting with the executive committee yesterday afternoon that I'd given the problem of taking Ramsey's job only fleeting consideration. But now the big guns were aimed at me, expecting an answer. In a matter of minutes, I would have to decide.

"Fine by me," Ruthie replied, putting down the phone, though obviously it wasn't. The names Ebert, Rollings and Guilden were royalty to Ruthie—as close to real glamour and power as she was likely to come. And though, of course, nobody actually bowed when they came by, one was certainly expected to jump. My failure to act appropriately must have seemed to her sadly irrefutable evidence that I would never be able to step into Ramsey's elegant Italianate shoes. Ruthie was no doubt conjuring up my expulsion, an onslaught of new people bringing in new staff and, inevitably, her own dismissal. So when she said, "Black, right?" it seemed more a comment on our future than on how I took my coffee.

"Yes, please," I replied, trying to sound a lot more confident and in charge than I felt. "Bring it into Ramsey's office when it comes. And do your best to give the impression that I'm still not in yet. I need some time to think, Ruthie."

"I see," Ruthie said, though from the righteous sniff that followed and the pained set of her thin lips, I had the feeling that she didn't see at all.

Ramsey had always insisted on being decorated with the trappings of power. Though not in a position of ultimate authority, star art directors, like certain key senators or businessmen, often wielded more influence than the ad execs, presidents and C.E.O.'s they worked under. It was at Ramsey's level that favor was curried, deals bartered, agreement wrung. And though the top creative people like Ramsey were looked upon as temperamental and childish by the Eberts and Rollings of this world—they were also handled like signed Steuben originals. Without award-winning creative, no big agency stayed big for long. Ramsey invariably got what he wanted.

He had managed to accrue all the stock options, profit sharing and bonus schedules reserved strictly for members of the executive board. Plus he had finagled one of the most spectacular offices in the entire P&Q building. It was a prime corner property with floor-to-ceiling plate glass windows that looked down grandly on the jumble of Midtown. He had demanded the eastern view because it included a large upward-thrusting slice of the Chrysler Building—the only example of civilized twentieth-century architecture, Ramsey used to claim, in the entire New World.

As I collapsed into his silky black leather Eames chair and swiveled it toward the window, I recalled snatches of Ramsey's infamous diatribes against Midtown's building room.

"Ugly utilitarian monoliths!" he would sputter, gesturing out the window at some rising new construction. "Soulless, unsophisticated beehives designed for drones. Life is too short, Peggy darling, for anyone to be surrounded by such mediocrity. We must strive," he would instruct me, pacing his bright little sea of imported French carpet, "for what is superior. Whether it's wine or architecture or something as pedestrian as this layout."

And then with the skill of the truly gifted teacher, he would show me how to turn my middling design work into a layout he would be proud to claim as his own. For five years he had coached me through inference and example to see and think about design the way he did. He had molded me in his image. Toward the end, hardly anybody could tell the difference between Ramsey's work and my own. But what happens to an image, I wondered, gazing out at the futuristic tracery of Ramsey's favorite building, when the thing it's reflecting is gone?

Of course I was afraid to take the job, I thought, remembering what Cursio had said the night before. I was afraid because I might fail . . . *and* because I might succeed. And I was terrified by the fact that no matter how I performed, the job would so absolutely change my carefully organized, stable life. If I accepted, I would be taking a risk. I would be putting my life, my relationship with Spencer—everything I'd worked so hard to build—in jeopardy. I would be reliving the agonies of my childhood with Theo. I would be turning back into the storm.

"Mark Rollings called again," Ruthie reproached me as she slipped into the room with a steaming container of coffee. "He wanted to know if you were always this late in the morning. And he sounded more than a little teed off, if you want my opinion."

"Thanks, Ruthie," I responded lightly. "Mind closing the door again as you go out, please?" I waited until she was gone before pulling the plastic top off my coffee and breathing in its fumes. Though black, as requested, it smelled acrid, even faintly burned. I blew on its murky surface and took a sip. The first sensation was heat, followed all too quickly by a strange chemical aftertaste. Damn, I thought, I should have reminded Ruthie to bring me sugar.

Then I remembered Ramsey's sweet tooth.

As long as I had known him, Ramsey had been on a diet. According to him, he had been at war with the bathroom scale ever since childhood. His wealthy widowed mother had been unable to deny the apple of her eye anything, especially the divinity and cream pies that had made him so very happy. And so very plump. Even as a full-grown, responsible adult, the only way Ramsey could keep himself from gorging on sweets was to keep away from them. With Teddy's help, he carefully monitored his sugar intake at home and while eating out. He made a rather public show of never having dessert during business lunches. I was the only one who knew about his sweet drawer.

I had caught him at it late one afternoon about a year ago. We had just pitched and won a four-million-dollar savings-and-loan account—and I had dropped by Ramsey's office on the off chance he'd want to join his junior design staff down the hall for some champagne. But Ramsey was doing some celebrating of his own. I found him hunched over his desk, his hands and mouth full of miniature Reese's peanut butter cups.

"Ramsey, what are you doing!" I'd cried. His face blanching to the color of confectioners' sugar, he had swallowed hard before answering.

"Eating, I'm afraid, darling. Rewarding myself for a job well-done. And, yes, behaving like an absolute pig. But you'll be a dear, won't you, Peggy, and keep this our dirty little secret? Teddy would be just beside himself if he knew."

He had looked so crestfallen that someone had found him out, I promised not to tell. Then with obvious relief and boyish glee, he showed me the bottom right drawer of his huge antique desk, which was laden with enough sweets to satisfy an entire Boy Scout troop on Halloween. Like an alcoholic who will guzzle the cheapest gin as eagerly as the best Bordeaux, Ramsey had no sense of discrimination when it came to his vice. Boxes of Jujyfruits were scattered among beautifully wrapped treats from Godiva. Hoarded packets of sugar were lost amongst imported French bonbons. To keep himself from indulging too often, he had the key to the drawer hidden across his enormous office under a potted fern.

I got up, retrieved the tiny key and fingered it sadly as I sat back down. Ramsey had certainly been the last person to touch it, I reflected. I turned it over in my hand. Poor, dear, Ramsey. I felt strangely honored that I had shared this harmless secret with him. But, oh, if I had known what a Pandora's box was waiting for me, I doubt I would ever have leaned over, jiggled the key into the lock and turned it until the drawer clicked softly open.

SIX

THE DRAWER WAS FLOODED with Almond Joy bars, Mint Patties, a half-dozen of those miniature Whitman's Samplers you see at airport gift counters, but no loose packets of sugar this time. I dug some more and uncovered handfuls of Mary Janes, a six-pack of Chuckles, hundreds of exotic-flavored jelly beans—a virtual candyland of goodies. I pulled the drawer out farther... and there it was: a small, badly worn, black leather notebook.

At the time, of course, I had no idea of its significance. But it looked so out of place in that brightly colored sea of packaged sweets that I couldn't help but notice it—and pick it up.

I flipped the notebook open. It contained perhaps twenty-five blue-ruled pages, each divided into three columns. About half the pages were filled with Ramsey's meticulous handwriting: the left columns with two or three capital letters, the middle column with dollar amounts ranging from five hundred and four thousand, the right column with dates divided by day/month/year. The date of the first entry was October 28 of the previous autumn... the last date was the day of Ramsey's murder.

I fingered through the entries several times, quickly figuring that the middle column roughly totalled fifty thousand dollars. Then I went back through the dated entries again. And then once more, very slowly, just to make sure.

Though it could easily have been coincidence, I was positive that it was toward the end of last October—about the time of his first entry—that I had noticed the beginnings of Ramsey's odd behavior and mood swings. There was something else about that date that bothered me, but I didn't have a chance to think it through. At that moment Mark Rollings stormed into the room.

"What in hell do you think you're doing!" he cried, his voice breaking like an adolescent's. His nose looked pinched. For the first time since I'd known him, his tie hung a little off center. "I've been asking for you since eight-thirty this morning."

"Yes, I know, Mark," I replied, slipping Ramsey's notebook into the side pocket of my pleated linen skirt. "I've needed a little time alone. To think."

"'To think,' she says! Who has time to think? Listen to me, Ms Goodenough," he sneered, the s on "Ms" hissing like an angry snake. "As we speak the father-and-son team of Bobbin and Bobbin are jetting north on their corporate Lear for an emergency meeting with their new 'creative team.'"

"Oh boy!" I gulped. "When was this scheduled?"

"Victor Bobbin's secretary called mine at eight-thirty to say they were on their way to the airport."

"But why? They signed off on the launch campaign weeks ago."

"I managed to talk to Victor briefly on his car phone," Mark replied, pacing back and forth in front of Ramsey's desk. "But the goddamn reception was so bad I couldn't make out what he was trying to say. Except that 'everything has to change.'"

"'Everything'?" I demanded, sitting up as straight as was possible in the low-slung chair. "What does that mean?"

"Well, we're not certain. But Phillip, Spencer and I talked it over this morning, and we're pretty sure it means . . . *you*."

"But just yesterday they were begging for me, right?" I demanded in something of a panic. It wasn't until that minute that I realized I had already decided to take the job *and* that I really wanted it.

"'Begging'? That's a bit strong," Mark responded. Sensing I was about to lose my composure, he managed to regain some of his own. A tight down-turning smile played at the corners of his mouth. Somehow, even his dimples seemed pasted on. "But, yes, Victor Bobbin had indicated he'd be satisfied if you were offered the position. First rule of advertising, though, Peg—clients, like women, are entitled to change their minds."

Only by digging my fingers deep into the soft leather of the chair did I manage to keep myself from leaping across the desk top and strangling Mark Rollings with my bare hands.

"All of us agreed, in any case," Mark forged on, "that we were at too sensitive a point with the Fanpan account not to have some exigency plans ready. So, we put calls in to Nathan Freeman at KRR&S and Miranda Fox at T&A. They're both ready to jump ship as soon as we give the word."

Freeman and Fox—two of the biggest stars on Madison Avenue. Even Ramsey, who rarely had had a kind word to say about his peers, had admitted to me privately that Nathan Freeman was a cut above "the rest of that pack of howling lupines." I had been kidding myself. I was out of this league. Without the Bobbins' support, there was no job for me here.

"So that settles it, I guess?" I sighed, swinging toward the window. "I step aside quietly... you roll the big guns into position. The battle is won."

"Well, yes. Precisely," Mark replied, flashing me his best Shiney Brite smile. "I knew you'd understand. But we all want you at that lunch meeting, Peg, to...you know...sort of show your goodwill."

"Right," I replied without enthusiasm. After he left, I stared out the window for several minutes without really seeing anything. If I'd jumped at the chance of taking Ramsey's job, I wondered, if I'd accepted it without hesitation—would it have been mine now? Was I becoming too cautious and conservative for my own good? A midday haze hung over the city. Far below, distant and as muffled as the noises of a grown-up dinner party heard from a child's bedroom, came the screeches and horns of crosstown traffic. Here and there a high window blazed with reflected sunlight, flashing unreadable signals. I thought it all through carefully, but I could find no answers.

After a while, I roused myself, stretched and stood. I closed Ramsey's sweet drawer, securing the key and the little black notebook in my shoulder bag. Then I took the elevator five floors up to Spencer's office.

The executive suites were the most subtly—and expensively—decorated in the company. Creams and beiges predominated. Wall-to-wall carpeting as thick and soft as leopard skin kept noise to a minimum, creating an atmosphere as rarified as most of the salaries up there. The executive secretaries, almost to a person middle-aged, severely dressed matrons, guarded their charges as diligently as Victorian chaperons. Spencer's secretary was no exception.

"You're not scheduled," she informed me, looking over her bifocals with obvious suspicion. Her large modern walnut work unit was built like a battlement around the entrance to Spencer's inner office. It was fanatically free of any sign of commerce: no memos to be typed, no papers to be filed, her typewriter gleamed like the large rectangular decorative piece it seemed to be.

"I know," I explained. "But he's been asking for me. Just tell him I'm here."

"You're not scheduled," she replied more severely. "And he hates to be interrupted. You should have called ahead for an appointment."

"But he *is* expecting me," I tried again, and after a few more unfriendly skirmishes over this familiar turf, she finally buzzed Spencer and informed him I was there.

"Ms Goodenough, thanks so much for dropping up," Spencer greeted me with formality for his secretary's benefit. But as soon as he'd shut the door behind us, he pulled me into his arms. Our kisses were sweetly exciting, tinged with illicitness and tasting faintly of coffee. He moved away first.

"Now what the hell are you doing here, Peg? I thought we agreed never to do this." But to show how he felt about my visit, he started to take delicious little bites out of my neck.

"I needed to talk," I tried to explain, curling into his arms. "And it just wasn't anything I felt like going into over the phone."

"Hmm," Spencer murmured, running his hand along the curve of my right hip. "Let me tell you what I feel like going into...."

"No, Spencer, please," I cried, pulling away. I took a step back, trying to clear my head. In every way, Spencer made me feel heady: he was handsome, steady, ambitious, self-assured. He knew what he wanted...and what he wanted of me. He saw us as a couple so clearly that whenever I felt confused about my life—or our future life together—I turned to him to borrow a little of that clear-sightedness. That's why I was there.

"It's this job business, isn't it?" Spencer replied, pacing the enormous sunlit room. The office was about the same size as Ramsey's, with the addition of a private bath and dressing room that opened off the far end. Like his secretary's, all of Spencer's office furniture seemed unused. The desk was a spotless slab of chrome and glass. Empty In and Out boxes sat on either front corner like sentinels. "Come over here and relax," Spencer commanded, patting the seat next to him on the large oatmeal-colored suede couch that was kitty-corner to his desk. "Come on," he added, "I promise to behave myself."

"Sure it's the job," I admitted, sitting down. "Or the sudden lack thereof. It's the job and the murder and the sort of scary fact that my apartment was broken into last night."

"Damn! You, too?" he cried. "It's turning into a real P&Q epidemic. Yours is the fourth. All from the Fanpan group."

"The detective I talked to thinks they're all related to the murder," I explained. "So the person who broke into my place could have been capable of... I don't like to think about it."

"You poor kid," Spencer replied, putting his hand over mine. "You must have had a hell of a night. First my rotten family...then this. If is helps any, babe, the entire Guilden clan couldn't think of enough nice things to say about you when I got home last night." There was something forced about Spencer's tone that made me momentarily question his sincerity. But I was in no mood to root around for unwanted truths.

"So I passed, huh?" I responded. "Well, that's a relief. Now there's just Theo to get through."

"And who cares what she says, right?" Spencer declared. "Who cares what anybody thinks? You know, I'm getting really tired of all this clandestine stuff. I'm fed up with tiptoeing around here, pretending I hardly even know your name. And I hate like hell this news about your place getting broken into. You know what I think?"

Yes, I knew. We had been over it all before. Spencer wanted us to find a place together and either set up house or go ahead and get married. But the former reminded me too much of the way Theo lived, and the latter...? Like the white picket fence, the backyard swing, the family car—like so many other things I had missed out on as a child—it was something I was looking forward to *someday*. But not just yet.

"Marry me, Peg," Spencer murmured, his hand squeezing mine. "Come on—now's the perfect time. We can find a nice little co-op on the East Side, and you can have a great time fixing it up. Why, with your design sense, we might not even need a decorator."

"And my job?" I demanded.

"What? Oh, you mean this Fanpan business?" Spencer asked. When I nodded, he replied, "Hey, don't worry. Nathan Freeman's ready to commit. I mean, it's sweet of you to take it so seriously and everything, Peg, but art directors are not exactly hard to come by these days."

"Tell me the truth, Spencer," I said. "You never thought I could handle that job in the first place, did you?"

"Hey, come on now, I've already told you that I think you could do anything you put your mind to." Spencer grabbed both my hands and gazed at me searchingly. "The real question is, why would you want to? I make more than enough to support us both. We've been together almost two years . . . and I don't know about you, but I'm getting tired of waiting. It's time to settle down, Peg. It's time to think about a family."

"Yes, I know, but . . ." My words trailed off. But. What did I know about being a wife? A mother? I'd never had a role model. I had only the vaguest sense, gleaned from a long rapid succession of maids and cooks, of what "keeping house" entailed. And it wasn't even the physical process that worried me, it was the mental one. What did a housewife do with her mind? Her energies? Her drive? Could I really be as happy picking out silver patterns for formal dinnerware as I had been working up ad layouts?

"What are you afraid of, Peg?" Spencer pressed me, kissing the inside of my right palm. He knew perfectly well what that did to my nervous system. I was starting to melt.

"It's just that . . . well, what would I actually *do* all day?" I asked, trying to pull my hand away—and myself together.

"I don't know," Spencer replied, his brow creasing as he concentrated on the question. "What do women do? You'll shop, of course. Go to the club. Take the kids to lessons. Entertain. You'll do what every mother does."

My mother had run for Congress on Maine's Communist ticket when I was seven. My mother had ballooned across India the summer of my thirteenth birthday. My mother's idea of shopping was to order by the case, the gross, the square mile anything that happened at the moment to take her fancy. Every house I had lived in with her had quickly turned into a warehouse for these flaring, quickly discarded passions. I knew for certain that I didn't want to live my life like that. I wanted solidity. Long-term love. Commitment. Everything, in fact, that Spencer seemed to be offering.

And yet, my mother was leaving her mark on this world. She was creating, doing, living. She had taught me early on the value of work. I loved the process of designing, of taking a block of white space or an empty half minute of airtime and turning it into a message. It was my way of saying something.

"Let me think about it," I said.

"What's there to think about!" Spencer exploded. He stood, marched over to the window and rocked back and forth on his heels, staring out across the city. "I don't get you, Peg. Either you love me and want to be with me, or not. What are you trying to tell me here?"

"You're asking me to give up my job," I countered.

"The way I see it, you're going to be out of that job in another—" he glanced at his Rolex "—forty-five minutes or so. I'm simply offering you another job. And a damned important one, if you ask me. Don't get all hung up in a lot of feminist bull, okay? You don't *need* to work. I do need a wife, a mother for my children. What's the problem?"

"I don't know," I replied weakly. "I really don't. I'm just not thinking straight. I'm still really messed up about Ramsey. And then, oh, I don't know, I think I was really sort of up on the idea of taking on the job. It's just that when Mark told me what had happened, I felt so let down."

"Hey, of course you did," Spencer said, his whole tone softening. He came back and sat beside me. "You're going through a lot of changes. It's not easy. And I'm not asking for a definite answer from you right now. But promise me this. After today's meeting with the Bobbins, after this whole Fanpan business is taken off your shoulders...tell me you'll say yes. Okay?"

Spencer's eyes are blue, the color of summer afternoons on the beach. The color of serenity. Peace. I looked into them. I closed my own eyes for half a second. I said, "Okay."

It came that close.

SEVEN

Lunch was served in the executive dining room by waiters in summer-white tuxes. The room, on the penthouse floor, ran half the length of the building. Its floor-to-ceiling windows faced north to the corporate majesty of upper Madison and the distant green patchwork of Central Park. Champagne-colored fabric swathed the remaining three walls. We were served gingered eggplant mousse and rolled breast of veal stuffed with tuna, accompanied by a crisp California Chardonnay. In any other situation, it would have been a delicious meal.

But things were not going well.

The Bobbins had arrived overheated and irritable, nearly an hour late. The traffic in from Kennedy had been the official cause of their delay and touchiness, though I also detected some undisclosed tension between father and son. J.J. tucked moodily into the meal. Victor, rebuffing various attempts at small talk on the parts of Phillip Ebert and Mark Rollings, toyed with his food and lit up a fat Cuban cigar long before the dessert trolley was wheeled in.

Besides Phillip, Mark, Spencer and myself, Fanpan's media director, a tall blond model-thin woman named Felice Clay, and the head of the research department, a Walter-Mitty-type character called Neal Meadows, had been invited to join the Bobbins. By the time coffee was served, even gregarious, loudmouthed Felice had subsided into a gloomy silence.

"Well," Phillip announced finally as the waiters cleared away our dessert plates, "what an unexpected—but welcome—surprise to have you join us today. It's always a pleasure to see you Victor . . . and J.J."

"Bull. You're shocked as hell, and I don't blame you," Victor grunted, sucking on his cigar.

"Yes, of course, we were a bit surprised by the rather short notice," Phillip continued smoothly. "But Mark explained that something rather, uh, critical has come up?"

"Critical? That's an understatement," Victor retorted. Meanwhile, J.J. ran his right index finger around the rim of his water glass, seemingly oblivious to his surroundings.

"Perhaps you could . . . fill us in," Phillip encouraged.

"Well, J.J.," Victor replied bitingly, "why don't *you* tell them what's happened?"

J.J. glanced up at his father, then down again, his face flushing. His embarrassment made him appear even more painfully oaflike and awkward. If it wasn't for the temper that I'd seen rage from J.J. on occasion, I would have thought him a gentle, simpleminded young giant.

"Come on, Pappy," J.J. complained, "it's not such a big thing. No one meant any harm. It's just some kind of a misunderstanding, is all."

"Tell them, J.J.," Victor commanded severely. "From the beginning."

"Oh, dang it all," J.J. complained, slapping his hand on the table. His water glass jumped. Silverware tinkled. Then he stood, slamming his chair back against the wall, and stamped over to the windows, his huge fists jammed deep into the expensive twill of his powder-blue pant pockets. His red hair flaming against the afternoon sun, his hulking frame outlined against the glass, he looked like some primordial being—half man, half beast. The casual dignity of his beautifully made summer suit gave him a strangely comic cast.

"I met a gal," J.J. began, not bothering to turn around, "at one of the fancy new dance places in downtown Macon. She was a pretty little thing. A redhead just like me. Don't usually go for them. But, my oh my, she was something special," he went on, addressing his words to the wide deaf vista of Upper Manhattan.

"Tell them what she did for a living," Victor interrupted.

"Advertising," J.J. replied, the end of the word turning into an unpleasant whine. "But how was I to know? She was so cute and pert. Seemed so interested in me and stuff."

"The 'stuff' my clever son refers to," Victor interrupted again, "being the theme and content of the launch campaign for Fanpan. It seems that J.J.'s little friend works for none other than Smiley's."

"The fast-food chain?" Spencer asked.

"Yes, indeedy," Victor replied. "This pretty, 'pert' little thing turns out to be their national marketing director."

"Now Pappy, how the heck was I to know?"

"You could have asked, I suppose," Victor replied, sighing. "*Before* you handed her the ad layouts."

"You, uh, actually gave this woman the designs?" Mark Rollings gasped, his face now a pale green.

"Of course not!" J.J. retorted, spinning around. "I just sort of sketched them for her on a cocktail napkin."

"Well now, we can understand your concern here, Victor," Phillip interjected. "But what makes you think this young lady would actually use this information against Fanpan?"

"That's right," Spencer added. "We try to keep security on launch campaigns as tight as possible—but little things do leak out. And we've never had a major catastrophe."

"You're looking at one now," Victor replied. "Unfortunately, J.J. was not content with playing advertising, he wanted to play house, as well. Our lady friend didn't. And, well, sometimes my son can play a little rough; just manhandling, you know!"

"She really led me on," J.J. mumbled, slouching back into his chair.

"We heard from Smiley's corporate lawyers yesterday," Victor continued. "They weren't smiling."

"Hey, you know, I did try to apologize!" J.J. exclaimed, leaning forward to stare down at his big freckled hands, as if he'd just noticed they were attached to his body.

"I had J.J. try to get through to her," Victor explained. "It was then that we learned the worst."

"She quoted me our new tag line. 'The Down-home Chicken with the Downright Delicious Taste,'" J.J. added. "She said to keep my eyes peeled for *Smiley's* new campaign. Then she laughed, really nastylike. And she had seemed like such a nice gal."

"You're right," Phillip commented. "The situation doesn't sound so good. But I think it's important for us all not to overreact."

"May I remind you," Victor announced, "that nationwide, Smiley's is Fanpan's biggest competitor."

"Oh dear," murmured Felice, who had been remarkably quiet throughout the proceedings.

"Jesus," Mark Rollings swore under his breath.

"I see no way around it," Victor announced. "We need a whole new, totally different campaign. I'm afraid we've just got to scrap everything."

The table fell silent as the necessity of what Victor proposed sank in. Knowing what Smiley's did about the Fanpan launch and factoring in the marketing director's understandable distaste for J.J., it would be commercial suicide to run with the approved material. Smiley's was no doubt repositioning their fast-food line, directly against our "down-home" theme. Months of work were down the drain because of J.J.'s one night on the town.

Spencer looked at Mark. Mark glanced sideways to see Phillip's reaction. Phillip cleared his throat nervously before commenting. "I'm afraid you're right, Victor."

"Yes, we're afraid so," Mark immediately repeated.

"It's going to mean a hell of a lot of work," Spencer noted, "under a particularly tight schedule. I suppose you still intend the first wave to break right after Labor Day?"

"Yep," Victor replied. "You all think that's going to be a problem? Speak up now, if so. Some of your competitors gave me a call after that unfortunate business with Farnsworth. Implied they'd be happy to take over the account." Victor didn't sound threatening, just businesslike. He recognized his value as a client, and he just wanted us to know he knew it.

"No problem at all," Phillip hastily assured him. "A few late hours here and there, a little overtime. Nothing that can't be done, of course. Right, group?" Phillip beamed around the table, and we all beamed at Victor.

"Terrific," Phillip confirmed. "Now Victor, that brings us to some account restructuring we'd like to propose."

"Restructuring?" Victor demanded, knocking the ash off his cigar onto his coffee saucer. "Wish you people would talk English. You mean changes, right?" When Phillip nodded, Victor replied irritably, "Well then, just say so."

"Changes for the better, of course," Mark Rollings enthused, "definitely for the better."

"You see, we value your business tremendously," Phillip began sonorously. "You offer new challenges to us as an agency. And the opportunity to do award-winning work. Our greatest hope is that together—our advertising and your product—will set new standards of excellence in the minds of the consum—"

"Yeah, I remember all this from the day you pitched us," Victor interrupted. "But let's get to the point, okay?"

"Of course," Phillip replied, smiling. "I was just getting there, as a matter of fact. I don't think any of us can overestimate the value of really dynamite creative work on your product."

"Fanpan?" Victor asked. "I'm the first to admit it's just fried chicken. But okay, dynamite always works fine by me."

"Ramsey's loss was quite a blow to the agency," Phillip continued solemnly. "His talent is just, well, irreplaceable."

"Sure," Victor agreed. "But we worked mostly with Peggy, anyway. I don't know, Farnsworth didn't seem to put in much of an appearance."

"Ah, but his *talent* was there, working behind the scenes," Spencer interrupted. That statement couldn't help but rankle me. I'm the first to admit Ramsey taught me everything I know, but it was also true that the dear man, for whatever personal reasons, did zero work on Fanpan. From beginning to end, the concepts were mine.

"Yeah? Well, I didn't see it," Victor responded.

I glanced at Spencer, then Phillip. Their expressions were set. Whether or not I could handle the job, they weren't about to take the risk. Spencer hadn't lied when he'd assured me I could do anything I put my mind to; that didn't mean he would help me do it. He'd been obliged to offer me the job; he had done his best to discourage me from accepting it. In his mind, it was a simple business equation. One did not take a chance when the bottom line was at stake. He wanted Freeman or Fox. He demanded a known entity. And along with Mark and Phillip, he was determined to convince Victor of this.

"Of course not, Victor!" Mark replied with a bright tinkle of laughter. "Talent isn't something you can *see*!"

"That's true," Phillip added, cutting short Mark's unnerving zealousness. "There are only a handful of top creative people in the business. Ramsey was one of them. And, Victor, we have some really terrific news for you...."

"Oh, yeah?" Victor replied, glancing around the table. He caught my eye. I immediately tried to change my expression to match Phillip's upbeat tone. But Victor must have seen my unhappiness. He winked at me.

"Yes!" Phillip responded. "Nathan Freeman is ready to head up our marvelous group. Freeman, as I'm sure you know, is one of *the* top creative names."

"Never heard of him," Victor declared, stubbing out his cigar in the dregs of his coffee cup. "What's wrong with Peggy, here? I thought we agreed to give her the job." He gave me a smile that lit up his craggy features. How could I help but smile back?

"But Freeman's a big name," Mark assured him. "Very big!"

"And Peg, well—" Spencer turned hopefully to me "—she understands that the position is just a bit out of her depth. Though she's very grateful for your offer."

"Can't Peggy speak for herself?" Victor demanded.

"Really, Mr. Bobbin," I replied, "everyone seems to think this is for the best."

"Including you?" Victor asked.

"It seems to be the general consensus," I hedged.

"You're not answering my question, Peggy," Victor pressed. "Can you or can you not do the job?"

"Hey, Pappy, why not work with this new bigwig?" J.J., who hadn't shown much interest in the proceedings, suddenly piped in. "What does Peggy know? She's just a girl."

"Sonny," Victor answered, sighing. "Remember it was 'just a girl' who walked off with our initial creative strategy, as if it were nothing more than a Neiman-Marcus shopping bag."

"But, Pappy—" J.J. started to whine, only Victor cut him off.

"And besides which, Peggy doesn't hand me a troughful of advertising palaver every time I ask a human question," Victor continued, his voice rising.

"Yes, but—" J.J. tried once more.

"And finally," Victor continued forcefully, "I think Peggy has the ability and patience to deal with you, J.J. And you know what, sonny? I think that's going to be more than half the job."

"So what do you say, Peggy?" Victor demanded again. "Can I count you in?"

I looked from J.J.'s flushed angry expression to Phillip's impassive but overly controlled features to Spencer's dark, foreboding look. What would I be giving up? What was I getting myself into? It didn't make any difference, because my answer was out before I could consider the consequences.

"Yes," I said, of course.

EIGHT

SPENCER AND I HAD never really had an argument before. There had been the usual harmless disagreements—which movie to see, whose friends to join for dinner—but never the full-fledged, all-out fight that ensued after the Bobbin lunch.

"But what choice did I have?" I demanded for the tenth time later that evening. We had brought a box of our favorite take-out pizza back to my apartment. The anchovy-and-sausage pie sat untouched between us on my coffee table. "Obviously the man wanted me to take the job. What was I supposed to say, Spencer?"

"What we had already agreed you'd say," Spencer retorted, giving Picasso, who had been inching gradually closer to the source of the anchovy aroma, an unnecessarily vicious kick.

"I don't remember *agreeing* to say anything," I replied. "Maybe you and Phillip and Mark had some sort of set script established. I was only told—somewhat brutally, as a matter of fact—that I was being taken off the account."

"For your own good," Spencer asserted. "Just this morning I thought we agreed that you'd resign. That we'd think about settling down together. Do you remember that, at least? Or has that unimportant conversation, too, slipped from your memory?"

"I can't believe how unfair you're being!" I cried. "I agreed to *think* about it if and when the Bobbins didn't want me. That's all."

"Obviously your work on this chicken account is more important to you than our life together," Spencer announced. He stood up, brushing imaginary cat hairs off his crisp, dark blue Armani slacks. Even though Picasso made a point of avoiding him, Spencer never left my apartment without thoroughly brushing off his clothes. Up until that moment, the habit had never bothered me.

"It's ridiculous to even equate the two," I protested. "You're being purposefully pigheaded about this. Just completely unfair."

"And you," Spencer declared, heading for the door, "are behaving totally out of character. I hardly know who you are. It's remarkable, as Mark Rollings pointed out to me after that horrible luncheon, what happens to a woman when she's given a little power. Just remarkable."

"Spencer, don't you dare leave on that chauvinistic note!" I cried, rising to stop him.

"I'm sorry, Peg," Spencer replied, not sounding the least bit sorry, "but that's the note you make me want to strike. Good night."

Theo had always put a lot of stock in "good clean contretemps between consenting adults," as she called them. "Nothing like a nasty fight to clear the air, get the blood flowing," she'd claim, and she'd be the first to practice what she preached. One of my earliest memories was of her throwing a frying pan across the kitchen at someone. My father? A lover? I didn't recall, but I did know from experience that she was not a person you'd want to go up against. Perhaps that was why I'd never had much of a stomach for battle; it didn't pay off. Theo had always won.

After Spencer left I thought I was going to be sick. I sat for several minutes on the edge of the couch, my head between my knees, going over the ugly words we had spoken. I knew I should be feeling remorse over my part in the argument . . . instead, I found myself feeling only bitterness toward him. But before long, still nursing resentment, I began to feel a lot better. Together, Picasso and I ate the cold pizza, Picasso claiming the lion's share of anchovy pieces.

Around ten o'clock the phone rang. Assuming it was Spencer calling to apologize, I took my time answering.

"Peg, you're home!" Teddy, Ramsey's live-in lover, exclaimed. "Oh, I'm ever so relieved. I've been in the lowest of low funks all night and was just hoping you'd be there to pull me out."

"Well, I'm afraid I'm right down there with you, Teddy," I replied, though I was smiling. Teddy, unlike Spencer, was always eager to discuss the sticky stuff of emotions. Our relationship was not unlike the one I used to have with my best girlfriend in seventh grade; we could spend literally hours dissecting our feelings. As an adult, only Teddy made me feel perfectly at ease to discuss such matters.

"Oh, dear heart, what's the matter? Tell Teddy."

"Spencer and I had an awful fight earlier," I confessed, pulling the phone with me to the couch. I settled down into the cushions, getting ready for a lengthy soul-baring session.

"I can hardly believe what I'm hearing!" Teddy exclaimed. "America's dream couple have finally had a spat? Do tell, Peggy, and don't hold back. I demand to hear all the sordid details."

"It's a long boring story—but I'm dying to talk to somebody. Sure you don't mind?"

"Angel, Peggy, this is Teddy here, remember? If you don't start crying on my shoulder immediately, I'll be terribly insulted. Besides, sweetheart, it will take my mind off my own little woes."

Poor Teddy, I thought with a pang of remorse. What was my silly squabble with Spencer compared to the abyss of loneliness and grief he'd been plunged into since Ramsey's death?

Ramsey and Ted had lived together for fifteen years, and in my mind were closer and more loving to each other than almost any straight couple I knew. Ramsey, the flamboyant, aggressive partner, supported sensitive, self-effacing Teddy, who for years had been struggling to establish himself as a sculptor in the cutthroat New York art scene.

It was not until last year that Ted finally managed to get a one-man show in a fairly prestigious SoHo gallery. Though the exhibit was only a modest success, it had bolstered Teddy's self-image immeasurably. A big reason Ted and I became such good friends, I think, was that we'd both gone through the trauma of living in someone else's shadow. He had heard me out endlessly on my problems with Theo. I, in turn, had listened to his struggle to gain an identity of his own—one that did not depend so much on Ramsey's emotional and financial support.

Now he would have no choice but to stand on his own, I thought sadly as I went into detail about my problems with Spencer. But I kept feeling that my concerns were lightweight and meaningless compared with Teddy's major emotional tragedy and, after a while, I started to edit my recitation.

"Whoa there," Teddy interrupted. "Back up just a second. What did Spencer *say* when you explained he was being unfair?"

"Oh, I don't know," I replied. "He just employed some typically effective upper-management tactic. Never get into an argument with an M.B.A., Teddy, it's like sword fighting with all three musketeers at once. You inevitably end up weapon-less, backed into a corner, begging for mercy."

"Doesn't sound to me like you did much begging tonight, Peg," Teddy observed.

"Actually, you're right," I replied. "I just felt so, I don't know, *justified* in what I was saying."

"I think you were, dear," Teddy said. "Spencer seems to be pushing very hard for you to make a commitment to him. Why, I wonder? Does he not want you to succeed on your own terms, perhaps? Do you threaten him, somehow?"

"Who knows, Teddy?" I answered. "It's so sweet of you to listen to all this nonsense—to care. After what you've been going through, my problems seem so silly."

"Hey, come on now, Peggy, don't get gushy on me," Teddy said, laughing lightly. "It does me a world of good to get caught up in someone else's life. At least yours are worries that, by combining our two fertile minds, we might be able to find solutions for. With mine, well—" his voice started to break, but he managed to catch himself and take a deep breath "—there's just not a whole lot I can do."

"I'm sorry, Teddy," I murmured as he lost control again and began to cry. "I'm so terribly sorry. Is there anything I can do that would help?"

"No, dear, but thanks for asking," Teddy replied heavily. "It's helping just to talk to a sympathetic soul. I'm so awfully tired of repeating myself to that blasted homicide detective."

"Cursio?" I asked. "You know, I've talked to him, too, just last . . ." I started to tell Teddy about the break-in, but stopped myself. He had enough to contend with as it was. Why burden him with that horror story, as well?

"He sure is the busy little bee," Teddy said with a sigh. "I can't imagine how he found the time to fit you in. He seems to spend most of his waking hours poking around here."

"I suppose we should be grateful that he's trying so hard to find the . . ." I found it impossible to utter the word *murderer*.

"Oh yes, I suppose. . . ." Teddy agreed. Then after a moment's pause, he added all in a gush, "I know this is just terrible of me, Peggy, but for a lot of reasons I'm really not sure that I want to know who . . . I mean, what if it's somebody we know? This Cursio keeps asking me these awful obvious questions about Ramsey's and my closest friends. He seems to suspect everyone. I mean, my God, he even asked me a lot of things about . . ." Teddy hesitated.

"Who, Teddy?" I asked stupidly.

"Why, *you*, dearest," Teddy answered softly.

"Me?" I gasped. "You've got to be kidding. What possible motive could I have for wanting to . . . That's just ridiculous!"

"Of course, it is!" Teddy exclaimed. "And I told him as much in no uncertain terms. It's his job to be suspicious, remember, though I have a feeling it's the man's nature, as well."

"I think you're right," I agreed with enthusiasm. "And he's hardly subtle about it." Teddy and I proceeded to spend several delicious minutes taking easy potshots at the character of Detective Dante Cursio. Then, his tone of voice growing serious, Teddy changed the subject.

"Actually, Peggy, I did call you tonight for a reason."

"Yes?"

"Now I want you to feel absolutely free to say no if what I'm about to ask is in any way an imposition," Teddy declared. "Promise?"

"Sure."

"Well, the thing is, I have to go out to the Fire Island place this weekend," Teddy explained. "I haven't been there since the . . . well, you know, and I hate to even speculate on the state of the houseplants. While I'm there I thought I would try to sort through some of Ramsey's things. I simply can't bear to have his belongings staring me in the face all the time. Anyway," he paused, sighing, "it's really not something I'm looking forward to. And you're such a good organizer. Oh, heavens, I hate to impose but—"

"Of course, I'll come," I interrupted him.

"You will?" Teddy cried. "Really? You wouldn't mind? I know it's a dreadful thing to have to ask somebody. But I would so appreciate not having to face it alone. Dear Peggy, I'd be eternally grateful."

"Say no more," I assured him. "When are you leaving?"

"The early train Friday morning, I think," Teddy said. "I'll try to pull the place together and have dinner on the table by the time you get there."

"Fine," I said. "I'll shoot for the 6:25, as usual." There was a brief silence between us as we considered the fact that there would be nothing usual about my visit this time. Some of my happiest moments as an adult had been spent out at Ramsey's summer house. Long hilarious nights on the deck drinking wine and listening to Ramsey recount the trials and tribulations of our week at P&Q. It was a house that laughter rang through as regularly as the chimes of a grandfather clock. It would be a very different sort of place now.

"Terrific, Peggy," Ted enthused, but the sadness in his voice could not be disguised. "I'm looking forward to it."

Despite the tragic circumstances, I began to look forward to the trip, as well. The week, which had started out badly enough on Monday, went straight downhill from there. We had endless meetings about what new creative approach to take on Fanpan. We all knew now that it couldn't be anything like the "down-home" theme. But what should it be? We were working in the dark. And nobody could agree where to find the light switch.

ON FRIDAY, Mark Rollings showed up uninvited at my afternoon meeting. Though it was none of his concern, he had plenty to say about the creative direction on the Bobbin account. "This is ridiculous," he declared. "You people are floundering. Come on, guys, what's your new strategy? Where's your work plan?"

"That's what we're trying to develop here, Mark," I replied irritably. "And if you can't contribute any ideas, maybe we'd be better off left to our own devices."

"Don't get snippy with me, young lady," Mark answered huffily. "I'm just trying to offer some much-needed direction."

"Keep calling me a young lady, Mark," I retorted, "and I'll start calling you things we'll both regret. You know, it's hard enough working up ideas with people who might actually have some—contending with people who clearly don't makes the job that much more difficult."

"Oh, you're going to regret that little comment, Ms Goodenough," Mark announced, his voice weak with anger. He pushed back his chair and stood. "People are going to hear about this."

"Bravo, Peg," one of the senior copywriters exclaimed after Mark had slammed the door behind him.

After that, the mood of the meeting improved—though the creative thinking didn't.

"Let's call it a day," I decided around four-thirty. "We just keep going around in circles. Get a good rest over the weekend. We're all going to need it on Monday."

A message from Spencer was waiting for me back in Ramsey's office. Though we hadn't spoken since the night of the Bobbin lunch, I wasn't worried. I knew it was just a matter of time before he realized that he'd been wrong. I already decided to be at my most tactful and gracious when he apologized.

"Yes, hello, Peg," Spencer answered the phone. "Listen, Mark Rollings just left my office. I can't believe what he's been telling me about your creative meeting this afternoon. I think I'd better hear your side of the story."

Chilled by Spencer's officious tone, it took me a moment to consider my response. "First of all," I began, "no one asked him to be there. Secondly, he was incredibly condescending. And finally, he was downright insulting. What was I supposed to do?"

"I have an answer for the first part, anyway," Spencer responded smoothly. "*I* asked him to drop by and see how things were progressing."

"Whatever for?" I demanded. "It was my meeting."

"You're new at this," Spencer replied. "And no matter how much Victor Bobbin likes you, it doesn't necessarily mean he's going to like what you produce. And if we're going to get anything into print by September, he'd better simply adore the first thing you come up with. I was only protecting our interests by having Mark there. Besides, I'd heard through the grapevine that you had hit a few dead ends."

"You sound almost happy about that," I observed dryly.

"Don't be idiotic," Spencer snapped. Lowering his voice, he continued, "Listen, I'm proud of the fact that I'm perfectly capable of keeping my personal and professional lives separate. As far as I'm concerned, you're nothing more than an employee of mine right now—and not a very promising one, at that."

"Why?" I demanded, bristling. "Because I didn't allow Mark Rollings to step all over me?"

"What's come over you?" Spencer demanded. "Whatever happened to my sweet loving little Peg?"

"I've never been 'little,' Spencer," I retorted. "And I'll tell you what's come over me. This is a chance to prove to everyone—including Ramsey's memory—that I can do this job. Without your interference. Without Mark's heavy-handed advice. Without—"

"Have dinner with me tonight, Peg," Spencer broke in. "Let's sit down someplace nice and quiet and talk this thing out like reasonable adults." There was a pleading, slightly desperate note in his voice that broke through my anger—and made me want to accept.

"I can't. I'm leaving in half an hour for Fire Island. Teddy invited me out."

"Call and say you'll be there tomorrow," Spencer instructed.

"I really can't," I insisted. "Teddy's having a very hard time facing the house again. I promised I'd be there tonight."

"So break the promise, damn it," Spencer shot back. "I'm having a hard time, too, as a matter of fact. And you're giving it to me."

"No. I'm sorry, I won't do that."

"You're just pissed off because of this business with Mark," Spencer countered. "If I hadn't sounded off about it before, we'd be on our way to dinner at Cavaliere's this minute."

"Oh, how wrong you are, Spencer," I lied. "You see, I'm also proud of the fact that I'm perfectly capable of keeping my personal and professional lives separate."

And that ended round two.

Twenty-five minutes later I was crushed into the smoking car of the 6:25 to Sayville. The first real heat wave of the summer had continued unabated through the week and, as usual on the Long Island Railroad, the air conditioning was down. We changed trains at Jamaica; the sleek inhuman orange-and-beige interiors of the Jamaica line were replaced by the nicked metallic green of the Patchogue train.

At Bay Shore we rattled through a brief, though ferocious, thunderstorm. Lightening crackled on the low-lying horizon, illuminating the scraggly tops of pines. After that the air cleared, and a smell of marsh grass and honeysuckle wafted through my open window. Just before the train slowed for Sayville, we passed the old abandoned windmill. I'd noticed it before on many earlier trips. Tonight it struck me as being almost human in form. Its useless arms seemed to open to the sky—beseechingly.

NINE

THE THUNDERSTORM left the air cool and clean smelling. I sat on the upper deck of the ferry, wrapped in my blue-and-red striped beach towel, and turned my face into the spray of seawater and wind. The sky had cleared to the west, and a semicircular afterglow of sunset lighted up the horizon. To the east, a few stars blinked on and off like fireflies as the departing storm clouds drifted beneath them.

The wind whipped my hair into wild tangles and burned against my cheeks. For the first time in many days, I felt aware of my body, the fine cool texture of my skin, the warm weight of my breasts. I found myself wishing that someone was sitting beside me...that someone's arms encircled mine. I realized with a little pang that though I'd no particular man in mind, I had not been imagining Spencer in the role.

Teddy was waiting for me at the dock, a shopping bag in one hand, a massive bunch of wild daisies in the other. Although I had seen Ted at Ramsey's memorial service, I was shocked at the amount of weight he'd gained. Tall frail Teddy, who had appeared almost wraithlike a month ago, had put on more than pounds—he seemed to have actually developed muscle. I could feel real biceps bulging beneath his polo shirt as I hugged him to me.

"Peg, you're a sight for sore eyes," Teddy exclaimed, holding me at arm's length to get a better look. "Why, you're positively glowing, dear."

"And you!" I cried, hoisting my duffel over my shoulder. "Have you taken out a membership at the Vertical Club? You could be a stand-in for Arnold Schwartzenegger." Laughing, we started back down the dock. Teddy unhitched the little red rusted house wagon and loaded our things.

"Well, I'll tell you," he said, lowering his voice, "this is bound to come as a surprise, but I *have* joined a gym. Not because I've suddenly gotten vain—I'm the first to admit that I'm not Robert Redford—but I've become, well, aware of the need to keep fit. I can't help wondering whether Ramsey, if he'd even really half tried to stay in shape, would have been with us to-night. Maybe he could have beaten his attacker off.''

I was touched by Teddy's earnestness. As long as I could re-member, he'd never given a thought to his own health, devot-ing all his attention to Ramsey and his eternal diet. Now, bereft of his lover, he was obviously turning that energy on himself. And even at a glance, I could see that it was doing him good. His long pasty face had filled out and taken on some color. Though his light brown hair continued its looping line of re-treat back from his forehead, there was a fresh glow of health to his exposed pate. Behind his rimless John Lennon-style glasses, his eyes seemed less tired, and the dark circles beneath them were gone.

''You can't keep thinking in 'ifs,' though, Ted,'' I coun-seled him. The wagon rattled behind us as we started down the long straight boardwalk. A million crickets whined. Now, away from the water, the air was heavy with the aromas of summer: marsh grass, wood fire, ferny undergrowth. Night fell quickly.

''I know, Peggy,'' Teddy's voice beside me was thick with feeling. ''I really am trying to live in the here and now. It's damn hard, though. I do miss him so.''

About half a mile from the dock, we turned right up the walkway to the beach. Ramsey's house, one of the original homes in the community, was built on the crest of a small hill that commanded views of both the bay and the ocean. It was a modest-size octagonal structure, with sliding glass doors and decks facing every direction. Though neither as large nor as dramatic as some of the newer houses, it was built with the materials and skill of a more caring era. It exuded charm and something rare in houses these days—the owner's unique character.

The eerie melodic song of Ramsey's collection of Oriental wind chimes greeted us as we climbed the wooden walkway to the house. As Teddy opened the door, I walked around to the front deck for my first unobstructed view of the ocean.

Though the storm had headed north, a heavy mist had been left in its wake. The thin sliver of new moon did little to illu-minate the humid night. Only the breakers, which roiled onto the beach in long foaming lines of attack, broke through the dense blackness. The air still carried something of the earlier disturbance, and sudden gusts of electrically charged wind whipped the chimes into frenzied singing. The evening dampness—or was it something else?—made me shiver. I was ready, when Teddy turned on the front porch light and slid open the double glass doors, to go in.

Teddy had brought fresh asparagus and strawberries from the city. He'd purchased the tiny rack of lamb, new potatoes and feather-light sponge cake from the excellent gourmet grocery at the dock. Practicing the smooth effortless choreography of a born chef, he put together a delicious meal. In the past Teddy had insisted on serving his dinners by candlelight at the long formal dining room table that overlooked the front deck and ocean. Tonight we ate at the small round teak table in the kitchen, with all the bright overhead lights left on.

"Some of tomorrow's work has been taken out of our hands," Teddy announced, pouring me a generous glass of Beaujolais Nouveau. "The NYPD paid this place a little visit last week. Our local sheriff stopped by here earlier and told me they hadn't given him much choice but to let them in."

"Cursio?" I asked, spearing a quarter of crisp pan-fried potato.

"From the sheriff's description, I would guess so," Teddy replied. "'A dark dour fellow,' was how he put it, I believe."

"Sounds like him, all right," I replied, thinking again of the few disturbing hours I'd spent in the detective's presence. "But why didn't he simply *ask* you to let him into the beach house? Seems ridiculous for him to break in without permission."

"Oh, these guys can do anything they like and dress it up as the law," Teddy responded, pouring more wine. "They already went through the loft with a fine-tooth comb and confiscated everything that interested them. And they did the same out here. Note, please, dear Peggy, that I could not provide you with a proper knife for your chop this evening. They walked away with half my silverware!"

"That's outrageous, Teddy!" I cried. "I'd be positively livid. What else is missing?"

"A lot of Ramsey's papers. Some books. Nothing I can't live without. It's the invasion of privacy that I find so disturbing. I never know when Cursio and his henchmen are going to pop up next. I haven't been able to do a lick of work since this whole thing happened. It's been driving me mad. I was just starting to feel that I was getting somewhere with that Plexiglas series."

For the next hour, over dessert and freshly brewed coffee, we talked about Teddy's sculpting and the art world in general. Though I often found Teddy's ideas about his craft too complicated and abstract to follow, tonight I encouraged him to discuss them. It was wonderful to hear his voice take on some of its old vigor, to watch his face light up with enthusiasm.

"In other words, art for art's sake or the whole clichéd concept of the ivory tower," Teddy explained as I followed along with only half an ear, "is really just another attempt on the part of the intelligentsia to keep the working class in cultural chains. That's why, in many respects, even a comic strip artist like Red Grooms makes a more valid statement to the world than any of the abstract expressionist types. Our dear Theodora Goodenough included."

It was an old familiar pastime of Teddy's to put Theo down on artistic grounds. Since, like Theo, I'd never involved myself with the intense, often passionate politics of the art world, I'd never minded his criticisms of her. Often, in fact, I welcomed them if they could help support some familial grievance of my own.

"She was devastated when I told her about Ramsey," I put in quickly. It was hard for me to gauge what Teddy really felt about my mother. They had met three or four times, and on those occasions I felt Teddy had very nearly fawned over her.

"Was she?" Teddy asked. "What did she say, exactly?"

"Oh, you know, how much she had liked him. How sorry she was for me...and you, of course."

"She mentioned me by name?" Teddy asked, his face brightening at the idea. "What did she say about me?"

"Teddy, I don't remember exactly," I answered, yawning. "Just something about her hoping you'd be okay. And if there was anything she could do, you know...."

"She said that, really?" Teddy exclaimed. "Anything?"

"Yes," I said, trying to stifle another yawn. It was unlike Teddy not to notice how weary I was. "I'm positive she did."

"That's marvelous, Peggy dear," Teddy enthused. He stood and started to clear our places, talking with animation. "You see, there is something I've been meaning to talk to you about for the longest time. I haven't felt comfortable asking until now, though, because of my rather strong convictions. I didn't want to say or act in any way that could be interpreted as two-faced or hypocritical. And, well, you know how I feel about Theo's art.''

I sat up, trying to shake the sleepiness away. "I doubt you could do something hypocritical if you tried, Teddy. You've got to be the most honest person I know," I said with real feeling. It was true, sometimes to an almost painful degree. Teddy was the first person to tell me if he thought a dress didn't suit me, or if a new haircut was less than absolutely flattering.

"Thank you, Peggy. Your opinion means so much," Teddy replied, vigorously rinsing the dishes and loading them into the washer. He was all keyed up. "And if what I'm about to propose bothers you in any way—I mean even the slightest—I want you to tell me. Promise me?'' He turned to me, his face beaming with anticipation. At the moment, glowing with excitement as he was, he seemed almost handsome.

"Okay," I replied, trying to dredge up some enthusiasm of my own. I really was so tired. "Come on then, out with it, Teddy.''

"Well, all right. I want to ask Theo if she'll help me find a new gallery.''

"Oh . . .'' I replied, stunned by the request. Teddy knew the struggle I'd had to escape Theo's shadow. He knew how I hated to cash in on her fame. And this seemed to me a blatant use of my mother's influence. For someone who was usually so sensitive to others' feelings, it seemed grossly out of character. Teddy was the last person I'd have imagined would ask such a thing.

"Oh damn," Teddy exclaimed, his smile collapsing. "You hate the very idea, don't you? You think it puts you in an awkward position, right? Damn it all, I was afraid you'd take it like that! I didn't mean for you to be involved at all, dear heart,'' Teddy continued, coming back to the table. He pulled his chair around to sit beside me. "I saw myself in the role of Ramsey's friend, you see, not yours. I meant to ask her directly—artist to artist. Oh dear, I didn't intend for your name to even come up. How ridiculous of me! I somehow talked myself into the idea that you'd see it as I do, that you wouldn't take offense. I've just been so miserable with Walden. He has the tastes of a Neanderthal, if that. And now, oh, I don't know, my mind's been in such turmoil. I thought it would be the right time for me to make a change.''

"Please, Teddy, give me a chance here," I interrupted him, recovering myself. Was I really too proud a daughter to be a good friend? "I think it's a fine idea! I'm surprised we didn't think of it years ago. And I'm sure Theo will be happy to do what she can." Though I wasn't really the least bit sure. Theo tended to fight her own wars and let others fight theirs.

"No, you're just saying that," Teddy responded, his shoulders slumping. "I can tell. I refuse to let anything interfere with our friendship. We'll just forget this whole thing right now, okay?"

"Not okay," I answered. "You're writing a letter to Theo this weekend, if I have to stand over you with a rolling pin."

"Positively not," Teddy replied, standing. "And I refuse to argue this any further. We're both exhausted. And it's going to be a long day tomorrow."

"Long enough to get you to change your mind," I answered, rising, as well. "I'm not through with this yet."

I slept in the guest bedroom. Its big double windows were angled toward the ocean, and through these I heard the roar of the surf all night. It invaded my dreams: as applause, as the wind, and finally as a vague foreboding of some unnameable but onrushing disaster.

TEN

"My dearest boy," I read quickly as Teddy went to answer the back-door bell. "How can I begin to tell you what these past few weeks have meant to me? What a change you have made in my life! I feel—oh, Ted, how trite all of this must sound—that we were meant to be together. Always."

THE LETTER WAS written fifteen years ago, less than a month after Ramsey and Ted first met at a civil rights rally in the Village. It was sitting on top of the carton of letters Teddy and I had been sorting through in the living room. I didn't mean to pry, but when Teddy left the room, my eyes automatically started to scan Ramsey's delicately penned words. I felt tears sting my eyes.

I got up and made my way around the boxes of books and letters scattered across the room to the sliding double glass doors that looked out over the front porch and beach. It was still raining, though the downpour that had woken us up that morning had diminished to a feather-light drizzle. Now mid-afternoon, we had been working since nine that morning, sorting through belongings of Ramsey's that dated back more than fifty years: from a childhood essay on garter snakes, to P&Q's stock option plan. It was heartbreaking work.

With painstaking care, Teddy had been poring over each piece of paper, trying to sort out what should be kept. Though I encouraged him to get rid of things, he was having a hard time parting with the most trivial items. I didn't blame him for jumping up eagerly when the back-door bell rang. He needed a break.

It was the delivery boy from the gourmet grocery store at the dock. I recognized his minitruck and the yellow bomber jacket with Marty's stenciled in red across the back. And I remembered the boy from previous visits. I didn't know his name, but his thatch of snow-white blond hair and round cherubic face epitomized summer for me. His mouth seemed to form a natural smile. With a smart wave to Teddy, he revved his minitruck and backed it down the walkway. I heard the back door slam as Teddy came in with the bags.

"It was just Sandy with the groceries," Teddy announced, entering the living room.

"Sandy," I said, turning back from the window. "So that's his name. How appropriate. He's always so sunny and good-natured. A walking advertisement for this place."

"Unlike me, I'm afraid," Ted answered. "I just realized that it's half-past three, and I haven't offered you any lunch. Really, Peg, you should have piped up hours ago. You must be absolutely famished."

"I'm really not hungry," I explained. "Somehow this kind of work—" I gestured around the cluttered room "—doesn't do a whole lot for my appetite."

"I know what you mean," Teddy replied, sighing. He came over and sat down beside me. He picked up Ramsey's letter and fingered it idly. "I'll tell you what. Let's put in a few more hours here, then I'll take you out to dinner at that chic new place at the dock. It will do us good to go out after being cooped up here all day.''

We worked until five-thirty, then showered and changed. The skies had finally cleared by the time we left the house, so we decided to walk by way of the beach to the landing. It was low tide. I took off my sandals, pushed my white jeans up to my knees and walked through the gently lapping waves. The water was glassy and warm. Sandpipers ran ahead of us, twittering.

Teddy and I could talk nonstop for hours. We were also perfectly comfortable sharing a companionable silence. We walked for ten minutes or so without speaking, each deep in thought.

Finally, I broke the silence. ''Did you know, I mean from the very beginning, that Ramsey was the right person for you?''

''What makes you ask, Peggy?'' Ted replied. I could feel him glance over at me quickly, then away.

''I just wanted to make sure.... I bet you did,'' I explained. ''You two shared a very special kind of love—deeper, I think, than most people will ever get to experience. It was so obvious what was between you. And, well, sometimes I wonder about Spencer and me.''

''What do you wonder about?'' Teddy asked gently.

''Whether there's enough tension, enough passion...'' I searched for the right word, but couldn't find it. ''I don't know, enough *drama*, I guess, between us.''

''I would have thought that Theo had put you off drama forever, dear,'' Teddy observed. ''You are the young woman who was looking for security and stability in a relationship, aren't you? Or have I mixed you up with somebody else?''

''Normalcy, yes,'' I conceded. ''But does that have to mean lack of excitement?''

''Is that what it means?'' Teddy demanded. ''You tell me. I always thought there were plenty of sparks flying between Spencer and you. What's really the matter, dear? Have you two been fighting again?''

I told him about the recent debacle with Mark Rollings as we started up the beach to the bay walk. ''It almost seems that Spencer is *trying* to make life difficult for me,'' I concluded. ''And now, of all times, when I need his support most.''

''It's often hard to watch someone you love grow...and change,'' Ted counseled as we started toward the landing. It was only a five-minute walk from the beach to the bay; already we could hear the usual racket of the evening cocktail hour as we approached the marina.

"But I'm *not* changing," I insisted.

"Well, maybe in Spencer's eyes you are," Teddy replied. "I think this new position of yours threatens him. Makes him feel that you don't need him as much as you used to."

The dock and boardwalks were crowded with pleasure seekers when we arrived, and we had to wait in line at the spacious new restaurant/bar/disco that overlooked the bay. Its two-story canvas roof flapped slightly in the evening breeze. Bamboo and fern plants in brightly painted plaster pots sat among the tiny round tables that were jammed together like bumper cars. Tina Turner was pleading love's cause on a sound system so loudly that glasses shivered above the bar.

Though the place was as noisy and humid as a jungle, the service had all the verve and snap of the best Midtown expense-account watering holes. Two chilled glasses of California sauvignon blanc materialized before us within seconds of our order. The menu—studded with specials, which our waiter recited aloud with great ceremony—leaned heavily upon the local catch of shrimp and sole.

I ordered the mélange of shellfish in puff pastry, Ted the scampi—and both were fresh, simply prepared, perfectly cooked. We each had another glass of the house wine with the meal, coffee after, and shared a delicious, freshly baked *tarte tatin* with *crème fraîche*. Our little table had a splendid view of the Great South Bay. As we ate, the last of the sun faded through light pastels into the dark indigo of evening. We had a second cup of coffee and watched lights blink on across the water.

"I never did answer your question," Ted said, breaking the contented silence that had settled between us after the meal.

"Which one?" I asked lazily, taking a last sip of wine.

"About Ramsey and me," Ted reminded me. "And whether I knew right off whether he was the one...."

"Well?"

"To be quite truthful," Ted answered unexpectedly, "no. I didn't. But Ramsey did. He was ten years older than me, past forty when we met, and he had been kicking around awhile. He told me later that he'd given up entirely finding that one perfect person. Not, of course, Peggy dear, that I'm perfect by any means. It really is all in the eye of the beholder."

"And at first you didn't see it?" I asked him. "How long did it take? When were you sure?"

"Sweetheart, you know something they never really tell you about love? The real thing *takes time*. This business about lightning bolts and so forth is all very nice, but that's just sex talking. And that wild electrical feeling—well, honestly, does it ever last much longer than a summer thunderstorm? That's what I felt for Ramsey when we first met—you know, just the old lure of the flesh."

"But he felt more?"

"He'd been around the block a few times, remember, Peggy. And, well, I was relatively new at it. After all, I'd spent most of my twenties holed up in graduate school and then on that grant to Madrid. Up until the time I came to Manhattan, I'd been so busy sculpting I didn't have the spare time to fall in love. So when I first met Ramsey, I tried to pretend for a while that it was just a little fling. Nothing that could really *affect* me." Ted took a sip of coffee and stared out into the darkness, then added, "God, was I ever an egotistical little fraud."

"What finally happened? How did Ramsey convince you?" I pressed him. I was thinking of Spencer's ultimatum to me the previous afternoon.

"He didn't," Ted replied. "When he realized that I was ambivalent about the affair, he left me alone. Later he told me he damned near committed suicide that month. He took time off from work, got the hell out of the city. Actually, I think he went down south to stay with his mother. So there I was—after six weeks or so of this incredible passion—left, as I had so adamantly demanded, entirely to my own devices."

"And?"

"It was awful," Ted replied. "First, I thought I was physically sick. I stayed in bed for a few days nursing this imaginary flu. Then, after seeing the doctor, I decided I was having some kind of mental crisis. You see, I couldn't think. I couldn't sculpt. My work just sat there in the studio, gathering dust. I went to see the shrink of a friend of mine, who put me through the usual paces. At the end of the session, he asked why I had put an end to my relationship with Ramsey. That simple question was all it took. And I, at last, came out with the truth—I was terrified of admitting that I loved him."

"I keep wondering if this parallels my situation with Spencer," I remarked. "Do you think it does?"

"Oh, Peggy, I don't think love is that systematic," Ted replied with a sad, knowing smile. "I doubt such similarities exist. Everyone is different—every case of love unique. Thank God I was lucky enough to discover in time that that was what I had—not a bug or a breakdown, but a case of love. And that was that. I got ahold of Ramsey, told him what had happened. We've been together ever since. I mean, we were...."

"And you two were so happy, so close," I observed. "You never argued."

"Hah!" Teddy cried, pounding the table. "We fought like cats and dogs. Just not in public, dear. We were both civilized enough to know that our problems were really of only passing interest to the world at large. Ramsey used to declare that people who worked out their traumas at dinner parties should be guillotined."

"But, obviously, you made the right choice," I added. We had paid the bill and were waiting for our change.

"I'm not sure a choice was involved, actually," Teddy replied. He sorted through the singles and coins our waiter had returned and left a generous amount on the table. Outside, the crowd had dispersed—to dockside restaurants, yachts or home—for dinner. The air was cooler, refreshed by the thunderstorms. Here and there a small bright early star pierced the darkened horizon. In a thoughtful tone, Teddy continued.

"No, I don't believe I was ever really *given* the choice to stay or not to stay with Ramsey. After I realized that I loved him, it was just the way it had to be. You know, people talk about committing themselves to a relationship as if it were something they had to do, some kind of effort. With us, it was almost the opposite. It would have taken a terrible wrenching effort not to stay together. Do you know what I mean?"

"Only sort of," I responded honestly. We were taking the bay walk home, a different route from the way we'd come the night before. The air was dense with the smells of the bay: salt marsh, dried kelp, gasoline. "I still feel there's some sort of decision I have to come to about Spencer and me."

We walked on for a moment or two in silence, then I added, "Maybe you're right, Teddy, about me changing. I think I *have* been seeing life a little differently since Ramsey... died. I used to be more careful. Now I think maybe I'm ready to take some risks, to... I don't know—*live* more."

"I wish I felt that way, sweetheart," Teddy murmured beside me. "I envy you."

When we got back, we sat on the front deck with snifters of Calvados and watched the summer constellations fill the night sky. Ramsey used to love pointing out his favorites: Libra, Scorpio, the Corona Borealis. We talked about Ramsey and the past for an hour or so as the crickets whirred in the underbrush. Finally, after Ted had refilled his snifter, I brought up a subject that had been on my mind all day.

"You and Ramsey have done so much for me over the years," I began. "You've been, well, more than friends—family, almost. I always thought that someday I'd have a chance to pay Ramsey back for everything he did for me. But now I never will. So, Teddy, really, I beg you, let Theo help you find the right gallery. Please? It would make me happy."

"You're a good person, Peggy," Ted replied through the darkness. His voice was tinged with sadness. "You're thoughtful and caring. Yes, I'll take you up on your offer. Thank you, dear."

I SLEPT BETTER that night, and in the morning my bedroom was flooded with sunlight. The sky was a fine ethereal blue. After breakfast, at Ted's urging, we went down to the beach for a swim. The water was glorious: cool, invigorating, as clear as a mountain lake.

"Dear, it would be ridiculous to try to work today," Teddy declared after we'd run, laughing, out of the surf. "I'm going to go up and get some towels and things. I insist we spend the day in the sun like normal, healthy hedonists."

We sunbathed, read the paper, swam and chatted all morning. Around three I went up to the house to shower and get ready to go. Ted came up a half hour later to see me off. I pulled him to me for a quick hug as I was leaving.

"Sit down and write that letter to Theo tonight," I called back over my shoulder as I started down the walk. "Promise?"

"Yes, you nag, I promise," Teddy called back, waving.

I was more than halfway to the dock before I realized that I'd left my beach towel drying on the front deck. I glanced quickly at my watch and figured I had just enough time to go back and get it before the four o'clock ferry left. I trotted back against the stream of weekend visitors heading for the dock. By the time I reached the house, I was hot and out of breath. I hurried up the walkway and around the side deck. I raced past the kitchen window. Then I stopped. I retraced my steps. I couldn't help myself. I stared in, unable for several seconds to fully register what I was seeing.

Teddy was leaning back against the kitchen counter, facing but not seeing me. His eyes were closed. And his arms were wrapped around the waist of Sandy, the delivery boy from the grocery store. The two men were kissing.

Neither one of them saw me go.

ELEVEN

"STAYING LATE AGAIN?" Ruthie asked as she was leaving for the night. She had already donned her Nikes for the walk home. And she was flanked by her customary totes—"Le Bag," which was fat with freebie newspapers and magazines from the media department, and the sadly worn Ralph Lauren giveaway stuffed with umbrella, sweater, books and who knows what else. An imitation Vuitton purse was slung over her shoulder. Without her workday heels and weighted down with the excess luggage, short, dumpy Ruthie could have easily passed for a bag lady.

Luckily, she had absolutely no idea of how she looked. An incurable reader of *Cosmo* and *Vogue*, Ruthie had been brainwashed through the years by endless how-to beauty articles. Because she faithfully did everything they told her—drank eight glasses of water a day, soaked her fingertips in liquid Dove, walked a brisk forty blocks a night—she believed that she resembled the tall gamine nymphs who danced across the glossy pages of the portable monthly installments of *her* Bible. She carried her lumpy little body as if it were an object of utmost desire. She eyed the most gorgeous, sought-after men as though they were well within her reach. Ruthie believed in her own beauty as passionately as Ponce de León had believed in his fountain of youth.

"Yes, I'm afraid I'll be here awhile," I said, leaning back and stretching. It had been a long day. A long week. It was

Thursday already, and the Fanpan creative was really no further along than it had been the previous Friday afternoon. Not that we hadn't been trying. I'd just gotten out of a three-hour planning session that had gone in circles. All our ideas seemed either too corny, too funny or just not original enough. And the longer we wandered around trying to discover an approach that worked, the less likely it seemed that we'd ever find one. I'd seen this kind of creative block at P&Q on prior occasions; I'd just never been in charge of breaking through it before. And a Fanpan account review—including sketches for the new creative—was scheduled for the following Monday afternoon.

"Anything more I can do?" Ruthie asked without enthusiasm.

"No, Ruthie," I replied, leaning forward again and staring at my oversize pad of tracing paper. It was blank. "You go on home."

"Well, okay," she said, making it sound as though I was forcing her out. "But don't stay too late now. I'll see you in the morning." And with that Ruthie swung her body and bags around and sashayed heavily down the corridor to the elevator banks.

There is nothing quite so suddenly, absolutely empty as a Midtown office on a summer evening. The silence was so severe after Ruthie had gone that I could actually hear the fine high hum of the overhead lights. I got up and walked over to the windows just to assure myself that there was still a world out there.

Thirty-six floors below, Madison Avenue was thick with buses, taxis, pedestrians streaming uptown. It was a Thursday night, after all, and for thousands of New Yorkers the beginning of an unofficial long weekend. It looked as though it was going to be a long one for me, as well, but for all the wrong reasons. Fanpan was actually the least of my worries.

Spencer and I hadn't communicated—except by copying each other on various memos—all week long. I had been sure that there would be a message from him waiting for me on my machine when I got back from Fire Island. There wasn't. I had been positive that when we met in the halls or at a meeting, one glance between us would precipitate an immediate truce. It hadn't. Spencer had looked right through me at the staff meeting on Tuesday afternoon. I was beginning to regret that I had turned down his invitation for dinner the previous Friday night. I was regretting a lot of things.

Teddy, for instance. The mental image of him and Sandy in the kitchen was haunting me. How could he speak so eloquently of his love for Ramsey, of their commitment to each other, and then turn around and do what he and Sandy had so clearly been doing? How could he—honest, forthright Teddy— lie so blatantly? And especially to me, one of his closest friends?

I kept trying to justify what I'd witnessed: Teddy was lonely; Teddy was seeking solace; Teddy was too grief-stricken to know what he was doing. But none of my excuses for his actions seemed to pan out. The fact of the matter was, Teddy had forcefully told me one thing, only to turn around and do quite another. Then, after I'd mentally gone over the situation with Teddy yet again, my mind would swing wearily back to the Spencer dilemma.

Too much time had elapsed without some kind of détente initiated between us, and I was afraid that our little misunderstanding was now in danger of hardening into a permanent grudge. I was beginning to wonder if Spencer would ever realize that he was in the wrong. Worse still, I was starting to question whether he actually was.

Hadn't I promised to think about settling down with him— marrying him, even—only to turn around and snap up the Fanpan job? Indeed, hadn't I, just like Teddy, said one thing and done another? As the week elapsed, my thinking about Spencer changed and softened. The whole blowup began to seem less Spencer's fault...and more like mine. I was the one, after all, who had to decide what I wanted to do. Spencer, as usual, already knew. It was my uncertainty, my waffling, that had brought on the argument in the first place. Wasn't it? I was so afraid of losing my one firm foothold in security, that by Thursday night I'd almost convinced myself that I alone was to blame for the fight.

My mind was so deeply entrenched in these concerns that I didn't hear the footsteps approaching down the hall or the first tentative knock on the door.

"Ms Goodenough?" The familiar voice sent an unfamiliar shiver through me. Anger? Fear? I whirled around.

"Oh, it's you," I replied without enthusiasm, taking in a far more groomed version of Detective Dante Cursio than the one that had first been presented to me more than a week before. For one thing, he'd gotten some rest. His dark eyes had lost their bruised, haunted look. The hospital-pale sheen of his complexion had been replaced by a healthier, darker hue. Though by no means tan, he looked as if he'd spent some time out-of-doors. He seemed fit, relaxed. This overall aura of well-being was helped by the handsomely cut, light beige gabardine suit he was wearing. I would never have pegged him as a cop.

"Am I interrupting you?" he asked, though it was rather obvious that I'd been doing nothing more than staring moodily out a window. "I was in the neighborhood," he added, taking a step or two into the office, "so I thought I'd drop by."

"What's in the neighborhood of the thirty-sixth floor of P&Q?" I asked sarcastically. I was feeling down enough as it was, the last thing I needed was Detective Cursio and his damned informed insights into my life. His comment about my being afraid of success because of Theo still rankled.

"The forty-second," he answered smoothly, moving across the carpet to the far wall, where a gallery of Ramsey's and my best work hung. "I had a meeting with your executive people, updating them on the investigation."

"Oh? Who was there?" I asked, thinking of Spencer. Was he still in the building? Had he been thinking of me?

"At the meeting?" Cursio asked, examining the print ads with care. "Let's see." He recited from memory, "All men. A gray-haired in-charge type called Ebert. Some sycophant named Rollings. And then this young pric—uh, prig, called, let me think just a second . . ."

"Guilden?" I asked unbelievingly. Though I didn't like Cursio one little bit, I knew from experience that his instincts were razor sharp. I didn't want this man to hold Spencer in low regard. "Spencer Guilden?" I repeated.

"Right," Cursio said, turning to face me. "He seemed to think I'm personally responsible for the effect this whole mess has had on your company. Gave me a hell of a time for not having the thing solved already. Not a whole lot of patience there."

"Well, how *is* it going?" I asked, deciding to cut short any further observations about Spencer's character. "You can sit down, if you like," I added, gesturing to the leather-backed director's chair across from Ramsey's desk. I gave up my post at the window and settled into the Eames chair. It felt oddly pleasant to take the position of power. I glanced across at Cursio to see if he felt the subtle weight of authority Ramsey's seat lent me. The smile he gave me touched his lips only briefly, but it lighted up his eyes. I decided again that he was a man who missed very little.

"Not well," Cursio reported gloomily, leaning forward slightly and running his hands through his dark, straight hair. A strand immediately fell back across his forehead. His well-groomed appearance did not hold up under close scrutiny. He badly needed a haircut.

"Can you elaborate on that a little?" I asked smartly. "I mean, in what way is it not going well? How unwell is it going?"

"You really want to know?" Cursio asked dubiously.

"Yes," I answered vehemently. "He was my *friend*, remember? He was my boss."

"This his old office?" Cursio asked, glancing around the room. "Whose work is that on the wall?" he continued, before I had a chance to answer the first question.

"Yes, it was his," I replied. "It's mine now. And those," I swung around so that we were both facing the ads, "are both of ours. Some Ramsey's, some mine. A few we worked on together."

"I think I can tell who did what," Cursio stated thoughtfully. He stood up and walked around the desk for a closer view.

"I kind of doubt it," I answered, though I was hoping he'd try. I was going to take genuine pleasure in seeing him be wrong. "Nobody we worked with could."

"Okay, for instance," Cursio continued undaunted, "that Crunchy King cereal one is yours. And that one on the far top row for running shoes...that's yours, too."

"You're just lucky," I snapped. "You're guessing."

"Well, let me keep guessing, then," he answered, pacing up and down in front of the pictures. "Pizza Palace is Ramsey's, and so is that big one for radial tires. You did the fuzzy wuzzy toy ad. Now I'm not sure about this mouthwash one," Cursio murmured, stopping in front of the ad that had won Ramsey his eleventh Art Director's Award. "But I think you two designed it together."

"You're right," I said. I was stunned. "How did you know? You must have gotten ahold of some old job sheets or something," I added, trying to explain it to myself.

"No, really," Cursio replied mildly, "I can just tell. Your techniques are similar, yes. But they're really far from identical. Ramsey was more practical, more interested in displaying the product, making the point. You, on the other hand, you're more artistic. Look at all that white space in the ad for the running shoes. You're trying to catch the reader's attention. You take more risks. Why, it's really quite obvious. And you know which are the best ads?"

"No," I retorted. I was both irritated and impressed by his observations. They echoed thoughts I'd been forming, in some unrealized part of myself, about Ramsey's work...and my own.

"The ones you did together," he asserted, not seeming to hear or sense my hostility. "They combine the best of both talents."

"Why thank *you*, Detective Cursio, for your most cogent insights into our humble work at P&Q," I replied bitingly. "Next time before you give a lecture, though, I'd appreciate some warning. I'd like to take notes."

"You can't take being told anything about yourself, can you?" Cursio demanded, turning on me and for the first time showing a glint of anger. "Or is it that you don't think you can learn anything from someone like me?" He began to really work himself up. "Hard to believe a dumb *cop* could tell you anything about your work, right? I apologize for any crimp I might have put in your obviously set ideas about life. And from now—"

"I'm sorry," I interrupted him. "Really, I am. You're right...about a lot of things."

"Oh," Cursio muttered, calming down. "Well..."

"But nobody can ever tell Ramsey's and my work apart," I tried to explain. "It's bound to be something of a shock to have you waltz in and just *know*. And, really, I don't think of you as a dumb cop, by any means. As a matter of fact, you kind of scare me. You're too smart."

"I only wish," Cursio replied, smiling. This time the smile lasted longer around his mouth, making him look almost congenial. "You may have noticed that I get very, well, defensive about being with the force. People automatically think you joined because you're too stupid to do anything else, or because you're trying to get rich quick on the take. But some of us have other reasons. Good ones." He didn't elaborate, and I didn't push. For the first time, Cursio had shown some chinks in his armor. I liked him better for it.

"Not to obviously change the subject," I answered, "but before we got sidetracked, weren't you going to tell me how the investigation was progressing?"

"Progress is not a word I'd used in this instance," Cursio answered. He looked tired again suddenly. "But I'd be happy to fill you in."

"Would you mind terribly if we got out of here?" I asked him. "It's been a long day for me. I could buy you a cup of coffee at the deli downstairs, if you like."

"Yes," Cursio replied with feeling. "Places like this make me nuts. I don't know why, but I start to itch the minute I walk into a big corporation. I've been longing to get this damn tie off. It's been killing me."

"That's too bad," I observed as we made our way out the door and down the hall. I pressed the buzzer for night service. "I was thinking before how much better you look in that suit than—"

"What you saw me in the last time?" Cursio finished for me. He laughed when I nodded. "No wonder. But I borrowed this baby from the wardrobe room in the undercover department so I could look like a big boy at the meeting this afternoon. I wouldn't be caught dead in this thing otherwise."

Pity, I thought, glancing at him as Joe took us down in the freight elevator. If he just dressed a little better...if he got a decent haircut...Detective Dante Cursio could definitely be considered a good-looking man. What am I thinking? I asked myself, momentarily alarmed. But by the time we reached the lobby, I had lost the train of thought.

As the detective had noted earlier, there were certain things about myself I simply didn't want to know.

TWELVE

"WE MUST BE AVERAGING around twenty-five crank calls a day," Cursio reported, sipping at the brim of his steaming coffee mug. I toyed with my iced tea. We were sitting at the counter; George's last two customers of the evening.

"What kinds of things do they say?" I demanded. His matter-of-fact description of the inner workings of the investigation had me enthralled. "How can you tell they're not for real?"

"Oh, they say things like, 'I killed the SOB because he was beaming messages from Uranus into the left ear of my Pekingese.' Or, 'I think my husband murdered him because he was sleeping with the ex-lover of my husband's second cousin.' And the problem is, there's no decent way *to* tell if they're murderous nuts . . . or just plain nuts. We waste more damn time following up these crazy leads."

"But it must be fascinating," I replied. "I mean, being able to enter into so many odd lives like that."

"Hardly," Cursio replied shortly. "Listen, after a few years you develop a kind of second sense about these people. By far the majority of them are harmless, lonely, really sort of pitiful human beings. But then there's that last little fraction—and you never know where they're going to be—who'll just as soon kill you as look at you. And the problem is, no matter how finely tuned your senses are, if you just once misread one of them—that's it. No, it's hardly fascinating work."

"I guess that sounded naive on my part," I apologized. "But your job is so different from mine. It sounds so much more real-life and grown-up. . . ."

"I got into it because I thought it would be," Cursio replied. "But, you know, I spend more time pushing papers around than anything else. That and doing my best to appease the captain, who's trying to calm down the commissioner, who's getting hell from the mayor. Well, you probably know what it's like."

"I do," I said, "and it's one thing about my job I didn't bargain for. I really think I'm going to be just fine when it comes to managing the work. But I don't seem to show much of a talent for answering to the higher-ups. I tend to get a little...cocky."

"I bet," Cursio answered, smiling. I liked him a lot more tonight than when we first met. He seemed less cynical, less probing. I couldn't help but wonder...

"Am I...I mean, have you decided whether or not I might have..." I couldn't think of a delicate way of phrasing it, so I finally asked outright. "You don't think I killed him, do you?"

"Farnsworth?" he asked. Cursio's eyebrows are dark, thick, every which way—giving him an almost constant quizzical look. "Well, I have to admit that I had more or less ruled you out, but then I don't have any other viable candidates. Are you volunteering yourself?"

"You're joking," I said uncertainly. His long face was a perfect deadpan.

"Yes, Peg," he said, smiling again. "Right at this moment I don't seriously count you in. One of my men checked your whereabouts the time of the murder. You were where? Out with some friends for a late dinner, or something?"

"Yes," I said, deciding not to mention that it had been Spencer and another couple I'd been with.

"And besides that," he went on, "you don't have much of a motive except professional jealousy. But who knows? My problem is, nobody seems to have a motive. Besides the fact that he was gay, nothing was off kilter about Ramsey's life. Nothing leads up to the murder...except vague indications from you—and others—that he seemed mildly depressed."

"Not so much depressed," I explained, "as distracted. His mind just seemed elsewhere most of the time, as though he were trying to work out something that had nothing to do with P&Q or his regular life. I...I really don't know how else to explain it. Ramsey was such a keen, sharp person. It was as though he'd somehow gotten dulled."

"We've ruled out drugs," Cursio commented. "He'd none of the right connections, and our undercover network can tell us within half an hour if someone's even looked sideways at a nickel bag."

"Oh no, Ramsey wasn't involved with drugs," I asserted.

"I don't think so now, either," Cursio responded, "but almost ninety percent of the crimes in this city *are*. It's one of the first things we check for. But here, like just about everything else in this damn investigation, drugs are a blind alley."

"It sounds like what I'm going through, in a way," I replied sympathetically. I didn't know what it was about Cursio, but despite his less than charming bedside manner, he was a remarkably easy person to talk to. It must have something to do with being an investigator—of always having your ear pricked for the false note, the harbored truth. In any case, I found myself pouring out the entire Fanpan story. And he listened as raptly as a child hearing Dickens's *A Christmas Carol* for the first time.

"You going home from here?" he demanded unexpectedly when I had finished detailing my professional woes.

"Well...yes, I guess so," I responded, disappointed that he had offered no insights into my problems when I'd shown such interest in his. Once again, I decided that no matter how perceptive Detective Cursio might be, he was basically insensitive and rude. I signaled George and paid for the check, my anger growing when Cursio didn't even pretend interest in paying his share. He was lost in his own thoughts.

"I'll walk you home," Cursio declared when we reached the sidewalk.

"It's more than forty blocks," I retorted. "I'm going to grab a cab."

"It'll do you good to walk," Cursio countered. "I walk everywhere I can—forty blocks is nothing, less than two miles. Besides, you'll never find a taxi around here this time of night."

He was wrong about the walk being nothing. I was not a naturally athletic person, and I had made no effort to join the rest of my health-minded generation in their headlong pursuit of the perfect physique. I liked my top-heavy, undermuscled, slightly overweight body just the way it was. At even a slow jog, my flesh tended to jiggle like a Jell-O salad just turned from its mold. I had no intention of joining Cursio in what would no doubt be a brutally brisk two-mile constitutional. On the other hand, he was right. Taxis seemed to be banned from Midtown streets from five to seven-thirty on weekday nights. There was nothing in sight.

"You can join me as far as the subway," I grudgingly replied, and we started to walk. Compared to the torpid weeks of record-breaking heat and humidity we'd had earlier in June, the night was blissfully cool and dry. And to my surprise, Cursio set the slow reflective pace of landed gentry surveying the back forty. I had no trouble keeping up.

"J.J. sounds like a perfect fool," Cursio commented out of the blue as we strolled across Sixth Avenue. "Is he all there?"

"I'm not sure," I replied truthfully, pleased that Cursio had been considering my earlier disclosures—and that he'd revived the conversation. Though I was beginning to think that the man himself was unreadable, I trusted Cursio's instincts about others. I felt certain he could add some perspective to my dilemma. "At first I thought maybe J.J. was a little slow," I continued, "but now I wonder. I've seen him get angry. He can really lose control, and when he does you get glimpses of a very disturbed, but not unintelligent, man hiding behind this dumb hulking mountain of a boy."

"What sort of situations upset him?" Cursio asked. "Do you remember?"

"Sure," I responded immediately. "He doesn't like his authority challenged. He almost attacked a top photographer who implied he was interfering. And he seems far from overjoyed about my promotion."

"How did he get on with Ramsey?" Cursio demanded.

"You know, I'm really not sure," I said. "I don't remember them ever talking directly. From the beginning I handled most of the client contact."

"You don't feel threatened by him, do you?" Cursio asked.

"No. But then I've never had to go up against him, either. I have an uneasy feeling, though, that my opportunity is fast approaching." We had reached the Fiftieth Street subway stop for the uptown Broadway local. I hesitated.

"Give me another ten blocks," Cursio said, "I'm working something out in my head. And it helps me to walk—and talk the thing through. Okay?" It was a statement, not a question. But because my feet were holding up surprisingly well, and more because I was interested in what he was "working out," I nodded, and we went on.

"You know, Peg, I think we *are* facing parallel problems," Cursio stated as we swung north on Broadway. The grim sidewalk and storefronts of Hell's Kitchen were softened somewhat by the setting sun. "We're both lacking a premise. You, as a basis for your creative strategy, or whatever. Me, as a way of constructing a motive for the murder. I'm not going to get anywhere if I concentrate on *who* killed Farnsworth. And by the same token, you're going to just keep on completing fruitless laps if you continue to worry about *what* this new ad campaign should be. Instead, we both have to concentrate on why.''

"I understand the need for a why when it comes to the murder," I answered. "But I don't see how it's going to help to hold on to and hopefully gain more market share. It's as simple as that."

"Of course," Cursio replied. "The toughest questions usually have the simplest answers. But I don't think you're working your side of this all the way through. Yes, it's a given that they have to advertise. What you're missing is the same necessity, the same inevitability in your creative approach."

"Yes, I *know* that already," I retorted. Cursio was starting to sound a little like Mark Rollings, and my knees were starting to ache. "All I've managed to work out is what it shouldn't be. There's nothing saying what it should or must be."

"But there is," Cursio stated simply. "It's obvious."

"Excuse me if I sound rude," I shot back with feeling, "but I have been worrying about this particular question for nearly two weeks now—almost nonstop. The answer is far from obvious."

"The ultimate answer, perhaps," Cursio conceded. "But the initial *premise*, your jumping-off point, is."

"Do tell," I replied, hoping my voice sounded as put out as I felt. Somehow, in the heat of the past few minutes, we'd passed Columbus Circle and were well into the Lincoln Center area. The pretheater crowd filled sidewalk cafés and waited in line for restaurant tables. The usual crush of sidewalk merchants—peddling everything from hand-tooled silver bracelets to self-help paperbacks—made walking and talking, let alone arguing, impossible. Cursio didn't answer me until we were past Alice Tully Hall.

"You had to scrap your original campaign because your competition found out what it was, right?" Cursio asked. "You figure they're going to somehow turn the tables on this 'down-home' theme. Right so far?"

"Yes," I answered impatiently. "I already told you all this."

"Okay, Peg, if those are the facts," Cursio continued, "there's only one right thing you can do... and that's find out what these people are planning and..."

I finished the sentence for him. "Turn the tables on them!"

"Right," Cursio said.

"You're right!" I cried. "You are absolutely right. That's the most sensible suggestion I've heard since I landed this job." I turned to him, smiling. We stopped.

"And that," Cursio said, taking a step toward me, "is probably the first totally nice thing you've said to me." Cursio's left hand reached out and cupped my chin. He took another step toward me. I moved toward him. We were on Sixty-eighth Street, in front of a Korean grocery store that had huge buckets of flowers on its sidewalk. The musty summery smell of daisies filled the air. Cursio's right arm found its way around my waist. I wasn't sure what we were doing, but it seemed—just what Cursio said my creative strategy must be—inevitable. He leaned over. He kissed me.

No, that's not quite the truth. We kissed each other. And it was that—my willing participation in the event—that made me break away so quickly. I was shocked. With myself.

"I've got to go," I mumbled, stepping back. I started to walk down the block.

"Peg," Cursio said, catching up to me. "Don't act like this. Where are you going?"

"Home," I sniffed righteously.

"Then you're going in the wrong direction," Cursio observed. I stopped to get my bearings and saw that he was right. I was heading downtown rather than up. I was furious.

"I am going this way," I improvised, "because this is a good corner to find a cab, which is what I'm going to do. Which is something I should have done an hour ago." I'll never know what god of transportation saw my plight and sped that golden chariot toward me. Nevertheless, a battered yellow Checker screeched to a stop as soon as I raised my arm. I scrambled in, but Cursio grabbed the door handle.

He leaned in and said, "It's incredible to me that Theo Goodenough's daughter could turn out to be a prude." Then he slammed the door and walked away.

I WENT RIGHT for the phone when I got back to my apartment and dialed Spencer. He answered on the fifth ring. "Yes?" he demanded irritably.

"Hi," I said. My knees, already shaky from Cursio's forced march, now almost buckled. I slid into the armchair. "Spencer, it's me."

"I recognize the voice," he answered, though not unkindly. He waited. Spencer had graduated cum laude from Harvard's B. School. There he'd been taught the fine art of management by intimidation. It was a lesson he'd learned well. He continued to say nothing as all my fears and self-doubts coalesced into one uncontrollable need. I tried desperately to remember why I had been angry with him, but it now seemed totally unimportant.

"I called to tell you," I managed at last, "that I know I've been behaving badly."

"Yes?" Spencer replied, wanting more.

"I've been awfully confused and pressured," I continued submissively. "I'm sorry if I've taken any of it out on you."

"You're saying you're sorry, then?" Spencer replied, getting to the point. "You're calling to apologize?"

"Yes," I mumbled, eating my words.

"That's great, babe," Spencer cried, magnanimous in victory. "I've been going crazy hoping you'd come around. God, I'm so relieved!" He didn't offer to take any of the blame for our spat, and I guess that by then I didn't really expect him to. Clearly, unlike me, Spencer had never doubted that he was in the right. It was one of the things that had drawn me to him initially. It was one of the things that had brought me back to him now.

All my life I'd been surrounded by confusion and uncertainty. All my life I'd longed for stability and control. With Spencer I was secure. I was safe. But from whom? It didn't occur to me until much later that with Spencer I was protected from the one person I was most afraid of really facing.

Me.

THIRTEEN

"MARK ROLLINGS HAS already called twice, and Phillip Ebert's secretary phoned to confirm your meeting for Monday afternoon, and—"

"Ruthie, call Information," I interrupted her in midsentence, "and get me the number for Smiley's corporate headquarters. I think they're in Atlanta." Ruthie's perfect mask of makeup did little to conceal her look of disapproval.

"Rollings wants you to call him *immediately*," she warned in a voice that said she wanted nothing to do with the consequences if I didn't comply. She added haughtily, "And some woman named Theo phoned. She said you'd know where she could be reached."

My mother hardly ever called me at the office, but when she did she made a point of not revealing our relationship. Did she guess that I was uncomfortable with the part of famous woman's daughter? Or was she simply unhappy with the role of mother? It was one of those subjects we managed never to get around to discussing.

I put a call through to the island estate in Maine where Theo usually held court during the summer months.

"Darling!" Theo cried when I'd finally worked my way through her maid and personal assistant to reach the great artist herself. Theo hated phones and most other modern conveniences. She generally shouted into the receiver, as if it were the deafened ear of some doddering old maid. Today was no exception. "How are you? Is everything all right?"

"I'm just fine," I assured her. Theo had always mistaken my staying in Manhattan for the summers as an early symptom of incipient insanity. She brushed aside my explanation—that I had a job, after all, that required I be here—as so much nonsense. I had long ago given up trying to convince her that my summers were not one long stretch on a torture rack.

"I guess I have to take your word for it," she answered, unconvinced. "Listen, Peg, I had a thought this morning while I was doing my laps." My mother swam in the ocean a half hour every day. Often through temperatures and weather that would keep lifelong sailors snug in their bunks. "You know, I'm taking off for Paris this afternoon and—"

"I didn't know," I cut in. Theo still assumed that I was as intimately informed about her affairs as when I lived with her. I don't think she's ever totally realized that I don't sleep under the same roof as her anymore. It was this very sort of self-involvement on Theo's part that had driven me out in the first place—and it still could drive me crazy.

"Didn't Elise send you my tour schedule?" Theo demanded. "It includes all the details of my European trip."

"Yes, I suppose I have it somewhere," I replied. My mother's private secretary sent me at least half a forest of papers every month. Catalogs and books featuring Theo's work. Magazines and newspaper clippings covering her latest exhibits and sales. I long ago stopped trying to keep up.

"Well, anyway, darling, what I was thinking is," Theo continued with her usual enthusiasm, "why don't you come with me? Wouldn't this summer be the perfect time? It's been ages and ages since we've seen each other. And, well, darling, after this terrible business with Ramsey, I think it would be a good time for you to get away. You haven't had a decent break in years..." Theo didn't usually run on so. I cut her off before she wasted any more breath.

"I can't," I said simply. "It's impossible right now." I knew it was the perfect opportunity to tell her about my promotion, but I hesitated. What if it didn't work out?

"Drat," she cried. "I was afraid you'd say that. I don't suppose you'd care to tell me why?"

"I would if I thought for one moment that you'd consider any reason of mine... more important than a need of yours."

"Oh really, Peg." Theo sighed. "Must you be so contrary? I only thought it would be nice for you."

"I know, Theo," I answered, then added quickly, "Look, I'm sorry, but I really have to run. I'm already late for a meeting as it is."

"God, Peg, and you used to complain about me never having any time," Theo said. "Well, take care, darling. I'll call you when I get back next month."

"Have a good trip," I said. Despite our differences, I always wanted to tell her so much more. Like, "I love you." And, "I'll miss you." But Theo tended to keep such endearments to a minimum, preferring the "darling" she used on everyone from the gardener to the First Lady. As soon as I hung up, Ruthie buzzed me on the intercom.

"I have that number in Atlanta you wanted," she said. After she gave it to me, she added a little desperately, "and I want to remind you to get back to Mr. Rollings, please. He's sounding positively livid."

"I've never heard him sound any way else, Ruthie," I said, and I wasn't positive, but I think I actually heard a snicker on the other end of the phone line.

"MARKETING DEPARTMENT, please," I demanded officiously when I'd reached Smiley's switchboard.

"Yes, hello, I'm a feature reporter for *Ad Week*, and I must talk immediately to the head of your advertising department," I said when the call was picked up.

"I'm sorry, Miss Woolfe is in a meeting at the moment," a gently tempered young Southern voice replied. "But if you'd care to leave a message, I can have her get back to you."

"I guess you didn't hear me the first time," I retorted fiercely. "I'm from *Ad Week*? In New York? I'm a feature writer? Get it so far?"

"Yes, ma'am."

"And I want to talk to your Miss Woolfe right now."

"Yes, but, like I said—"

"Better tell her who's on the phone, sweetheart," I warned. "She may never forgive you for causing me to leave her out of my piece." There was a pause as my message sank in, then another delay during which I was put on hold. But not even a minute later, a husky, honey-sweet voice cooed at the other end.

"Tricia Woolfe speaking. May I help you?"

"Trish, glad I could finally get through to you," I replied irritably. "Listen, we're almost at deadline here for a piece we've been putting together on fall ad plans for the big fast-food chains."

"I'm so pleased you're including Smiley's in your article," Tricia purred. "I'm usually so disappointed by the lack of coverage we in-house agencies get from the New York media."

"Well, frankly, Trish, I *was* going to leave you out. But my editor insisted. As you've probably heard, Fanpan decided to dissolve their in-house ad staff and take their account to one of the big four in New York."

"Yes, I heard about the move," Tricia replied with a smile in her voice. "P&Q's the agency, I believe."

"That's right. I've just been over there for an interview with their creative team. They've developed an absolutely dynamite campaign, positioning Fanpan as the 'down-home' chicken. I got to tell you, Trish, P&Q does beautiful work."

"I couldn't agree with you more," Tricia murmured. "They're real pros. But I do think it's time the advertising community began to realize that good strong creative thinking can also be done outside New York and the big agency scene."

"That's an interesting statement, Trish," I replied thoughtfully. "Mmm, yes, I think I'm going to use that in a sidebar quote. Do you think you could courier me up a photo of yourself this afternoon, Trish? We may just want to give Smiley's more of a stake in this piece than we'd first imagined."

"Of course!" Tricia's soprano trilled. "Who should I send it to?"

"Ruthie Tupper," I replied, and gave her a fictitious address on Third Avenue to send it to. "Now, I've a few more questions, if you don't mind."

"Quest away!" she cried girlishly.

"Well, as I told you, we already have a thorough rundown on what Fanpan is planning to roll out come September. I know in-house agencies tend to work a little more, uh, slowly. I don't suppose your plans are actually set?"

"In stone," Tricia replied proudly.

"Care to fill me in, Trish?" I asked casually, trying to sound only vaguely interested.

"It would be my pleasure," Tricia crowed. "But first, I'd like to say that Smiley's has a totally different attitude toward the American consumer than Fanpan. We believe that today's fast-food customer is bright enough to know that neither Smiley's nor Fanpan will ever serve them a 'down-home' meal. We feel that's just blatantly puffery—pure Madison Avenue poppy-cock."

"Hey, you're a terrific quote, Trish," I urged her on.

"Smiley's is catering to the two-career household. To mothers too hassled with work and chores to get dinner together on their own. Now we think it's just bad psychology to sell our products as 'down-home.' Why make the poor woman feel guilty that she can't be all things to all people? No, instead, we're positioning Smiley's perfect-every-time take-out chicken as . . . are you ready?"

"Baited breath, Trish," I said, and it really wasn't far from the truth.

"A luxury! Smiley's is the place to go when you want to treat yourself! Now everyone knows that Smiley's and Fanpan cost just exactly the same. So, if you were a harried mother and career woman, and you had to choose between take-out chains, which would you go for—the one that reminds you that you didn't have time to do it right yourself . . . or the one that encourages you to pamper yourself with their delicious food?"

"Smart, Trish," I said with feeling. "Very, very smart." Now all we had to do was be a little smarter. "Listen, I want to thank you for your time—and your insights. I've got to tell you that you've opened *my* eyes, at least, to the kind of top-notch strategizing some in-house agencies can do. I just might want to do a follow-up piece on your shop. Would you be interested?"

"Ruthie, I'd be honored," Trish answered. "It's been a real pleasure chatting with you."

FOURTEEN

"So, what have you got?" I asked, looking around the conference table at the six weary, defeated faces that constituted my creative group. Nobody spoke. Jon, one of the writers, lit a fresh cigarette off the one he'd been smoking. Tracy and Sean, a writer/artist team famous for wacky trendsetting work, looked at each other and then away. Everyone managed, one way or another, to avoid my gaze.

"Okay, I'll rephrase that," I tried. "Who'd like to go first?" At the end of yesterday's meeting, I had suggested that we all separate and work up individual ideas. But I could tell by the expressions around me that even this last-ditch effort hadn't succeeded.

"Come on, someone," I pleaded. "Leon? You always manage to come up with something." I turned to the writer I'd been teamed with most often during Ramsey's reign. Though he'd won numerous awards for his distinctively playful headlines, Leon continued to be a hardworking productive journeyman.

"Well, of course, Peg, I've a few lines," Leon retorted. He looked at the single sheet of typing paper he had angled toward him, then winced. "Shall I read them?"

"Yes, please," I encouraged. Leon cleared his throat and swallowed audibly. "First, uh, I thought maybe we could play off the idea of 'there's nobody here but us chickens.' As a visual I see a Fanpan outlet, you know, run entirely by real chickens. Of course, the special effects might be a little tricky. And I'm not totally firm on the headline. But, well, the concept is sort of interesting."

"No, Leon, it isn't," I replied. "It's terrible."

"I know," Leon answered, sighing. He looked down at his typed sheet. "But the others are a lot worse."

"Anyone else?" I asked, glancing around the table. I caught Tracy's eye. "Anything?" I begged.

"Well, Sean and I did have a thought," Tracy began slowly. Tracy's high-pitched voice could generally carry with ease over a takeoff at La Guardia. This afternoon I could barely hear her.

"Yes? Go on...."

"Okay. Here goes," she mumbled. "The headline reads, 'Fanpan...everything You Always Wanted in a Chicken, but Were Afraid to Ask.' You see, our thinking is... Well, Sean, what was our thinking?"

"I don't remember," Sean replied. Normally morose and introspective, today Sean looked positively saturnine. He sat slumped in his chair, moodily taking off and putting on his bifocals. "Frankly, I don't believe any thinking *was* involved. Listen, it's clear to me we're just all too close to this. We've lost perspective...and judgment. Shit, I even had a dream about chickens last night. They were closing in on me—a huge yellow chirping army of them—"

"Okay, that's enough," I cut in, standing up and pushing back my chair. "I wanted to hear you all out before I told you my news." I paced up and down at the head of the conference table. "Through, uh, certain secret sources, I've just this morning discovered Smiley's new product positioning. And the creative direction they plan to take in their fall campaign."

"You've what?" Leon gasped.

"You're kidding!" Tracy cried.

"Good God," Sean murmured.

It was a little like announcing to a class of high school seniors on the verge of flunking that I had all the answers to the final exam. I told them everything Tricia Woolfe had told me.

"How in hell did you find all this out?" Jon demanded. "It's just incredible!"

"Well, I can't tell how I found out," I answered. "But now that we all know what I discovered, I'd like to give you my thinking on how we could best capitalize on it." I sat back down again and opened up the drawing pad I'd brought with me to the meeting. "Okay, we know that Smiley's is going to tell the world that their chicken is a luxury item. What we have to do, simultaneously to their campaign, is position Fanpan as the ultimate luxury food."

"Absolutely," Leon stated.

"Good," Sean confirmed.

"A chicken, in fact, so delicious, so wonderful," I continued, turning my pad to them, "that it's the one the great restaurants of the world bring into their kitchens when they want to send out for fast-food." Before the meeting I'd sketched a master chef, several cooks, waiters, a sommelier and busboys clustered around a huge box of take-out Fanpan. The setting was obviously the kitchen of an expensive, prestigious restaurant.

"Wonderful!" Tracy cried. "I love it!"

"It's good, Peg," Jon answered, nodding and smiling. "And it will roll out well. I mean, we can use the Four Seasons to start . . . then go to Lutèce, maybe Windows on the World . . ."

"And all on location," Sean added. "We want the real McCoys. Actual cooks and waitresses. Yes, and I visualize one of those beautiful black-and-brown duotones—with only the box of Fanpan in vivid four-color."

"Yes," I responded. "Like the Dewar's ads. That's exactly what I had in mind for print. But, I'm also wondering if we shouldn't consider television. I know it's a lot of money. But wouldn't it make a great thirty-second spot?"

"The Bobbins can only say no, right?" Sean demanded. "Listen, let Tracy and me work up some storyboards. We'll really go to town."

"Good," I replied. "Now, Jon and Leon, I think we need both headline and body copy on the print campaign. Maybe even several headline approaches—you know, just to show them how flexible and far-reaching our concept it."

"And a good strong tagline," Leon added, jotting something down on his notepad.

"Right." I nodded. "Good." I smiled.

"*You're* good, kiddo," Leon replied, smiling back. "Who'd a thunk it? Our little Peggy Goodenough, a real live creative director."

"He's right, Peg," Tracy added. "You know, I think we all kind of wondered when you got the promotion if there wasn't something funny going on between the Bobbins and you."

"What do you mean, 'wondered'?" Sean demanded. "We had bets out on which one of those good old boys had a thing for you."

"I'm not going to ask you the odds," I said, laughing. "And I really don't blame you for feeling that way...as long as you've changed your minds now."

"Don't worry," Jon replied.

"Not after this afternoon," Tracy added.

"Okay," I said, taking a deep breath to keep my soaring feelings in some kind of check. I felt so light-headed and proud at the moment that I was almost convinced I could levitate. "Well, now, down to business. I've a Fanpan account review with upper management Monday afternoon. So I'll need all your preliminary layouts and copy drafts by no later than eleven that morning. I'm afraid it's going to mean coming in tomorrow." A Saturday. During the summer. Not the easiest thing to ask.

"Hey, better than presenting 'nobody here but us chickens'!" Tracy cried, snorting with laughter.

"Or what about your god-awful 'everything you always wanted' line?" Leon retorted. "It's a toss-up which is worse."

"Will you be coming in, Peg?" Jon asked. Though he put the question casually, I felt the subtle ripple of tension his words sent around the table. All too often in the past, these creative people had worked overtime and weekends to put together an award-winning campaign, only to have their superiors swoop down and take all the credit. Ramsey had done it to me on more than one occasion during his final months. It had left me with a feeling of outrage mixed with futility.

"Of course," I replied simply. And the meeting broke for the first time with everyone in a positive mood.

The next evening, after a long productive day in the office, I volunteered to make dinner for Spencer at his studio apartment on East Seventy-ninth Street. Spencer spent more time down at his parents' Gramercy Park duplex—they kept his childhood bedroom always ready—than he did in his own apartment. And it showed. The refrigerator contained only condiments—half-used jars of ketchup, mustard, soy sauce— ice cubes and beer. The kitchen cupboards were sparsely stocked with such bachelor favorites as canned baked beans and boxes of instant macaroni and cheese.

"Where's the flour?" I cried, having searched through his sadly lacking stores. "And the salt, pepper, butter and milk?"

"How should I know?" Spencer called back from the living room. He was relaxing on the couch with a beer, watching a Mets game on television. "You know I don't cook, Peg."

"I'm not talking about exotic herbs and spices, Spencer," I replied, making my way into the living room. "I'm referring to your basic survival supplies. Do you realize that you don't even have a coffeepot? How do you *eat* here?"

"I don't, babe," Spencer retorted. "I eat out, or at home. You were the one who elected to play chef here tonight. Listen, I'd be happy to take you out when the game's over."

"No," I replied. "I promised you I'd cook something. I'm just going to have to go out and buy some things first."

"Okay, great," Spencer replied without glancing up from the television. "I'll see you later."

It took me an hour and a half to shop, another fifteen minutes to put everything away, and a bit more than two hours to prepare and cook the stuffed supreme of chicken and spinach soufflé. In my own, plodding, strictly-by-the-cookbook way, I like to bustle around a kitchen. I was raised in a household where all of this was done behind closed doors by anonymous ever-changing hands. I find that I enjoy the measuring out and mixing of ingredients, the poking for doneness, the carving up and garnishing with parsley. Flushed with pleasure and exertion, I served my meal to Spencer by candlelight. It was just past ten-thirty.

"Hmm..." Spencer made appreciative little noises as he ate. "Worth the wait."

"Well, if I'd started out with an actual kitchen," I shot back, "we could have eaten two hours earlier."

"Listen, when the time comes," Spencer replied between bites, "I'll buy you one that will make Betty Crocker go green with envy. You just tell me when, Peg."

"Yes...I know," I replied, putting down my fork. "I'm afraid that...I'm just not in the mood to talk about the future yet. There's so much going on in the present."

"Like?" Spencer demanded.

"Well, Fanpan, of course," I replied. "And the murder investigation..." I hesitated a moment and then asked, "I saw that detective the other night after he had his meeting with you."

"Cursio," Spencer retorted, accentuating the first syllable. "You know I'm really starting to understand what Dad keeps going on about. The law enforcement in this city is a total disaster. This Cursio comes on like he's some sort of Columbo, but you know what he's accomplished? A big nothing.''

"These things take some time," I volunteered.

"Oh, this guy's just a bundle of hot air," Spencer complained. "A lot of empty posturing. He literally hasn't, as far as I can tell, got a clue.''

"What he needs is a premise," I replied.

"Is that what he told you?" Spencer demanded, laughing scornfully. "He really knows how to dish out the old psychobabble, doesn't he? What else did our brilliant investigator have to say?''

"This business about a premise actually makes sense, Spencer," I argued. "It certainly helped me solve the Fanpan situation." And then I went on to tell Spencer what I'd been waiting to reveal all evening: my call to Smiley's, my breakthrough with the creative; I even confessed a growing concern I was having about J.J. after my talk with Cursio.

"Are you actually trying to tell me," Spencer interrupted me at one point, "that J.J. murdered Ramsey?''

"I'm just saying," I countered, "that considering what we know about J.J., it's not entirely out of the question.''

"Does our little buddy Cursio buy this nonsense, too?" Spencer demanded.

"He did seem interested in J.J. when we last spoke. I'm pretty sure he considers him a suspect.''

"Then he's an imbecile!" Spencer cried. "J.J. wasn't even in town when Ramsey was murdered. He happened to be in Macon. He told me that himself. And as for you going around accusing clients of killing people—hey, Peg, somehow I thought you were a whole lot smarter than that.''

"I don't see how being a client can lessen the probability of being a suspect," I replied stiffly. The dinner that had taken me so long to prepare was quickly turning as chilly as the atmosphere in the room. And all my pride and relief at solving the Fanpan creative was trickling away.

"That's hardly the point," Spencer shot back. "Read my lips, Peg, okay? It's not your job to solve Ramsey's murder. That's up to our friendly local homicide detective, right? So then why are you, someone J.J. Bobbin's father handpicked, for chrissakes, to head up his creative, going around construing motives and framing accusations about his son?''

"Look, I'm only trying to say. . ." I began, but once again Mr. M.B.A. had so rattled my cognitive capabilities that I didn't exactly know where my thoughts were heading. I tried again. "J.J. could be dangerous. That's all I'm trying to say. Who knows how rough he actually got with that woman from Smiley's?"

"Peg." Spencer sighed, throwing down his napkin and leaning back in his chair, "What was my main reservation about you taking this job when the question first came up weeks ago?"

The answer stuck in my throat; something difficult to swallow. It didn't help to see that Spencer, once more victorious, was offering me a forgiving, knowing smile.

"J.J.," I said.

FIFTEEN

IN THE END, though a staff of thousands might have helped in the preparation, the creative director stood alone when new work was being presented. It was not unlike an actor playing Hamlet, delivering his "to be or not to be" soliloquy on opening night. The creative was always the question upon which everything else—media, research, account services—depended. There was nothing potentially nobler, or more deadly.

Through the years I had watched Ramsey prepare for presentations hundreds of times. And even Ramsey Farnsworth, one of the greats, was invariably as jittery as a bride before the first chords of the wedding march. A few days before the event, he'd start pacing his long office, mumbling lines, gesturing, frowning. One or two days before the meeting, he'd call the staff together for a run-through, an exercise not unlike a full-dress rehearsal.

I, unfortunately, was to have no opportunity for fine-tuning the already hastily assembled creative. The account management review originally scheduled for Monday was delayed—due to a migraine developed by Mark Rollings—until late Wednesday afternoon. And at the beginning of that meeting, Phillip Ebert announced that the Bobbins were flying up to see our new work. This Thursday. Nine o'clock sharp.

"But that's tomorrow!" I gasped, staring unbelievingly around the table. Phillip, Mark and Spencer all stared grimly back. Felice Clay from media and research's Neal Meadows sympathetically looked away.

"Clever girl," Mark replied. "If you keep at it, soon you'll be able to count to ten, as well."

"Stop it, you two," Phillip declared, though his glare came to rest on me rather than Mark. "I'll allow no infighting among my staff. Let's direct our energies toward more useful ends, shall we? I don't think I have to remind any of you of the importance of tomorrow's meeting. The Bobbins must walk out of this building absolutely *thrilled* with P&Q. We simply have to ebb the current flow of bad feelings about this agency."

Phillip was referring to the lead article in the latest issue of *Ad Age*, headlined, "The Great Exodus, or, Whatever Became of P&Q?" It was a detailed, depressing piece about the two major and four minor accounts that had deserted us since Ramsey's murder. Although generally fair-minded and accurate, the article had managed to make Phillip Ebert sound slightly accusatory—the police were dragging their feet, loyal clients were a dying breed, etc.—and more than a little desperate.

"Absolutely," Mark echoed. "And as I know you're well aware, Phillip, the Bobbins have always been pleased and most complimentary with the work they've been getting from account services. It's, well, obviously in other areas—" he glanced through lowered lids at me "—that our problems lie."

"Thank you, Mark," Phillip answered smoothly, "for your astute but totally unnecessary and clearly self-serving remarks. Regardless of how efficient and organized your staff may be, it's become clear to me in the several meetings we've all had with the Bobbins, that Victor doesn't *like* you or Spencer, or to be thoroughly honest, me. I believe he finds our, well, professional approach somewhat daunting. That's obviously why he fixed on Peg as a replacement for Ramsey. She's young and a little green, and Victor feels comfortable with that. So, my suggestion is that tomorrow becomes basically Peg's show. I'll lead in with a few introductory remarks. Neal and Felice will take a few minutes to review the media and research the Bobbins already remember from our initial presentation to them, then Peg will take the floor."

"Of course, I should summarize account's role in the preparation of the new creative," Mark stated, flashing Phillip one of his most boyish and appealing smiles.

"No, Mark," Phillip said with a sigh. "I have something far more important for you to do."

"Yes?" Mark preened.

"You'll shut up," Phillip replied simply, and without missing a beat, he continued, "Now, Peg, let's see what you've got."

Leon, Jon, Tracy, Sean—in fact everyone—had done a terrific job. The comps were so tightly rendered they looked almost typeset. The copy was crisp, funny, perfect for the concept. Though I'd been concerned that the idea wouldn't translate well into television, the storyboards turned out to be just as strong, if not stronger, than the print campaign. It was good work. It was directly on our new competitive strategy. It was creative that, if produced as shown, could win its share of OBIEs and CLIOs. What I hadn't taken into consideration was that it was not, at all, the kind of work P&Q did.

Every advertising agency had a distinctive creative attitude that attracted certain kinds of accounts. Often a client would decide on a particular agency by reputation alone. A huge corporate packaged-goods mogul like Procter & Gamble wouldn't be happy at some wild and crazy little creative boutique. It was a match of personalities as much as anything else. New aggressive businesses tended to gravitate to the more risk-taking and flamboyant shops; mainstream blue-chip companies to the more conservative research-oriented agencies. P&Q was a long-established leader of the latter school. Our clients preferred the test-marketed focus-grouped tried-and-true approach.

That didn't leave room for a whole lot of humor.

"But, Peg," Phillip objected as soon as I finished my presentation, "it almost sounds, well . . . funny."

"It's supposed to," I explained, glancing around the table. Everyone, including Spencer, looked puzzled and more than a little alarmed.

"Oh dear," Phillip continued, adjusting his perfectly positioned tie. "Well, what else do you have? What's your backup approach?"

"We didn't prepare one," I announced. "I felt this was so strong that offering alternatives would be a waste of time. Listen, believe me, this is *exactly* what Fanpan needs right now.

It's a terrific positioning statement, and competitively it just blows Smiley's out of the water."

"Perhaps," Phillip conceded. "But, Peg, I really have to ask, is it us? Is it P&Q?"

"That's what's wrong with this agency, Mr. Ebert," I shot back with feeling. "We're always asking that question, instead of the far more important one—is it the right approach as far as the *client* is concerned? The more we worry about us at the expense of them, the faster they're going to be walking out that door." Suddenly overcome with conviction, I pulled all my stuff together, stood up from the table and started that direction myself.

"Where do you think you're going, Peg?" Phillip demanded as I reached for the doorknob.

"I don't know," I answered, turning around to survey the table. I read only one thing in the faces that looked back at mine: fear. "I guess I'm going someplace that's smart enough to take risks, if that's what is going to make business grow." I started to push open the door.

"Then you're staying here," Phillip announced. I turned to stare at him.

"You mean that?" I demanded.

"You don't leave me much choice, Peg," Phillip answered, sighing. "The Bobbins will be here tomorrow morning. I can't see us redoing the entire campaign now, can you? So, present it as is. But I want you to know one thing...."

"Yes?" I asked.

"I don't like it." And neither, I sensed, did anyone else. Though it was hard to tell. In advertising we live by the herd instinct. Follow the leader, stay with the pack. Or you're liable to get trampled. Well, I was a stray now. Setting off on my own. And though Mark Rollings could hardly control his smirk, I read concern in Spencer's look. Pity in the others'. But I didn't want their sympathy. I didn't need their support. I'm the first to admit I'm no maverick. I'm no radical. I'm not like my mother. But the point was, as far as the Fanpan creative went, I *was* right. And that was all there was to it.

"More coffee, Victor?" Mark asked. "J.J., how about another Danish? These cheese-filled ones are just delicious."

"I didn't fly all the way up from Macon to get fed," Victor grumbled. I heard the end of this exchange as I hurried into the executive conference room. It was more like an arena than a room, really. A luxuriously decorated little contemporary Roman coliseum designed for throwing various things to the lions. Me, for instance, I thought as I hurriedly set up my flip charts on the small center stage.

I had been up since five that morning, composing my thoughts for this very moment. I'd downed about a gallon of coffee as I formulated and memorized what I needed to say. My nerves were wound as tight as a yo-yo string. I was up. I was ready. I'd stopped caring about the dangers that faced me. I was ready to roll.

"Good morning Victor, J.J.," I said, sitting down between Phillip Ebert and Felice Clay at the speaker's podium. Besides our two visiting dignitaries positioned front and center, the rows of seats facing me were filled by all the P&Q employees even remotely concerned with the Fanpan account. Everyone from the secretaries to the junior account people to the assistant paste-up artists was expected to attend.

This long-standing P&Q tradition of stocking the theater was designed as a show of force to the client in question. Look, the tiers of anonymous bodies said, at all the people we've got working just for you. It was also traditional to so fatten clients with rich pastry and coffee before the presentation that they were too groggy to fully grasp the proceedings. But the look of irritation and impatience on Victor's face convinced me that none of our usual techniques was working this morning.

"Ladies and gentlemen," Phillip began at last. I listened to his preamble and the remarks from Neal and Felice with only half an ear. Instead, I concentrated on observing J.J., seeing him for the first time as the terrible thing he might actually be: a murderer.

His freckled face was wide and flat. The nose slightly pug, the lips full, soft, darkly pink. With his tightly wired orange-colored hair and his thickly freckled, highly colored flesh, J.J. looked like something in negative: dark where he should be light. This morning his two-hundred-plus pounds were stuffed inside a peach-colored linen jacket and stiffly laundered pin-striped shirt with a high white collar. His neck spilled out over his shirt top in a rich fleshy fold, like ice-cream over the lip of a cone.

So intent was my scrutiny, it took me a moment or two to realize that a new element had emerged in my watch: J. J. Bobbin was staring back. With a start, I looked away. Then, ever so slowly and casually, back. Oh heavens, yes, he was glaring straight at me!

"And now, Peg Goodenough will tell you a bit about what we have in mind for you creatively," Phillip announced, scraping me from the frying pan and casting me into the fire. At last, I stood, walked over to my easel and began.

My memories are fleeting of that half hour in hell. In the beginning, I remember a voice—high-pitched, reedy, not my own—talking with admirable conviction about a subject my poor tired mind had suddenly completely forgotten. As time went on and the voice grew more familiar, the situation less surreal, I began to wonder what sort of effect my words were having on the audience. As I worked my way through the flip chart, I tried to glance now and then into the seats. They seemed to be occupied by life-size stone statues. No one coughed or sneezed or whispered. But worst of all, no one laughed.

I had decided early that morning when I prepared the speech to make it in the spirit of the creative. Or, in other words, humorous. That's not to say I told any jokes. I just kept it light, breezy, hopefully fun. If anyone out there was enjoying it, however, he or she was masterfully disguising the fact.

"Our headline, then," I concluded, my voice still strong though my heart had long ago sunk, "is, 'Guess What the Staff at Lutéce Brings in When They Want the Best in Take-out Dining?'"

Silence. Deadly deafening silence. I glanced at Victor. He was stony faced, unmoved. J.J., his eyes glazed slightly over, seemed to be napping. Nothing moved. Nobody spoke. Days, weeks, years seemed to crawl by. I managed to walk back to the podium and sit down shakily. I was so relieved to hear a human voice that when someone finally spoke, I didn't even care that it was Mark Rollings.

"Well, of course, as everyone knows," Mark began snidely, "creative attempts are just that—attempts. What Peg has given us is just the, uh, first stage, a rough idea, of what we might develop into a full-fledged effective campaign. At P&Q, we like to work closely with our clients as we start to, well, flesh out these initial ideas. We like to hear your input first—then move on to more fully realize the potential of what we've presented. So, in other words, if you, Victor, or you, J.J., would care to comment on what you've seen and heard, we could then—"

"It's fine," Victor declared. He stood and stretched.

"Oh, well," Mark replied. "Of course. But what, exactly, Victor, did you like? What should we change? Where do we go from here?"

"The whole thing's fine," Victor responded shortly. "Come on, J.J., can't be lazing around here all day, sonny boy."

"Yes, b-but," Mark stuttered, "what do you like best—the print or the air? How far into the fall should we book? And which schedule?"

"Listen, mister, haven't I made myself clear?" Victor retorted. "I liked everything. Print. Radio. Television. Even those billboards are fine by me. Book the works, damn it, straight through till Christmas. Good work, Peg. That's my gal." And with that, Victor Bobbin stomped out of the conference room and J.J., hoisting himself awkwardly out of his chair, lumbered slowly behind.

SIXTEEN

THE SATURDAY AFTER the Bobbins' visit and my triumph, was the Fourth of July. It was one of those breezy, high visibility, sharply sunny days Manhattan can be known to produce when it decides to be on its best behavior. The city was surpassing itself in appearing patriotic—American flags snapped proudly from wind-whipped poles and window ledges—and, even more surprisingly, the denizens were behaving with uncharacteristic warmth and uncitylike charm.

"Here you go, lady," my taxi driver announced cheerfully as he pulled to the curb down the street from the Guildens' duplex. "Afraid I can't get any closer. Looks like its gonna be quite the party." Limos were lined up two-deep down the block. Combo music and female laughter drifted with the smell of cigarette smoke and perfume onto the square. Though the luncheon invitation had specified dress—informal—I now knew the Guildens a little better than that. Miriam's idea of a casual picnic would be a sit-down affair for a hundred people.

I wasn't far off the mark. In the end, 112 of Manhattan's politically conservative movers and shakers dined off Miriam's floral-patterned Limoges. Both pink and white champagne flowed as swiftly as the Hudson after a heavy rain. It wasn't until the toasts and speeches—from a New York state senator and a powerful Manhattan court judge—that I grasped the fact I was attending a political fund-raiser. For Jacob Guilden. For mayor.

"It is highly appropriate then, that on the very day we celebrate this country's most sacred precepts," the rotund judge, jowls shaking with feeling, concluded his remarks, "we also celebrate a man whose belief in the constitutional values set forth by our founding fathers is unrivaled in this city, the state and, perhaps, dear friends, even in this great country of ours."

I'd been standing between Martin Guilden and Spencer during the speeches. As the warm applause began to die down, I turned to Martin and asked, "Does this officially mean your father is running?"

"Heavens, no!" Martin replied, his pasty face going a shade paler at my suggestion. "We won't announce until the very last minute. Really, Spence, you should give Peg a crash course in politics. It's unsafe to have her wandering around with such naive thoughts in her head. Who knows what she might say?"

"Don't worry, Marty," Spencer answered in a conciliatory tone quite unlike the one he usually used with his hectoring older brother. "Peg and I haven't talked about the race at all that much yet. I'll fill her in about what she should know."

"Best tell her what I told Tracy," Martin advised, glancing toward his wife. She was standing across the room, the center of a tight little group of equally lovely, blond, perfectly dressed women—a ready-made photo essay for *W*'s "What's Happening in Manhattan?" page.

"Which was?" Spencer asked, following Martin's gaze. What did he see in me, I wondered, when he could have his pick of that fragrant bouquet of debutantes? Though I'd gotten some advice from a "personal shopper" at Lord & Taylor, I sensed that once again my costume fell short of expectations. Or, more to the point, it went too far. I'd opted for a red, white and blue, wide-striped linen blouse, a finely pleated white skirt and flat fire-engine red patent leather shoes. At the time I made the purchases, I felt supremely confident that this wardrobe would help me slip unnoticed into the Guildens' rarefied social circle. In fact, I stood out like a tugboat hooting full steam through a calm sea of pleasure yachts.

"I simply told Tracy," Martin explained, his tone both proprietary and fond, "to keep her pretty little mouth shut when it came to Father. Tell Peg to do the same."

"I'm right here, Martin," I objected, irritated by his acting as if I was both deaf and dumb. It didn't help matters that he seemed to see his wife in the same terms. "You can speak to me directly, you know. I think I'm capable of following along."

"Really, Spence," Martin sniffed. Over his horn-rims he gave me a hard disapproving look and strode away.

"What's with you, Peg?" Spencer whispered urgently as we watched Martin's slightly balding head disappear into the crowd. "This is a big day for the family. A time we should all pull together. Don't go spoil it with a lot of hard-nosed opinions, okay?"

"If asking to be treated like a human being—rather than a designer's dummy—is asking too much," I replied in hurt tones, "then maybe I should head home right now." Spencer's attitude was confusing—and alarming—to me. In the past he had always claimed an opposing renegade position to his family and its political aspirations. He spoke with disdain of his father's single-minded drive to make Gracie Mansion the next Guilden residence, and he belittled his brothers for fueling Jacob Guilden's fanaticism on the subject. His extreme distaste for the campaign had, in fact, bolstered my confidence about facing the clan. I, like Spencer, my thinking went, remained untainted by this political fervor. I, like Spencer, stood in the wings, watching the silly drama unfold. Now, suddenly, I felt that I was standing there alone.

"Oh, come on now, babe," Spencer answered, taking my hand. "Don't be so damn sensitive. Poor Martin probably didn't even realize he was insulting you. He's so used to living with that pea brain, Tracy, he doesn't know how to act in front of an intelligent female."

Spencer's little speech was no doubt calculated to comfort and compliment. And though I sensed this, it didn't stop me from eating up his soothing words like a hungry baby gobbling pablum. He filled me with a renewed sense of confidence, causing the rest of the afternoon to pass in a bright glow of well-being. It was hard not to feel special and pampered when being entertained by the Guildens. The events of the af-

ternoon were, of course, arranged for the benefit of possible
high-rolling Jacob Guilden supporters, but I managed to enjoy them thoroughly just the same.

The luncheon was only the beginning. After coffee and
speeches, chartered limousines carried us to the Seventy-second
Street boat basin where a luxury cruiser, equipped with a full
bar and Dixieland jazz band, waited. To the tune of "Happy
Days Are Here Again," we floated downstream on the Hudson. The river was awash with sailboats and speedboats, yachts
of varying sizes and condition, but the cruiser the Guildens had
chartered was by far the grandest of the lot. Spencer and I
sipped champagne and danced to "The Saints Go Marching
In" with a kind of happy abandon I thought I'd never feel
around my prospective in-laws. We drifted below Battery Park
and up the East River, the hot sun turning the harbor into a
dazzling arena of dancing light. By the time we disembarked at
a landing in the East Fifties, I felt a warm glow, fueled only
partially by fermented French grapes, toward the entire Guilden family.

The limousines again waited. This time they conducted us
with portentous slowness into the dark lush interior of Central
Park. Though most traffic was being redirected down Fifth, the
Guilden cavalcade was waved through the Sixty-sixth Street
entrance by rows of policemen dressed in parade uniform.

"What's going on?" I whispered to Spencer as the chauf-
feur threw open the door at the Sheep Meadow. A large empty
podium decorated with red, white and blue bunting sat in the
middle of the field of green. When the crowd that had been
milling around the stage spotted the limousines, they started to
applaud. "What in heaven's name is going on?" I asked again.

"A sort of surprise," Spencer replied, grinning. "I only
found out last night, and thought I'd better keep it from you
until the last minute. It's entirely up to you, Peg. You can sit
with us or not. I just don't want to see you throw one of your
fits in front of Father. So you decide."

"But what am I deciding, Spencer?" I demanded as the
Guildens and their guest started to stream toward the waiting
crowd. I saw a camera flash across the lawn. "You still haven't
told me what's going on!"

"A speech," Spencer explained excitedly, grabbing my hand
and trailing along behind his brothers. "Dad's giving a speech,

and he wants us all to sit with him on the dais. You, too, if you like.''

"Oh," I murmured, wondering again at Spencer's sudden enthusiasm for his father's cause. With his free hand, he waved to several people I didn't know. His gorgeous smile flashing, he called hellos to several more. I felt the dynamism and charisma he emanated. I saw the women who naturally swayed toward him; flowers turning their faces toward the sun. Who could blame them? I glanced proudly at the masculine prize who held my hand so possessively. His dark blond hair seemed to draw the sun to it like a mirror, glinting with red-and-gold highlights. His green-checked linen sport jacket, off-white shirt and gray rough-weave linen slacks all fit with the kind of casual low-key elegance money alone can't buy. Spencer projected style, assurance. He had that "star quality" Hollywood craved.

"Come on, everybody," Martin was officiating at the podium, "let's take our places. Louis, you and Cecilia here. Mother, dear, take the seat to the right of Father. Spencer? Peggy? Hurry up now, kids, we're supposed to get under way before six."

It was more that I didn't want to let go of Spencer's warm hand than that I wanted to climb up behind the bunting. In any case, feeling rather like a fool, I joined Spencer's handsome wealthy family on the dais. I was so embarrassed by my position that I didn't hear a word of Martin's introductory remarks, though I rose with the others when Jacob Guilden took the microphone. I, too, applauded. What else could I do?

It was a loud vehement long-winded speech, and after the first flowery sentence or two, I didn't listen. Though late afternoon, the sun was still very much with us. A residue of champagne and overexertion flooded my limbs with a tingling fatigue. And though I didn't actually doze off, I did let my mind wander.

I thought about my Fanpan presentation. About Victor's compliments and J.J.'s brooding presence. I tried to analyze what I felt toward J.J. Fear? Revulsion? I conjured up his face: the broad flat forehead, the small eyes bulging from their fatty sockets. And then, the weirdest thing happened. I actually *saw* those eyes staring at me from the sun-drenched crowd that surrounded the podium. J.J.'s eyes! But it couldn't be! I squinted into the sun.

He was standing toward the back, wearing a white visor cap that shadowed his face. The man was big, beefy like J.J., with a camera strap slung over one shoulder. He clutched a can of beer in his hand. I told myself I was imagining things. I told myself it couldn't be J.J. Then something else happened that took my mind totally off the junior Bobbin. Jacob Guilden smacked the podium.

"And I say to you, ladies and gentlemen, that if Ramsey Farnsworth had been allowed to carry his own registered firearm, that man would be alive today!"

A wave of applause rippled through the crowd.

"And I ask you, friends, if we cannot protect ourselves, where are those men who we—honest taxpayers—support to keep law and order in this city for us? Where were they when Ramsey Farnsworth was murdered? Where are they now? Who is looking for this man's slayer? Who is guarding the gates to our city?"

The applause swelled. Several people cried out their approval to Jacob Guilden. Finally, he had to raise his arms for silence.

"What are we asking for, my friends?" he continued, subdued. "What is our simple demand? Let me tell you what it is. It's nothing more or less than our constitutional right. Anyone who loves this country, anyone who believes and follows the Declaration of Independence, the very document that created this land of our, knows this to be true. Constitutionally, we are granted the...right...to...carry..." He paused before each word to lengthen the suspense and build drama. His pacing drove the crowd wild.

"Arms!" he screamed, the crowd stamped and cheered. The mayhem continued for several seconds before he once again leaned into the microphone. "Thank you. And God bless you," he said with feeling, then he reached for Miriam's hand, and together they stepped down from the dais and hurried to their waiting limo.

"Thank you all for coming," Martin was saying as I started to recover from Jacob's diatribe. I scanned the thinning crowd for the man I thought was J.J., but he was gone.

"Spencer, who are these people?" I asked as he helped me down from my seat. "Is this some kind of organization?"

"Wake up, Peggy," Spencer replied, once again securing my hand in his. He led me around so that I saw the front of the dais for the first time. A large sign hung among the patriotic bunting. It read, The American Rifle Association Welcomes Jacob Guilden.

Suddenly I felt dizzy and more than a little sick. It was not just that I was raised by a woman who numbers among her pet causes that of legislating for stiffer gun-control laws. Somewhere along the line I, too, began to believe in them. Somehow during the past few years, I'd found myself *believing* in a lot of things Theo taught me. And everything Jacob Guilden had said that day went against this deepening moral grain in me.

"What's the matter, babe?" Spencer asked with concern. "You look a little ill. Too much champagne?"

Clearly he didn't see anything wrong with what his father had said or with the issue that would no doubt become a plank in Guilden's political platform. His sea-blue eyes gazed into mine. I saw us on the deck that afternoon, dancing. I remembered the looks of other women as he passed. I squeezed his strong warm hand and said, "No, really, I'm fine."

Well, what else could I have done?

SEVENTEEN

"So, HOW DID DAD'S SPEECH hit you, Spence?" Martin asked, leaning across me as he posed the question. I was wedged between the two men in the back of a limousine that was edging downtown through thickening traffic. We were about to complete the last leg of the Guilden political triathlon: a huge cocktail party at Beekman Place, which promised superb views of the fireworks on the East River. As the brothers spoke, they inched closer and closer to each other, squeezing me in on either side. I began to feel—both physically and emotionally—rather like a large damp sponge.

"Frankly, Martin," Spencer answered, "I though it was heavy on the issues . . . and light on the inspiration."

"But, Spencer," Martin responded, "that was just what we were shooting for. We wanted to prove that Dad's not afraid of tackling these problems head-on. Unlike the mayor, who hides behind a lot of double-talk and statistics. Unlike the other unannounced candidates, who're spouting the usual liberal non-sense. Jacob Guilden is laying his opinions on the line. He's saying what he thinks is wrong with the city—and telling people what should be done."

"That's fine," Spencer retorted, "and I know it's damned important and all that. But let me ask you something, aside from the special-interest types who were there today, who in hell cares? People want a little charm...a little sparkle. They want to be wooed, not dictated to."

"Nobody was dictating," Martin replied defensively. He turned and glared out the window at the traffic light five cars up that was turning red for a second time; we'd inched forward a tricycle-length, at most.

"Hey, listen, I'm not saying that what happened this afternoon wasn't absolutely fantastic. My God, that crowd couldn't get enough of him. It was a terrific coming-out reception. And I think you should all be congratulated. But be sensible, Martin. That speech would go over like a lead balloon before a more general audience."

"I don't know about that," Martin countered. "Perhaps Lou, Dad and I have a slightly higher opinion of the American public than you do, Spence. We happen to believe they care about these issues, that they'll listen."

"Oh, spare me!" Spencer moaned. "Public perceptions, consumer awareness—that's *my* territory. It's what I do for a living. Don't kid yourself, brother. You're selling something here. It's not all that terribly different from peddling car wax or breakfast cereal. Only you're pushing a man, you're plumping for a—listen to me, Martin—public image. The great unwashed couldn't give a flying fig about Dad's beliefs—they want to know if he likes baseball, if he loves his wife, what he watches on TV."

In fits and starts we edged forward. Though heavily air-conditioned, the atmosphere in the back seat was far from cool. Beneath Martin's deodorant-perfumed aroma, I could smell a danker, more heated body emerging.

"I think you're exaggerating your point," Martin responded judiciously.

"And I think you're not listening," Spencer shot back. "There's nothing wrong with a campaign of conscience, but it can't be *just* that. You need to wrap it in a patina of personality, give it a little human interest. You need to make Dad more than just a one-dimensional public speaker. You have to give him a persona—put some blood and guts behind all this politicking."

"I have to admit that your argument has its merits," Martin conceded thoughtfully. "It worries me from time to time that Lou, Dad and I live in too rarefied an atmosphere. I mean, we spend our days with other articulate intelligent business-oriented people. I'm not sure if we're really connecting with your 'great unwashed' American consumer."

I'm afraid that Spencer was too excited by the fact that he was making an impression on his older sibling to hear the derisive undercurrent of what Martin was saying: the lawyer brothers and father were "more rarefied, more articulate and intelligent" than Spencer.

"Of course, what Spencer says makes sense," I blurted out protectively.

"Oh?" Martin sniffed, flashing me a cold "what do you know" look. "I'm sure you're right," he added, obviously not meaning it. My little outburst effectively ended the conversation, and we traveled the rest of the way in a thoughtful silence.

I'd lived with Theo in some pretty sumptuous surroundings. We'd rented castles in Scotland, châteaus in Switzerland, luxury estates in Connecticut. But for sheer size and ostentation, not even Theo's voracious appetites would be able to swallow the Beekman Place cooperative where the Guildens' evening reception was held. It took up an entire floor of one of the hideous high rises that have started to shoot up along the East River like so many silent sulky monsters. Whereas the exterior was a pink marble and supershiny brass fantasy à la Trump Tower, the lobby plunged one immediately into the lush crimson atmosphere of a turn-of-the-century American West bordello.

Night had fallen by the time Spencer, Martin and I entered the fiftieth-floor penthouse, and Queens and Brooklyn—gray wastelands by day—had transformed themselves into magical kingdoms of light. Downriver, the Brooklyn Bridge glittered with all its old heart-tugging promise. The highway and river were flooded with the lights of incoming traffic as millions of New Yorkers converged on the East Side to participate in the culminating event of Fourth of July in Manhattan: Macy's fireworks.

Though there were probably more than two hundred guests, the apartment was so large that everyone who wanted to see the show had managed to find a spot somewhere along the windows or floor-length balconies that overlooked the river. Spencer and I edged our way through the crowd.

Spencer stood behind me, his arms around my waist as the first orange spirals of light shot through the night and all of New York gave out a collective "aaah!"

"Having a good time?" he whispered in my ear as purple and pink plumes of light exploded before our eyes. "Hasn't this been a day, though?" he added rhetorically. And I nodded, the back of my head rubbing against his shirtfront, but my agreement was only that it had been a day, all right. What kind, exactly, and how much I'd really liked it, I was still trying to decipher.

"Spence..." I began, shifting slightly so that my question wouldn't be overheard by those around us, "did you, uh, agree with everything your father was saying today?"

"What do you mean, agree?" Spencer demanded, his arms tightening around me as he spoke. "You heard what I said to Martin. I saw a lot of room for improvement, obviously."

"Well, yes, I understand what you meant about your dad humanizing his image," I replied, now turning around in his arms so that I was facing him. "But did you agree with what he was *saying*?"

I saw red, white and blue fireworks reflecting in the eyes of the man I thought I loved. I watched them fade, like shooting stars, as he replied, "You missed my point, Peg. My argument isn't with what he said, you see, it's with the way he said it. He needs to lighten up. Make his speeches more personal, less pedantic."

"Forget about your dad and the campaign for a minute," I responded, my voice rising, "and just answer for yourself. Are you telling me that you really think gun-control laws should be banned? Is that what you're saying?"

"Hey, babe, settle down," Spencer urged quietly. "People are starting to look at us."

"I don't care," I shot back, though I tried to lower my voice. "You haven't given me a straight answer yet. Do you agree with him?"

"I don't really know," Spencer answered simply. "I haven't given it a whole lot of thought. But in general, I guess, sure, I think he's on the right track."

"That's not exactly true," I responded. "It seems to me that until very recently, you haven't agreed with him about this campaign. It seems to me that, unless my memory is really going, less than a week or two ago you were calling it 'a load of bull.'"

"Don't get sarcastic," Spencer snapped, his eyes flaring with an explosion of golden plumes. Above the chorus of "oohs" and "aahs" that surrounded us, he continued, "It's true that I have had some problems with the way he first started this thing. But, recently, there have been some changes. You see, Peg, both Lou and Dad have started to ask for my... advice."

"About what?" I demanded, unmoved by the self-satisfied grin that was pulling at the corners of Spencer's handsome mouth.

"About the kinds of things I was trying to explain to Marty tonight," Spencer replied. "You know, public perception, issues versus image, that sort of thing. It's really hit home to me during the past few weeks that I know something Dad and the guys don't. I mean, Peg, Dad and Lou are finally beginning to see that I'm an expert in an area they know nothing about—but really need to."

"And what about Martin?" I asked. "You seem to be leaving him out of this."

"That's because he's the problem," Spencer answered. "Martin is supposed to be handling the public relations side of Dad's campaign—Lou and Dad, the internal issues and planning. But, well, Martin doesn't really know anything about PR. He's floundering."

"And you wouldn't?" I demanded. "Spencer, are you telling me that you're actually thinking of joining your Dad's campaign at some point?"

"Oh, no, Peg," Spencer answered convincingly. "The question hasn't even come up. They're just turning to me for advice now and then. And, well, I guess all I'm trying to say is... I'm a little flattered. I've always been the odd man out in the family, you know."

"I always thought you wanted it that way," I replied, looking into his eyes. They were glassy in the dark, pools of blackness into which fireworks exploded. Was this maybe all that was there? A fine polished surface on which things could be easily reflected. Had I just been seeing myself in Spencer all this time?

"Don't look so dejected, Peg," Spencer replied with a short laugh. "Just because you can't forgive your mother for being such a strong personality, doesn't mean I shouldn't deal with my father being one."

"Is that what you're doing, Spence?" I demanded. "Dealing with it? Or giving in to it?" The minute I blurted the words out, I was sorry. Everyone has a weak spot in their lives; for both Spencer and me it's our parents. It was one of the things that had drawn us together, that had nourished our love. I didn't want it to be the thing that ended it.

"I take that back," I raced to add, giving him a hug and whispering in his ear, "We're going to just strike that from the public record, okay? And we're going to drop this silly conversation right here. As you were saying, it was some day. Let's make it some night, too, all right?"

"You got it," he said, hugging me back, and I wasn't sure if it was the sound of the fireworks—or of his heart—but my ears filled with a thunderous joyful rat-a-tat-tat.

We went back to his apartment later, giggling with too much champagne and excitement, and made brief urgent love on his unmade bed. I am an overly modest person; I prefer lowered blinds and plenty of sheets to hide beneath. Spencer, unfortunately, likes yards of brilliant sunlight and naked flesh on naked flesh. Our most successful moments are spontaneous, unstudied, fleeting. That's the way it was that night. Afterward we lay exhausted, satisfied and still almost fully clothed in each other's arms.

Spencer walked me to the corner later and found a taxi for me. "Make sure she gets in the door safely," he told the driver, crumpling some bills into the man's palm. It was a smooth fast drive through the park. The lush jungly smells of midsummer rushed through the open windows. Cries and music of late-night revelers drifted on the air. I was weary, relaxed, pleased with myself for retrieving the evening from the brink of disaster, where it had been tottering during the fireworks.

"Good night, lady," the taxi driver called after me as I unlocked the front door. I suppose it was his way of making good on Spencer's tip. If I hadn't turned around to wave good-night in return, I would never have seen the Chevy sedan parked across the street. Or the man in it. He was wearing a white visor. He was looking over at me. Yes, it was J.J.

EIGHTEEN

"DON'T TELL ME *he's* your boyfriend," the tired angry voice at the other end of the line announced bluntly after I'd said "Hello?" It was the Tuesday after the Fourth. A little past nine o'clock, and I'd just gotten into the office.

"What?" I asked, trying to get my bearings. Then I recognized the voice. Dante Cursio. "What are you talking about?"

"The photo spread in the *Daily News*," Cursio retorted. "Someone who looks a hell of a lot like you is standing beside Spencer Guilden and his father, grinning like a deranged Miss America."

"Oh, my God, it's in the paper?" I gasped.

"What did you expect, Peg?" Cursio shot back. "I heard that the Guilden crew invited the entire Fourth Estate out to hear that god-awful speech. But answer my question, because I just can't believe what I'm reading. You're identified here as a 'friend of the family.' Tell me that's not true."

"Why should I deny it?" I demanded. "Yes, if you really care to know, Spencer Guilden is my boyfriend—he has been for over a year. And, as a matter of fact—"

"Christ, you've got to be kidding," Cursio cut in. "Peg, I really don't get it. The guy's nothing but a smart-assed self-satisfied little—"

"He's my fiancé," I interrupted him boldly, hardly caring that my words came out in an angry high-pitched warble.

"Oh," Cursio responded. There was a long moment of awkward silence in which I could hear both of us breathing too deeply and too fast. "Listen," he continued at last, "I'm sorry. I . . . didn't know. Forget what I said. It's your life."

"That's right," I replied evenly, though I was hurt by his chilly tone. "It certainly is."

"Let me ask you one thing, though, just for the record. . . ."

"Of course," I answered magnanimously.

"Do you support what Guilden was saying?" Cursio demanded. "I mean, that business about the cops—that means *me*, you understand—not doing the job? You agree with that?"

"No," I responded at once. "No . . . I think he's really a little misinformed about the murder investigation."

"I see," Cursio retorted. "That didn't keep you from taking a seat up there with the man, though, did it? Little Miss Anti-Gun-Control of 1989. God, your mother must be so proud."

"Now you listen to me, Dante Cursio," I exploded, my voice cracking like an adolescent's. "How I choose to live my life— and with whom—is none of your business. But, just for your information, I didn't know until *after* that speech was over what the whole thing was about. I didn't *knowingly* sit there condoning what Jacob Guilden said. I was dragged onto the stage at the last minute."

"Dragged?" Cursio snorted. "You? Listen, Peg, maybe you *couldn't* have foreseen what Guilden was going to say. But why did you stay on the podium after he'd started in on us? I mean, couldn't you have at least made a gesture of protest and stepped down?"

"May I remind you that Spencer is my *fiancé*," I answered. "I think he, and his family, would have found it highly embarrassing if I'd made such a move."

"Well, I find it highly embarrassing," Cursio answered with a sigh, "that you didn't." And he hung up.

My phone rang immediately. It was Mark Rollings, his voice oozing with vitriol. "Saw your pic in the *News*," he announced. "So you and Spencer are finally going public, huh?"

"What do you want, Mark?" I demanded. "I'm busy."

"Oh yeah?" Mark replied snidely. "Well, you may not be for long. You can be damn sure that Ebert's going to see the photo spread of the Guilden rally. And we all know how the board feels about office romances, now don't we? If I were you, Peggy, I'd spend the rest of the morning polishing up the old résumé."

This time *I* slammed down the phone. Then I picked it right up again, dialing Spencer's interoffice number.

"I'm sorry," his secretary responded to my request to speak with him, "but Mr. Guilden was called into an emergency meeting first thing this morning."

"With whom?" I demanded.

"Mr. Ebert and—" the woman paused reverently "—the chairman of the board." Oh God, I thought, old Ironsides himself! Rosco Peabody, nephew and heir to the founder of Peabody & Quinlan, only made the trip in from his horse ranch in Westchester if a major bloodletting was about to take place. Though totally ignorant as to how the agency was run, Rosco would take sudden terrifying interest when he thought it was being run badly. He was rather proud of the fact that he knew nothing practical about the business. He saw himself as a figurehead for the corporation. A moral leader. He did not smoke, drink, swear or gamble. And he expected his employees to follow his example—at least during the workday. He once fired a senior vice president for ordering a second martini at the annual executive Christmas lunch.

It was Rosco who had set the hard-and-fast rule outlawing interoffice romance. No, I decided as I hung up the phone, it was definitely not going to be a good day.

By noontime I'd heard from another dozen or so people about the newspaper article, most implying that the linkage of Spencer's and my name was hardly news.

"For heaven's sake, Peg," Sean told me blithely, "you know how this place is. I probably knew Spencer had a thing for you before *you* did. I'm just surprised it didn't blow up in your faces sooner. I mean, my God, you two were hardly the soul of discretion."

"That's not fair," I retorted hotly. "I thought we tried very hard to keep it under wraps."

"Peg, I've passed you two kissing in front of that Xerox place in Grand Central," Sean answered laughingly, "at least a hundred times. C'mon, everybody knew."

"Not Ebert," I objected.

"Don't kid yourself!" Sean shot back. "He just didn't say anything because he can't afford to lose either of you. The only person who gives a damn is that crazy old loon Rosco. He's got so many bees in his bonnet I swear he could set up a honey farm."

"Yeah, and it's *me* who's going to get stung!" I replied, near tears with the injustice of it all.

"Maybe Spencer will take the rap," Sean tried to comfort me.

"No," I answered, sighing, "we already agreed that if this ever happened, I'd be the one who'd go."

Only now it didn't seem fair. At all. At twelve-thirty, with Spencer still behind closed doors, I decided I needed to get out of the office. Breathe some heady pungent exhaust fumes. Feel the comforting crush of noontime Midtown. Brush shoulders with people whose major worry was whether to spend the lunch hour shopping at Saks or Macy's.

Without consciously thinking it through, I found myself gravitating to the Museum of Modern Art. To the second floor, to be exact. There, in a stark white room turned over entirely to their violent symbolism and pure bold beauty, hung three of Theo's largest, most dramatic oil paintings. I sat down on the low-slung leather bench facing the largest one and, almost immediately, I felt better.

My relationship with Theo had always been a stormy one. Most mother-daughter relations were, but mine was compounded by the fact that Theo herself was volatile, opinionated and more or less impossible to live with. I'd tried with varying degrees of success for more than twenty years. It was not until I finally set sail from the seemingly rocky mother ship, mapped a course, grew sea legs of my own, that I realized how steady a hand Theo had been at the helm. Despite her idiosyncratic way of life, Theo had somehow imbued me with a strong sense of right and wrong. I was able to judge circumstances and people. She had—in a way only a good parent or teacher can—given me vision. The funny thing about Theo, though, was that she never tried to teach me by example. Everything she wanted me to learn was evident in her paintings.

I stared at the flood of blue and aqua washes facing me, the violent undercurrents of purple and black. The one canvas took up nearly the entire wall, missing the ceiling by inches, dominating the room to such an extent that everything—floor, benches, windows—seemed slanted toward it.

"What does it mean?" I'd asked Theo once of a painting—not this one, but one equally chaotic and disturbing—as we watched two of her assistants stretch it on boards for framing.

"Mean?" Theo had demanded in the abrupt irritated tone she took with me when I, as I so often did, somehow failed to come up to her expectations. "Do you really expect me to answer that, Peg? Paintings that have meanings—I mean pat little morality lessons—aren't paintings at all. They're pictures. Real art, like life, defies that sort of easy analysis. You should know that by now," she'd finished dismissively.

"But . . ." I tried again, "aren't you trying to say something? Aren't you thinking of something when you work? I . . . I watch you sometimes, and you're so intent on what you're doing that you don't even know that I'm there." It often seemed to me during those years—we were living in Paris at the time and I was unhappily attending L'École des Beaux Arts— that Theo didn't know I was there even when she wasn't painting.

"I'm not actually thinking, darling," she'd answered more gently. "I'm feeling. I'm, well, there's no good word for it. . . . I'm *perceiving* the world when I paint. I believe that if I do that clearly enough, and if I'm honest about what I see, then perhaps a little bit of truth will be translated onto canvas. But it won't mean anything, Peggy darling. It will just be there. Like, well, a mountain or a lake."

I'd thought several times since how appropriate that analogy of Theo's was. Sitting in front of one of her paintings, or seeing any work of art, for that matter, was like looking into a sudden unexpected landscape. One rich with imaginary mountains and lakes of deep feeling. Perhaps it had no single intrinsic meaning. But there was truth to be found there, comfort and counsel, if only one looked hard enough.

Against the backdrop of Theo's passionate blues, I thought about Spencer . . . me . . . P&Q. And, just as Theo tried to perceive her painterly world, I tried to perceive my personal one. How could I give up the job just when I had solved Fanpan's creative problems? It seemed grossly unfair, especially considering that it was association with Jacob Guilden—not Spencer—that would cause my dismissal.

I had told Cursio the truth: I disagreed with Jacob Guilden about the investigation. I didn't actually see eye-to-eye with Spencer's father on much of anything. I didn't like the possessive condescending manner in which he and his two eldest sons handled their wives. I objected to the upright holier-than-thou attitude they took with anyone, Spencer included, who stood outside their tight little men's club. That Spencer was being drawn into this inner circle, that his advice was being solicited, bothered me.

No, more than bothered. It terrified me. It forced me to question who Spencer was, what he valued, where we were headed. Could I love a man who believed in things I didn't? Could he love me?

I thought of our lovemaking the night of the Fourth, of Spencer's smile, of the pride that flowed through me at the sight of him. This was love, wasn't it? And love would smooth out the various wrinkles of our differing opinions. Wouldn't it? And if it was more than a matter of opinions that separated us, if real deep-set values divided us—what then?

Well, wasn't everyone full of contradictions? I asked myself. Wasn't life itself? Wouldn't it be boring if we were all the same? And surely it would be possible, I decided, to love the parts of Spencer that I loved and simply overlook the rest.

That seemed an excellent plan for the long haul, but what about the short term? How could I justify going back—like a lamb to slaughter—to get the ax, while Spencer stayed on unscathed? Why had I so spinelessly agreed to leave P&Q if our relationship came to light? It was Spencer's fault, after all, that this had happened. It didn't seem right that I should be the one who faced the consequences. No, suddenly, it didn't seem right at all.

Nervous about what I now knew I had to do made me get up and start to pace the room. I'd stood up for myself and this job before, and I would stand up again. I would explain to Spencer that just as my position at P&Q had changed since we made our little pact, so had my mind about agreeing to leave. I wanted to stay. We would fight it out.

I stopped in front of Theo's huge masterpiece. The swirling ocean of color seemed triumphant now, rather than chaotic. I now saw that Theo had painted a glorious affirmation of life, one that accepted and embraced the dark side of existence, one that recognized the hard choices that had to be made.

I almost ran back to the office, eager to confront Spencer with my decision. It was so important that we argue this out, I realized as I elbowed my way across Fifth. I couldn't wait to face him. I took the elevator straight up to the executive floor. What did it matter now? Everyone knew about us. I raced down the thickly carpeted corridor, nearly colliding with one of the building janitors who was directing two assistants in the removal of a large glass-topped desk. I hurried down the hall.

There was a small crowd in front of Spencer's office. I spotted Mark Rollings in the group, which consisted of an odd mix of maintenance men and top-level personnel. As I approached I realized that Spencer's usually stiff-upper-lip secretary was openly weeping. Then I noticed that the maintenance men were carrying things—chairs, wastepaper basket, files—out of Spencer's office.

"What's happened?" I demanded as I reached the scene. I looked from the ravaged face of Spencer's secretary to Mark's dumbstruck countenance. "Was he . . . fired?"

"Haven't you heard?" Mark gasped, his expression a warring terrain of alarm and confusion. "I thought for sure *you'd* know."

"No! Tell me!" I demanded, fearfully taking in the carnage of Spencer's dismantled office.

"Spencer quit about an hour ago," Mark answered slowly, staring at me in a kind of awe, "so that you could keep your job."

NINETEEN

"I wish you could have been there!" Spencer exclaimed. He loosened, then tugged off the madras plaid Polo tie he'd been wearing and undid the top button of his starched pink cotton shirt. I caught a glimpse of golden chest hair and glistening flesh. Though almost eight-thirty in the evening, the temperature was still hovering near the ninety-degree mark, and the humidity was such that my wiry head of hair had doubled in bulk and density. It foamed around my head like a dark unruly cloud. The rest of me felt heavy and damp—an unfortunate study in contrasts with the elegant and unruffled man at my side.

We were standing on Amsterdam Avenue in the eighties waiting in line with a good portion of hip young New York to get a table at the tiny home-style Italian restaurant down the street. Until six months ago, Narcisco's had been an unpretentious hole-in-the-wall favorite of the neighborhood, which specialized in underpriced and oversize plates of pasta. Simultaneous rave reviews in *New York* and the *Times* had changed all that. The line down the block tonight was almost as long as one for a new Woody Allen film. And I had been too concerned over my fate at P&Q to have had anything for lunch that day. Now I was starving.

"I wasn't invited," I pointed out as I breathed in heady pungent waves of fresh Parmesan and garlic. "And I can't really say I'm sorry."

"Well, it was totally bizarre," Spencer informed me. "I'd never actually met old Peabody before. My God, Peg, what a big bag of hot air that man is! I don't think he has the vaguest notion what an advertising agency does. He was certainly unable to grasp what I did for the company. Believe me, it was a real circus."

"How did Ebert behave?" I asked as we edged forward toward the mesmerizing aromas. A chalkboard on which the day's specials were listed sat out in front of the restaurant: spaghettini col pesto di ricotta, tagliatelle carbonara, ziti alla boscaiola... I couldn't continue reading for fear I'd faint dead away with hunger.

"Like a complete toady!" Spencer declared bitterly. "I've never seen such a display of brownnosing and yes-manning in my life. You know, I'm really beginning to see what this business is all about . . . and it's not nice." His dismal tone touched my heart. He had sacrificed his career at the agency for me. His bright star had swiftly fallen. It was no wonder he was depressed. I reached over and grabbed his hand. I held it tightly, forgetting my hunger for the moment.

"Why don't you tell me everything that happened," I prompted him, "from the beginning."

"Well, Ebert called me in first thing this morning," Spencer began. "He had the paper spread out in front of him. He was very solemn—you know how he gets—very much in his 'Mr. Clean' mode. He said he was shocked, deeply shocked, by what he had just read."

"Sean told me he was sure Ebert already knew about us," I interjected.

"Peg, honey, he *did*, that's the whole point," Spencer explained. "The two of us discussed it ages ago—when you and I first started seeing each other. I brought it up, and he said at the time that he didn't really give a damn so long as we were discreet about it."

"So then why the charade this morning?" I demanded, my stomach grumbling as we edged another step forward in line. I could now hear the muffled noise of people eating—the tinkle of glassware, the din of cutlery—and it was not unlike the distant chords of a lovely rhapsody.

"To establish his cover before old Peabody got there," Spencer retorted. "He was making his position clear—he didn't intend to be on my side. I more or less knew that from that moment on I was dead meat. I was hauled in there just so the two of them could beat up on me."

"You make it sound so—" I sighed, squeezing his hand "—so ugly."

"Well, it was, Peg," Spencer declared vehemently. "You know, sometimes I think you live in a kind of fantasy world. I don't think you actually *see* how most human beings treat each other. You wander around on the sunny side of the street, looking for silver linings—and in the meantime your friends are being murdered. Your boyfriend's forced out of his job for the most archaic of reasons—"

"Oh, please, Spence," I interrupted him, "I didn't mean to sound like a Pollyanna. I'm sure it was awful. I worried like crazy about you all day. As soon as I heard you were holed up with Peabody, I prepared myself for the worst." Spencer still hadn't told me under what precise circumstances he'd resigned, and I decided not to push him. The rumor mill at P&Q had quickly and broadly cranked out the story that Spencer had quit so that I could stay on. And though initially it seemed like the most logical—and certainly the most chivalric—scenario, I was beginning to wonder why Spencer didn't come right out and take credit for his deed. It was most unlike him.

"I don't mean to attack you," Spencer replied, putting his arm around my shoulders. "I guess I've just been on the attack all day." Up close, Spencer invariably smells of deodorant and shaving cream, clean socks and newly laundered shirts. Even on one of the hottest nights of the summer, he still managed to emit a crisp fresh air. I, on the other hand, felt like some damp thing that had been left in a gym locker for several weeks. Even my elbows felt clammy. I breathed in Spencer's aroma and the mingled scents of our promised dinner, and sighed.

"I know," I assured him, leaning my head back against his supporting arm. I felt faint and a little off balance suddenly. My skipped lunch was catching up with me, or was it something else? "So what exactly happened?" I persisted. "I mean, what did old Peabody actually say?"

"What didn't he say!" Spencer snorted. "Do you realize that I was holed up in there for nearly five hours? I think the entire time I was lucky if I got half a dozen words in edgewise. It was like the Grand Inquisition, Peg. Ever been in the board-room?'' he asked, and when I nodded he continued, ''So you know how that long teak table runs nearly the full length of the room. Well, I was at one end of the table . . . they were down at the other. My God, the way Peabody went on, you'd have thought that at the very least I was having it on with his wife or something. I mean, he seemed to take our affair as some kind of personal affront.''

''We should have been more careful,'' I declared. ''I should never have gotten up on that stage.'' That was certainly true, for more reasons than one. I had involved myself in something I didn't believe in, and now I was forced to pay for it. Though I hadn't really had time to dwell on it, Cursio's phone call had been haunting me all day. It no doubt went back to my life-long inability to deal with authority figures—namely Theo—but I had wanted Cursio to approve of my future husband. That he more than disapproved, that he seemed to actively dislike Spencer, was hard for me to swallow.

''Hey, come on now,'' Spencer replied. ''This is not your fault. It's not my fault. I wouldn't have done one damn thing differently. We're just dealing with a lunatic, that's all. Pea-body clearly enjoyed his sermonizing. He got all flushed and excited. Threw his hands around a lot. There was enough spit flying to act as a sprinkler system. He probably has had a se-cret yearning to be a minister all his life. I believe he could have ranted and raved all day. In fact, he seemed absolutely let down when I told him that I quit.''

''How did it happen, Spencer?'' I asked, turning to him. My low heels gave me about half an inch on him, so I was able to look down into his soft opaline blue eyes. Spencer's gaze never failed to send a warm shiver through me. At that moment I felt as though I were about to dive, naked perhaps and in the moonlight, into the dappled calm of the Mediterranean. ''We agreed that I would be the one who left,'' I continued gently. ''You didn't have to, you know.'' Despite my words, it was hard not to hear the gratefulness—and relief—in my tone.

''I know what we said,'' Spencer answered gruffly, looking away. ''But a lot has changed since we made that agreement. And, well, when the time actually came, I just couldn't put you on the spot like that.'' He had been thinking of my promo-tion, of my hard work and excitement over the job. At the mo-ment when his own future hung in the balance, Spencer had been thinking of mine. I hugged him to me, silently, lovingly. At just that moment Spencer's name was called for our table.

Originally, Narcisco's had consisted of six round tables draped in red-checkered cloths and positioned down a long narrow strip of a room, not much wider than a hallway. The walls had had a dingy spackled grotto look and on them, at odd intervals, yellow candle-shaped electrical torches flickered. It had offered quiet friendly refuge from the chaotic culinary storm that was raging up and down the Upper West Side.

But now someone had clearly "gotten hold" of Narcisco's and transformed it into a clean chic ultramodern eatery. The walls were a brilliant lacquered white along which raced thin tubes of red and green neon. A dozen tiny square tables had been herded into the same space the six round ones had once occupied, and no amount of geometrical tinkering could make the new arrangement a comfortable one. But then, I realized almost as soon as Spencer and I were seated, no one was coming to Narcisco's these days for its comfort—or perhaps even for the food. By whatever odd alchemy of publicity and rumor these things are determined, Narcisco's had clearly become a place "to go." The room was cheek by jowl with people who followed these trends: lawyers, brokers and, yes, admen. Spencer waved offhandedly to a man swathed in pale green Georgio Armani.

"Who is that?" I asked, shaking out my enormous white linen napkin.

"Gilbertson from K. W. Masters," Spencer answered, naming an agency that was presently considered "hot." Though small and less than a year old, it had already managed to pry away several top accounts from larger agencies, including one from P&Q. "He's a V.P. of something or other—account services, maybe."

"How do you know him?" I asked, glancing over at the gentleman in question. He smiled back at us sympathetically. I felt for sure he already knew about Spencer's situation.

"The way most people get to know each other in this city," Spencer answered. "He belongs to my health club. We ended up squash partners a couple of times. He has a very weak return."

"Maybe he could do you some good now, Spence," I suggested, breathing in a powerful aroma of anchovy and olive that emanated from the next table. I had to swallow hard to keep from drooling.

"Please, Peg," Spencer replied, examining the wine list with a curious intensity. "I don't think I've yet reached the point where I have to start groveling in front of squash partners to get a job."

"I didn't say anything about groveling," I retorted, stung by his sarcasm. "I only meant to imply that K. W. Masters might not be all that bad a place for you to consider."

"Consider for what, Peg?" Spencer demanded, setting aside the *carte de vins*. His blue eyes were flat and distant, a frozen-over pond. "Another V.P. slot where I would spend the next year or so jostling for position among the other V.P.s? And then, fingers crossed, be promoted to some senior executive slot?"

"Well, yes," I admitted, "if you want to put it that way. I suppose a certain amount of jostling is required in any job."

"And what if," Spencer continued, "having played all my cards right, having towed every line, I end up facing off against some egomaniacal know-nothing like Peabody again?"

"I seriously doubt there are two Peabodys in this world," I tried to assure him. I picked up the menu and immersed myself in its contents, hoping to change the subject. "Hmm... Cappelletti di pesce—that's a favorite of yours, isn't it?"

"I'm fed up with advertising," Spencer announced.

A secret part of me had been dreading those words. Slowly, I put down my menu.

"I'm thinking of getting into another field," he added.

A pang—like gnawing hunger—shot through me. Had I ruined his career? "What... what other field?" I demanded.

"Have you decided yet?" a harried waitress interrupted, her pen already poised above her notepad. We ordered, our thoughts elsewhere, and waited impatiently as she jotted it all down.

"I'm not sure, Peg," Spencer answered, toying with his water glass. "But something with more purpose to it. I need a job I can believe in, something I can really commit myself to."

"I can understand how you might feel that advertising isn't fraught with meaning," I sympathized. "But for whatever crazy reason, it's something you do well. What else is there, Spence?"

"Well, I've been thinking about public relations," Spencer replied, glancing up but not quite meeting my gaze.

"Wouldn't that be jumping out of the frying pan into the fire?" I demanded. "From what I hear, PR's a lot sleazier than advertising. I mean, if you're looking for commitment . . . I'm not sure that's the place to start."

"It would depend, of course, on who I'd be working for," Spencer replied. "If I can find a cause I really believe in . . . I think it could be quite a challenge."

"But aren't PR firms like ad agencies?" I asked. "I don't think you get to decide which accounts you're going to handle."

"Well, maybe I won't join a firm," Spencer answered, as though considering it for the first time. "Maybe I'll hook up with an organization—directly."

"Do you have any, uh, organizations in mind?" I asked, though I decided with a sinking heart that I already knew the answer. Hadn't a part of me known since I heard the news about Spencer resigning? Hadn't I really suspected weeks ago that it would come to this?

"Well, I have had an offer, Peg," Spencer replied. "A very generous one, as a matter of fact. An exciting one, too. In fact, I think it might be just what I'm looking for."

So, of course, none of it had been true. Spencer hadn't resigned because of me; I had just been a well-timed excuse. How long had he been planning to leave P&Q? I wondered. "With whom?" I asked. But I knew the answer.

"My father," Spencer replied. "I'm going to head up public relations for his campaign drive."

Our plates of pasta arrived at that moment: steaming, redolent of garlic, tomato, anchovy, sausage. The waitress set them in front of us with a flourish. I picked up my fork. Then I put it down again.

I had lost my appetite.

TWENTY

MY APPETITE HAD IMPROVED somewhat by the following Tuesday when I asked Tomi Tabor out to lunch to discuss the upcoming Fanpan photo sessions. Spencer and I had spent the intervening weekend together at the Guilden family compound in the Berkshires. With the rest of the family off politicking, we had the run of the ultramodern five-bedroom house built on a wide U-turn of the Housatonic. The solitude and serenity helped mend my frazzled nerves and blur the importance of Spencer's decision to join the Guilden crusade. In any case, I came back to the city refreshed and somehow reassured about our love. I suppose I saw the coming campaign as a kind of final test: if we could endure that, my thinking went, then surely we belonged together for life.

I met Tomi downtown near his studio at what once had been a ribbons and trimmings warehouse and was now a sleek high-ceilinged restaurant catering to the rag trade. Anorexic blond female giants nibbled crudités alongside balding pudgy impresarios of fashion who had a hard time fastening the middle buttons of their hand-tailored three-piece suits.

"Sorry to drag you so far away from your cabbage patch," Tomi apologized as the maître d' showed me to his table. "But I'm in between sessions for a new frozen dessert product."

"This is fine, Tomi," I assured him. "It's sort of nice to get out of Midtown for an hour or two. You're looking well." Though still a mass of facial twitches and nervous mannerisms, Tomi did look a great deal better than the last time I had seen him at Ramsey's memorial service a few days after the murder. Someone had recently forced him out into the sun; a pleasant bronze flush disguised his usual mushroom-colored pallor. Though physically small, almost petite, Tomi emanated an aura of power and success that made him seem much larger. Balding, narrow faced, with slightly upward-slanting eyes, his expression—especially when behind the camera—was foxlike: wise, on guard and more than a little world-weary.

"Thanks, Peg," Tomi responded with a small smile. "I've been feeling fairly good recently. At least up until this morning. Wouldn't you know that this damn ice-cream shoot involves two of the most dreaded elements in still photography—children and dogs.''

"I don't envy you, Tomi," I answered with feeling. "Remember that shoot we did for Summertime soft drinks? We must have had seventeen little brats on our hands that day. Now that was a nightmare!''

"Whose genius idea was that setup, anyway?" Tomi demanded, lighting a cigarette with tremulous hands. Tomi always seemed to be quivering slightly all over, as if he were suffering from either constant chilliness—or continuous fear. And yet his photography never failed to be the essence of calm composed perfection.

"Ramsey's, I believe," I replied, trying to remember the exact details. "Or... I don't know, I think maybe we developed it together. We worked very closely.''

"Yeah, I know," Tomi said, exhaling heavily. "He used to tell me how tight you two were. He thought a hell of a lot of you, Peg. Trusted you with everything, didn't he?''

"In terms of business, yes, I think he probably did," I answered, thinking how I wished he had trusted me as much with his personal life. If I had known what had been troubling him so much at the end, maybe I could have done something. Maybe I could have helped. I still remembered vividly the look on his face when I saw him last, the night before the shoot at Tomi's. He had been reaching into the bottom drawer of his desk when I knocked on the door of his office. He jumped when he heard me and glanced up with an expression that had been so frightened, so bewildered and somehow lost. If only I had pushed him *then* to tell me what was wrong. If only... I would live with that regret for the rest of my life.

"So you know how he organized everything, then?" Tomi asked, eyeing me carefully through his cigarette smoke. Tomi and Ramsey had both taught at least a generation of art directors their trade. Year after year they'd watched the latest crop of bright young graduates from Carnegie Tech and RISOD start their climb through the rough ranks of creative departments, from assistants to associates... right up to the top. It must be painful, I thought, to know that the people below you, the people to whom you're lending a hand, want nothing better than to usurp your position. It must be difficult for Tomi, I realized suddenly, to see me in Ramsey's place now.

"Oh yes," I assured him brightly, "I think I have a pretty good idea how everything's done. You don't have to worry, Tomi."

"Good, that's good," Tomi answered, reaching for the menu. "I'm glad we understand each other."

Though Tomi only picked at his plate of Cajun shrimp and potato fritters, I devoured my blackened redfish with gusto and generously helped myself to the napkin-covered basket of warm corn bread and biscuits. Tomi lit up another cigarette as soon as he sensed my appetite was flagging. Through a screen of smoke, he scrutinized me with that wary knowing look of his.

"I've heard around town that you're doing okay, Peg," he declared. "I'm not surprised. You're bright, and you had a damn good teacher. But, you know, talent and perseverance are only part of it. You've got to be tough, kid, and damn careful. It can be a nasty sort of business."

"I know, Tomi," I replied, swallowing the last bit of my fish. "Ramsey used to tell me the same thing, and I always thought that he was just being dramatic. But lately I've been learning the hard way—experience." And then, over a pot of rich black espresso, I told him about Spencer's dismissal, omitting the fact that Spencer had been waiting for just such an opportunity to make an exit.

"Peabody's clearly nuts," Tomi declared. "But at least with someone like him you know where you stand. The ones you really have to watch out for are the two-faced types—you know, the account supervisors who tell you that you're the greatest and then turn right around and complain to their creative directors that you're losing your touch."

"Well, surely that can't happen to you very often," I replied. "Come on, Tomi, everyone knows you're the best."

"Oh, you're a sweetheart, Peg," Tomi replied, flashing me a brief, but for the first time thoroughly genuine, smile. "And I'm not going to burden you with my problems. But, believe me, times have been better. I invested a hell of a lot of money when I bought the new space. And, well, you know, a bigger studio means more expenses, a larger staff. Hell, I was doing better financially when I was in that hole-in-the-wall down on Houston."

"Why did you expand?" I asked.

"I had to," Tomi answered, lighting a fresh cigarette off of a dying one, "to support my growing reputation. I couldn't just *be* the best—I had to *look* it. Photography is a very simple process, really. It's the eye, the vision that counts. But because you ad agencies can charge your clients an arm and a leg for a simple setup shot, all of the top studios have to make the business appear complicated, mystical and *très cher*. You see? I couldn't work out of a tiny darkroom and demand the usual ten thousand a pop. I had to fancy the place up with leather couches, secretaries, catered lunches.''

"And now you're finding that all this window dressing doesn't pay?'' I asked.

"Oh, sure, in a way it does,'' Tomi responded, but there was an undertone of bitterness in his voice. "Or it would, if there weren't so many other payoffs involved.''

"I'm sorry,'' I answered as sympathetically as possible, though I really didn't understand. Every business has its unique set of problems. What looks so simple to the uninformed—a click of a shutter, a squiggle of pentel—is actually the end result of hours of painstaking thought and planning. "I'm afraid I can't change the business,'' I added, "but maybe I can help matters a bit. I've a couple of major shoots coming up for Fanpan. And if we can work things out, I'd like you to handle them for us.''

"That's great, Peg,'' Tomi replied hastily, "and don't get me wrong. I don't mean to sound ungrateful. I owe my success to advertising—I'm the first to admit it. Without Madison Avenue, I'd be shooting passport photos in some dusty walk-up off Times Square.''

I refilled our cups with espresso and told him about the new Fanpan campaign. He listened carefully, obviously taking mental notes; his small slanting eyes agleam.

"I'd like to start with the Four Seasons,'' I explained. "It will probably end up the centerpiece of the campaign, as it's the most famous of the restaurants.''

"Hmm,'' Tomi replied, nodding to himself as he thought the situation through. "We'll have to work around their schedule, of course, which means early morning or very late at night. It will all be interior lighting, of course, but I think we should shoot for early morning. You say you want to use their actual staff, right?''

"Don't you think that would be best?'' I asked.

"I guess,'' Tomi replied. "But it will take a lot longer. More time with makeup. And plenty of shooting time. There's something about amateurs that's just, well, amateur. They don't know how to stand up straight or their smiles look frozen or they blink all the time." Tomi himself was blinking rapidly as he visualized the upcoming carnage at the Four Seasons. The left side of his lower lip twitched repeatedly. I looked away across the room, uncomfortable with the sight.

"I suppose we should settle on a price," I suggested, noticing that the room was starting to clear out. Tomi would have to head back to his ice-cream people soon.

"Well, they'll both be on location," Tomi said, "and at offhours. I'll need a full staff of makeup people, stylists and assistants. And I'll need plenty of setup time. It's not going to be cheap, Peg."

"I didn't expect it to be, Tomi," I answered smoothly. "But can you give me a ballpark figure? I want to get some preliminary production estimates to the client before we start."

Tomi named a number that seemed reasonable though perhaps on the high side. I was signaling for the check, assuming our business was concluded, when he added in a somewhat shaky voice, "Ten percent, right?"

"I'm sorry," I answered, somewhat confused as our waiter brought over our bill. For a moment I thought Tomi was telling me to tip the waiter only ten percent, which seemed cheap to me, considering the excellent service. "Ten percent of what?"

"Your take," Tomi answered, his voice low and suddenly ominous. "Ten percent, just the way it used to be with Ramsey. I . . . I just can't go any higher, Peg, not right now."

I gulped. I didn't say anything, grateful that I could hide my expression while I pretended to busy myself with adding up the bill. *Ten percent. My take. The way it used to be with Ramsey.* Oh my God, I thought, feeling goose bumps rising up my arm. So that was what Tomi had been talking about before: payoffs. Agencies gave Tomi the high-ticket jobs so long as he gave something back: ten percent commission. I wasn't naive. I'd heard that this kind of thing went on in our business. But never among the people I knew, I thought desperately. Not only was it illegal, but it was patently immoral. Oh, Ramsey! I felt sick with the knowledge, shaken to my core.

"Peg, don't give me a hard time about this," Tomi was saying. "I appreciate the work, believe me. But I simply can't make ends meet if I offer any more than ten."

I continued to be silent, my mind racing as I figured in a tip and signed my credit card. It was so unlike Ramsey, I thought, so totally out of character. He couldn't have needed the money, not on his salary, I speculated as I carefully ripped out the carbons in the receipt and tore them up. Why had he done it? Why had he risked both his job and his reputation? I wondered. What had Ramsey been thinking of? Somehow I managed to smile as our waiter leaned over and picked up the receipt.

"Peg, are you going to hold out on me?" Tomi demanded, desperation clear in both his voice and his haunted eyes.

"Did Ramsey?" I replied, turning to face Tomi head-on. "Is that why you're so worried about me? You think I'll pull the same thing?"

"Well...yes," Tomi admitted miserably. "At least he tried. But, Peg, I couldn't. I can't. You don't have any idea what my overhead's like these days! Nobody who works on salary can. It's just awful. There's the mortgage and the rent. Then the insurance and the payroll. My God, it just goes on and on. And then you guys come along wanting your juicy little slice. It's just too much...too much!" Tomi's head dropped into his hands, and he suddenly started to sob, his shoulders shaking convulsively.

Though my heart went out to him, I was too confused and concerned over Ramsey's part in this ugly situation to do anything more than stare at the weeping man across from me. Finally the sobs subsided and, with his head still lowered, he fished around in his pocket for a Kleenex. He blew his nose lengthily and sat up. The small eyes were red rimmed, bulging slightly. They had lost all their earlier warmth and animation.

"I apologize for that despicable scene," Tomi muttered, burying his nose in the Kleenex once again. "I'm, well, under a great deal of pressure right now. It was ridiculous of me to let off steam in public, in front of you. Totally unprofessional. I'm dreadfully sorry. I hope you'll find it in your heart, Peg, to keep this between the two of us."

"Of course, Tomi," I replied gently. I could imagine the fears now forming in his mind: word sweeping up and down Madison Avenue that Tomi Tabor was totally losing it and no doubt on the verge of a nervous breakdown. Tidbits about our little lunch, whispered in the wrong places, could seriously wound Tomi's reputation. If I chose to, I could probably ruin him. That he thought for an instant I might, made me feel almost physically sick. I reached over and patted his arm. "Really, Tomi," I reassured him, "I'm not going to say a word."

His little eyes drilled into mine, plumbing their depth, searching frantically for reassurance. Tomi must have found some, because he leaned back, suddenly more relaxed, and sighed.

"Listen, Peg," he said, shakily lighting up a cigarette. He exhaled gratefully before he continued. "Listen, maybe we could work something special out. I mean, you're in a pretty powerful position these days. I know you'll be handing out a lot of work. And, well, besides, I like you. You're real people, you know what I mean?"

What he meant was, he wanted me in his back pocket. Now that he'd regained some of his composure, I could see his mind working ahead, busily figuring. He couldn't afford to lose me right now, neither as a client nor as an unexpected confidante. He couldn't afford to take my word that I'd keep quiet about the scene at lunch . . . he could only afford to offer me cash to do so. I felt sorry for him, for Ramsey, for the whole business.

"What do you have in mind?" I asked.

"Twelve and a half?" Tomi suggested.

"How would you arrange it?" I demanded, suddenly needing to know how it was done. It was like discovering someone you loved was an alcoholic or a drug addict. I wanted to know all the sordid details. In what form did Ramsey get the payoff? How was it delivered?

"I thought Ramsey filled you in on all this?" Tomi asked, suddenly suspicious.

"Just tell me," I demanded, "tell me how it's done."

"The usual way," Tomi answered simply. "Half up front. Half after the client okays the prints."

"How do you get me the money?" I pressed him. "In a check? Money order?"

"Are you crazy?" Tomi demanded. "I thought you said Ramsey let you in on all this. I figured you got your cut of the cash."

"Where do you send it?" I continued ignoring his growing confusion and alarm. "To the office? To my home?"

"God, of course not!" Tomi snapped. "To the P.O. box at Grand Central."

"Oh," I said blankly. It was like stumbling upon the empty vodka bottle, the discarded needle. He had just given me final, irrefutable evidence. "I see."

"Hey, what did Ramsey tell you, anyway?" Tomi asked. "You don't seem to know much about this."

"Nothing," I answered simply, staring across the table into Tomi's startled gaze. "I had no idea either of you were involved with payoffs until today."

"Oh, sweet Jesus...." Tomi whispered, slowly comprehending. "You mean...?"

"That's right, Tomi," I replied, standing up. I dropped my napkin on the table. "I wanted to hire you because I thought you were the best. I didn't expect anything in return."

"But, Peg," Tomi cried, scrambling up, as well. "You can still have it. You can have twelve and a half, if you want it! Peg, really, you can have anything you want!"

What I wanted was not to know about any of this. About Tomi's willingness to give...or Ramsey's to take. For many people, the simple exchange of money for favor was an acceptable, in fact common, modus operandi. Payoff. Giveback. You scratch my back, I'll scratch yours. People would tell you that was simply the way the world worked. That's how it was. But even in the most hardened grasping heart, a person knew the truth. The first payoff accepted was the first step down a path that led to growing greed...and crime...and, I wondered briefly as I stared again into Tomi's hard narrowed eyes...murder?

TWENTY-ONE

PERHAPS THE ATMOSPHERE in which Theo raised me was ultimately *too* open, *too* honest, but she was always straight with me. I knew where we stood with each other. And I had always thought that Ramsey and Theo were alike in that way. Ramsey always spoke his mind; he was constantly decrying the easily frightened, the wishy-washy, the deceivers in our midst. And due to the volatile nature of the ad business, most agencies were staffed with examples of each. But from the start, Ramsey taught me to be different.

"I don't care if you've made a mistake," Ramsey lectured me my first month on the job, after I confessed that I'd missed an important closing date, "just never lie to me about it. And never try to blame it on someone else when you know it's really your fault. So we missed the damned deadline! Let the ad run next week, instead. The world won't come to a screeching halt. But it would have become a darker, more confusing place if you hadn't been up-front with me just now. Always be up-front with me, Peg, okay?"

And I had been. I had been more than just honest with Ramsey; I had opened my heart to him. He knew my worst fears . . . and my highest aspirations. He was the first person I confided to about my affair with Spencer. And though I did not burden Ramsey with all the intimate details of my life that Teddy seemed to treasure, I believe he knew me as thoroughly as I knew myself.

But had I ever really known him?

After my lunch with Tomi, I went back to the office and made a few phone calls.

"Denny? Hi, it's Peg Goodenough at P&Q."

"Peg! Hey, I've been meaning to call to congratulate you on your promotion." Dennis Manfred, one of the photographers Ramsey used on a regular basis, was big and bearded—a physical throwback to the late '60s. He specialized in "real life" shots, and half the time even the client couldn't tell if Denny took a crew on location to Colorado or shot the cowboys smoking cigarettes round the campfire in the back of his studio. I'd worked with Denny at least half a dozen times and liked his gruff practical attitude. He favored checkered work shirts and overalls and wore his shoulder-length ink-black hair pulled back in a ponytail.

"I've been meaning to call you, too," I answered, "just to say, you know, that I intend to continue using all the outside vendors Ramsey had developed. You've always given us top-notch work, Denny. I hope we can keep doing business together."

"That's great, Peg," Denny replied, though his voice sounded wary. "You, uh, know all about how Ramsey used to set things up? I mean . . . financially?"

My heart sank.

"We're talking ten, right?" I said.

"Yup," Denny replied. "That was the deal."

I paused a long moment, letting the unwanted truth settle in, then I said, "Listen, Denny, I'm not interested in anything back. All I want from you—from anyone I do business with— is the best work you can give me. You understand?"

"I sure do, Peg," he replied, "and I can't tell you how relieved I am. You really had me worried for a moment there. Thought you'd gone over to the wolf pack. You have no idea how much palm greasing I have to do these days! This business is getting to be as dirty as politics."

"Why do you do it, then?" I demanded.

"Oh, the usual lousy reasons," Denny answered, sighing. "Everyone else does it. Its the only way I can get steady work. Didn't the Watergate burglars say something along the same lines? The whole thing makes me feel awful, believe me, and not just because of the financial burden. Psychologically, it's the pits."

"Well, I just stumbled onto this whole thing," I admitted. "And I've got to tell you that I'm pretty shocked. I mean, Denny, I knew this kind of thing went on, but I just never thought that *Ramsey* would ever—"

"Peg, believe me, I felt exactly the same way when he first hit me up. I was stunned. Ramsey Farnsworth was one of the last great hopes for civilization, as far as I was concerned. In fact, I was so surprised when Ramsey first broached the subject, I actually thought he was kidding. Some fool me, huh?"

"How long ago was that, Denny?" I asked. "Do you remember?"

"Oh, a year, maybe," Denny replied. "A little longer, perhaps. I could look it up, if you like."

"You kept records?" I gasped. "I hope the IRS doesn't get wind of that information."

"C'mon, Peggy, I didn't track payments or anything," Denny exclaimed. "But I always hike up the total bill a bit to cover any percentage I have to give back. As usual, it's your trusting clients who have to eat it."

"Well, if there's some way," I said, "of you checking when Ramsey first asked for ten percent . . . I'd appreciate you calling me."

"Sure, Peg, I'll see what I can do."

"And, one more thing, Denny.... Did Ramsey ever try to up the ante on you? Did he ever ask for fifteen?"

"Ramsey? No," Denny replied. "But some of the other bastards—yes."

"And do you give it?" I asked.

"Like I said, Peg," Denny replied, "it's turning into a hell of a dirty business."

I called Marcia Gibbs, Seymour Friedman, Ricardo Prince. All the photographers Ramsey worked with frequently, and they all told me the same thing: Ramsey had been taking kickbacks for months.

"In a way I feel partly responsible," Ricardo told me over the phone.

"That's crazy, Ric," I assured him. "Ramsey was apparently demanding ten percent—and sometimes even more— from all his photographers."

"Yeah, I know," Ricardo said, "but I think I planted the idea in his head. About a year ago, I guess, I stupidly complained to him about a group head at K. L. Immersol who had started to ask for a little something on the side. Ramsey was such a straight-ahead kind of guy, you know, I was sure he'd be shocked—and sympathetic. And at the time, he was. Then I guess he went home and kind of slept on it. The next time we worked together, he told me that he'd be wanting his little something on the side, as well."

"How did he put it, Ric?" I asked. "Do you remember?"

"Oh, sure," Ricardo said. "Ramsey had come up to the studio to check the set for the next day's shoot, and I was showing him some test Polaroids that I'd taken. He glanced through them, smiled, and then said something like, 'Ricky, old chum...' Well, you know how Ramsey talked.... 'I'm afraid I must take advantage of your generosity, after all.' Well, of course, I didn't know what the hell he was talking about. 'Remuneration, Ricardo,' he replied. 'A little monetary token of your appreciation. Ten percent will do fine.'"

"Did he seem at all embarrassed by what he was saying?" I demanded.

"No," Ricardo answered, "he just seemed sad."

I didn't get much work done that afternoon. I felt drained after I hung up with Ricardo, physically exhausted, soul sick. I sat at the desk Ramsey had once occupied and faced the fact that a man I thought I had known...had been a stranger. I swiveled around in his chair and stared out over the summery haze of Midtown. A man I thought I had loved...had been a liar, a thief. I sat there for nearly an hour, staring listlessly, trying to think the thing through. In many ways this news was more horrible than that of Ramsey's murder. Then, some outside unknown force had struck; now, only Ramsey was to blame. But why? I kept wondering. *Why?*

I was relieved when Spencer called at the end of the afternoon to say he'd have to cancel our dinner date; Guilden, Senior had been asked to address an antidrug rally at the last minute, and Spencer was working frantically on the speech. He was too preoccupied to ask me how my day had gone, and I decided not to volunteer the information. I didn't much feel like telling him about Ramsey's kickback scheme—only to have Spencer seize upon it as another example of the kind of dirty dealing that had forced him to leave the advertising business.

I decided, in fact, not to tell anyone what I had learned about Ramsey. What would be the point of besmirching his reputation now? Who could possibly benefit from such information? I went home earlier than usual, shared half a cold roasted chicken with Picasso and curled up on the couch to sort through the thick envelope of press clippings and catalogs Theo's secretary had forwarded from Europe. As usual, there was no actual letter from my mother, but there was a short, hastily scrawled note.

Your friend Teddy Maynard wrote me about helping him get into a new gallery in SoHo. God, Peg, you know I hate that sort of thing! But if you really want me to, I'll see what I can do. Save me the bother, darling, and tell him for me. All's going fine here, though I wish you had come.

Theo.

I called Ted a few minutes later to tell him the news and he was, as I expected he would be, ecstatic.

"You are a dear heart, Peg!" he cried. "An absolute angel!"

"Honestly, Ted, I didn't do anything," I assured him. "I haven't spoken to Theo since she left for Europe. This is all Theo's doing."

"What did she say exactly?" Ted demanded, his voice sliding up an octave in excitement. "Read it to me."

"Oh, she just says she'd be happy to help," I lied. "It's really just a note from her. Theo is not a world-class letter writer by any means."

"Words are obviously not her favored mode of expression," Ted answered a bit pompously. "I can appreciate that. I often have a hard time writing down—or even saying—what I want to express. But my work, my sculpture, always speaks from my heart."

It amused me that Ted thought he could explain Theo to me. I may not be a fine artist, but I am, after all, a Goodenough. Theo's reluctance to commit herself to paper has very little to do with art and clarity... and a whole lot to do with laziness. Theo can't be bothered with things she doesn't do brilliantly.

Ted and I spent nearly half an hour catching up on each other's lives. Though we'd talked on the phone a few times, I hadn't actually seen him since my visit to Fire Island. For a moment the image of Ted and Sandy embracing in the kitchen flashed before my eyes, then it faded. I had never told Ted what I'd seen, and he had never alluded to a new love in his life. It was one of those things, I decided, that was best forgotten. He told me about his progress on the new sculpture series; I filled him in on the recent events at work—and with Spencer. But as usual with Teddy and me, we ended up talking mostly about Ramsey. He was always there between us—almost alive again— a warm known beloved presence. And it was that Ramsey, Ted's and my Ramsey, I wanted to remember. Not the man I had discovered that afternoon.

"Peg, darling, have I mentioned to you that I'm thinking of renting out the Fire Island place during August?" Teddy said after our conversation had started to wind down.

"No, you didn't," I answered. "I always thought that was your favorite month out there."

"Well, it is, actually," Teddy admitted. "Or it was.... The problem is, I'm in a sort of cash-flow jam right now. Things will probably be a bit tight until Ramsey's will gets settled."

"But what about his checking account?" I asked. "Wasn't it in both your names? Surely that can see you through for now."

"If only," Teddy said with a sigh. "I was caught unawares myself, you know. But apparently dear old Rams kept us living rather hand-to-mouth. There's simply nothing here, Peggy, dear. Letting the place in August seems to be the only thing to do. So if you hear of anyone who's looking . . .''

"Of course," I responded. "I'll let you know, Ted." Then after a second's pause, I said, "Weren't you . . . well, shocked that Ramsey didn't keep a more careful eye on his bank balance? He always struck me as being so canny about that sort of thing."

"I was upset, of course," Teddy explained. "I mean, it puts me in an awkward position right now. But surprised? No. Ramsey couldn't stand to talk about money. He referred to it as the 'great green monster.' He'd go into an absolute swivet if I so much as asked about his finances."

And for good reason, I thought sadly as I hung up the phone. The great green monster had cornered Ramsey. How and why Ramsey had let it . . . I couldn't imagine. Ramsey had been so smart, so knowing. And yet, what was the point of kidding myself any longer? Ramsey had allowed himself to be stalked—and trapped—by greed.

TWENTY-TWO

THERE WERE THREE Dominican dishwashers in spotless white-aproned uniforms, two busboys in bright red tailored jackets, a pastry chef cradling a large stainless steel mixing bowl, a butcher brandishing a long paper-thin filleting knife and the great chef himself, Seppi Renggli, in his high white hat, looking a little sleepy eyed and disgruntled as he smoothed down his handsome graying moustachio.

It was four forty-five on a Tuesday morning and, while the rest of Manhattan slumbered on through air-conditioned darkness, these volunteers from the Four Seasons staff stood beneath Tomi's blinding bright lights and smiled bravely into the camera. They were grouped together in front of a jumbo-size box of Fanpan's Famous Fried Chicken—one of the busboys, in fact, actually clutched a large drumstick in his hand—while behind them one of the most famous kitchens in the world gleamed pristinely with the promise of culinary delights.

"Say *fromage*, gentlemen," Tomi exclaimed merrily as he started to click his way through his fifth roll of film. I knew by his tone of voice and relaxed manner that Tomi felt he'd already "gotten it." We'd been set up since 3:00 a.m., and shooting for nearly an hour. And though I'd been on shoots that required a full day to capture something far less complicated than the scene before us, I shared Tomi's attitude that the shot I wanted was in the can. It was a good thing, too, I decided as I watched Adriano Pesce, the butcher, swallow a yawn; our little team was starting to tire. While Tomi and I and our crew would be able to take the afternoon off, these men had a long full day ahead of them.

"Juan, could you perhaps lift the chicken leg up a bit?" Tomi asked the young busboy, "as though you were actually going to take a bite of it?"

"This?" the slim uniformed man replied, holding up the drumstick. "You mean people actually *eat* this sort of thing?" It seemed a harmless enough joke, especially considering that the Four Seasons made a policy of feeding their staff from their own kitchens. A normal lunch for Juan could consist of grilled tuna steak with red pepper and coriander sauce and perhaps some fresh raspberries with *fromage blanc* for dessert. It was the promise of two hundred dollars an hour gratuity for each of the volunteers—as well as perhaps the even more alluring possibility of seeing themselves in print—that had gotten Juan and the rest of them out of bed for us. The cold, crusty, slightly oily-looking chicken leg that Juan was displaying with such disdain certainly held no attraction. Everyone laughed, including me.

"What's so funny?" The high wheezing voice behind me was unmistakable. I wheeled around to find J.J., resplendent in a canary-yellow sport jacket and white cotton ducks, lumbering toward us. Victor, intent on getting his first cigar of the morning unwrapped and going, followed a few steps behind. Had they heard? I wondered, searching J.J.'s flat freckled face for some kind of clue. But as usual his expression was impassive, if slightly pouty, his pale blue eyes as empty as a clear summer sky.

"Oh, nothing really," I responded, flashing J.J. my best, most reassuring smile. "We're all just having a great time here.... In fact, we're almost done." I introduced the Bobbins to the Four Seasons staff, who quickly caught on to the fact that chicken-leg jokes would no longer be found amusing.

"But how can you be done?" J.J. demanded, staring hungrily around at the camera and lights. "We all just got here. You promised, Peg, that we'd have a chance to set this up just the way we wanted."

"You did approve the final layout, J.J.," I reminded him soothingly. It was never advisable to have a client making decisions on the set, especially one consisting of nonprofessionals, so I had made sure to invite J.J. and Victor to visit the kitchen toward the end of the shooting. "And as you can see," I continued, gesturing toward our little group, "we've brought the sketch to life. Don't you think, Victor?"

Victor Bobbin was no fool. He undoubtedly knew what I had done—and why I'd done it. It was growing increasingly clear to me that he'd given J.J. the job of marketing director just to keep his rather slow-witted, easily angered son occupied. This big lummox of a boy was simply the burden Victor had to bear in life. And though I think Victor probably loved his offspring, he was far from respectful of his opinion. Sometimes I wasn't even sure he listened to what J.J. said.

"Looks jim-dandy to me, Peg," Victor responded, smiling through his veil of cigar smoke. "But I know you.... Of course you'd make it work. Why don't you wrap it up here and let J.J. and me take you out to breakfast?"

"No," J.J. cried, stepping over the electrical cables to reach the set. J.J.'s shoes left fat gray smudges on the white backdrop paper Tomi's assistants had carefully spread over the floor. "This is all wrong. The box shouldn't be sitting on a table like that," he continued, picking up the huge, meticulously arranged carton. A chicken breast tumbled out and plopped greasily to the floor. "Someone should be holding it." J.J. then thrust the box of chicken into the arms of the master chef Seppi Renggli, who stood looking down at it with an expression of panic mingled with horror.

"What the hell are you doing?" Tomi cried, straightening up from his position behind the camera and then scurrying onto the set to save it from further disaster. J.J. towered at least two feet above the diminutive photographer.

"I'm doing my job," J.J. replied, glaring down at Tomi. "Or don't you know who I am? I'm the marketing director here.

The guy who pays the bills. And I'm not about to leave till the job that I'm paying for is done *right*!"

"It's already *been* done," Tomi practically hissed. "It's been taken care of, the way it should be, by professionals. Now, if you'll kindly step over to the side—" Tomi made brushing motions, as though he were ridding himself of a small irritating insect "—we can finish up this last roll of film and call it a wrap. Okay?"

"No," J.J. declared emphatically in the tone of a stubborn child who refuses to give up a favorite toy. "We're gonna do this *my* way now. I'm sick and tired of being pushed around by you advertising people. Peg promised me I'd have a chance to arrange this the way I liked...and damn it, that's just what I'm gonna do." With that, he turned his back on Tomi and started to distribute pieces of chicken to the dumbstruck Four Seasons staff.

"Get a good grip," J.J. instructed, passing a second joint to the pastry chef. "I want each of you to be holding one of these things up. The way the kid was doing before."

"Don't be absolutely ridic—" Tomi started to sputter, but I cut him off.

"That's fine, J.J.," I called over Tomi's protests. "You go right ahead with what you think is right. And, uh, Tomi, could I see you for a minute here?"

Bristling with anger, Tomi marched over. "I can't believe you're letting him get away with this charade!" Tomi whispered under his breath so that Victor wouldn't hear.

"You can speak up, Mr. Tabor," Victor suggested mildly. "Though I can imagine well enough what you're saying. My sonny boy's a damned nuisance, all right. I'm the first to agree with you. But I don't think Peg's going to take any of his handiwork seriously—she's just letting him have a little fun. Right?"

"That's right," I answered, grinning at Victor, pleased we once again instinctively understood each other. "C'mon, Tomi, be a sport, okay? Play along?"

"Talk about a waste of money!" Tomi cried, stamping back to the camera. Tomi's earlier relative calm was shattered. He paced up and down in front of the set, twitching and shrugging, while we waited for J.J. to complete his arrangements.

"Okeydockey," J.J. declared happily about five minutes later. He had lined the group up in one tight uncomfortable-looking row and made them each hold up a piece of Fanpan fried chicken in their right hand. All in all, the group looked like a bizarre rank of soldiers presenting arms—only their weapons were chicken wings, legs and thighs. Victor snorted, I had to stifle a laugh, but one glance at Tomi told me he was far from amused. He was crouched rigidly behind his tripod.

"Half the group winds up outside the frame," Tomi declared, the irritation obvious in his tone. "You'll have to either bring them closer or do with less people."

"I want them all in," J.J. retorted. "And I want them to be just the way I've got them here."

"Well, it's impossible!" Tomi cried. "The lighting, the reflectors, everything is set up for the kind of grouping we had before. You'll just have to change it. Or, better yet," Tomi paused to jerkily light up a cigarette, "forget the whole idea."

"I ain't forgetting any idea of mine, buddy," J.J. answered, turning to face the bright lights and Tomi. "You'll just have to change *your* stuff, is all."

"That's insane!" Tomi exploded, gesticulating wildly as he came out from behind the camera. "It takes hours to break down and change a set like this. And if you took a little time to learn your damned job *before* you started dictating to others how to do theirs, you would already have known that."

"Tomi, knock it off!" I warned. I'd seen J.J. angry before. His ruddy complexion goes beet red, his shoulders seem to swell like a wave about to break, his breath comes in short asthmatic bursts...but I'd never seen him quite this crimson, puffed out and heaving before. He looked like a bull about to charge.

"J.J., you just calm down now, sonny," Victor cried, seeing what I saw and not liking it, either. "No point getting into a tussle over some little snapshot." Both Victor and I took a few tentative steps toward the two men. A couple of people among the Four Seasons staff, I noticed, were taking a few steps tack.

"I know my job," J.J. was saying, apparently not hearing his father, "one whole helluva lot better than some little jerk like you."

"'Jerk'?" Tomi cried, his voice high and crackling. "You're so stupid you don't even know how to *insult* people decently. 'Jerk'? I haven't heard that word since Dobbie Gillis went off the air!"

"Why you...you..." J.J. sputtered, trying to find a word— the right word—with which to humiliate Tomi, whose vocab-

ulary of abuse, when unleashed, was one of the most extensive
I'd ever known. But poor J.J., whose name-calling seemed not
to have matured beyond a fifth-grade level, couldn't find the
insult he was looking for. Instead, blustering, flushed to the
roots of his frizzy orange hair, he glanced sideways and found
something else: Adriano Pesce's long, lovingly sharpened filleting knife. The butcher had left it on the tabletop when J.J.
insisted he brandish a chicken wing, instead.

"Put that thing down, boy," Victor commanded sharply after J.J. grabbed the shiny stilettolike butchering tool. "I mean,
put it down this very instant."

"You stay away from me, Pappy," J.J. warned, not taking
his eyes off Tomi. The knife flashed under the bright lights as
J.J. flourished it in front of him. "This is my problem. My
fight. I don't want your help."

"Tomi," I whispered, "say you're sorry, for heaven's sake.
Apologize to him."

"Juan," I heard Seppi Renggli murmur calmly, "I think it
might be advisable for you to telephone the police." Like the
excellent busboy Juan no doubt was, he suddenly melted like
butter into the depths of the kitchen.

"Listen to me, J.J.," Victor continued as he edged his way
toward his son. "You're giving everyone here the wrong
impression, boy. They might think you actually want to hurt
somebody with that knife. That's called assault, J.J., assault
with a deadly weapon."

"Back off, Pappy," J.J. retorted, shifting his gaze from Tomi
to the glistening knife in his hand. "I can take care of myself,
for once. I know you think you have to watch every goddamned thing I do. But I'm gonna handle this one all on my
own."

"Whoever said you couldn't take care of yourself?" Victor
continued gently, taking another casual step toward the two
men. Tomi seemed hypnotized by the knife in J.J.'s hands. He
hadn't moved an inch, had hardly seemed to breathe, since J.J.
grabbed it from the tabletop. "All of us here know how capable you are. Good heavens, boy, everyone appreciates your
importance. Right, Peg?"

"Uh... of course!" I cried hoarsely, realizing that Victor
wanted me to distract J.J. temporarily so that he could inch
closer to his son. "I wouldn't have invited you here unless I
thought so. I'm surprised at you, J.J."

"Yeah?" J.J. retorted. "Didn't think I'd stand up for myself, did you?"

"Oh, it's not that," I continued. "I'm just a little shocked that someone like you doesn't fight fair. I mean, there you are—a big strong healthy guy—out to get puny little Tomi. And you even have that knife."

"She's right, J.J.," Victor said. He was now only a foot or two away. "You don't need it," Victor continued, taking the final step. "Hand it over, sonny."

For one tense frozen moment, nobody—J.J., Victor, Tomi, none of us—moved. Then J.J. looked down at his father, then at the knife, then at Victor again. He shrugged as if giving up on a difficult question.

"Dang it," he muttered as he slapped the knife back down on the tabletop. "Can't anyone around here take a little joke?"

I don't know how long the police had been there, or how they had managed to get in so quietly. But within seconds of J.J. releasing the knife, they were swarming all around us. A young fair-haired cop, already going to fat around his midriff, took my statement. At the time, of course, I didn't know why Tomi refused to press charges, graciously explaining to the cops that it was all a silly misunderstanding. I was grateful, of course; I couldn't imagine explaining to Ebert how P&Q helped put one of his top clients behind bars. In any case, Victor and J.J. departed in a flurry of handshakes and smiles.

Later, as we broke down the equipment, Tomi explained that compassion had been the last thing on his mind when he let J.J. off the hook.

"No, Pappy had a quick chat with me," Tomi said, sliding his camera into its fitted leather case, "while the cops were concentrating on sonny boy. My forgiveness, believe me, did not come cheap."

So there it was again. A payoff. This time hush money. It seemed to be all around me: grasping hands, whispered promises, an accumulation of seemingly harmless lies. But I was slowly starting to believe that somewhere, running beneath it all, was the truth about Ramsey's murder.

TWENTY-THREE

I WAS THE LAST of the crew to leave, taking a few extra moments to thank Renggli and his staff once again for their time...and to smooth any feathers J.J.'s outburst may have ruffled.

"Oh, we're quite used to temper tantrums," the pastry chef confided, nodding toward the front of the restaurant and giving me a knowing smile. "After all, what we do here is an art, no? So emotions and opinions naturally run high. The same is obviously true in your field, as well. It's trying sometimes, I agree, but who would really want it any other way?"

Me, I responded silently as I made my way down the hall and into the huge darkened arena of the famous Grill Room. I had fled the kind of chaotic involving artistic life the pastry chef referred to, when I'd left Theo. I'd had my share then of flying insults and hurtled kitchen utensils, of passionate avowals and overwrought denouncements. I had come to Madison Avenue seeking solace and sanity. And until Ramsey's murder, I thought I'd found it. Now I was beginning to realize just how illusory that sense of security had been.

I stood for a moment at the top of the stairs leading down to the ground floor anteroom and took in the cool spacious elegance of the empty restaurant. I'd dined here with Theo on numerous occasions and had always relished the room's monotone masculinity. Now the early morning light cast a pale pink sheen over the cream-colored napery and along the paneled walls. A water glass on a table near the window winked brightly with the sun's first direct rays. It wasn't quite seven o'clock in the morning, and I already felt exhausted. I leaned against the banister for a moment and sighed.

"It's beautiful, isn't it?" a voice called up from the landing below, and I turned abruptly to make out the contours of a man standing in the shadows of the huge sculpture that adorned the restaurant's entryway.

"I'm sorry?" I responded nervously. Who could blame me that after recent events with filleting knives I was a little jumpy about conversing with strangers in darkened restaurants? I tried to judge the distance back to the kitchens—and just how fast my unathletic body could carry me there.

"The Lippold, Peg," the man continued, his tone now growing more familiar. I tried hard to place it, realizing as I did so that its associations made me feel both anxious—and excited. "The sculpture right above you. Phillip Johnson commissioned it when he first designed this room."

"Oh," I replied, placing the voice at last. I glanced up at the elaborate construction of bronze rods suspended above us. "Yes, of course," I continued, starting down the stairs, "but I'm not in much of a mood for art appreciation, Detective."

"I wouldn't think so, Peg," Cursio responded, taking a step forward to meet me. For a brief awkward moment, I thought he was going to embrace me. Or was it that after what I'd been through that morning... I wanted him to? He stood looking down at me in the ghostly half-light, his pale features craggy in the shadows, his deep-set eyes searching mine. "Are you okay?"

"Yes, sure," I murmured, glancing away. His nearness was a little unsettling; I could hear his breathing, smell the faint though tart aromas—so unlike Spencer's elegant spiciness—of lime-scented shaving cream and sweat. "But why are you here?" I asked, coming to my senses. "How did you know where I was?"

"One of my men heard the call come in over the car radio," Cursio said. "I put a few things together after I heard the names Bobbin and P&Q and decided to drop by. I was talking to a patrolman outside—he told me you really used your head."

"Oh, it was nothing," I responded sarcastically. "I just helped Victor Bobbin talk J.J. out of deadly assault. He attacked my photographer with a butchering knife."

"Yes, I heard," Cursio replied. I could feel his gaze on me again—hard and searching. "Are you sure you're okay?"

"Of course, why shouldn't I be?" I demanded, turning away from him and starting down the steps to the ground floor. "We got some wonderful shots... and Tomi Tabor refuses to press charges, so my client's off the hook. All's well that ends well, right?"

"Come off it, Peg," Cursio retorted, following me down the stairs. "That's hardly better than saying that the end justifies the means. What happened back there, anyway? What are you so angry about?"

"Nothing," I lied, striding across the marble floor to the front door. The anteroom was as cool and dark as a wine cellar. I pulled hard on the heavy door as Cursio came up behind me.

"Don't hand me that," Cursio said, wedging his foot against the jamb. "I know you too well. You're holding back on me, Peg."

"Come on, I'm tired," I answered, sighing, pulling futilely on the door handle. "Let me go."

"I will as soon as you tell me what's really the matter," Cursio replied stubbornly. Maybe it was because I *was* tired. Or maybe it was because so many frustrations—Spencer's decision to join the Guilden campaign, the news about Ramsey's dirty dealings, the events of the morning—had built up to the point where *something* had to give. In any case, I leaned my head against the door, sighed deeply and answered Cursio's question honestly.

"The world's a pretty ugly place sometimes, you know?"

"Yes, Peg," Cursio answered gently, then he opened the door, adding, "I know." Together, we stepped out into the fresh, damp, but rapidly warming July morning.

We walked without speaking down Fifty-second Street until we reached Lexington Avenue. Then Cursio touched my arm.

"Listen, I owe you a cup of coffee. There's a place I go to not far from here. Could I buy you some breakfast?"

I glanced up at him speculatively. "Breakfast, fine," I replied. "But I'm really not in the mood for one of your third degrees. Understand?"

"Sure," Cursio answered lightly, though his eyes studied me with a look of unsettling intensity. What did he see? I wondered. Or, perhaps more to the point, what did he want? Too tired and depressed to worry further about his motives, I concentrated on matching his long strides as we headed north on Lex.

"Peg, I want to apologize for the way I acted on the phone the other day," Cursio announced after we were settled into a back booth at the Cosmopolitan Coffee Shop. The restaurant—with its plastic ferns, Formica-covered tabletops and orange plastic dinettes—was like a thousand others in the city. Its one distinguishing quality as far as I could tell was the owner's unabashed affection for Detective Dante Cursio. The stocky Italian had greeted Cursio at the door as enthusiastically as if he'd been Sylvester Stallone—whose photo hung with obvious reverence over the cash register. With a flourish of menus and a wide toothy grin, we had been conducted to a choice window booth at the rear of the restaurant.

"I'm sorry?" I replied, glancing over the enormous breakfast listings as well as a list of a dozen or so specials paper clipped to the plastic menu.

"You know, the day that piece came out in the papers about the Guilden rally," Cursio continued. "I shouldn't have taken it out on you, but you can't possible realize the pressure Jacob Guilden's law-and-order crusade is putting on City Hall. It's hard enough trying to get a case like this solved—having the commissioner breathing down my neck doesn't exactly help matters any."

"I can imagine," I answered, thinking of my dealings with Rollings and Ebert. In the end, wasn't every bureaucracy the same? "And you're entirely forgiven, by the way, as long as I can get you to see that even though I shared the stage that day, I don't by any means share the Guildens' political beliefs." At Cursio's suggestion, we both ordered plates of pancakes and sausages, coffee and orange juice, while the owner stood by scribbling illegibly on a notepad and smiling his vast unqualified approval.

"I'm curious about something then," Cursio replied after the owner had bustled off. "Doesn't that make for some, uh, awkwardness between you and Spencer?"

"Of course not," I retorted. "We don't let politics interfere with our relationship."

"Then you don't mind him leaving P&Q," Cursio continued, "and joining his father's campaign?"

"How do you know about that?" I demanded. "I don't see how that's any of your business."

"To the contrary, Peg," Cursio replied, stirring milk into the cup of coffee that had been placed in front of him. "It's entirely my business. As is everything that happens to anyone remotely connected with Ramsey's murder." We waited in silence as the breakfast plates were distributed. Then, as Cursio poured syrup over his steaming pancakes, he observed, "You haven't answered my question. Do you mind Spencer leaving?"

"I don't see what possible bearing my feelings about this matter have on your case," I replied haughtily, spearing a sausage link and slicing it in half. "Besides which," I added, "you promised me a nice quiet breakfast. Do you realize that you haven't stopped asking me questions since we sat down?"

"You know, you're right," Cursio replied, sitting back and staring out across the room. He seemed lost in thought. "It's a bad habit I've gotten into," he added. "I think I've almost forgotten how to carry on a normal conversation." We ate in silence for a few minutes, both of us seemingly intent on our meal, although my thoughts were all on the man across from me.

Dante Cursio did not strike me as a person who acted on whim. It was no accident that we'd met in the darkened restaurant, I decided. No impulse that he had invited me out for breakfast. But what did he want? I wondered again, watching him out of the corner of my eye as he gestured to the waiter for more coffee. In the flat, early morning sunlight his face looked worn, chiseled with fatigue. Two little lines were etched on either side of his mouth; the remnants of laughter, of happier times. Once again it struck me that Cursio knew more about the intimate details of my life than most of my closest friends, and yet I knew nothing about him. As the waiter refilled our cups, Cursio glanced up and saw me looking at him. He waited until we were alone again before he said, "What's the matter, Peg? You seem sad."

"That's funny,.... I was just thinking the same thing about you."

"Well, at least I'm *supposed* to look halfway serious," Cursio replied. "People don't have a lot of faith in homicide detectives who go around grinning from ear to ear. But you, that's a different story. You're bright, pretty. You've got a great new job, a fiancé. But something's wrong. I could tell as soon as I saw you this morning...and it's not just J.J.'s knifing attempt."

"You're prying again," I observed, though not angrily. Because, as usual, Cursio was able to read my feelings—as easily as if they'd been on one of the restaurant's catsup-stained menus. I was a naturally happy person. Even in the heyday of my problems with Theo, I had been able to see the bright side of the situation. Spencer accused me of being a Pollyanna, and I suppose I was, but it was an attitude that came naturally to me. I guess I was just born with a sunny disposition. But ever since I discovered that Ramsey had been taking kickbacks, a melancholy—like a blanket of cold damp fog—had settled over me. And I couldn't seem to work my way out of it.

More than my faith in Ramsey had been shaken, for he had represented to me all that truly mattered in this world. If Ramsey had been a sham, I was forced to conclude, then everything I most treasured in this world—honesty, intelligence, kindness—was a pretense, also. It was a realization that would surely cloud the brightest of outlooks.

And yet, despite my anger at and disappointment in Ramsey, I was not about to share what I'd learned with the NYPD. Ramsey had obviously been willing to risk his reputation—but I had no intention of seeing it destroyed. Though half a dozen photographers around town knew better, I wanted Ramsey to be remembered with love...and respect. And I would do what was necessary to see that this happened, I decided, including skirting the truth with Dante Cursio.

"But you're right," I added at last, sighing into the grounds of my empty coffee cup. "Something has been bothering me...or, more to the point, *someone*."

"You want to tell me about it?" Cursio asked, signaling for the check. "Or am I overstepping my bounds again?" Before I was able to answer, a friendly argument started between Cursio and the Italian owner over whether or not our breakfast was on the house. But Cursio remained adamant and eventually, after a great deal of arm waving and carrying on, he paid the bill.

"You always get that kind of treatment?" I asked when we were back out on the sidewalk. The mercury must have climbed ten degrees in the time we were inside. Now, at nine o'clock, the sidewalk was clogged with commuters and the air had the gaseous miragelike density of a midsummer noon. Cursio shrugged his way out of his trademark rumpled seersucker jacket, unhooked the top button of his white cotton-blend shirt and slid down his tie—a wrinkled, pale blue stripped affair, which looked as though it had been picked out of the bottom of a firesale bin.

"I did the man a favor once," Cursio replied simply, fishing out a pair of smudged dark glasses. He glanced down at me for a second before slipping them on and added, "This may come as a surprise to you, Peg, but I'm in this business to *ease* the sordid burdens of this world, not add to them."

"How can I possibly forget the importance of your work?" I demanded. "You remind me of it every time we meet."

"What's that supposed to mean?" Cursio demanded, striding north through the rush-hour crowd. I had to hurry to keep up with him, so my words came out in short breathless bursts.

"That . . . that you are often more than a little arrogant," I gasped, growing angry as his pace forced me to run awkwardly alongside him, "and rude . . . and probably one of the most secretive, most condescending—"

"My God, Peg, that's amazing," Cursio interrupted me without breaking stride. "Do you know that precisely the same things could be said about you?"

"That's ridiculous!" I cried.

"No, it's not," Cursio retorted. "You've been nothing but haughty, moody, uncooperative and snide since the moment I met you. Okay, okay, I *know* your job is a big deal, I *know* you're a busy important woman. I don't think that gives you any excuse to treat me like the hired help."

"But I don't!" I shot back. "I think I've shown you every possible courtesy. I thought you were this tough hardened cop, Detective Cursio. I had no idea you were so sensitive."

"Oh, put a lid on it!" Cursio replied. "God knows what possessed me to drop by that damned restaurant this morning. I've got to be subconsciously masochistic."

"Why *did* you stop in?" I asked. "I'm sure you had your reasons. Men like you never act without some well-worked-out advance plan."

"Yeah, I had a reason," Cursio replied, slowing his pace as we reached the crowded intersection at Fifty-ninth Street where Bloomingdale's and various mass-transit stops form one of the noisiest cross streets in the city.

"Well, what was it?" I cried. We were jostled right and left as subway riders streamed out of the Sixtieth Street exit. For a moment I thought I couldn't have heard his reply correctly.

"What?" I cried over the traffic. "What did you say?"

"I said," Cursio replied, stopping and grabbing my elbow. I looked up at him, his gaze unreadable behind dark glasses. "That I guess I was worried about you. You're a goddamned pain in the ass, Peg. But I wouldn't be able to forgive myself if something happened to you now."

TWENTY-FOUR

"WHAT DO YOU MEAN 'happen'?" I asked, squinting up at him through the blinding morning sunlight. "What could possibly happen to me?"

"I'm not sure," Cursio replied, letting go of my arm. We started to walk up Lexington Avenue again, but this time more slowly and side by side. "But until we find Ramsey's murderer, everyone's at risk."

"In what way?" I asked casually, though my question was far from disinterested.

"You might stumble onto some evidence of your own," Cursio replied. "You might not even realize it—but Ramsey's murderer will. And he or she might attempt to...you know what I'm trying to say...take you out of the picture, as well."

"And you thought something like that could have been happening this morning?" I demanded faintly. "You mean, you think J.J. might have actually meant to..."

"Kill Tabor?" Cursio concluded for me. "I don't know, Peg. But it was you, after all, who first planted suspicions in my mind about J.J."

"Yes," I replied. "I can see why you were worried. But what happened this morning was so spontaneous. So unrehearsed. Not that J.J.'s a harmless innocent. In fact, what I was saying before—about someone being on my mind—well, that was J.J. The more I know about him, the more he...frightens me."

"Listen, Peg," Cursio replied. "Why don't we call a truce? Let's stop sniping at each other. We both want to find out who killed Ramsey. And if you tell me what you know, or feel, about J.J., we might get this thing solved that much faster."

"Okay," I agreed, realizing as I did so what a relief it was going to be to share my suspicions.

"And if you're not heading back down to the office, let's get off this blazing sidewalk. How about a walk through the park?"

Central Park during weekday-morning hours is a different place from the weekend afternoon madhouse I know. Cursio and I entered under its warm dense green canopy at Fifty-ninth

Street to discover a placid paradise of strollers, balloon ped-
dlers and well-dressed young mothers proudly observing the
antics of their various offspring.

"I suppose you'll be one of them soon enough," Cursio said,
nodding toward a clutch of young women and babies.

"Suppose so," I replied, trying to fight back the wave of
concern that automatically washed through me these days at the
mention of my future marriage. *Would* that be me in another
year or two? I wondered, watching as a mother cradled a new-
born in her arms. Would I, too, be wearing a look of such self-
satisfied parental bliss? I simply couldn't imagine it, and my
inability to visualize my future was beginning to worry me more
and more. Was it simply because Theo had never provided me
with a proper role model? Or was the reason more serious,
more sinister than that? We walked slowly around a lake flut-
tering with miniature yachts and speedboats. Cursio stopped as
a small boy, no older than three or four, threw his remote control unit at the sidewalk and let out a loud agonized wail.

"What's the matter?" Cursio asked, stooping down to pick
up the gadget. He remained down, rocking back a bit on his
heels, eye level with the child.

"It's broke," the boy mumbled, hiccuping through his tears.

"Let me take a look at it," Cursio said, picking up the toy.
He turned the black plastic rectangle over, pried off the back
and fiddled with the inside for a second. After snapping the
thing back together, Cursio stood up and handed the unit back
to the boy.

"There you go," Cursio said. "It should work now."

And it did.

"He could have said thanks," I observed dryly as we walked
on leaving the boy engrossed in his toy.

"Oh, you can hardly expect it at that age," Cursio replied
sagely.

"You sound like you talk from experience," I replied,
somewhat puzzled. Cursio came across as such a loner. "Are
you married?"

"Not anymore," he responded bluntly. "But I do have a
daughter. She's six. Lives with her mother in London."

"Oh," I replied, somewhat stunned by this new side to Cursio, which I hadn't in the least suspected. "It must be hard on
you," I added stupidly. "I mean, not being able to watch her
grow up."

"That's right," he answered curtly. We walked on without speaking as I reflected on how little you can judge a person by appearances. Here was Cursio, for instance, who I'd decided at first glance was a cold cocky sort of man, suddenly showing every indication of being a good father. You could just never tell.

"Listen, I don't mind talking about it," Cursio announced rather loudly, breaking the silence. The funny thing was, I hadn't even hinted that he did. He continued almost to himself, "I mean, it was just one of those things that happens in life."

We had wandered far off the subject of J.J., but I realized that I was rather enjoying myself. Men, especially strong silent types like Cursio, so seldom confide. And I couldn't help but feel a shiver of feminine pride that he'd decided to open up to me.

"Were you married long?" I asked, hoping the innocuous question would lead us to more interesting terrain.

"Three and a half years," Cursio answered. "But most of that time I was working on getting my M.F.A. at Columbia. Between my thesis and my part-time job down at One Police Plaza, I guess I didn't give the marriage much thought." I imagined a younger version of the dark-haired man beside me, sitting down to dinner with his books, totally oblivious to his young bride's culinary endeavors. But I had it all wrong.

"Gwen was counting on me settling into a steady academic existence once I got my teaching degree," Cursio continued. "She was already a full professor of psychology at Barnard when we got married. You see, she was one of those whiz kids who graduated from high school at fifteen or so. To her, teaching—the whole academic scene—was just it. Nirvana. Writing for all those damned elitist scholarly journals. Making nice with those old windbags on the tenure committee..."

We had reached the paved pathway that led out of the park to Fifth Avenue and the Metropolitan Museum of Art.

"The museum should be opening about now," I interjected. "It's nice and cool there in the summer. Let's head in."

"I'm boring you with all this," Cursio announced as we made our way up Fifth. "I don't know what got me started, but we should get back to business."

"Hey, come on," I objected, "you were just saying at breakfast that you've lost the knack of normal conversation.

That's what this is. A conversation. Now, go on. What happened after you finished your thesis?"

We paid our entrance fee, pinned on our MMA buttons—baby blue that day—and started up the long front staircase toward the huge Venetian masterworks.

"I got a job teaching part-time at Waldsom," Cursio continued. "It's a private boys' school stocked with a lot of rich bored spoiled kids who could give less than a damn about art. I spent most of the time in the classroom just trying to keep the most cursory kind of order. It wasn't at all what I'd had in mind."

"Why didn't you teach at the university level?" I asked as we headed, by silent mutual consent, toward the impressionist galleries.

"Ah, there's the rub!" Cursio responded bitterly. "I couldn't get a position. At least not in Manhattan at any of the first-rate institutions. It's a crowded competitive kind of world, Peg, not so different from yours, I imagine. Anyway, as far as Gwen was concerned, it was more prestigious to take the Waldsom position than to settle for something at Queens College."

"But she didn't like it any more than you did?" I guessed.

"That's right," Cursio responded. "A part-time position at Waldsom just doesn't have a terrific ring to it when everyone's flaunting their academic credentials at a cocktail party. And in the meantime, Gwen's first book got a rave review in the *New York Review of Books*. I started being introduced as brilliant Gwen Master's husband."

"I know how that feels," I sympathized, stopping in front of my favorite Pissarro landscape. "I've been Theodora Goodenough's daughter all my life."

"Well at least you had some early training," Cursio said with a sigh. "I wasn't at all prepared for failure. Or, perhaps worse, for mediocrity. I was forced to look at myself—my life, my goals—pretty hard. And you know what I decided?" Before I could think of a reply, Cursio went on, "I realized that my old drab routine clerk/typist job with the police department meant more to me than any college position I might attain. Because it meant dealing with real issues, solving real problems. Really *helping* the world somehow. Sounds pretty idealistic, huh?" Cursio commented, glancing around to see if we were being overheard. But the museum was almost empty at that early hour.

"Yes it does," I replied honestly, "but I don't see anything wrong with that." We moved on to the long Degas gallery with its lovely faded pastels of ballerinas. "So you quit teaching and joined the police force..." I continued encouragingly.

"And Gwen got pregnant with Eva and—" Cursio cleared his throat and added "—all hell broke loose. Poor little kid. The only thing she heard the first year of her life was her parents fighting. I just wasn't fitting into Gwen's grand scheme. She had banked on a brilliant, perhaps slightly absentminded academic...and she ended up with a totally unacceptable cop. It got worse day by day. So when the big grant from the British Sociological Society came up, it just made sense that the two of them go.... I stayed here."

"And she's still in England," I remarked.

"Oxford. She fell in love with a don, of course. What a Gwen-like thing to do. He's a nice enough guy, I suppose, and he clearly dotes on Eva. They're bringing her up beautifully. I got to see her last Christmas. They all came over for a convention in Boston. This well-mannered, very serious, somehow very British family. It's odd, my daughter having an English accent."

"Yes," I replied, at something of a loss, "it must be. But you're not sorry, are you? I mean, you couldn't have changed anything, could you?"

"No, I couldn't have," Cursio answered, gazing down at me with a somewhat distant expression. "I'm doing what I was meant to do. You know, I think everyone carries around a private little dream image of who he is." He smiled at me, his look now thoroughly focused, and said, "I'm the guy in the white hat."

"I see, Detective Cursio," I responded, smiling back. We had come around the back of the gallery and were passing one of Seurat's famous oil studies. "I wonder what my dream image is?"

"You don't know?" Cursio demanded, his heavy brows joining. "Isn't it to be the most perfect of wives for one Spencer Guilden?"

"Stop making fun of that!" I snapped, turning away from him and setting off again at marching speed. "I really don't think that's very funny."

"I'm sorry, Peg," Cursio replied, hastening after me. "Really. That was rude. I'm sorry." In a less cordial atmosphere than before, we retraced our steps to the grand staircase. Halfway down, Cursio asked, "How do you think *J.J.* secretly sees himself?"

"Hmm," I murmured. "Interesting question. Probably as some kind of advertising wunderkind—a marketing genius."

"Maybe he killed Ramsey out of jealousy," Cursio reflected. "Professional jealousy. It's a motive, at any rate. I've come to realize that behind the most gruesome murders, the most inhuman kinds of acts...there's always a very human motive."

I told Cursio then what I'd learned about J.J.—his history of manhandling, his bursts of uncontrollable anger, the feeling I had from time to time that he was following me. Unlike Spencer, who had discounted my fears about J.J. almost before I'd had the chance to voice them, Cursio listened to me. Very carefully. We walked back down to Seventy-ninth Street, where I decided to take a crosstown bus home. I'd been up since two o'clock to get ready for the shoot, and I was dead tired. Cursio waited with me under the bus shelter, out of the heavy glare of the late morning sun. He'd slipped his dark glasses back on and, despite the long confessional morning we'd spent together, seemed his old distant enigmatic self. But I'd seen a different side of him, and I knew now that there was a vulnerable man hidden behind his cool facade.

"What are you grinning about?" he demanded as he caught my smile.

"You," I replied, laughing. "In your white hat."

"Hey, remember, that's privileged information," Cursio replied, helping me onto the bus. "And Peg?" he called after me. I turned around. "Be careful now, okay?"

I dozed a little on the bus, the heavy shadows of trees rushing past. I thought of Cursio; how open and honest he became when he finally got talking. Men were like that, I decided, smiling sleepily. Then I thought of Ramsey and the lies he'd told. For a moment I felt a twinge of panic and guilt that I'd kept all that from Cursio. Surely what I knew would affect the investigation somehow. But how could I tell Cursio about it without miring Ramsey's memory?

No, I was right to keep it to myself, I decided once again. But the malaise—the fog that had lifted during my morning with Cursio—engulfed me once again.

TWENTY-FIVE

"Darling, it's absolutely fabulous to see you!" Theo cried, crushing me to her. I breathed in a heady combination of turpentine and Chanel and winced as her huge silver-and-turquoise squash blossom necklace spiked various parts of my diaphragm.

"It's good to see you, too, Theo," I replied, gently extricating myself from her embrace. "You're looking great." Theo was too tall and bony, dark skinned and heavy browed to be considered classically beautiful. Instead, not unlike one of her own studies of angles and planes, my mother was stunning. Today she had her mass of shoulder-length hair—with its thick streak of skunk-tail white flashing through it—piled loosely on her head. When she let her hair down, though she was now a few years shy of sixty, teenage boys followed her around like homeless pups.

"And you, darling," Theo announced, taking me in with her usual piercing concentration, "look exhausted. Is the channel churning again? God, I remember how seasick you used to get!"

"Theo," I began with a sigh, realizing how long it had been since I'd come up against one of my mother's famous exaggerations, "the only time I was ever ill on the water was that six-day cruise we took on the Indian Ocean when I had the mumps."

"Exactly, darling," Theo replied, turning back to the massive canvas that took up half the length of her barn-size studio. "I'd never seen a person turn that particular color of green before—or since, for that matter."

There was no use arguing, I knew. Theo was a natural force—a hurricane or eclipse, perhaps—sometimes terrifying, sometimes fascinating, causing havoc or delight in equal measure. It'd taken me years to realize she had no real sense of her own power; she meant no harm. She saw herself as one of the world's last great humanitarians. And yet, I know of one man who attempted suicide because she left him and another who gave up a fabulous career in medicine and moved to Australia to get her out of his system. And then, of course, there was me. But Theo didn't see any of us as her victims. We were her circle. Her beloved. Her audience. And I was the one with the front-row orchestra seat.

Well, I knew what I was getting into when I decided—on an odd last-minute impulse—to fly up to Theo's Maine island retreat for the weekend. Though she had been hounding me to visit ever since her return from Europe, I probably would never have come if Spencer hadn't been forced to spend the next five days at some Guilden political powwow in Washington.

"I'll fly down with you," I announced when he told me of his travel plans. "I haven't seen the new wing at the National Gallery yet. You can do all your meeting stuff—I'll do some sight-seeing—and we'll be together at night."

"No way, Peg," Spencer responded. We were watching the David Letterman show, both naked in his double bed, having just finished making rather perfunctory and not particularly satisfying love. It had seemed to me that Spencer's performance had been nothing more than the final item on his packed daily schedule. I could almost hear him mentally ticking it off, another job well-done.

"Why not?" I asked, hurt by his rebuttal and irritated by the fact that he could look so good after our recent exertions—his skin glistening with health, his hair endearingly tousled—when I felt like someone who had just hit the wall in a marathon.

"Because, I'll be working every goddamned minute, Peg," Spencer had replied impatiently. "We're going down there to hustle federal support for Dad's proposed municipal reform platform. And that means nonstop meetings, lunches, dinner engagements—you name it. And when we're not actually in sessions, I'll have to be working the phone. I don't think you have any idea how demanding this job really is, Peg."

"That's not true," I responded gravely. "I can see the terrible toll it's taking on you physically," and with that I laughed and leaned over to squeeze the little roll of fat that had started to grow around his stomach since he joined the Guilden crusade.

"Hey, cut that out!" Spencer had retorted irritably.

The following morning I had decided a little fresh sea air would do me some good.

Theo bought Windsong Island five years ago and had spent every subsequent August here. It lies about ten miles up the coast from Seal Harbor and half a mile out to sea, a square acre or so of craggy granite and mossy pine forest topped by a sprawling shingled whale of a mansion that has more gables, turrets, widow's walks and balconies than I'd ever actually had the courage to count. Local legend had it that the place was thrown up in the twenties by a German film tycoon who had fallen in love with a Hollywood starlet. It had been called Windsong after the one apparently dismal film the hapless girl had appeared in. She'd jumped off the cliffs one night—some say as a prank, others claim out of desperation over her failing career—and was never seen again. There remained about the place an air of loneliness and longing.

Like all of Theo's abodes, Windsong was perpetually open to her troupe of artist "friends" and hangers-on. Though there must have been at least ten guest rooms in the place—not counting the sleeping porch and master bedrooms—most August weekends the house was packed. Maddie, the head housekeeper, told me I was lucky that the poet occupying my favorite garret room had left unexpectedly the day before.

"Poor soul," Maddie clucked as she led the way up the winding creaky stairs. "He was a goner, all right. Spent all day up here writing villanelles to your mother, and she, well, you know her, she hardly bothered to read them. I found one on the dining room table the other morning.... Theo'd written out a shopping list on the back of it."

"I hate to sound unfeeling," I replied, "but I can't say I'm sorry he's gone. Windsong just wouldn't be the same if I didn't get this room."

"Come now, Peg, honey," Maddie retorted, "you know Theo would insist you sleep in here, even if it meant tossing out one of the regulars."

"It's sweet of you to think so, Maddie," I answered with a sigh, "but to tell you the truth, I doubt Theo's even fully aware I've arrived. She's so involved in that new canvas, she hardly said hello before she was turning back to it."

"Oh, you two!" Maddie scoffed. "The worry and bother you put each other through. You're both so stubborn and touchy. You're like two damned porcupines, sitting side by side, waiting to see whose quills are gonna prick whom first."

"It's just that we're too different," I tried to explain to her as I started to unpack my weekend bag.

"No, ma'am," Maddie retorted as she turned to go back downstairs. "That's what you'd *like* to believe. Truth of the matter is, you're too much the same."

As usual, Theo spent all afternoon cloistered with her canvas and oils while the rest of us—a baker's dozen by my count—sunbathed on the rocks and took turns making fools of ourselves with various pieces of nautical equipment. Though Theo made an expensive habit of stocking her boat house each June with the latest models from Chris Craft, few of her guests ever had the least notion what to do with the sunfish or catamarans, canoes or kayaks she put at their disposal. Theo's crowd was primarily comprised of aging artists—writers, composers, choreographers, playwrights and actors of every stripe and gender. It was a group whose idea of truly strenuous exercise was a full-length game of badminton or croquet. The one notable exception this trip out was Cal, a bronzed hunk of a man in his late twenties, who practised dives off the dock with eye-riveting grace and expertise.

"Who's that?" I asked Felix Northfield, a music critic of national renown, whom Theo had had a fling with twenty years ago. He had patiently, some feel pathetically, carried a torch for her ever since. Felix had always been something of an uncle to me.

"Who?" Felix demanded, lowering his copy of *Opera News* while simultaneously raising his glass of vodka and tonic. "Oh, you mean that walking muscle in the string bikini who just jumped off the dock?"

"Not jumped, Felix," I replied, "dived. And beautifully. Who is he? I don't think I've seen him up here before."

"Well, sweetheart, then this must be your first visit all summer," Felix retorted bitterly. "The man's practically part of the furniture. Need I say more?"

I could tell immediately from his tone what he was driving at, but I still couldn't believe it.

"You mean . . ." I whispered, "he and Theo? But, my God, Felix, he's my age! If he's that."

"Oh, these damned professional athletes take forever to age," Felix said with a sigh. "I read somewhere that Cal's thirty-five. Heavens, if I looked like that at eighteen . . . how different my life might have been!"

"But you still haven't told me, Felix," I reminded him, "who is he? What does he do? What's his last name?"

"You mean to tell me you've never heard of Calvin Hotchner?" Felix demanded. "Olympic gold medalist? He set a new record in the freestyle competition back in the seventies. My God, Peg, he's been the darling of Madison Avenue ever since. You people have his gorgeous biceps plastered over everything from frozen orange juice to bran flakes."

"Of course," I murmured, vaguely connecting Cal's face with the front of a certain cereal box. "I wonder how they met? He seems a bit out of Theo's usual line, don't you think?"

"Oh, I don't keep up anymore, Peg." Felix sighed, turning back to his magazine. "I simply don't have the energy."

Around five-thirty the sun slipped around the cliffs, the cove fell into shadow, and most of the guests started to climb back up to the house to shower and change for dinner. I wandered out to the end of the dock to watch the sunset, grateful for a chance to be alone. I breathed in the sharp sea air and sighed, admitting at last that the rotten mood I'd hoped to shake by coming up here had tagged along.

Part of it was Spencer, of course. We were drifting, ever so slowly, apart. I was noticing things about him—silly things, like the condescending way he talked to taxi drivers, or his habit of massaging the lobe of his right ear when he was thinking—that I didn't much like. Also, knowing how little I cared for his new job, he no longer confided in me, as he used to do, about the events of his day. Now there were long silences between us. Where we once had been spontaneous and silly with each other, we were now careful and courteous. I still *loved* him, of course. But, as I supposed happens in all long-term relationships, the romantic veneer was beginning to wear thin.

And then, of course, there was the murder: the fact that it was still unsolved, the possibility that I might be holding back information that could aid the investigation. Or, perhaps more to the point, help Cursio. I knew he trusted me, or he would never have poured out the story of his divorce. He saw me as an ally, a confidante, and I doubted he had many. The fact that I wasn't being honest with him kept nagging at me. Was I wrong to try to protect Ramsey's reputation? What was the right thing to do?

"Penny for them."

"What?" I whirled around. Calvin Hotchner had somehow managed to creep up soundlessly behind me. "Oh, it's you. You scared the daylights out of me!"

"Sorry," Cal answered, ducking his chin. He appeared to be genuinely apologetic and more than a little shy. "I didn't mean to frighten you. I ... I just wanted to officially say hello, you know, before dinner. I couldn't stand the thought of Theo introducing us with that entire house looking on. I'm—" he held out a large tanned hand "—Cal Hotchner."

His grip was warm and firm. His gaze direct, if a little wary. It occurred to me suddenly that he'd been afraid of meeting me. Worried about what I'd think. I liked the fact that he'd been concerned, that my opinion would matter to him.

"Yes, I know who you are," I said, returning his smile.

"We're so happy you could make it up," Cal replied, letting go of my hand. "I've been hoping every weekend that you'd come. I've been afraid that, well, maybe it was me, or something. I mean, oh, you know, the fact that Theo and I ..."

He was now thoroughly embarrassed, his face a deep red beneath his tan. Despite his confusion, he managed to convey a certain steadfastness and dignity. He wasn't ashamed of his affair with my mother, just concerned about my feelings.

"Oh, not at all," I hastened to assure him. "In fact, I didn't even know until this afternoon about Theo and you. I've just been terribly busy at work. And, maybe Theo didn't tell you, but a close friend of mine—my old boss, actually—was ... well, murdered at the beginning of the summer. And I've been pretty caught up in that, too."

"Yes, I heard," Calvin replied, digging his hands into the pockets of his khaki shorts and rocking back on his sneakered heels. He hesitated a moment, looking out to sea, and then added, "Ramsey Farnsworth. I worked with him once, years ago, when I first started to do commercials. He was very kind to me during a time when I really needed a friend. He gave me some advice then that I'll never forget."

"Yes?" I asked, scanning Calvin's tanned perfect features. Up close you could see the web of fine lines around his eyes and mouth. You noticed the weariness lurking under the deceptively sunny blue of his gaze.

"His exact words were—" Calvin cleared his throat "—'Never screw around with something you don't believe in.'"

"Umm, sounds like Ramsey, all right," I said.

"Yeah ... if only I'd followed his advice," Calvin added with a short disparaging laugh. If only Ramsey had, too, I thought sadly as Calvin and I walked up to the house together. It was dark by the time we reached the front yard. The first fireflies of the evening winked off and on in the juniper bushes. We heard voices on the long screened-in front porch. The tinkle of ice against glass. And, drifting above it all, the sound of my mother laughing. I heard Calvin sigh at the sound, and I glanced swiftly up at him. He was smiling a little. His face expectant, hopeful. With a pang—of what? Jealousy? Concern? Envy? I recognized the expression of someone in love.

TWENTY-SIX

IT TURNED OUT to be one of the most beautiful weekends of the summer. Sunday was a dazzling sun-soaked day that felt like a time out of childhood: fragrant with the smell of sea air and pine, filled with laughter and the high echoing call of gulls. The golden afternoon seemed to go on forever.

Cal and I swam off the dock, then later took the kayak out for an exhilarating sail. We practically flew around the island several times—our waists level with the water—the two of us as light as feathers picked up on the wind. Cal had an innate sense of the sea. Water was his second home, and it showed in the way he swam and dove and handled boats. For the first time in many, many years, I found myself liking one of Theo's lovers. I found myself hoping that, despite the differences in their ages and backgrounds, somehow it could work out between them.

"Tell me about Spencer," Cal said later as we lay side by side on the warm rocks. "Theo can't figure out why you don't bring him up. Why you won't introduce him. Is there something you're not telling her? Is he a nudist, or something, Peg?"

"Worse," I said with a sigh, sitting up and hugging my knees to my chest. "He's, uh, politically conservative. He's, well . . . kind of staid. Respectable."

"Oh, gee, I can see the problem," Cal answered. "In other words, he's just the opposite of Theo. You don't think they're going to hit it off, is that it?"

"I'd be very surprised if they didn't absolutely despise each other on sight," I answered simply.

"Well, I'm . . . sorry, Peg," Cal murmured. After a moment he added, "Mind if I ask what you see in him? I mean, considering your upbringing, isn't it kind of funny to be drawn to someone like that? And, hey, if I'm prying, tell me to go stick my head in a hole.''

"No, it's okay to ask," I replied. "I'm just not real sure of the answer. Why do you fall in love with somebody? Are there reasons? I don't know. The only thing I can tell you is that I think I was first attracted to Spencer because of the way he smelled.''

"I've heard stranger explanations," Cal responded.

"He smelled so absolutely clean, Cal," I went on, dreamily remembering the first wonderful weeks Spencer and I were together. "He seemed so, I don't know, safe...secure.''

"You're talking in the past tense," Cal interjected, "do you realize that?''

"I'm what?" I demanded, coming out of my reverie. "Oh, yes, I see what you mean. Well, we've been together awhile, you know. I mean, after you've been with someone for a year or two, things have a way of changing.''

"Like?" Cal asked.

"Nothing important," I replied, and when I saw his unconvinced expression, I added, "No, really, Cal, everything's fine between Spencer and me. That's not what's bothering me.''

"But something is," Cal observed, squinting up through the sunlight at me. "Want to tell me about it?''

"I guess I should talk to someone," I said sighing. I looked down gravely at Cal and asked, "How are you at keeping secrets?''

"That depends on who I would have to keep them from," Cal answered without hesitation.

"How about the police?''

"I can deal with that," Cal replied. "In fact, I could probably hold back on just about anybody these days...except Theo.''

"Well, you can use your discretion there," I answered. "I doubt she'd care one way or another.''

"Why do you say that?" Cal demanded. "You know damn well Theo would want to know about anything weighing on your mind.''

"Whatever you say, Cal," I replied patiently. "But Theo's not the issue, in any case. This has to do with Ramsey....''

I told him everything I'd learned from Tomi, Dennis and the others about Ramsey's kickback schemes. As I heard myself reciting the straight facts, I became even more convinced that Ramsey's double-dealing and Ramsey's murder were somehow interconnected.

"And I guess I'm feeling guilty about not letting Cursio in on what I know," I concluded. "He's been so straightforward with me. I just feel . . . bad."

"Hmm," Cal responded. "You know, if this Cursio's half as smart as you say he is, he probably already knows about all this. Christ, he probably thinks he has to keep it from *you* so that you won't be disillusioned about your old boss unless it's absolutely necessary."

"I don't think so, Cal," I replied. "Cursio wants this case solved, over with. I think if he knew about the kickbacks, he'd tackle me immediately with questions. He may have an M.F.A. in art history, but believe me, when it comes to police work the man's about as subtle and sensitive as a crane operator on Fifty-seventh Street."

"Well, I don't know what to say, Peg," Cal answered, deliberating. "But I'll tell you one thing—I don't like the sound of any of this. I mean, Ramsey's murderer is still loose, right? You could be in danger."

Cursio had said the same thing. But the fact that I could be threatened by an unknown killer seemed totally unreal to me at this point—ridiculous.

"No, I think I'd go to the police," Cal continued, shaking his head. "What's the point of you hiding it?"

"You knew Ramsey," I answered softly. "And even though you didn't know him that well, you already admitted that he affected you. That he was there for you when other people weren't. Well, Cal, Ramsey was *always* there for me. He helped me through some hard times. He was the best teacher I ever had. And, in his own way, the best friend. Don't you see? If I told Cursio what I knew, it would be as though I were turning on Ramsey, betraying him."

"I hear what you're saying." Cal sighed. "But Ramsey's gone, Peg. You're still here. It's you I'm worried about. And I believe your mother would agree with me. I think we better hear what she has to say about this, okay?"

Poor Cal, I thought later that evening as I watched him and Theo at the dinner table. He had a quiet dignity about him, an inner resolve that I guess came from being an athlete, and yet his love for Theo was absolutely transparent. It was as though you could see through his broad bronzed chest straight to his heart. He breathed for her. I'd seen a lot of men smitten by Theo. They were generally dumbstruck, lolling. And not unlike Odysseus's men in front of Circe, they became animallike, piggish for my mother's attention.

But Cal was different. He didn't seem to want anything from her. I could see in his gaze, his movements, his talk just how determined he was that she be happy. He directed the conversation so that she could relax, get outside of herself, shake off the concentrated aloneness that takes over her when she's working. I could see that he knew, instinctively, how best to take care of Theo. I envied his skill with her, his understanding. His love seemed so uncomplicated. And I wondered if Theo had any idea how lucky she was to have found him.

"Cal says you want to talk to me, darling," Theo announced later as coffee and liqueurs were being served on the porch. It was a clear night, the stars brilliant and close, the moonlight a dancing pathway out to sea.

"Not here, Theo," Cal broke in gently. "Let's take a walk. Come on, I'll get us each a brandy."

We took the west trail, out to the bluff. Here the huge bald cliffs faced inland and south, to responsibilities, to real life. No one came out here much, as the rocks were hazardous. It was rumored that this was the spot the starlet chose to jump to her death. On a night like this one, though, with the full ceiling of stars and the distant coastline glittering with light, the bluff seemed majestic in its isolated beauty.

"So, darling," Theo began after we'd settled ourselves on the rocks. "What's all this nonsense about Ramsey being on the take?"

"It's not nonsense," Cal interjected. "Peg has stumbled upon some pretty damaging evidence. It's quite serious."

"I know, dearest," Theo answered, touching his arm, quieting him. "Now, go ahead, Peg. Tell me what you know."

I repeated it all again. Tomi's revelations. Denny's collaboration. I explained how Ramsey had set it up: the ten percent "commission," the P.O. box numbers. But somehow this time in the telling, the story sounded less ominous. Maybe it was the comforting whir of the crickets in the background or the rich definite aroma of Theo's perfume, but for the first time I felt maybe Ramsey's escapades were harmless, after all.

"And you have no idea why Ramsey would pull this sort of stunt?" Theo demanded when I'd finished.

"None," I answered. "He made a lot of money. He bought that loft years ago...and could probably turn it around and sell it for five times what he originally invested. Same with the beach house, I'd guess."

"Maybe he just liked the thrill of it," Theo suggested. "Perhaps he was bored . . . and these little dealings gave him something of a boost."

"Theo, he was *stealing*," Cal insisted. "He was knowingly breaking the law. Time and time again. You can't tell me that it doesn't seem an odd coincidence that the same man who was taking kickbacks also got murdered."

"I know what you're saying, darling," Theo responded patiently, taking Cal's hand and squeezing it. The affectionate gesture surprised me; Theo was usually standoffish with her lovers. "But I'm a little older than you, God knows," Theo went on with a sigh, "and I recognize how jaded people can become. They get hooked into going from thrill to thrill, needing bigger and more risky ones as time goes on. Who knows? Maybe Ramsey started out cheating a little on his expense accounts . . . and, before he knew it, he needed big-time excitement."

"You know, he did seem depressed, distracted a lot of the time toward the end," I responded. "Maybe Theo's right. Maybe life had lost its luster, and he was just trying to cheer himself up."

"So now you're saying," Cal demanded, "that you don't think any of this has to do with Ramsey's murder?"

"I . . . just don't know," I muttered.

"And if we're not sure," Theo continued, "and Peg goes and tells the police everything, and it all comes out in the papers . . . what good will that have done?"

"It will keep us from worrying about Peg," Cal answered.

"Oh, I'm not worried about my Peg," Theo responded with a knowing laugh. "She's my daughter. She can handle it."

It was stupid of me, but I felt a sudden rush of pride. Theo so rarely acted or sounded like a mother, I sometimes thought she'd forgotten that she was one. I wanted to take her other hand and squeeze it tight. I took a sip of my brandy instead, and asked, "What do you think I should do, Theo?" I felt closer to her at that moment than I had in years.

"Hmm," Theo murmured. She stood up then and walked over to the edge of the cliffs, her brandy snifter dangling from her right hand. In the moonlight, her sheer silk shift became transparent; I could see her firm tall figure outlined against the sky.

"Careful, Theo," Cal called after her into the wind, though not quite loud enough for her to hear. He knew better than to stop her or to let her see that he was worried. We waited several moments in silence as Theo stood, looking out to sea, thinking. Cal and I sat side by side, not saying anything, two people who had been strangers a day ago, now bound together because of Theo. For the first time in my adult life, though, my mother's gravitational pull didn't anger me.

"Aiiieee!" Theo cried suddenly, throwing her arms up in the air. Cal scrambled to his feet and stood, tensed, ready to run to her.

"Aiiieee!" she cried again, then she turned and walked back across the cliffs toward us.

"What the hell was that all about?" Cal demanded, relieved. He grabbed her hand when she got close enough. "You're a crazy woman, do you know that?" he told her, pulling her to him. I expected her to push him gently away, but she didn't. She stepped into his embrace as one would into a beloved old coat.

"I was communing," Theo replied, laughing, "with my own personal gods. Asking what we should do about Peg's dilemma."

We. It wasn't a word Theo used very often.

"And?" Cal demanded, his arm tight around her waist. "What did they tell you, Theo?"

"Can't you hear them?" Theo asked, turning back to the sea. "Listen." But all I heard was the whine of the crickets and the explosion of the waves as they hit the rocks below.

"They're saying *act*," Theo muttered. "Act."

"That sounds great, Theo," Cal said as we made our way through the moonlit trees back toward the house. "But what the hell does it mean?"

"Whatever Peg decides it should," Theo replied grandly, gathering up her skirt behind her as though it were a train. "All I'm saying is that she's reached a point in all this where she just has to make some kind of move. It's obvious. She can't sit there and let this fester."

"You're right," I said, stumbling along behind her. Theo's shadow blocked the moonlight, obscuring the path before me. "I don't want to turn to Cursio...and yet I have to turn somewhere. I have to do something."

"Darling, why don't you try a little poking around on your own?" Theo suggested mildly.

"Theo!" Cal gasped, stopping dead in his tracks. "Theo, listen to me. This is a murder investigation. A serious matter."

"Peg and I know that," Theo responded. "Don't we, darling?"

"Yes," I answered. Yes, of course! Why involve Cursio at all? I'd look into Ramsey's dealings myself. Now it seemed that everything had been leading up to this conclusion. That Theo had only given voice to something I'd known all along. For the first time since I'd discovered Ramsey's secret, I felt confident, freed. And for practically the first time in my life, Theo and I had agreed on something.

"This is crazy, Peg," Cal pleaded, dropping back beside me. "Take what you know to the police. It's dangerous, stupid...it's insane going off on your own. Don't you see that?"

"I'm afraid not," I answered gently. We'd reached the herb garden at the back of the house. The air was fragrant with the smell of mint and thyme. The house lights beckoned through the trees. "What I see is a chance to get to the bottom of Ramsey's indiscretions without the entire world finding out."

"That's my girl," Theo said, laughing, and she threw her arm around my shoulders as we walked up the steps into the porch light.

"You're both crazy," Cal fumed behind us. "I thought you were halfway sensible, Peg. But now I see you're as bad as Theo."

As bad...or as good? I thought about what Cal had said as I boarded the early ferry the next morning. For years now I had been waging silent war against Theo's stubbornness, her vagaries, her fanaticisms. I had yearned for her to be like my friends' mothers: to manage bake sales, head up the clothes drive, join the PTA. I had wanted her to be normal...because that's what I had wanted to be.

But since Ramsey's murder I'd slowly begun to realize that life wasn't normal. It wasn't fair. There were times when the sensible and safe solutions—the answers I always thought I wanted—just wouldn't do. Theo had little patience for tradi-

tional values in her work...or in her life. She went her own way,
setting her own standards and goals. She took a kind of vigi-
lante approach to justice. She believed in fighting fire with fire.

It's funny, I reflected as I watched Windsong disappear into
the morning mist, whoever would have thought that I'd come
to believe in it, as well?

TWENTY-SEVEN

"OH, GOD, Simmons's work is becoming so terribly gauche,"
Teddy whispered as we moved through the packed gallery.
"This one is like some six-year-old's imitation of early Francis
Bacon. And that horror across the way—can you believe that
cattle skull?—Georgia O'Keeffe is undoubtedly turning over in
her grave."

"I don't think they're all *that* bad, Ted," I demurred, sipping from the chilled champagne flute that a tuxedoed waiter
had just slipped into my hand. It was Teddy who had insisted
we meet at the Simmons opening before joining Spencer for
dinner. And though I was not particularly impressed by the
SoHo artist's latest paintings, I had a hard time criticizing his
work while taking advantage of the gallery's catering.

"Oh, yes, you do, sweetheart," Teddy insisted. "You're just
too polite to be honest. Heavens, look at that Pollock rip-off.
This guy's no better than a thief!"

"Well, if you really feel that strongly, Teddy," I replied,
lifting a tapenade-covered toast square from a passing tray,
"let's go. We're supposed to be meeting Spencer in less than an
hour, anyway."

"But I wouldn't dream of leaving without seeing the whole
show, Peg!" Teddy exclaimed. "I'm not at all sure yet just how
thoroughly I hate it. No, we can't leave until my negative opinion is totally formed."

"Oh, all right," I said with a sigh, allowing him to steer me
through the crowd. "Whatever you say." It had been a mistake, I realize now, to let Teddy talk me into this gallery opening. My hope had been to get him alone for an hour or two
before my date with Spencer, but as soon as he learned I was
meeting my fiancé, he insisted on coming along.

"I haven't seen Spence for months, sweetheart," Teddy had exclaimed that afternoon on the phone when I had tried gently to talk him out of joining us for dinner. "Not since, well...you know..."

Ramsey's murder, of course, was what he meant. And though Teddy never complained to me directly, I knew he felt I'd been ignoring him of late. It had been more than a month since we'd actually gotten together, though we still spent our requisite five hours or so a week chatting on the phone.

"It's just that I haven't seen Spencer myself since his Washington trip," I tried to explain. "And, well, I want to see you, too, but I think I'd really rather see you alone. We haven't had a good heart-to-heart in ages." And there were things—specific questions I'd devised about Ramsey's financial dealings—that I wanted to sound Teddy out on.

"Why don't you just come right out and say it, Peg?" Teddy had responded. "Spencer doesn't like me, does he? That's why you'd rather I not tag along."

"Don't be ridiculous, Ted!" I'd retorted. "Spencer thinks you're terrific. C'mon, you know that." And though I tried to imbue my words with the utmost confidence, I wasn't terribly sure that they were true. Spencer never had given me his reading on Ted, though I knew his feelings toward Ramsey had always been somewhat cool.

"Then be a sweetheart, Peg," Ted had pleaded, "and let me join the two of you? I've been so damn down in the dumps lately. I just need some human companionship. You understand, don't you?'

"Of course, I do, Teddy," I'd answered. And I did. It was Spencer I was worried about. From the brief talks we'd had on the phone since Spencer's return from Washington two days before, I'd gathered that the Guilden political lobbying had not gone as well as hoped. I knew he was looking forward to cataloging his woes at dinner that night, and that he would hardly appreciate Teddy horning in on his personal sob session. To make matters worse, I had been unable to reach Spencer all afternoon to explain—and hopefully defuse—the situation.

Of course, it didn't help that Teddy and I couldn't find a taxi. Or that we arrived at Bandillo's nearly three-quarters of an hour later than Spencer expected. But the venomous look Spencer shot in my direction when we finally did rush breathlessly through the door made me want to crawl backward to the sidewalk on my hands and knees.

"You're late," Spencer fumed. "And we've lost the table. We'll have to go somewhere else, and I hate every other restaurant in this area."

"I'm sorry," I mumbled. Spencer had every right to be upset; but it seemed unnecessary for him to be so rude to me in front of Teddy.

"Oh, it's all my fault, Spencer," Teddy exclaimed, his hands tracing helpless circles in the air. "I detained poor Peggy at this dreadful gallery opening . . . and then forced her to bring me along for dinner. Please, don't be upset with her. I'm the one to blame, Spence. And the one who's so horribly—"

"Okay," Spencer snapped, cutting Teddy off. "So here we all are at last. Anyone have any suggestions about where we're going to find something to eat? The maître d' has assured me that there are no tables available here until after ten o'clock."

"Actually, yes, I know of a place," Teddy answered, composing himself after his breathless apology. Knowing how low Ted was feeling these days, I felt awful that Spencer was being so unpleasant. Ted had asked to join us, after all, seeking friendly company. Now it seemed he'd walked into the middle of a mine field. "There's an absolutely fabulous vegetarian place just around the corner from here," Teddy plowed on valiantly. "It's supposed to be one of the best in the city."

"I despise anything cooked with tofu," Spencer retorted.

"And I do, too!" Teddy cried. "Ugh! The stuff was created for people with the palates of Teflon frying pans. No, this restaurant isn't a typical veggie place at all. There are tons of pasta dishes. I think the *Times* gave it two stars. And Gael Greene's *New York* piece had me practically drooling."

The magic word *pasta* changed Spencer's thinking, and soon the three of us were settled into a small, brightly lighted booth at the back of the Green Planet Natural Food Restaurant. Spencer was so hungry that he insisted we order as soon as we sat down. Barely glancing at the menu, he asked for the Naturally Spicy Lasagna Special. Teddy and I settled for steamed vegetable platters with cheese sauce. Then we sat back and waited.

And we waited. Of the two dozen other tables in the room, only half were occupied, and those diners seemed well into their desserts and coffee by the time we arrived.

"What the hell can be taking so long?" Spencer demanded after fifteen minutes had elapsed. "Are they back there *growing* the damn vegetables, or what?"

"It's a little late, Spencer," I reminded him. "The kitchen was probably slowing down for the night, and now they have to get back up to speed."

"Well, they shouldn't have seated us," Spencer complained, craning his neck around to glare at the kitchen door, "if they didn't think they could handle the job. Damn it, Ted, you sure this place was recommended by the *Times*? It looks like an old Village fly trap to me."

"Gosh, I'm sure this is the restaurant," Ted murmured, glancing around the half-empty room uncertainly.

"What does it matter now?" I added lightly. Then, determined to change the subject, I said, "Tell us how your new sculpture series is coming along, Ted. I'm dying to see what you've been up to."

"Well, I think you're gong to be pretty impressed," Ted began eagerly. "I can't help but feel that I've finally found a style—and a statement—that's totally individual. You know, I've been experimenting with marble for nearly a year now, but it's only been the past few weeks that I've finally felt a total master of my materials...." As I had expected, once Ted started, he couldn't be stopped. Another ten minutes passed. "So what I'm hoping to do," Ted rambled on, his gaze inward and enraptured, "is to totally alter our current conception of shape versus contour. In my way of thinking, you see, shape *is* contour. Or, to put it in laymen's terms..."

"What the hell are they doing back there!" Spencer demanded, slamming his fist down on the tabletop. "I've been sitting here starving for nearly an hour, listing to this goddamned crap about—"

"Spencer," I breathed, kicking him under the table.

"Oh, I'm terribly sorry," Teddy mumbled, his face ashen with embarrassment. "I guess I just forgot myself. How rude of me. How vulgar." He shifted in his seat, then suddenly stood up, tossing his napkin onto the table. "Listen, I think I'm going to take off. I'm really not that hungry...."

"Ted, don't be crazy," I cried, grabbing his arm. "Don't go. Spencer didn't mean any harm. He's just irritable because he's tired and hungry. Right, Spencer?" I added, glaring at him across the table.

"Yeah, I'm sorry, Ted," Spencer muttered, not meeting my eye. "It's been a long day, you know? Come on, stick around and have some chow. You've waited this long."

But Ted, like me, could easily detect the lack of warmth in Spencer's offhand apology. Ted smiled wanly down at me and replied, "I don't mean to disappoint you, darling, but I really do think I'd better be running along. I ate a ton of goodies at the opening. I'll be fine." He leaned over and kissed me on the cheek. "I'll call you tomorrow, Peg, darling. Bye-bye, Spence."

I waited until Ted was out the door before I said, "You know, you couldn't have been ruder."

"That's not true, babe," Spencer retorted. "I could have been a whole lot worse. I'm starving, I'm annoyed you brought him along in the first place, and then I have to sit here and listen to the guy practically foaming at the mouth. No, I could have been a hell of a lot ruder. Believe me."

"Ted is going through a hard time right now, Spencer," I replied quietly. "I'm surprised that you lack the sensitivity to see that... that you're unable to show a little sympathy."

"Peg, I don't know how to break this to you," Spencer retorted, "but Ted's *always* going through a hard time. The first week I met you, I heard all about your dear unappreciated little friend Teddy. If it wasn't some nonsense about not getting a show, it was some trouble he was having with Ramsey. And I've been hearing about Ted's problems ever since. Frankly, I'm sick and tired of Ted and his damned little complaints."

"You should have said something a long time ago," I sniffed. I was furious at Spencer, yet at the same time a part of me had to admit that what Spencer said was true. I'd never known Ted to be totally happy.

"Yeah, well, you're entitled to your friends," Spencer grumbled. "I just wish you wouldn't inflict them upon me."

At this moment, luckily, our dinners arrived: huge delicious-smelling platters of steaming hot food. Spencer's portion of lasagna looked generous enough for a family of six. He tucked into it immediately.

"Hmm," he purred a moment or two later. "At least one thing Teddy said made sense—this food is terrific! Too bad he had to leave."

"You mean too bad you drove him out," I corrected. "I hope now that your appetite's somewhat sated, you have the grace to feel a little badly."

"All right already, Peg. I'm sorry. I was pretty ugly. But I still can't figure why you let him tag along. You know damn well I wasn't in the best of moods."

"Yes, well, there was something I wanted to talk to him about," I said. "I was hoping to get to it before we met, but it just never happened. And then he seemed so down, I just couldn't bear to say no."

"My own little Miss Lonely Hearts," Spencer chided, though not unkindly. It was amazing what a good dinner could do to a bad temper. He smiled across the table at me and asked, "What sensitive little issue did you want to discuss with our fragile Teddy?"

"Uh, well, it's sensitive, all right," I replied. "It's something I've actually been meaning to talk to *you* about for a while, but... we've both been so busy."

"Well?" Spencer asked, pulling Teddy's untouched platter of steamed vegetables over from across the table. He breathed in the rich aromas of cheddar and broccoli, then added encouragingly, "Go ahead. I'm all ears, Peg."

I shouldn't have done it. I didn't think it through. I should have realized what daily exposure to Guilden, Senior's law-and-order ideas had done to Spencer's objectivity. In any case, I stupidly went ahead and told Spencer everything I'd discovered about Ramsey's kickback schemes. Of course, I should have known better.

But then I guess we all have twenty-twenty hindsight.

TWENTY-EIGHT

"I DON'T BELIEVE this! I just don't believe this!"

Spencer was as angry as I'd ever seen him. His upper lip was a thin pinched line of white. His usually serene blue eyes were clouded and fierce. He was yelling. In public. Something he'd never done in front of me before.

"You don't have to shout at me," I told him.

"Oh yes, I do!" he retorted, though I noticed he immediately lowered his voice and glanced around the room. Everyone who'd been staring at us turned quickly back to their meals. "What else can I do? I don't believe this, Peg."

"I can understand why you find it so incredulous," I replied. "I agree that it was totally out of Ramsey's character to do something like this. But it doesn't do any good to scream at *me*."

"Let's get something straight," Spencer retorted. "I don't give a damn about Ramsey. Or his character. That's not what's bothering me. You really don't understand why I'm so upset, do you? You just aren't getting it, are you, Peg?"

"I thought you were concerned because, well . . . because of me."

"God, that's so typical of you, Peg," Spencer snapped. "You have this incredibly narrow personalized view of the world. And you keep totally missing the big picture. The reason I'm so upset—and I find myself getting even angrier because I have to explain something that should be obvious to you by now—the reason I'm so mad is, well . . . Let me ask you something, okay?"

"Fine."

"You admit that what Ramsey did was against the law, right?"

"Of course, listen, I already told you that—"

"Now just be quiet a second," Spencer interrupted me, "and answer a few questions, all right? You admit he broke the law. And further, you'd agree to the fact that most people at P&Q and elsewhere thought of you and Ramsey as friends. Is that a correct impression?"

"You know it is, Spencer. But I don't see what all this is leading up—"

"And, further," Spencer continued, his voice rising again, "you'll agree that everyone we know thinks of us as a couple. I mean, even though nobody knows we're engaged, we're still generally thought to be going together, right?"

"Well, I certainly hope so."

"Now add to that," Spencer cried, "the fact that I'm working for my father, who's running for mayor on a law-and-order platform, Peg. What do you get?"

"I can understand that you're sort of upset, Spence, but—"

"But nothing! What you've got is one big royal screwup. God, if the press ever gets ahold of this . . . ! I mean, if they ever connect you and Ramsey and me. . . . Oh, Jesus, will they have a field day! I'll be washed up in politics before I even get started. Dad's going to kill me! He's going to literally crucify me. What the hell am I going to do?''

"I don't understand why your dad—or anyone else, for that matter—has to know."

"What do you mean you don't understand?" Spencer demanded. "Didn't you just tell me Cursio uncovered this mess? Listen, Peg, believe me, once the cops get ahold of something, you might as well advertise it on the front pages."

"Cursio doesn't know about this, Spence," I countered. "At least not as far as I know. I was the one who stumbled onto it. Just me. And I've only told you and Theo and Cal about it, so far."

"Who's Cal?"

"Calvin Hotchner. He's, uh, a friend of Theo's"

"Oh."

"And I don't intend to tell anybody else."

"Oh." Spencer breathed an audible sigh of relief. "Well, that's different. That's better. But what exactly *do* you intend to do?"

"I don't know," I admitted. "Poke around a little in the files. Talk some more with the photographers Ramsey had deals with. I just want to try to get a better sense of *why* Ramsey got involved with payoffs. There's got to be a good explanation somewhere for his behavior. I just know there does. And I want to find out what it is before the police—or the public—get any closer to the facts.

"I'm all for that, babe," Spencer replied. "I don't think I have to tell you what could happen if this news leaked out. It could seriously injure Dad's chances, not to mention my standing within his organization. Really, Peg, you've got to keep a lid on it—for *all* our sakes."

I didn't dare tell Spencer so at the time, but I didn't give a damn anymore about Jacob Guilden's mayoral bid. In fact, a big part of me was rooting against it. It was more than just a problem of my not liking the Guildens' conservative attitudes. The fact was, I actively disliked what the campaign was doing to Spencer.

For one thing, my movie-star handsome fiancé was getting fat. Spencer was not a big man to start with, so a few extra pounds could make a lot of difference. And recently he'd put on more than a few. His shoulders and thighs were practically busting the seams of his hand-tailored Italian suits. He wasn't even pretending to button his collars anymore. His ties sat askew beneath his Adam's apple, as though they couldn't get comfortable in their new expanded headquarters. His face was looking puffy and flushed.

And it wasn't just his physical appearance that was bothering me. It was his whole mental attitude. Slowly but surely he was turning into a Guilden. His attitudes were starting to harden. He measured his words with care, as though the entire press corps were waiting to pounce on his least utterance. But, worst of all, the only thing that seemed to matter to him anymore was the campaign. His reaction to my news about Ramsey had been that of public relations director...rather than fiancé.

It apparently never even crossed his mind that my clandestine research into Ramsey's dealings could get me into trouble. But, to be honest, it hadn't really occurred to me, either.

I SPENT MOST of the next afternoon at the office, sorting through the long strips of chromes Tomi had pulled of the Four Season's shoot. Tomi had marked his favorites with an *X* in orange grease pencil, but I went through the whole lot myself, anyway. Tomi evaluated his work from a technical end. I was looking for that more elusive quality of spontaneity and humor that makes people stop at a print ad...and take another look. There were literally hundreds of frames, and finding the perfect one was about as easy as finding a low-priced rental apartment on the Upper East Side.

At five sharp, Ruthie stood in my doorway, flanked by her usual army of shopping bags and totes.

"I'm off, then," she announced, then added grudgingly, "unless, of course, you need me for anything." I knew from previous discussions I'd had with her that Ruthie was facing a long busy night ahead. This being Thursday, she had her weekly pedicure to administer, plus a half hour mud-pack facial, followed by a homemade steam bath—this involved huge vats of boiling water and crouching over the stove—and another half hour of face massage. It seemed a terrible pity to me that Ruthie's face inevitably looked its worse on Fridays: the ministrations of the night before showing splotchy and raw through her layers of makeup.

I glanced up from my light table, then leaned back and stretched. Yes, there was something, but I didn't want to sound too eager.

"No, that's all, Ruthie," I said, waiting until she was a few steps down the hall before calling after her. "Listen, where could I find Tomi Tabor's invoices from last year?"

"The photographer's?" Ruthie asked, turning back around. I nodded and she said, "Well, that would depend on when last year. They've put a lot on microfiche, which you'll find in accounting. The rest are down the hall there to the left, in those red filing cabinets."

"Thanks, Ruthie, I may take a look later."

"Don't bother," Ruthie sniffed. "You probably won't be able to find what you're looking for. I'll get it for you in the morning. That's my job, after all."

Ruthie naturally assumed that anyone in a position of authority had the organizational abilities of a moron. She insisted proudly to everyone that I still didn't have the least idea how to operate our rather complicated phone system. And I heard her gossiping in the ladies' room once, when she didn't realize I was in one of the stalls, about my inability to discern the difference between my In and Out box. She wasn't being nasty, I knew; she just wanted me to be incompetent. It gave her something to do.

I pretended to pore over the chromes while the cleaning service made their desultory way through the empty offices. When I heard them rattle their cleaning cart onto the freight elevator, I turned my light table off. I had long ago found the shot I was looking for—with Renggli smiling bemusedly and Juan brandishing the drumstick as though it were a sword. What I stayed late to look for was going to take a much longer time.

A life was comprised of so many seemingly meaningless pieces of paper: letters, receipts, bank statements. Teddy and I had sorted through most of Ramsey's personal effects, and I had come across nothing that seemed out of the ordinary. I couldn't ask Teddy to let me see those papers again without letting him in on Ramsey's secret. So I decided I'd try to sift through Ramsey's business files. Somewhere, somehow, I'd have to find that wrong number, the misplaced decimal, that single clue that would help me unwind the string leading into the maze of Ramsey's wrongdoing. I had no idea how long it would take me . . . or how far.

I had asked Ruthie about Tomi's bills to find out where *all* the photographer's invoices were kept. Because I needed to go through each one. A typesetter's bill is a simple list of typesettings, changes to galleys and number of proofs pulled. A photo house merely indicates the number of halftones, the kind of velox or negative requested. But a photographer's invoice is a virtual catalog of items: props, assistants, stylists, model's fees, setup and breakdown costs, transportation, film and processing—and all that before any mention of the photographer's personal fee. Not only did I not know what I was looking for, but I had picked myself the most complicated hunting ground in which to search.

By nine-thirty that night my eyes ached from looking at lists of items and numbers. I had found nothing unusual, and I'd only made my way through the N files. I decided that I was on a wild-goose chase, put all the folders back and went home.

The next night I begged off my regular Friday night date with Spencer, explaining that it was for the good of his cause, and plowed through to the XYZ file. Again nothing. Or, more to the point, nothing I could see. I went home tired, grumpy and hardly in the mood to find Millie peeping out of her doorway, obviously lying in wait for me.

"My, you look pooped, child. Come in, and I'll make you a cup of tea."

"I'm exhausted, Millie," I replied. "And Picasso hasn't had dinner yet. For that matter, neither have I. Another time, maybe."

"You haven't eaten?" Millie cried. "Why, aren't you the lucky one. I just happen to have a good half of one of my homemade quiche Lorraines sitting in the icebox waiting for some hungry soul. Now, you run and get Picasso, and I'll have the two of you fed in no time flat."

I'd love to say that I took Millie up on her offer because I knew she was lonely and in need of company. The truth of the matter was, I'd had her quiche Lorraine before, and it happened to be a particularly delicate work of art.

I had seconds on both the tart and the tea, and was just sitting back with a contented sigh when I noticed Millie peering into my cup with undue interest.

"Oh no, not that Millie!" I cried, sitting back up.

"Now don't be a silly," Millie responded, pulling my cup toward her. "Whatever harm can it do?"

"Listen, I've told you a hundred times already, I don't like to have my fortune read. I don't want to know."

"Mmm," Millie hummed.

"You know what I think?" I went on, practically yelling at the angelic-looking diminutive white-haired lady opposite me. "I think you invited me in here under false pretenses. Admit it, Millie, all you cared about was reading those damn tea leaves, right?"

"I'm just trying to help," Millie answered sweetly.

"Help with what?" I demanded.

"Whatever all this trouble is," Millie responded, staring intently into the cup. "I see long rows of numbers, dear. What could those be?"

"What trouble, Millie?" I demanded. "What makes you think anything's wrong?"

"It's not what I think, it's what I feel. And, if you must know, I've been feeling these very disconcerting vibrations emanating from your apartment. Don't you tell me nothing's wrong. Now what *are* the numbers, dear?"

"I don't know what you're talking about," I retorted, though I wondered if she'd somehow picked up the fact I'd been searching through invoices all night. But how could she know? It was crazy.

"I see rows of numbers, quite distinctly," Millie continued, unperturbed. "Like in an accounting book, you know? They seem . . . yes I think they're written by hand—"

"Millie, listen, I really have to go," I interrupted. "I'm bone tired. I don't mean to be rude, but really. . ."

"And, yes, I see letters, as well. Rows of initials, next to the numbers."

"I don't know what you're—"

"And black. A book, no a folder. Wait a sec . . . It's a little black notebook. That's what I see. Ring any bells, dear?"

TWENTY-NINE

I DIDN'T BELIEVE in any of Millie's mumbo jumbo about auras and spirits and "the other side." Her tea readings and séances, in my opinion, were the harmless preoccupations of a lonely old woman. Her heart was in the right place when she roped me in for dinner that night, but I just couldn't take her dregs-inspired vision of a black notebook seriously.

When I got back to my apartment, though, I did sort through my top dresser drawers looking for the notebook I had found in Ramsey's desk the morning I moved into his office. I'd emptied it out of my bag the day I'd discovered it and hadn't thought of it since. It was a coincidence—though an odd one, I had to admit—that the notebook Millie described managed to resemble Ramsey's in every detail.

I found it under a pile of tangled panty hose and carried it with me into the living room. Picasso, his stomach expanded to bowling-ball size from Millie's overly generous repast, curled up on the couch beside me. It took me half an hour of flipping through Ramsey's neatly columned pages to finally figure the mystery out. Over and over again, I went back through the spidery list of initials, dates and amounts.

T.T.	12/6	$3,600.
D.H.R.	12/19	$2,400.
S.S.	1/12	$1,900.

Suddenly in a flash of insight, I broke the code. As soon as I did so, I was ashamed of myself for not figuring it out sooner. The initials were those of the photographers Ramsey was accepting kickbacks from, the dates those of the payoff transactions, and the dollar figures, well, that was sadly obvious.

The next evening I went back to the original invoices just to check that the amounts recorded in Ramsey's notebook were approximately ten percent of the bills submitted by each photographer. Every single one of them worked out to be just that, except for the very last entry in Ramsey's book.

T.T.   6/16 $5,250.

With Ruthie's desk calculator, I checked and rechecked my figuring, and each time Ramsey's take came to fifteen percent of the total bill.

I PHONED TOMI Monday morning. "You know, I think you and I have a little bone to pick, Tomi."

"Whatever about, sweetheart?" Tomi demanded. "Didn't you like my selections on the Fanpan shoot? I promise you, I pored over those chromes for hours. I thought they looked splendid."

"It's not that, Tomi," I replied. "Remember our lunch a month or so ago? And our memorable little talk about dear Rams?"

"Yes," Tomi answered. There was no warmth in his voice.

"Well, I've just stumbled upon something that doesn't quite gibe with what you were telling me. Does the number fifteen mean anything to you?"

"Shit." Tomi sighed.

"Yes, that's what I thought, too. Listen, Tomi, I want to hear the whole story. The *real* story about what happened when Ramsey upped the ante. Understand?"

"But not *now*," Tomi complained. "Not on the telephone, for chrissakes!"

"But soon," I insisted.

"Okay, come down to the studio tonight," Tomi agreed grudgingly. "Around eight. I'll be here alone then."

"Fine." It would mean canceling my date with Spencer, but then hadn't he urged me to settle this matter discreetly? And I sensed that if I could understand why Ramsey suddenly decided to up his take by five percent, then I would discover his reasons for demanding kickbacks in the first place. Also, I couldn't help but feel that Tomi knew more than he was telling me about Ramsey's motivations... and perhaps his own, as well.

Not that I thought for an instant that Tomi was the murderer. He might have had a motive, but I knew he didn't have the nerve. Tomi fainted at the sight of a paper cut. It would have been physically impossible for him to watch Ramsey bleed to death.

Tomi's name came up again later that day. And again, not in a particularly flattering context.

"It all looks fine to me, Pappy, so long as we don't have to work with that little son of a bitch Tabor."

J.J. and Victor Bobbin, Mark Rollings, Phillip Ebert and I were just finishing dessert after a leisurely two-hour lunch at Windows on the World. We had been laying out our fall advertising ideas to the Bobbins, who, except for J.J.'s final quibble, seemed to like what we had planned.

"Now, you listen, J.J.," Victor replied. "I told you before we came here to let sleeping dogs lie. Lordy knows, the man could have given us a bushel of trouble. But he didn't."

"We were just devastated when we heard how Tomi behaved," Mark Rollings asserted. I stared coldly across the table at him. When I'd told the executive committee what had happened at the Four Seasons, they had all agreed we were lucky Tomi Tabor wasn't suing. Mark's attempt to impress Victor at Tomi's expense made me furious. "It was simply unbelievable," Mark crooned on, "unforgivable. Of course, we'll never use the man again."

"Yes, we will," I countered, trying to keep my voice steady and reasonable sounding, though my temper was at full boil. "Not on Fanpan, of course. There's no point in that if we don't all get along. But Tomi's the top of the line. If the budget's there and the project's right, I'd go with him any day of the week."

"Really, Peg," Mark answered sternly, "I doubt Victor or J.J. particularly relish hearing your high opinion of Tomi at this point. I think you should keep your thinking on this matter to yourself."

"You're wrong there, Rollings," Victor announced. He chewed off the tip of the cellophane encasing his cigar and spat it out on the plush carpet. "I like Peg because she speaks her mind—she doesn't mouth whatever she thinks I want to hear. And I'll tell you something else—Peg's right about Tabor. The man knows what he's about. That Four Seasons batch came out darn nice."

"I couldn't agree more, Victor," Mark bubbled, his boyish smile turned to high intensity. "Actually, I think we all agree that Tomi's something of a genius. But that's hardly the issue now, is it?"

"In my mind it is," Victor replied, puffing rapidly to get the new cigar to catch. He blew a cloud of smoke in Mark's face and continued, "When I sink as much money into a project as I'm doing here, I want to know I've got the best plugging for me. If Peg thinks Tomi's it, then I say we go with him. Personal problems be damned."

"But Pappy!" J.J. cried, his face reddening with a rage that by now seemed almost familiar to me. His huge bulk—today swathed in a safari-style outfit that made him look like an oversize baby—trembled under the strain of his labored breathing. Anger caused his asthma to flare up.

"'But Pappy' nothing," Victor retorted. "Whether or not we use Tomi is not for you to decide, J.J. I leave it entirely to Peggy. And that's that. Now I say we all have a snort of brandy and celebrate a job well-done."

"I like your thinking, Victor," Phillip replied suavely as he signaled for the sommelier, though I knew how much he hated drinking at lunch. He'd barely touched his wine. "Bring us a Darroze Armagnac, Pierre, and just leave the bottle, please."

The party lasted nearly another hour, though I doubt anyone besides Victor had a particularly good time. As Phillip sniffed at his Armagnac, Victor regaled him with stories of his early hardscrabble years in the franchise business. Mark, whom Victor made a point of not including, glumly swallowed his postprandial drink and poured himself another. And then another. While J.J., shamed to silence by his father's words, glared across the table at me. I spent the time trying to avoid J.J.'s menacing gaze.

"So then I said to the son of a gun—" Victor laughed as he concluded a particularly long anecdote "—'You can take your five tons of chicken feed and throw 'em into the Old Missu, for all I care!'"

"Ha!" Phillip cried, trying to look jolly and impressed. "Well, you have quite a colorful history, Vic. Honestly, I wish we could just stay here all afternoon...and finish this fine bottle. But I'm afraid the three of us have to get back to the barracks. Mark? Peg? I think we better push off."

"Whaa?" Mark muttered, staring glassily around him. I think we all realized at the same instant that Rollings had become drunk. "I don't feel too good...." Mark added thickly.

"Overextended himself," Phillip, ever the diplomat, explained smoothly to the table. "Victor, would you mind awfully taking an arm and helping Mark to the gentlemen's?"

So that's how J.J. and I ended up together. Alone, for the very first time. I knew how an inexperienced matador must feel facing off against his first bull. J.J. loomed across the table, a mass of flesh, anger and frustration. This was a dangerous, perhaps deadly, man. I steadied myself for his charge, but it never came.

"You don't much like me, do you?" he said.

"Well, I..." I was caught totally off guard. *Like him?* I was terrified of him! How in the world was I supposed to respond?

In any case, I hesitated too long, because he added, "No, you don't like me. I can tell."

"Don't be silly, J.J.," I replied, collecting myself. "Of course, I like you."

"Nope. You're just saying that to be polite."

"That's not so," I persisted, feeling ridiculous. This was like talking to a five-year-old! "I think you're...very nice."

"Don't lie to me, Peg," J.J. said, and for the first time I met his gaze. The pale blue eyes were innocent, questioning.

"Okay," I answered. What the hell? I thought. What could he do to me here, in the middle of a crowded restaurant? "The truth is, sometimes I find your temper tantrums a little scary. Your behavior at the Four Seasons was enough to put anybody off."

"I know," J.J. muttered. "Pappy told me I should never have done it. It's just that...that Tomi got me so mad. And, Peg, you'd *promised* me I could help. I was just trying to do my job. To show Pappy that I could do it right."

Could he really be this simpleminded? I thought, meeting his gaze across the table. Did he really mean no harm? Had I misjudged him all this time? And then, just as quickly, I remembered the look in his eye when he went after Tomi...the roughing up he had given the Smiley's woman.

"I just think we'd get along a little better, J.J.," I continued, trying to sound soothing, "if you got a firmer hold on your temper. Real professionals learn to control their feelings. I'm sure you only want to do your job. But, believe me, nobody's going to take you seriously if you don't act businesslike."

"That's just what Pappy says."

"Your Dad's a pretty bright guy, you know. I'd certainly take his advice."

"I try," J.J. responded, his face clouding. "I like being advertising manager, and I think I could be good at it . . . but you know Pappy never gives me a chance. Whenever I have an idea, he tells me to just shut up and listen. How can I show him I can do my job, Peg, if he never lets me prove it?"

Once again it struck me how childlike J.J. seemed. I was so used to being afraid of him that his straightforward plea for understanding astounded me.

"Well, I guess you just have to keep trying," I suggested lamely. "That's all anybody can do."

"If . . . if I try," J.J. stuttered, "if I do better . . . do you think you'd like me then?"

"Sure," I said, smiling over at him. His wide blue eyes lighted up, and he grinned back at me.

"Promise?"

"Of course."

"Oh, that's great!" he cried, and suddenly a fat damp hand clasped mine.

"I said *like*, J.J.," I reminded him as I tried to wiggle my fingers out of his grasp. He stared across the table at me, grinning like a child who'd just been handed a surprise present.

"You're so pretty, Peg," J.J. went on happily. "I like your hair. And I like your eyes. But most of all I like your big boobs."

"J.J.!" I cried frantically, pulling back my hand. Several late diners turned and stared over at us. "Don't say those things!" I hissed. "Don't misunderstand what I said. . . . I only said that I'd *like* you. Don't get any ideas about me. I'm engaged. I'm going to get married soon."

"But you promised," J.J. answered, his wide smile wavering.

"Only that we'd be friends," I tried to explain.

"No," J.J. insisted, his hand squeezing mine so hard my knuckles cracked. "You promised."

"Let go of my hand. You're hurting me."

"No, you're hurting *me*," J.J. wheezed, his asthma building with his emotions. His face was flushed again, his eyes filled with tears. "You lied to me. Everyone lies. That Tomi Tabor lied, too. I know. Don't think I'm so dumb."

"If you don't let go of my hand right now," I warned, "I'm going to scream."

"I know he didn't have film in his camera," J.J. went on, oblivious to my threat. "He just pretended. And you did, too. You think I'm so dumb, but you'll see."

"Please, J.J.," I begged, "let go of my hand."

"You'll see, Peg. I'll show you and that Tomi—"

"Come on, you two!" Victor's voice boomed as he crossed the room toward us. "We're gonna skedaddle now. We got that milk toast Rollings back in human condition," Victor added, chuckling as he reached the table.

"Everything okay here?" he asked, glancing from my no doubt ashen face...to J.J.'s beet-red countenance. My just-released hand throbbed beneath the table.

"Yes," I lied, reaching for my bag.

Windows on the World was on the one hundred and seventh floor of one of the World Trade towers. Even in the building's ultramodern, room-size elevator, it took more than three minutes to reach street level. Minutes that went by like hours, because J.J. refused to take his eyes off me. Not that he met my gaze. No, his wide blue stare was fixed firmly on the part of my anatomy he said he most admired. Gone was all sense of his innocence, any feeling I might have had that he was naive. There was only one thing in the look he gave me. Well, if looks could kill, I would have had a knife in my heart.

THIRTY

IT WASN'T UNTIL I decided not to tell Spencer about J.J.'s advances that I finally faced the fact I wasn't telling him much of anything these days. I didn't know when exactly I'd started to edit the subject matter of my life for him. Had it been since he'd joined the Guilden crusade...or before? In any case, I found myself painting a bright picture of my lunch with the Bobbins when I spoke to him on the phone later that afternoon.

"And Rollings was sick as a dog all the way back in the taxi," I confided cheerily. "Phillip was just livid!" It had been a gruesome ride, actually, one in which I tried several times to explain what had transpired between J.J. and me. But both men were so preoccupied with Mark's condition that my comments were ignored. I'd arrived back at the office feeling frustrated . . . and more than a little frightened. By rights, I should have been telling Spencer all this. But I didn't.

"Oh, yes, and honey," I went on, "I'm afraid I'm going to have to skip the movie tonight. I've a late meeting with Tomi. To . . . go over some estimates." Another skirting of the truth, I realized.

"Just as well," Spencer answered. "I've a load of letters to get out for the next fund-raiser. And last-minute changes to make on Dad's farm bill speech. You know that dinner's Thursday night."

"What dinner?"

"Why, the Dairymen's Association Banquet. Don't tell me you've forgotten? I told you at least three weeks ago that Dad expects us both on the dais. These farmers put a lot of stock in family. Dad really wants a strong showing."

I didn't remember, but then I didn't want a fight. It was becoming more and more clear to me that Spencer and I were no longer listening to each other. I wasn't angry, just sad and confused, and my conversation with him only aggravated my sense of frustration. After we hung up, I paced my office, clenching and unclenching my fists, trying to wipe away the memory of J.J.'s touch. Finally, desperate for advice and sympathy, I phoned Teddy.

"Now, angel, you just sit right down and tell Ted all about it," he instructed me kindly.

"Oh, it's not really fair to lay it all on Spence," I hedged after I'd talked a while. "It's just been a bad day."

"I know how that can be," Ted replied comfortingly. "What made today so particularly grim?"

So poor patient Teddy heard all about my lunch with the Bobbins.

"Honestly, dear," Ted interrupted at one point, "the man sounds like an absolute brute, a Neanderthal. What swamp did he crawl out of, for heaven's sake?"

"I'm not sure he's to blame, Ted," I tried to explain. "I mean, I'm really beginning to think he's not all there. I kept getting the feeling I was talking to a child. It was eerie."

"A child with a decidedly lustful eye," Ted reminded. "And a rather grown-up temper, if you ask me. Oh, do be careful, Peg, dear. I don't like the sound of this J.J. at all."

"Well, I don't, either." I sighed. "I keep wondering...do you think I should call Cursio? He did tell me to watch out for J.J. But then—I don't know—what would I say? The guy was trying to put the moves on me? What can the police do?"

"You've got a point," Ted agreed. "They can't exactly arrest him for holding your hand. But why was Cursio warning you off J.J., Peg? Does he think...I mean, is there evidence that..."

"J.J. killed Ramsey?" I finished Ted's question for him. "No evidence as far as I know. Just a history of sudden temper tantrums, a tendency toward violence. Also, my growing impression is that J.J. doesn't really understand the basic difference between right and wrong. Maybe he's a...what are they called?"

"Sociopath?"

"Yeah."

"Hmm," Teddy ruminated. "But why Ramsey? What harm did Ramsey ever do him?"

"None intentionally, of course," I replied. "But J.J. is extremely sensitive about his abilities as an advertising executive. He's convinced neither his father nor anyone at P&Q respects him professionally."

"Well, they don't, do they?"

"Of course not. But we all put on a good show. Maybe Ramsey didn't understand the game. Maybe, early on in our relationship with Fanpan—sometime when none of us was around to intervene—Ramsey let old J.J. have it. You know how brutally frank he could be when it came to clients interfering with creative."

"Heavens, yes. He'd come home ranting and raving if an account so much as suggested a different layout possibility."

"Right. So all I'm saying is...perhaps Ramsey did something to set the man off. You should see the way J.J.'s reacting to Tomi Tabor these days. You know Tomi, don't you?"

"He's one of your photographers, right?"

"Probably our best," I replied. "An old crony of Ramsey's, who has just about Ramsey's tolerance level when it comes to interfering clients. Well, J.J. got so mad at him during a shoot at the Four Seasons that he went after Tomi...with a knife."

"Oh, God, Peg!" Ted gasped. "You're not kidding. This man *is* dangerous. Listen, I've changed my mind. Call Cursio.

Tell him you just want to update him on the situation. I think he should know.''

"Maybe you're right," I said with a sigh.

"You *know* I'm right," Ted corrected me. "And if you don't do it, I will. I won't sleep tonight thinking of that monster grubbing for your hand across the table. And Spencer acting an officious ass, to boot. You poor kid.''

"Well, thanks for hearing me out on all this," I replied gratefully. "I feel a lot better now. You're such a good friend, Ted. I don't think I tell you that enough.''

"Now, don't go getting sentimental on me, Peg," Ted responded, though I could tell he was pleased by what I'd said. "Listen, if it would make you feel better, why not come down here for dinner after work? I've a delicious-smelling cassoulet on.''

I explained I had a late meeting with Tomi.

"Well, how long can that go on, dear? Drop down here afterward. His loft is on lower Fifth, right? You'll just about be in the neighborhood, anyway.''

"Let's see . . . I'm going down to Tomi's around eight to discuss some estimates," I thought aloud. "It shouldn't take more than an hour. Sure you won't mind a late dinner? Because I'd love to come." Ted was just the remedy I needed for the mood I was in. He offered unquestioning loyalty and support. And dinner alone with him would give me the chance to feel him out a bit on Ramsey's finances, as well. Who could say? I thought as I hung up the phone. Perhaps, with the information Tomi was going to supply, along with a little help from Ted, I'd have the mystery solved by the end of the evening.

MANHATTAN IS A DECEPTIVE TOWN architecturally. The blandest graystone apartment building on Park Avenue discreetly houses the most fabulous private collection of Impressionist paintings in the world. The dingiest cast-iron facades of SoHo conceal the most glamorous and sought-after lofts. It is a city you have to know from the *inside* before you truly understand its wealth and power. No one would guess, for instance, after a quick glance at the grimy windows of the carpet showroom on lower Fifth Avenue, that the second floor had been converted into a commercial photographer's dreamland. Only a small brass plaque, hardly larger than a postage stamp, alerts you to the fact the the famous Tomi Tabor held professional court above.

I rang the outside buzzer around ten minutes after eight and waited for Tomi to ring me up. Though the day had been clear and mild, the oncoming evening was bringing an unexpected chill with it. Ominous-looking clouds were swallowing up the sunset, and there was a distinct dampness to the sudden breeze. I shivered, wishing now that I'd worn a jacket over my sleeveless white linen dress, and rang Tomi's bell again.

Nothing. Damn, I thought, rubbing the goose bumps on my bare arms. Had something gone wrong with Tomi's intercom? I held the buzzer down for a good fifteen seconds. Still *nada*. Perhaps the door was jammed, I decided, and so I put all my weight against the heavy oak front . . . and pushed. It fell open so abruptly that I nearly fell with it, and then it slammed shut behind me.

Well, the fact that the door hadn't been closed was obviously why the buzzer hadn't worked, I realized as I steadied myself against the banister. Damn, but it was dark. Tomi's overhead light must be out, I decided as I made my way up the stairs by touch alone. I stumbled once or twice, swearing to myself under my breath, determined to give Tomi a piece of my mind. "The least he could have done," I grumbled audibly, "was to leave a light on."

It wasn't until I got to the top and pushed open the studio door to find the whole place in darkness that it occurred to me that Tomi may have forgotten our date. But he would never have left his front door ajar, I told myself as I flicked on the bank of light switches to the right of the entrance. The vast, sparkling clean studio shimmered in its sudden shower of light.

"Tomi!" I cried, dropping my purse on the receptionist's desk. "Tomi! I'm here. Where are you?"

Everyone in advertising was quick to agree that Tomi now owned the largest best-equipped studio in the business. He had the most—and the highest quality—equipment. He could supply the widest range of backdrops and sets. Everyone in the business knew you needn't travel any farther than Tomi's. And yet, there was something in the very vastness and variety of what Tomi had to offer that implied a certain folly.

Did we really need three different bathroom sets to choose among? Would any consumer actually catch the difference between the corniches above Nice as opposed to those above

Menton in Tomi's collection of Riviera backdrops? I didn't think I was alone in the feeling that Tomi was able to supply his clients with more than we could ever use. In his attempt to go further than any other photographer had in giving agencies the best possible photography studio, I think a lot of people secretly agreed that Tomi had gone too far.

"Tomi?" I cried again into the jumbled worlds that faced me. Here, angled to the door, was a spacious new kitchen, fixtures glistening, totally useless except as a showcase for the aluminum cans of Merkin's Cocoa Mix that were spaced along the counters. There, right behind it, was a Paris street scene, the Eiffel Tower in the distance and a fully equipped cafè in the foreground. Containers of Viva yogurt were scattered among the glasses and coffee cups on the tabletops. There was a sadness, a loneliness to the place at night. It was like an empty Hollywood back lot or a huge department store swept free of customers.

"Anybody here?" I cried, and for the first time I heard my words echoing hollowly back at me. The half dozen arching windows that faced Fifth Avenue had now darkened completely, reflecting the vast chaotic room. "Tomi?" I tried again. "Hey, Tomi, where are you?"

The darkroom, I thought suddenly, remembering the little warren of private offices and storerooms Tomi had built at the back of his studio. By necessity Tomi had to work with the door shut while he was developing film; that was why he hadn't heard me come in.

I zigzagged my way through various sets toward the back of the studio. One scene in particular looked familiar; it took me a few seconds to recognize the kitchen from our first aborted Fanpan shoot. But there was the table and the red-checkered cloth. I ran my hands over the fabric. That morning now seemed a lifetime ago. Well, a lot had changed since Ramsey's murder, I thought, and not the least of it was me. It was more than just the confidence I'd gained from my success at P&Q; something more fundamental had happened. It was somehow connected to the realization that if someone as obviously good as Ramsey was capable of crime, then we all carried that potential in us. I was no longer so quick to blame others: Tomi, Ramsey, Spencer and perhaps most of all, Theo.

I guess what had happened, I realized as I opened the door leading to Tomi's private offices, was that I had taken a giant

step toward growing up. And in doing so I'd come to see that
being a responsible adult wasn't nearly as easy as it looked.

"Hey, Tomi?" I called as I walked down the corridor to his
darkroom. As I'd expected, the flashing red "occupied" button was on; the door closed.

"Tomi, I'm here!" I cried, knocking loudly on the door.

The red light, no bigger than a human eye, blinked back at
me with bright rapidity.

"C'mon, Tomi!" I shouted, banging with both fists. "Open
up in there. I haven't got all night."

The red eye winked. Silence.

"Tomi?" I asked, pushing open the door. "I hate to inter-
rupt, but..."

The darkroom was small, pungent with the smell of developing fluid, lined with crowded shelves. The entire room was
bathed in the rich crimson glow of Tomi's work light. On the
far wall, rows of prints—like laundry—hung along a plastic line
to dry. For a moment I thought the room was empty, then I saw
the sack on the floor next to the sink. I stepped in and to one
side, letting the light from the hallway fall onto that area of the
room. I took another step toward it, nearly slipping on some
fluid that had slopped onto the floor.

In a single second my mind registered about a million things.
This wasn't a sack—it was a person. This wasn't developing
fluid I was standing in—it was blood. This wasn't just anyone—it was Tomi. And he was dead. His upward-slanting eyes
stared vacantly at the ceiling. His hands curled on his chest, half
grasping something. It was a knife, a long-handled carving
knife, and it had been thrust straight into his heart.

THIRTY-ONE

"DID YOU TOUCH anything, Peg?" Cursio asked gently as we
stood together outside the darkroom and watched Cursio's men
carefully prowl around the tiny room that contained Tomi's
body.

"No," I answered numbly. Then I forced myself to think
about Cursio's question. "Well, actually...I guess I touched
the countertop and sink when I..."

"When you got sick," Cursio finished bluntly. A few seconds after I had discovered Tomi's body, I found myself retching violently into the darkroom's shallow developing basin. As soon as I'd gotten control of myself again, I'd groped my way back to the reception area and phoned Cursio. He had arrived within ten minutes of my call, accompanied by a half dozen men, including—ironically enough—a photographer, who was swiftly documenting the awful scene.

"Listen, that's nothing to be ashamed of," Cursio added kindly. "It's a normal human reaction. Believe me, all of us—" he gestured broadly at the six men working nearby "—have had our moments."

"Yes, well..." I muttered dismissively, unable to find much comfort in his words. "Besides that, no, I don't think I came in contact with anything. Except the doorknobs, from the street right on through to here...."

"Tell me about that, Peg," Cursio said, fishing around in his jacket pocket for a pen. "You said the door was open when you arrived?"

"Are you taking my statement?" I demanded coldly, glancing from his poised pen to his attentive, almost eager, expression. "Because if you are, maybe I should call a lawyer. Come to think of it, maybe I should have called one in the first place." My voice sounded high and reedy, edged with hysteria. Two of Cursio's men turned to stare at us. "I don't know why," I continued loudly, "but for some reason I thought you'd react with just a little bit more sensitivity."

"Tom, take over, would you?" Cursio called over to one of the men watching us with interest. "I want the place scoured, understand? And when the guy from the M.E.'s office gets here, I want you to give him the royal treatment, but tell him we needed the lab report yesterday. I'm going to see Ms Goodenough home. I'll call you from her apartment."

Cursio grabbed my elbow and wordlessly steered me along the corridor, through the studio and down the now well-lighted stairs. A dark blue sedan in serious need of a wash was parked in front of the building. Cursio yanked open the passenger door for me, then slammed it shut after I'd climbed in.

Periodically, the police radio crackled with voices or static, but besides that we rode together in silence for almost eighty blocks. The quiet was nearly a palpable thing between us. I had no idea what he was thinking or feeling, but I was benumbed by a totally unreasonable avalanche of anger: all of it heaped upon Cursio.

I had never been so terrified in my life. How could he react so coldly, so clinically? I needed comfort, advice, and he—good God—all he cared about was taking my statement! He didn't give a damn about me; he probably didn't give a damn about anybody. I inched away from him so that I was almost cringing against the door and breathed in the car's sad smell of smoke and sweat and cheap upholstery. Here, or in another car like this one, was where Cursio spent half his life. Waiting, watching. And what was it he wanted? What was he looking for? To have his own worst suspicions about human nature confirmed. Only a cynic could want this job. Only a man who could continue to exist with every possible illusion about life stripped away. I closed my eyes, trying not to see the bloody bundle in the darkroom, and told myself that I hated Dante Cursio.

"Thanks for the ride," I said coldly when he stopped in front of my brownstone. I started to open the door.

"If you think for one goddamned minute that you're going up there alone, forget it." Without waiting for me to close the door again, Cursio backed roughly into a parking space next to a fire hydrant. Continuing the stony silence, we made our way up to my apartment. Cursio insisted on unlocking my door, turning on all the lights, rummaging briefly through the closets.

"Just what is it that you're hoping to find?" I demanded from the kitchen, where I was opening Picasso's dinner. "I'm not sure I like you going through my things like that."

"And I'm suddenly not sure," Cursio responded, as he came into the kitchen, "that I like a lot of things about you."

"What's that supposed to mean?" I leaned over and emptied the cat food into Picasso's dish. My cat, who had up until this point pretended ecstasy at my return, now engrossed himself in the true object of his affection.

"You're developing an unseemly attraction to murder, that's what."

"I don't believe you're saying this!" I cried, slamming the empty can into the garbage pail.

"What do you think it is that I'm saying?" Cursio asked, walking across the room to my broom closet. He opened the narrow door and stared into the dark jumble of brooms, ironing board and stepladder.

"You know perfectly well what you're saying. Don't think you can trick me with a load of policeman's psychology." I was almost shouting now. "I'm not so dumb, Detective. I know what I'm doing."

"I'm sure you do, Peg," Cursio replied, shutting the door to the broom closet and turning to face me. "But what I'm interested in is what you *were* doing. At Tomi's studio. At nearly nine o'clock. When I'd think all good little creative directors should be long finished work."

"We were supposed to go over some estimates together."

"What estimates? Why so late? Why not wait for a more reasonable time?"

"Both Tomi and I are busy people. Keeping late hours is just part of the job."

"You're lying, Peg." Cursio sighed, rubbing his eyes wearily. "What do you think I've been doing for the past couple of months? I know damn right well what time you and Tomi both leave work as a rule. At six on the button, Tomi Tabor is usually angling his way through crosstown traffic en route to his Long Island estate. And, yes, sometimes you do work a little late. But not every night. And not nearly as long as you've been staying the past few nights. What's up, Peg? Why the lies? What happened tonight at the studio?"

"Just what I told you," I snapped, turning my back on him to face out the little window above my sink. It offered me a tiny slivered view of the Hudson and the distant, deceptively glittering rise of New Jersey. "The door was open. The place was dark. I called for him, but he didn't answer. I finally went back to look for him in the darkroom. I found him there...just the way you saw him. That's all. I promise."

"Promises," Cursio retorted. He came over and stood behind me at the sink. "I don't believe in promises anymore, Peg. They're for children. I believe in facts."

"I've given you the facts," I answered, though my voice was unsteady. I could feel his breath against the back of my neck. His nearness increased my anger and frustration. Why couldn't he just leave me alone? Didn't he see that I was nearly overcome with grief...and what else? Suddenly I had to ask myself what was really behind my bitterness. Wasn't it more than just Tomi's horrible death? Wasn't it the possibility that I might be partially responsible for it? What if some third party had learned Tomi was going to tell me something—something I shouldn't know—about Ramsey? What if my snooping around had precipitated his murder? Yes, I was overcome with grief. But I was also—perhaps even more so—consumed by guilt. Cursio's hands came to rest lightly on my shoulders. Slowly, he forced me to turn around. To face him. But I couldn't meet his gaze.

"No, I don't think you killed Tabor... or Ramsey," Cursio said softly. "But I do think you know a hell of a lot more than you're telling. I think you're holding back on me. Peg—" his voice turned sharp "—look at me."

As soon as I did so, I knew that any hope I'd held of continuing to protect Ramsey was extinguished. And it finally occurred to me that even if I had managed to get to the bottom of Ramsey's dealings, what good would it have done? No matter what I would have discovered, I would never have been able to accomplish what I truly wanted: no one could change the unalterable fact that Ramsey had been on the take. I had only succeeded in lying to myself, as well as to Cursio.

"Okay," I said, sighing. "You're right. I'm sorry. Come back into the living room. I want to show you something."

We sat on the couch, and I opened my purse and took out Ramsey's little black notebook. I'd carried it down to Tomi's intending to confront him with the evidence. Now I flipped through the pages to that last damaging entry, and handed it to Cursio.

"That," I said, pointing to the final amount, "might have been the reason Tomi was killed." And then I told Cursio everything I'd been able to piece together about Ramsey's kickback schemes. As I talked, Cursio turned slowly back through the pages, then closed the notebook and sat staring at the worn leather cover as if it were a star witness who had just refused to testify.

"I'm not surprised," Cursio murmured. "It explains a lot, actually. I got the feeling from almost all the photographers we'd interviewed that they were covering something up. I half suspected something like this myself. Damn—" he slapped his knee hard with the notebook "—I should have pressed them harder. I should have pressed *you*."

"I'm sorry. I thought I could protect Ramsey. I just had to try to get to the bottom of this myself. I never thought it could lead to another murder. It was stupid."

"The best intentions often are," Cursio said, absently taking my hand. "It requires a certain awful brilliance and imagination to carry through on the evil ones."

"Gruesome to use that knife," I said, shuddering with the memory of Tomi's hands curled around the long bone handle. It had turned out to be the knife used as a prop during the first Fanpan shoot.

"Yes, and perhaps a bit poetic," Cursio mused. "Everything in this case leads us back to that first photo session when you learned Ramsey had been killed. The murders are obviously related."

"Do you think it's also a coincidence that both Ramsey and Tomi were knifed?"

Cursio looked down at my hand, then back at me. "I'm not at liberty to say," he said, releasing his grasp. He stood up abruptly and stretched.

"Peg, I advise you not to stay alone tonight. I don't mean to scare you, really, but I would feel better if you had someone here. Why don't you call a friend? I'll wait until someone arrives."

"Why are you closing down on me like this?" I demanded. "Why can't you tell me about the knifing? Is it that you don't trust me anymore?"

"Words like *trust* and *promise* don't have a whole lot of meaning for me," Cursio responded, running his hands through disheveled hair. He looked tired and hot. "I just think the less you know about all this, the better."

"That's an incredibly condescending thing to say," I retorted, standing up to face him, "considering what I just handed you in the way of evidence."

"Don't start in on me, Peg. Please, just don't start. Now, do as I say, and call somebody up. I'm not leaving until you do."

"Then you better plan on spending the night. I refuse to be ordered around in my own apartment."

"Fine. Okay," Cursio replied, throwing up his hands in exasperation. "This couch looks plenty comfortable to me. I'd like to make a few phone calls first, if you don't mind. And, I hope this won't sound too much like an order, but do you suppose I could borrow a towel and a few sheets?"

Fuming, I made up Cursio's bed on the couch while he called headquarters. I brushed my teeth and went into my bedroom, closing the door tightly behind me without so much as a good-night to him. I smiled to myself, thinking of the lumpy pillow I'd given him and the tendency of my couch cushions to slide onto the floor under too much weight.

I fell into a light comfortable sleep almost immediately. But not for long. The next thing I knew—and it turned out to be less than half an hour later—I woke up to the sound of someone screaming. It was a woman's voice. I sat up in bed, gasping for breath, just as Cursio burst into the room and snapped on the light.

"What is it?" he cried, glancing quickly around.

"I don't know," I said, looking around the room, as well. "Someone was screaming. Didn't you hear it?"

Cursio sat down heavily next to me. He'd taken his shirt off. His well-muscled chest was matted with hair.

"Yes, I heard," he said, looking at me oddly. "It was you, Peg."

"Oh."

"It must have been a bad dream. Do you remember?"

"No," I said, trying to work back through the web of my waking thoughts. "I can't remember a thing."

"Good," Cursio said, smiling. "You going to be okay?"

"Yes."

"Sure now?" Cursio demanded. I felt his eyes on the low-cut neckline of my flimsy sleeveless summer nightgown. I didn't blame him for staring. My breasts, free from the daytime shackles of a bra, swayed saucily beneath the sheer fabric. I could just as easily have had nothing on.

"Yes," I said again, but I didn't want him to go. No, it wasn't that I was afraid. I reached over and touched his chest. The black hair was springy and strong. I heard the quick intake of his breath. I heard him swallow. Then I felt strong arms around me. "Yes," I repeated as he held me fiercely to him, "I think I'm going to be just fine now."

THIRTY-TWO

I'D NEVER BEEN a particularly spontaneous person. I was well aware that in my lifelong struggle to steady myself against Theo's erratic ways, I'd become somewhat overly analytical and cautious. I was not, I suppose, what you would call a passionate woman. In some shut-up secret part of myself, I think a certain fear of frigidity lurked. It was not that I didn't enjoy sex, it was just that it wasn't always on the very top of my "to do" list.

It came as something of a shock to me, then, that as soon as Detective Dante Cursio and I had finished making love, I immediately wished we could do it again.

"Sweet Jesus," he said, pulling my tangled hair back off my shoulders—we were both sweating like marathoners—and kissing the damp, undoubtedly sodium-rich nape of my neck. "You really are something, lady."

"You're not so bad yourself, Detective," I said, pulling the sheet up over my breasts. We'd left the light blazing. I felt suddenly shy.

"Dan. My name's Dan, okay?"

"Oh." I looked at him, trying to put all the disparate things I knew and felt about him together into one man. "I thought it was Dante."

"C'mon, Peg. I'm a cop, not a poet. The last person who called me Dante without snickering was my mother."

"You want to know the ugly truth about me?" I asked, running my left index finger along the thick dark curve of his right brow. I had a sudden odd impulse to kiss his eyes. "My real, legal name is...Margaret. Ugh."

"I already knew that. And I know other, even worse, things. Like the fact you were arrested in the summer of your fourteenth year for driving, not to mention the fact it was under the influence of alcohol."

"I'm surprised a good detective like you doesn't have his facts straight. I wasn't driving. Kenny Price was. I do confess to being a little tipsy, though."

"Kenny Price, huh? Man, you must have had them jumping through hoops." His right hand slid under the covers and along my waist. "You still do," he added, pulling me to him again.

I was, indeed, surprised by my reaction—which was immediate, swift and total. In the bright, hot, overly feminine confines of my room, we made love again. I simply forgot myself. I simply let go. And for the first time in my life, I think I really realized what passion was all about.

We got up later and took a lukewarm shower together, then climbed back into my rumpled bed and slept in each other's arms. Sometime early in the morning, I must have had another bad dream. I woke up crying.

"Hey, it's okay," Dan was saying. He kissed the tears that ran blindly down my cheeks. "I'm here, Peg. It's going to be okay."

Around six in the morning, I woke up again. Dan was sitting on the edge of the bed, tying his shoes.

"I'm going out to get the papers and some bagels. I've already checked, you've got coffee and milk. How do I shut that damned cat up?"

"Little Friskies. Top shelf of the refrigerator. Half a cup, at most. Ignore all ploys on his part to get any more out of you."

"Right." Dan leaned across the bed and kissed me. "Listen, think about things while I'm out, okay? We've got to talk when I get back."

I tried to do as he suggested. I got up and dressed, brushed my hair and put on a little makeup—the whole time doing my best to think. Instead, I only remembered the incredible lightness of Dan's touch, the heady power of his kisses. I was just getting around to recalling the more intimate of his finer qualities when he came back. A tall dark-haired man with a pale narrow weather-beaten face. Why had I never realized before, I wondered, how incredibly attractive he was?

"You just became famous," Dan said, handing me the *Daily News*. "Page 7. Bottom right-hand column."

The short paragraph, headlined, "Manhattan Photographer Found Slain," was obviously pieced together from police reports.

The body of Tomi Tabor, one of Madison Avenue's most respected still photographers, was found knifed to death in his spacious second-story lower Fifth Avenue studio last night. Peg Goodenough, art director at Peabody & Quinlan, discovered the body when, according to police reports, she stopped by the studio on a business matter.

It ended by saying that I was being held by the police for questioning and was unreachable for comment.

"That's odd," I said. "Nobody even tried to get me here."

"They might have tried," Dan called to me from the kitchen. I could hear him filling the coffeepot with water. "I had your calls recircuited down to headquarters last night after I called in. I had to while I had the bug set up."

"And who gave you permission to do that?" I demanded, marching into the kitchen.

"I did," Dan replied calmly as he measured coffee into the filter. "You're being held by the police for questioning. Didn't you read the full story?"

"Yes, damn it, I did. But that still doesn't give you the right to effectively cut me off from the world. What if Spencer or Theo has been trying to get me?"

"Or the murderer? Don't forget our mysterious little buddy, Peg. Listen, what I did was for your own good. From now on, we're going to monitor all your calls. We're getting close, I can feel it. But the nearer we get . . . the more dangerous our friend becomes. It's no time to be careless." He stood at the stove pouring boiling water into the Melitta, his dark gaze intent on some complicated inner riddle.

"What did last night mean to you?" I demanded abruptly.

"Mean?" Dan asked, slowly putting down the coffeepot and turning to face me. "That's a loaded word, *mean*. I'd be a lot happier if you rephrased the question."

"You know what the question is, no matter how I ask it. And I'm afraid I already know the answer."

"I doubt it," Dan replied evenly. "Since *I* don't even know the answer. I don't know what I think, or what I feel. A hell of a lot has happened in the past few hours."

"You're not convincing, Dan," I replied. "I'm sorry, but it just doesn't wash. So why don't you just admit it? It wasn't *me* who got you excited last night—it was the damned murder. I just happened to be conveniently underfoot and—"

"Better watch it, Peg," Dan interrupted, turning back to the stove. He turned back to me almost immediately, holding out a steaming cup of coffee. "Let's get into the living room. You'd better be sitting down for what I'm going to say."

I sat on the couch, the coffee warming my hands, though a chill swept through my heart.

"You ready for some statistics?" he asked, pacing the throw rug in front of me. "Over seventy-five percent of police marriages end in divorce. I've already contributed to that percentage. I see guys every day adding their numbers to the pile. It's no accident, Peg, that we can't keep our families together. There's a damn good reason—we're devoted, the way a soldier or priest is, to what we do. There's no glory in it, and, I seriously fear, no heavenly reward. But it's all I have. It's the job. It's what there is. It's what I *do*."

"I wasn't asking you to marry me, Dan," I countered. "I simply asked if—"

"You *meant* anything to me," he finished for me. "Well, what do *you* think, Peg? What do you want me to say?"

"I just want you to be honest," I answered. "I just need to know what you feel."

"Why? So that you can decide whether or not to break off with Spencer? So you can figure out if you want to throw in your hat with me?"

"Yes, that has something to do with it," I snapped. "Regardless of how I behaved a few hours ago, I've never run around on Spencer. I've never done anything remotely like...we did last night. And I don't intend to do it again. I have to make up my mind.... I have to decide between—"

"Whatever you do," Dan interjected, sitting down abruptly beside me on the couch, "don't decide between Spencer and me. Decide, instead, what kind of future you want—what sort of person you really want to be."

"You simply are the most arrogant man. I know perfectly well who I want to be."

"Then you don't need any commitment from me to decide," Dan answered.

"No," I said. "But needing and wanting are two different things."

"Yes," Dan replied, looking across at me, "and if it makes any difference to you, I've been wanting you like mad all summer."

"But not needing."

"Nope. I gave up on that about the same time I joined homicide. Life's a lot more bearable without it."

The phone, which wasn't supposed to ring, suddenly did. Dan jumped up and got it.

"Yeah?" he demanded. "Already? Good. Yeah, go ahead. From the top. No, I'll remember. Just read it to me." After a few seconds of silence, he added, "Fine. No, I'll be there. We're just about through here. Tell the commissioner to keep his pants on. Right, thanks."

"Let me guess," I said dryly as he hung up the phone. "It was the local Girl Scouts trying to sell you a carton of chocolate mint thins."

"They just got the lab report in. Tomi bled to death. Massive invasion of the left ventricle. Stab wound killed him."

"That can't be much of a surprise," I observed. "And I guess that reinforces the assumption that Ramsey's and Tomi's murderer are one and the same."

"Actually, no, Peg," Dan said, staring over at me intently. "For your own protection, I think you should know the truth."

"About?" I didn't like his comment about protection, but that could wait.

"How Ramsey really died."

"He was stabbed, just like Tomi was," I answered. "There were lengthy detailed reports in all the papers."

"Yeah, reports we put together downtown," Dan replied. He came back to the couch and picked up his cup of coffee from the table and took a sip. It must have been ice-cold, but he swallowed it anyway, his thoughts elsewhere. "The fact of the matter is, Ramsey was killed by a blow to the head from a heavy beveled object of some kind."

"But . . . what about the knife wounds?" I demanded. "All those gruesome descriptions of him being as carved up as a Sunday roast? I know you guys didn't make it all up. Remember, I was the first one to talk to Teddy after he'd found him."

"Oh yes, knife wounds were definitely discovered all over Ramsey's body. But they were entirely superficial. And they were inflicted at least several hours after Ramsey had died."

"But that's crazy. Why would anyone do such a thing?"

"To cover up the real cause—and perhaps time—of the murder. And not so crazy, really. It had the medical examiner's office stymied for quite some time."

"So then there's no reason to believe that the two murders are connected," I thought aloud.

"Except for what you told me last night," Dan replied, "about Ramsey taking kickbacks from Tomi and the others. That information would have put Tomi at the top of my list. But we can strike him now."

"I don't know," I mused. "I just can't imagine any of the others harboring that much hatred. Denny, Seymour Friedman, Marcia Gibbs—believe me, they may have been involved with kickbacks, but they're really all nice people."

"Historically, Peg, some of the nicest people have committed some of the ugliest murders," Dan replied. "Lizzie Borden was thought to be an absolute peach of a girl."

"But I just can't see it," I muttered. "Why? Where's your motive, Dan?"

"Anger. Greed. Envy. Any one of the seven deadly sins would do just fine."

"But you don't know these people. To you they're just suspects. They're colleagues to me. None of them did it."

"Okay, Miss Marple, who did?"

"I've no evidence," I declared.

"But you do have a gut feeling."

"Yes. Actually it's more than a feeling . . . it's hardened into conviction now."

"Okay, let's have it."

"Isn't it obvious?" I replied. "Anger...envy...perhaps even a strangely perverted kind of greed. Who else would have wanted to see them both dead?"

"J.J.?"

"Of course. I didn't have the chance to tell you before, but I had the most hair-raising lunch with him yesterday." I quickly explained what had transpired at Windows on the World, adding, "He promised that he'd 'show us all,' but I got the feeling he meant Tomi, in particular."

"A damaging episode," Dan agreed. "But it still doesn't get around the fact that J.J. had an airtight alibi for the night of Ramsey's murder. He was with his father the entire evening. And Victor corroborates his story."

"But don't you see? Victor's always protecting J.J. The boy's a little wacko, Dan, believe me. He's really not all there. And I think Victor assumes it's his parental responsibility to go around covering up for him."

"Even if it means covering up a murder?"

"I don't know," I answered. "I...like Victor. I respect him. But who can say what a person will do when it comes to protecting someone they love?" Later, I would remember those words and realize how very right I had been. But for all the wrong reasons.

THIRTY-THREE

"MARK ROLLINGS CALLED twice. Phillip Ebert *himself* dropped by to see if you were in. Spencer's been phoning every five minutes or so. And—" Ruthie fanned a fistful of pink message memos in my face as I walked into my office "—Teddy Manfred is on line five right now."

"Peg, oh, thank God!" Teddy cried, "I've been frantic! I've been trying to reach you since nine o'clock last night when you didn't show up for dinner. Around midnight I got the goddamned police department, instead, who said they were taking your calls but closed up like little blue-uniformed clams when I tried to find out why. And then, heavens, the news in the paper this morning! Peggy, are you all right? You must be *so* shook up. God, what an awful thing. I—"

"Teddy, I'm fine," I interrupted, trying to stem the near hysterical flow of words. "Really," I said, collapsing into my black leather swivel chair. "Believe me, I'm going to survive."

"I'm *so* relieved," Teddy said with a sigh, his voice more controlled. "I don't know what I'd do if something happened to *you*. And...you're absolutely sure you're all right? I hate to sound like a fussbudget, but are you sure you should be working? After all you've been through?"

"Yes, Ted," I tried to reassure him. "It's the best thing for me, really. Listen, I've a million problems to deal with right now. I'll call you later, okay? When I'm a little more sane."

I put down the phone just to pick it up again as Ruthie put my next call through.

"Phillip Ebert's office calling. Hold on, please." A secretary put me on hold for the requisite thirty seconds Ebert always made his underlings wait.

"Sorry to keep you," Phillip said as he came on the line. "I was on a transatlantic call. Peg, I wanted to speak to you about poor Tomi. I talked to the police earlier. Awful thing. Tragic terrible business."

"Yes," I said, wondering what he wanted.

"You're all right, I hope. What a frightening experience for you."

"Yes, I'm okay," I replied.

"That's good. That's excellent. I don't think I need to tell you how valuable you are to us right now. The Bobbins obviously dote on you, Peg."

"Thank you."

"And," Ebert continued, his voice lower and confiding, "I don't think I need to remind you how important the Fanpan account is to us, either."

"No," I replied, "I realize that."

"Right. So you understand that nothing, and I mean *nothing*, should happen to jeopardize our relationship with them."

"You mean you don't want me reminding the police that J.J. once attacked Tomi with a butchering knife? Or that he was verbally abusive toward him only yesterday at lunch? Is that what you mean?"

"Well, let me rephrase what you've just said," Ebert replied calmly. "I don't see why it's your responsibility to make these, uh, unfortunate details public right now. I'm not asking you not to be absolutely truthful. I'm merely suggesting that you be a bit selective in what you reveal, that's all."

"I'm sorry, Phillip. But I'm afraid it's too late. I already told Detective Cursio about J.J., and I also told him that I think— no, frankly, I believe—J.J. is a murderer."

"I see," Ebert replied. "Considering the detective's line of questioning this morning, I should have known. What a pity you didn't turn to me for advice first, Peg. You should have realized this incident is bigger than merely Tomi or you—why, it affects the entire agency." And in Ebert's mind, P&Q pretty much defined the boundaries of the universe.

"I'm sorry," I said, "but I'm afraid it's too late now."

"Not really," Ebert answered smoothly. "You could always explain to the police that in the confusion and heat of the moment, you made some accusations that you now regret. Tell them you were overwrought, that you didn't know what you were saying. Apologize, and retract your statement."

"I couldn't do that, Phillip. I'm sorry."

"I'm sorry, too, Peg. Surely you must understand that Victor's hardly going to want to keep you on the account when he learns how you feel."

I hadn't thought of that. But, of course, it made sense.

"And I'm sure you understand that I can hardly offer you another position when you've acted so irresponsibly in this one."

"Telling the truth is irresponsible?" I demanded.

"When it hurts your agency and one of its top clients, yes," Ebert replied vehemently.

"What about the rest of the world?" I demanded. "You really believe that turning J.J. loose at this point is a responsible action?"

"Frankly, I believe that it's not my concern. What I do care about, what I *am* responsible for, is the health and prosperity of this agency. It's my business to keep the stockholders happy, Peg. And I intend to do that—over your wishes, I'm afraid."

"And over a few dead bodies," I snapped.

"Think about it, Peg," Ebert continued, as though he hadn't heard me. "Think of what you're risking . . . for the very little that you'll gain."

"I don't consider a clean conscience a little thing."

"I'm just warning you now," Ebert replied. "The moment J. J. Bobbin is charged . . . you're fired."

I slammed down the phone just as Ruthie poked her head in the door and said, "Spencer's been holding on line three for the past five minutes. He sounds like he's absolutely desperate to talk to you."

"Put him through," I told her, trying to steady my nerves with long deep breaths. The image of Dan and me in my bedroom throbbed before my eyes. There, too, I had risked everything and gained nothing. What was I doing with my life?

"Have you seen the late edition of the *Daily News* this morning?" Spencer demanded as soon as I'd said hello.

"No, I haven't had time. It's been positively—"

"She hasn't had the time!" Spencer cried, cutting me off. "She has all the sweet time in the world to go around stumbling over dead bodies in the middle of the goddamned night. She had all the time in the world to single-handedly try to screw up her fiancé's career and life, but *no* when it comes to reading how—"

"Please, Spencer, just tell me what it says."

"Well, let's see," Spencer started. He read what sounded to me like a simple recap of the early edition's report. "But now here's the really juicy part, Peg,

> Sources close to the investigation have told us that Peg Goodenough, the art director at P&Q who discovered Tabor's body, is an intimate of Jacob Guilden's tight political family. Guilden, an undeclared candidate for mayor, has been campaigning aggressively in recent months for a return to law and order. Among his pet peeves with the current administration is its seeming inability to solve the brutal murder earlier this summer of Ramsey Farnsworth, formerly Ms Goodenough's boss at P&Q. The Guilden organization has refused to comment on these findings."

"I'm sorry," I said, sighing.

"You're sorry," Spencer repeated. "That's all you can say?"

"I told you I'd try to get to the bottom of Ramsey's double-dealing. And I tried."

"Tell me something," Spencer said. "Tell me why you're so incredibly good, so amazingly talented at screwing me up? Huh? You want to tell me why that is?"

"That's not fair, Spencer. None of this is my fault—you've got to realize that. I'm sorry, really truly sorry that it backfired on your career. But you've got to see that I didn't have anything to do with it."

"That's not true, Peg—you've had *everything* to do with it. Every time I turn around you're involved in some new scandal—Ramsey's murder, Ramsey's kickbacks, now Tomi's death. Whether you want to be or not, you're tainted with it."

"But . . . but that's only because I care. I've been trying to help. I've been trying to *do* something. That's the only reason I discovered Tomi. I was going to confront him with something I'd learned about his deal with Ramsey. Really, I was just there to ask—"

"I don't want to hear about it!" Spencer cried. "I don't want to know! I am not, I repeat, *not* involved with any of this."

"You sound like you're giving a press conference."

"I'm about to," Spencer replied. "And I wanted to let you know what I intended to say."

"I think I already know," I answered sadly. "You'll tell reporters that though it's true you once had a fleeting relationship with Peg Goodenough, reports of some kind of, uh, ongoing 'intimacy' are totally fallacious."

"Well, yeah, something like that," Spencer muttered.

"And you'll add that you're terribly upset to hear of her recent problems. You know her to be an outstanding individual, though her unorthodox upbringing might indeed have contributed to a certain instability in her character."

"Yes . . . I did have something like that in mind," Spencer admitted. "You . . . understand, then? I mean, you see that I have to do this?"

"Cut me loose in order to keep the Guilden platform afloat?" I demanded.

"To keep it above any hint of scandal."

"Yes, I see why you think you have to," I told him.

"And once all this blows over—say in two or three months— once Dad's in position, we'll be fine. And if we're careful and discreet, I see no reason why we can't go on as before."

"But I do."

"Oh? What's that?"

"It's not a what, it's a who, Spencer. It's you."

"What about me, Peg?"

"You've changed, or I've changed, or we both have. Or perhaps I just never really faced who you were before. Or who I was—"

"Listen, babe," Spencer cut in impatiently, "I've a press conference in exactly fifteen minutes. Mind getting to the point?"

"Sure. It's as simple as this—I just realized, just this morning, that I don't love you anymore."

"Now, come on," Spencer answered soothingly. "You're upset. You're tired. You don't know what you're saying."

"No, actually I've never been more sure about anything in my life. I don't love you. And I don't think I ever did."

"Peg, I'm sorry, but I simply don't have time to listen to your hysterics right now. I'll try to call you later, maybe from a pay phone, and we'll work this out. In the meantime, I think you should go home and get some sleep. You're in no state to work."

But somehow I did. I answered my calls, met with Felice Clay over Fanpan's new media schedule. Sat through an hour-long presentation by one of the top magazines about their new gatefold capabilities. I got back to my own office a little after five o'clock to find my In box stacked with a neat pile of pink message memos. On the top was one from Detective Dante Cursio. At last. It was the only call I'd wanted to answer all day.

"Hi there," I said when his switchboard put me through to his office.

"Well, hello. Hold on a second while I get these derelicts out of my office." I heard Dan giving some kind of muffled instructions to his men, then he spoke gently into the phone. "So, hello. You okay?"

"Never been better," I said, and in a funny way I meant it.

"Listen, I just got the transcript of the Guilden press conference this morning. They...denied knowing you particularly well."

"You mean Spencer did," I said. "Yes, I know."

"Oh. I'm sorry."

"I'm not," I answered truthfully. "And, you know, I've been thinking about something you said this morning. You were right. I want you to know that I didn't choose between anything—I mean you or Spencer—but *for* me. So don't you worry, Dan Cursio, you're off the hook."

"I'm not sure if that's a good place to be," Cursio replied, but without explaining what he meant by that, he continued, "Listen, I called you because I want you to know that J.J.'s disappeared."

"What do you mean, 'disappeared'?" I asked. "He's a big boy, Dan, hard to misplace."

"We tried to contact him and Victor to get a reading on their whereabouts last night. We reached Victor in his room at the Plaza, absolutely panicked because J.J. hadn't come back from an afternoon movie. We've a full alert out on him."

"So what do you say to my theory now?" I asked. "J.J.'s looking a little less than innocent, I'd say."

"And a whole lot like trouble, Peg," Dan added. "I've got a car coming to get you after work to take you home. The boys are going to make sure you get in safely and that the apartment's all right. I want you to be careful, Peg."

"It doesn't sound as if you're giving me any choice."

"I hope not," Dan conceded. "I wish I could be there with you, but I've got to coordinate things from here. Stay in. Take it easy. I'll call you later to see how it's going."

"You think he's going to come after me? In my apartment? Is that why your men are coming with me?"

"It's a possibility, yes. Though not a particularly likely one. The boys are just a precaution. A safeguard. Listen, they may hang around outside for a while. You won't even know they're there."

"And if I want to go out?"

"I can't stop you. But do me a favor, and let my men know where you're going. As I said, it's just a precautionary measure. I'm getting nervous in my old age."

"I'd say you've a ways to go before you're over the hill, Dan," I answered, laughing. "Quite a ways."

I was about to hang up when he said, "Peg, there's just one other thing. About this morning, again. About something I said..."

"Yes?"

"It did mean something to me, you know." There was a moment's silence, and he added, "You be careful now, all right?"

And that was the last time we spoke to each other for what seemed like years.

THIRTY-FOUR

DAN. DANTE. Detective Cursio. I tried to imagine how I would introduce him to my mother.

"I'd like you to meet Mr. Cursio, Theo. He's a homicide detective with the NYPD, and he's my lover." God, knowing Theo, she'd probably laugh, hold out her hand and say, "Marvelous to meet you, darling! I'm so delighted Peg's finally running around with somebody *interesting*. She's been desperate for a little color in her life, don't you think?"

Dante. Dan. Detective... I turned the various images I had of him over in my mind as the unmarked police car inched its way uptown through rush-hour traffic. I was in the back seat, separated by a heavy metal grate from the two young police officers who were seeing me hold.

"Okay, so say this J.J. *did* do Tabor," the cop on the passenger's side said to the driver. "And let's say he did Farnsworth, too. First with our as-of-yet-unidentified heavy beveled object, then dicing him up a bit for effect. So then, tell me this, Tom..."

"Yeah?"

"How come he only *knifes* Tabor—just one fast clean incision? How come no window dressing this time?"

"I don't know, Kev.... Maybe he didn't have time. Maybe he heard Ms Goodenough coming up the stairs. Maybe he had to split before he did his fancy work."

"I don't think so," I said, leaning forward and speaking through the grate. "I had my ears pricked for Tomi...and I didn't hear a thing. I mean the place was utterly—and now that I think about it—eerily silent. J.J.'s not only a big guy, he's clumsy, too. I can't imagine him finding his way out of there without making something of a racket."

"I'll tell you what, then," Kevin asserted. "I don't think this J.J. did it. And I don't think Cursio does, either."

"Oh yeah?" Tom retorted, swerving in between a taxi and a tow truck to move us forward another six feet. "You and the lieutenant comparing notes, are you? He been asking you for your considered opinion?"

"Okay, give me a hard time, I don't care," Kevin retorted, throwing up his hands. "I'm just telling you that it feels too easy pinning both sinkers on this guy. Something's not clicking. I keep feeling like we're missing something, something right under our noses."

"What makes you think Detective Cursio agrees with you?" I asked.

"Excuse me, ma'am," Kevin answered, turning around toward me, "but the lieutenant and I have worked a lot of cases together. I know him—I know his moods. When he's closing in on something, you can kind of feel the tension, the excitement jumping off him. I don't feel that right now. I think he's worried. He's still looking. I don't think we've got it yet."

"Don't pay any attention to him," Tom said, meeting my gaze in the rearview mirror. "Kevin fancies himself the next Colombo. The lieutenant told us before we picked you up that we were free to discuss the case in front of you—I'm just sorry the discussion has been so simpleminded this far."

"Get off my back," Kevin grumbled, slouching forward again. "I've got a right to my opinions, you know."

More as a way to keep the two men from bickering further, I asked, "What about this beveled object Detective Cursio mentioned? What did it look like exactly? Can you say?"

"If we knew that, we'd be home free," Tom replied. "The only description we've got now is the one from the M.E.'s office. Apparently, the weapon was plenty heavy—twenty-five pounds or so—rounded and beveled. You know, little imprints—like ball bearings—all over it."

"Ballistics has spent weeks trying to figure out what it was exactly," Kevin added. "They've come up with zilch."

"No idea what it was made of?" I asked, trying to picture the bizarre murder weapon myself.

"Nope," Tom said. "Had to be some kind of metal, though, something that heavy."

Tom and Kevin walked me up to my apartment, unlocked it and searched it carefully. But, just as I expected, they discovered only how untidy the back of my closets are . . . and how irritable Picasso can be around six o'clock when he hasn't been fed. As they were leaving, Millie popped her head out her door.

"Everything all right, Peg?" she asked.

"Oh, yes . . . nothing to worry about."

Millie waited until the two men were clomping down the stairs before she announced in her small bright voice, "I glanced at your chart earlier this afternoon, dear. I didn't much like what I saw about tonight."

"Now, Millie—" I sighed "—I know you mean well. I know you're trying to help, but we've gone over this a hundred times. I don't want to hear about your charts or your tea leaves, or any of that business. Even if it's true. Millie, I just don't want to know."

"I saw a big man, Peg," Millie went on, as though she hadn't heard me. "Very big and, I think, fair haired. He's determined to hurt you, dear."

"Millie!" I cried, staring into her innocent faded blue eyes. "How on earth did you hear about that?"

"I didn't *hear* about anything," Millie retorted, pulling herself up to her full five feet. "You know perfectly well that I don't believe in voices. Automatic writing, sometimes, yes. But, if you ask me, people who purport to hear voices are just plain kooks.''

"No, I mean, how did your learn about . . . this man?"

"I told you, dear," Millie replied patiently, "it's all in your chart. He's unmistakable. I'm surprised I didn't see him before. In any case, I wanted to warn you."

"Thanks," I told her, trying to smile reassuringly. "I'll be careful."

But what else can you be when you're locked into your own apartment with two policemen outside watching the front door? What else can you be with nothing more dangerous to do than sorting the mail and flipping through the latest issue of the *New Yorker*? Well, you can be—and I was—scared. Of course it was ridiculous. I knew I could hardly be any safer. And yet the tiniest noise—the ice cubes tumbling out of my ice maker in the freezer—made me jump. J.J.'s bulky form kept lumbering through my thoughts. His brute force, his childishness, his terrifying bursts of anger—his entire outsized presence took over my imagination. It seemed perfectly likely that he'd come bursting through the door at any moment. It didn't occur to me until Picasso leaped up beside me on the couch—and I screamed, thinking god knows what—that if I stayed cooped up in the apartment any longer, I'd surely go crazy.

So I called Teddy.

"Where are you, dearest?" Teddy cried. "I was just about to call you myself. I've the most wonderful news!"

"Oh, Ted, it's so good to hear a happy normal voice. I've been surrounded by gloom and doom all day. And now I'm back in my apartment—with a police guard, no less."

"Good heavens. . . . What do they think's going to happen?"

I briefly explained about J.J.'s disappearance and the growing agreement that he was responsible for Tomi's death at the very least.

"Peg, dear," Teddy asked in a hushed frightened voice, "do you think he might have killed Ramsey, as well?"

"I do, Teddy," I responded. "In fact, I'm sure of it. But I'm not positive the police agree. In any case, J.J.'s on the loose. And they think he might be headed here."

"And, good God, they have you just sitting there waiting for him? What are they thinking of? You must be going nuts!"

"I am, actually," I conceded. "But I'm also just as frightened of going out. What if J.J. follows me? And gets me alone? At least here I've a couple of cops underfoot."

"You could always come down here, Peg," Teddy suggested. "I'll make you that dinner you missed last night. I've already got some champagne, as a matter of fact. I've something marvelous to celebrate—and I'd love it if you'd share it with me."

"What is it, Ted?" I asked, already feeling better.

"Let's keep it a surprise until you get down, okay?" Teddy suggested, his voice eager with excitement. "Now, what I want you to do is call the car service Ramsey used to use. I still have an account with them. They'll come right to your door and whisk you down here without any possibility of J.J. intervening. Here, take down this number. They're usually there within fifteen minutes."

"Okay," I agreed. "If you're sure you don't mind."

"Don't be ridiculous. I'm putting the Perrier-Jouët on now to cool."

I called the service, then changed into my clean white Calvins and a loose-fitting short-sleeved cotton shirt. The thunderstorms of the evening before had done little to alleviate the sultry August weather, and more storms were forecast for later. I grabbed an umbrella and hurried downstairs to wait for the car. Tom and Kevin were parked down the street. I waved to them, then walked over. Tom rolled down the window as I came up, and a wall of air-conditioned coolness washed over me.

"Going out, huh?" Tom said, glancing down at my white jeans with an appreciative eye. I wondered briefly if any of Cursio's men guessed what we had been up to the night before.

"I was just going crazy up there," I started to explain, "and a friend of mine invited—"

"Yeah, we heard," Tom interrupted, nodding at the dashboard's complicated electronic accoutrement. He saw my puzzled expression and explained, "You're bugged, ma'am, remember? We heard every word."

"Of course," I said, feeling foolish. "So you know where I'll be."

"We already checked it out with the lieutenant," Tom replied. "He says it's fine to let you go alone. We're supposed to stay put and watch for J.J."

"I don't envy you," I said, straightening up again. "But I'll tell you one thing, you'll know him when you see him."

"Right, ma'am," Tom replied, smiling. "Enjoy your champagne."

It was a swift, almost nonstop ride down the West Side Highway, with Midtown on my left a blazing forest of light. The business heart of the city that by day is so dirty and drab seemed a completely different place at night. I don't think that I'm a particularly romantic person, but the skyline—that ragged mountain of glass and neon—suddenly filled me with thoughts of Fred Astaire movies, of the Crystal Room at the Waldorf, of being in love. "Put on your top hat," I hummed to myself, trying to imagine what Cursio would look like in a tux. Was I kidding myself? I wondered as we sailed past the Seventy-ninth Street Boat Basin. Was there any possible future for Cursio and me? Or was I, as Spencer had implied to me on the phone, simply going through some kind of hysterical episode?

I'd always been sensible solid Peg. I was invariably the logical sober one. I'd played straight man to Theo's flamboyant routines all my life. Yet, during the past few days, I'd been anything but sensible. And though I'd never felt less in control of the situation, though I'd never been at greater risk—I'd also never felt better. Was I just letting go of inhibitions? Or was I actually falling in love?

For reasons I didn't yet grasp, Teddy, too, seemed in a strangely exalted mood. He was waiting for me in front of his loft building, a flute of champagne held out toward me as I stepped from the car.

"Welcome, dear heart!" he cried, kissing me on the cheek and handing me the glass. We walked up the three short steps to the front door. "I trust you had no problems getting down here?"

"Oh yes, it was fine," I replied gaily, sipping the champagne. "I can't tell you how marvelous it feels to get away from that apartment—and the lurking specter of J.J.!"

"Well, you're in liberty city now, dearest," Teddy told me as we got into the elevator. He pressed the button for his floor. "You know what Ramsey used to say, 'We only allow good people and good times here.'" I could almost hear Ramsey's voice as Teddy said it, and suddenly it struck me how sad and ironic those words were. I gulped at the champagne. Whoever knew what was going to happen to you in life? It was in this loft, after all, where Ramsey had allowed only good people and good times, that he'd gone through the very worst moments anyone could possibly imagine: his last.

THIRTY-FIVE

RAMSEY'S LOFT occupies a third of a floor in one of the biggest turn-of-the-century cast-iron buildings in SoHo. It has twenty-foot-high ceilings, double arching windows and one of the most stupendous views of Lower Manhattan and the Hudson bay I've seen. And whatever the loft lacked to start with, Ramsey had added on: a kitchen that would make the most sated gourmet drool, a marble bath with Jacuzzi and whirlpool, a library area lined floor to ceiling with books and, of course, Teddy's very own studio.

"We'll save my sculptures till later," Teddy told me, waving toward his huge workroom, now carefully locked. "Let's get you something to nibble on, first. You must be famished, dear."

"Actually, yes, I am," I conceded as I followed Teddy down the hall toward the open living area. "I haven't given food much thought the past few days and—oh, Ted, you shouldn't have—"

"Now, really, I just put out a few hors d'oeuvres...."

"Hors d'oeuvres! Teddy," I said as I surveyed the feast, "this could feed an army of sumo wrestlers for a month."

"Well, then you'd better tuck in, or it will start getting stale. And here, hold our your glass, Peg, we've still got tons of champagne left."

I collapsed onto the low-slung black leather couch that faced the arching central windows and the view of the Hudson. The loft was exactly as it had been when Ramsey was alive: clean, white and spare. Ted hadn't altered a thing, not even the freshly cut flowers that Ramsey had always insisted decorate the coffee table. A vase full of fresh liliums sat there now. Everything looked the same, and yet nothing was. There was a coldness about the room, an emptiness—as though no one had been living there for many months—that even the low crackling fire in the glassed-in hearth couldn't remove. The chill struck deep: Ramsey was gone forever.

"Try the taleggio, dear," Teddy urged, holding out the cheese tray. "And do knock back that bubbly before it goes flat. I can't stand it when a good champagne isn't treated with proper respect."

"Oh, I'm sorry," I said, dutifully tipping back my glass. "It's just that, well, I haven't been here since Ramsey died, you know. And I . . . do miss him."

"Of course," Ted murmured, refilling my glass. "I should have realized. It was awful for me in the beginning to wake up here . . . alone. To walk where he walked. Touch the things he touched. I found it incredible—I still do, actually—that he's gone . . . and that the coffee cups, the toothbrushes, all those things are still here. He was so full of life! Why should these silly inanimate objects—" Teddy held up his half-filled champagne flute as an example "—continue to exist . . . and not him? For that matter, I suppose, why should I? Ramsey was worth at least ten of me."

"That's not true, Ted," I asserted. "It's ridiculous to think that way," though I'd had the same thought several times: why Ramsey and not me?

"In any case, it's futile," Ted agreed, spooning caviar onto a pumpernickel round. "The one thing I have been able to finally face is that he *is* gone. And I'm still here. And, I suppose, to be quite trite about it, the show must go on."

"I know," I replied, staring down into my champagne.

"Do you? Really?" Ted asked me. "Sometimes I think you're even less able than I—to let go, Peg."

"Why do you say that?"

"I'm not sure, exactly," Ted replied honestly. He got up, flute in hand, and paced in front of the coffee table. "I just can't help but feel that you're more involved with Ramsey's death—by that I suppose I mean this debacle of a murder investigation—than you should be."

"Well, I have been doing what I can to help Cursio," I replied. I should have realized that supersensitive Ted would have picked up on my concern over Ramsey's finances. Whatever happened, I really hoped Ted would never have to be burdened with the knowledge of what Ramsey had done. I certainly didn't intend to tell him now.

"No, it's more than that," Ted continued. "I get the feeling that you're still extremely focused on the whole thing. It's weighing on your mind, when it shouldn't be. Peg, listen, you're going to have to finally accept that what happened was *not your fault*. Do you understand what I'm saying? I get the feeling that you're still blaming yourself. I know I did for the longest time."

"And you got over feeling that way? How, Ted?"

"I got back to work," Ted replied. "I did what Ramsey would have wanted me to do. I turned all my energies, all my talent toward the one thing I do best. I got on with my life. And I think it's time you did, too."

"I *am* working, Ted," I replied somewhat defensively. "Very hard, as a matter of fact."

"Tell me this, then. What were you doing down at Tomi's studio? You know, even when you told me last night you had some estimates to go over with him, I wondered, why so late? And now, since his murder, I keep going back to that question. You know what I think?"

"No...." I said, hoping he hadn't somehow guessed the truth.

"I think that Cursio has somehow roped you into helping him with the investigation. I don't know how, but I get the feeling he's using you."

"Oh, no, Ted!" I replied, laughing for the first time that night. "If anything, believe me, he wants me to steer clear of the whole thing. Teddy, listen, he's not the ogre we used to think he was."

"No?" Ted demanded, facing me. "What made you change your mind?"

"I ... I've just gotten to know him a little better, that's all. He's really quite a wonderful person."

"You could have fooled me," Ted retorted, emptying the rest of the champagne into his glass. "And I think, for some odd reason, that that's exactly what you're trying to do. Am I so terribly off base, Peg?"

I looked across the room at my friend, probably my very best friend. He stared back at me searchingly, concern obvious in his eyes. I decided I couldn't lie outright.

"Okay." I gulped. "There is something—it has to do with Ramsey's case—that I can't tell you about right now. It's something I discovered ... and that I took to the police. It's no tremendous big deal, believe me, Teddy. But it wouldn't do either of us any good if I told you more."

"Did Tomi's death have anything to do with it?"

"I'm not sure," I answered truthfully. "But I wouldn't be surprised."

"Oh, dear heart, how I hate all this!" Teddy cried, coming to sit beside me on the couch. "I hate the violence and the lies and the endless, endless questions! When is it going to end?"

"Maybe sooner than you think, Ted," I answered soothingly. "Everything points to J.J. And now that he's disappeared, he looks that much more suspicious."

"Suspicions are one thing, dear," Ted pointed out, "but what about evidence? I mean, Cursio can't very well arrest the man because he didn't come home to Daddy one night."

"Well, I already told the police that I'm willing to testify against him. It may all just be circumstantial, but J.J. did threaten Tomi with a lethal weapon. And he made it clear to any number of people that he hated his guts."

"I'd do anything to get him behind bars!" Teddy announced bitterly. I understood how he felt. I didn't like to admit it to myself, but a sense of vengeance had been motivating me just as much as a desire for justice.

"Any more champagne, Ted?" I asked abruptly. I knew it was my fault that the conversation kept swinging back to the murders and J.J.—the very subjects I'd come down to the loft to escape. Teddy was right. I couldn't change what had happened or control what would. At some point I was just going to have to give up and get on with my life.

"Indeed, yes," Ted said, standing. "But how about a nice Bordeaux, instead? Are you hungry yet? I found some lovely looking veal shanks this afternoon at the market, so I threw together an osso buco. I hope you'll like it."

"If that is what's responsible for those delicious aromas that keep wafting through here, I don't think you have anything to worry about."

And, of course, he didn't—the veal was tender and spicy. Halfway through the meal, I saw Teddy opening yet another bottle.

"You know, if I didn't know better," I said, "I'd think you were trying to get me sozzled."

"No. Just trying to get you to relax," Ted replied, filling up my glass, "and put you in a mellow receptive mood for some extremely good news."

"Of course, your surprise!" I cried. "Oh, I'm sorry, Teddy. I just totally forgot."

"That's all right," Ted assured me. "I feel a little scared about it, actually. After all we've both been through, to finally have something to celebrate . . . it seems unbelievable."

"Enough with the guilt number, okay? Tell me what it is!"

"It's a where, actually," Ted replied, his eyes glistening. "As of next month, I'm switching galleries. To Greene Street, Peg. Can you believe it? Greene Street Gallery called me this morning. I talked to Sven Soderberg himself! He said they'd be delighted to take me on as soon as it could be arranged."

"That's great," I replied, wondering what strings my mother had had to tug in order to pull this one off. "So they've seen your new work? This marble series you've told me so much about?"

"They haven't actually seen anything yet," Teddy explained. "Sven was very understanding about my hesitancy to present the series unfinished. I told him I'd be ready to bring him up here before the month is out. And, Peg, we even discussed the possibility of a show this October."

"That's wonderful, Ted," I responded. "This is really great news." I was indeed happy for him, though also a little annoyed that he hadn't mentioned Theo's—or my—rather important role in his new triumph. No gallery as prestigious as Greene Street would take Ted on—sight unseen—without some pretty powerful patronage. Theo had really come through.

"You know, if I do the show in October," Teddy went on proudly, "it would mean two major exhibits within a year of each other. That's not a bad record now, Peg, is it?"

"No, it's not, Ted," I agreed, thinking back to his first show. I'm the first to admit that I don't have a great knowledge of sculpture. I can tell a Henry Moore from a Michelangelo, a Giacometti from a Calder, but I'm just not equipped with enough sculptural understanding to spot fresh new talent when it comes on the scene. And yet, even as one of Teddy's closest friends and strongest supporters, I knew that the pieces I had seen in the Walden Gallery last October were far from extraordinary. It was an uneven collection—ranging from huge metal-rod constructions resembling ruined jungle gyms, to tiny paper origami-style pieces—that seemed to encompass all of Ted's efforts during the ten preceding years.

"Isn't it wonderful!" Ramsey had greeted me at the opening. "Ted's already sold three major pieces. What a success!"

The art press, as I recall, had been far less enthusiastic. *ArtNews* had called the show "derivative at best." The *Times* had termed it "eminently forgettable." But Ramsey—even more than Teddy—had pooh-poohed their criticism.

"Listen, nobody understood what van Gogh was up to in the beginning, either," he had declared. "Or Picasso. Or...or any of the great ones. Give them time. Genius is always a little frightening at first. Believe me, years from now people will remember this October show as the start of a new chapter in the history of art."

October...I thought suddenly. What else had happened last October? There was something . . . something important. I was on the verge of recalling was it was when Teddy said, "Well, I'm ready if you are, dear."

"Ready? For what, Ted? Dessert?"

"No," Ted replied solemnly, pushing back his chair and standing. "I mean, I'm ready to show you the series. Despite what I told Sven, it is essentially finished. I've been working nonstop the past couple of weeks. I don't know why, but I've been filled with just an incredible amount of creative energy."

"I know you've been working hard," I said, tossing down my napkin as I stood. "I can't wait to see what you've done."

As I followed Ted back down the dark corridor that led to his studio, he continued to expound upon the artistic burst that had helped him complete his marble series.

"I don't know, it's just sort of amazing to feel this way," Ted explained. I walked behind him, trying to stifle a yawn. I shouldn't have had all that wine, I realized. I could have leaned against the wall then and there and fallen asleep. I yawned again, cursing myself for not asking Ted for coffee before visiting the studio.

"It's almost as if—" Ted paused to unlock the heavy metal door and switch on the bank of overhead lights "—this amazing drive, this force comes from outside of me. I know this sounds a little crazy, but I think I'm really starting to understand what they mean by 'divine inspiration.'"

My first impression was one of blinding whiteness. A snow-covered field on a blazing winter's day. And then, as the metal door slammed shut behind us, I was aware of the huge room's dense heat and animal smell. Ted's studio runs the length of the loft and, like the rest of the building, boasts a twenty-foot-high ceiling. The similarities ended there. I hadn't visited Ted's studio since Ramsey's death, and I was shocked by its transformation. The room was packed with junk: ladders, tools, paint cans, rope, coils of rusting metal. Where the rest of the loft was almost antiseptically clean, the studio was quite obviously filthy. Dirty rags, moldy sandwich ends, unwashed plates and cups lay scattered on the floor and tabletops. A roll of army blankets that looked as though they'd been used as a makeshift bed sat crumpled in a corner.

"Ted," I exclaimed, trying to keep the disgust out of my voice, "you really shouldn't leave rags around like this. It could be dangerous in a fire."

"Come here, Peg," Ted cried, ignoring what I said as he made his way across the room toward the far cluttered wall. I followed, stepping around thick slabs of marble, boxes full of plaster chips, plastic garbage bags filled with God knows what. The place seemed so entirely alien to Ted's careful nurturing personality. I reeled after him, unable to decide if I was a little drunk . . . or simply stunned by what I was seeing.

"Right here, Peg," Ted urged me. "Come stand over here." I came up and stood beside him. We were facing a wall of wooden shelves along which, in three-foot intervals, rounded marble shapes—approximately the size of human heads—were positioned. Each was white. Carved out of marble.

"Well?" Ted breathed in. "What do you think?"

The shapes were all amorphous, bulky, one could even say ungainly. There was really only one word for them: repulsive. I wanted to back away, but Ted pushed me forward.

"Here," he said, "I want you to hold one. It's only then that you get the full effect." He held one of the rounded white objects out. I took it into my hands. It was heavier than I anticipated, twenty-five pounds or more. And it was, despite the warmth of the room, cold. But what struck me first, what would stay with me forever, was its strange contour.

The rounded piece was beveled all over. The indents the size of ball bearings. I held it with a growing sense of fear and dread and revulsion. It took several seconds before I let my mind register the truth: I was holding Ramsey's murder weapon in my hands.

THIRTY-SIX

I'M STILL NOT SURE where I found the presence of mind to hand the cold ball of marble back to Teddy and calmly ask, "Are they all beveled like this one, Ted?"

"No, just a couple right now," Ted replied, carefully returning the sculpture to its place on the shelf. "I'm in something of a quandary about the surface work, actually. At first, I thought it was an interesting effect. Then I smoothed one of the first ones down, and I liked that, as well. I guess I'm still of two minds. What do you think, Peg?"

What I was thinking, of course, was, is Ted a murderer? It's not the kind of question you can pop on a friend, though. And in my present situation—alone in a locked room with the man—obviously not a particularly clever one to pose. What was clear, however, was that Teddy had no idea the police knew Ramsey had been struck down by one of his marble sculptures. Killer or not, he would never have shown me the series if he knew what I did about the real murder weapon.

"I'd leave them just as they are," I suggested, starting to back away from the shelves. More and more the rounded shapes were taking on the look of severed heads...and fear and panic were starting to get the better of me.

"Some tooled and some not?" Teddy asked, scanning the long shelf. "Hmm...I hadn't thought of that. But, yes, it could be interesting, I suppose. In any case, as I'm sure you're aware, it's the shape, the contour that matters. You see what I've done, don't you? I think it's something of a breakthrough. He turned back to face me, and for the first time he must have seen the look of horror in my eyes.

"Peg, what's the matter?" he demanded, taking a step toward me. I automatically took one back. "You look as though you've seen a ghost."

"Oh, no, I...just feel a little queasy," I lied faintly, trying to pull myself together. "I'm afraid that I overdid it at dinner. Too much wine, I guess."

"Are you sure that's all?" Ted demanded, taking my elbow. I had to resist the temptation to pull away. At least he started to steer us toward the door. Toward freedom. "You look positively ashen, dear heart."

"Yes, well, it came on suddenly," I answered truthfully. "I think I should go home . . . and climb into bed. I'm sure I'll be okay tomorrow."

"Why don't you stay here?" Ted suggested. "I'll put you up in the spare bedroom."

"No!" I cried, then quickly tempered my reaction by adding, "When I feel like this all I want to do is crawl into my own bed in my own apartment. It's sweet of you to offer, Teddy, but really, I think I'd rather just get home."

"Well, let me at least call the car service," Ted replied. "I want to make sure you get back safely."

"There'll be a million cabs going up Sixth Avenue," I countered. I couldn't stay another moment in the loft. "I'll grab something there. Thanks, though," I added hastily as I practically ran down the corridor to the front door.

It wasn't until I pushed open the door to the street and was confronted with a splashing wall of rain that I realized the thunderstorm had broken. And that I'd left my umbrella in the loft. Good riddance, I thought. I wasn't about to go back and ask Teddy for it now. I ran down the street through the deluge, searching blindly for a cab. The rain was so heavy, most cars were pulled up to the curb, waiting for the storm to pass. When I saw the green balloon light of the Spring Street subway, I realized I didn't have much choice. I dashed across the street, down the steps and into the train that was just pulling into the station. It was headed downtown.

I had lied to Teddy; I had no intention of going home until I told Cursio what I'd discovered. And though I didn't know exactly where One Police Plaza was, I had a vague sense that it was on the southern edge of Chinatown. I got off at Chambers Street and started to walk east through the hard pelting rain. I asked for directions three times, lost my way twice and finally stumbled into the huge brick complex a half hour after I'd left Teddy's.

"Where could I find Detective Cursio?" I asked at the front desk. The reception area was brightly lighted, as impersonal and tired as the glance the policewoman gave me when she looked up from her paperwork.

"Who, hon?" she asked, looking me over. I didn't really blame her for staring. I was drenched, my hair plastered to my head. I was dripping all over the tan brick floor.

"Cursio. Dante Cursio. He's with homicide."

"Yeah, Dan. I know him," she said, picking up a receiver. "Who should I say wants him?" I gave her my name and waited, shivering now, as she dialed a number and asked for Cursio.

"I see," the receptionist spoke into the phone. "Well, there's a Ms Goodenough out here asking for him. Yeah, that's right. Okay, I'll tell her."

She put her hand over the receiver and said, "He's not in. Want to leave a message?"

"It's, uh, urgent that I speak to him as soon as possible," I said, mindful of the pool of rainwater that was forming around me. "Is there any way he can be reached?"

The question was relayed, and the answer came back with a sympathetic shake of the head, "Sorry, hon. He's out right now, that's all they know. But he's bound to be calling in sometime tonight. I'll make sure he gets the message that you're trying to reach him, okay?"

"Would you?" I begged, realizing what a sorry picture I must have painted. "Would you tell him that I found the—the big beveled object he was looking for? It was at Teddy's. And that he should call me as soon as he can."

"Okeydoke," she said, scribbling my message on a pad. "Where will you be?"

"Home," I said, turning to go. As I pushed my way back through the revolving front doors, I saw the policewoman's reflection in the glass. She was shaking her head. God knows what she thought my story was.

If anything, the storm had worsened while I was inside. I headed north through Chinatown, through streets washed clean and running with rain. Plastic tarps were pulled across the storefronts on Canal Street, giving the stalls an eerie underwater look. Occasional thunder rumbled overhead. The city felt abandoned.

I finally found a cab on Mott Street, and we headed uptown. It wasn't until I'd paid the driver and was starting up the front steps that I remembered Tom and Kevin. I turned back to where they had been parked down the street, but they were gone. Getting drenched once again, I searched up and down the block. Nothing. Emotionally depleted, dripping and exhausted, I slowly climbed the stairs to my apartment. I was so desperate for simple human contact that I stopped at Millie's and knocked, but even she was out. Feeling desperately alone, I turned my key in the lock and opened the door.

"Surprise!" Teddy said, slamming the door behind me and ripping the keys out of my hand. "You have company."

"T-Ted...." I whispered. I took one look at him and knew. His pale eyes burned with malice. "How did you get in?"

"Oh, I've had duplicate keys for quite a while now, dear heart," Teddy explained as he bolted the door behind me. "You see, I've felt this urge to drop in on you from time to time when I knew you'd be out."

"Why, Ted?" I asked, determined to sound normal.

"Oh, just to look around," Ted replied, "see what's new, what's up. See where you might have hidden a few little things that didn't belong to you. Piece of marble? Black notebook?"

"So it was you who broke in the week after Ramsey...died?"

"Honestly, no need to be so delicate with me, Peg. What you mean to say is the week after Ramsey was murdered, right? Bludgeoned to death with a marble statue and then hacked up with a kitchen knife. Why mince words, dear heart?"

"Why, Ted?" I asked. "Why you?"

"Oh, it's a horribly long story, dear," Ted said with a sigh. "Bound to bore you to absolute tears. I don't intend to go into it all now."

"What do you intend to do, Ted?" I asked weakly. "Kill me, too?"

"I sincerely hope not, Peg, dear. Despite what you may presently think, I really don't have the least taste for bloodshed. Nor, I suppose, a particular aptitude for it. As you made obvious earlier when you were silly enough to show me that you recognized the marble piece."

"Was all that a test, then? To see if I knew?"

"Oh, heavens no!" Ted chortled. "Really, Peg, I'm not nearly that devious or clever. I had absolutely no idea the cops had seen through my little ruse until you nearly fainted on me tonight."

"Silly me," I murmured.

"Yes," Ted agreed. "Silly you. Now, do me a favor, dear heart, and go sit down on the couch. I can't have you prowling around near the door. And also, Peggy, love, don't do anything foolish. I have a knife in my pants pocket. And we both know I've used it before.''

"Tell me something,'' I said as I sat down on the edge of the couch. "Why did you let me leave the loft if you knew I knew about the marble?''

"Ah, you see, that's where silly you was at your silliest,'' Ted replied. "You almost had me fooled, love. I was nearly convinced that my delicious osso buco had been too much for you. And then, Peg, I watched you hurry across the street to the subway entrance. The one going downtown, dear. Not up. I knew you'd been lying. You went and paid a visit to our good friend Mr. Cursio, right?''

"Yes, Teddy,'' I said. "He knows all about it now, I'm afraid. They're probably breaking into your loft as we speak.''

"Too bad for you love,'' Teddy replied. "I do wish you'd been more broad-minded.''

"About what?'' I demanded harshly. "You killing Ramsey and Tomi? Is there some liberal interpretation to the crime of murder that I've somehow overlooked?''

"Don't be snide with me, Peg,'' Teddy warned, turning to look at me. "Don't get me riled. It would be a serious mistake. Surely you must understand that I wouldn't have hurt Ramsey unless I absolutely had to. Or Tomi, either. The trouble was, dear heart, that it got to the point where I had no choice. You see, they were standing in my way.''

"In the way of what?'' I asked.

"Why, my work, of course,'' Ted replied easily, as though he were explaining a simple arithmetic problem to a child. "The work I was sent to do. I never wanted to harm Ramsey. Believe me, Peg, but I really had no choice.'' He is mad, I realized as I stared into his pale but luminous gaze. Absolutely mad. "Actually, Ted, I don't understand,'' I answered carefully. "I wish you'd explain it to me. Tell me what happened. What Ramsey and Tomi did wrong. Help me to see. . . .''

"Well, it's simple really,'' Ted replied, continuing to pace back and forth in front of me, "though I'm afraid it sounds a little dramatic. You see, Peg, I have been sent to prepare the way.''

"Sent? By whom, Ted? For what?''

"Call it what you will. The Second Coming. The Third Millennium. I don't trust easy definitions. I'm not associated with any of those crazy Fundamentalist groups...nothing like that. It's just been revealed to me slowly over the years—I've been chosen to show the way. My work, well, it's like the writing on the wall at Babylon.''

"Like...a warning?" I asked, seeing again those strange bulbous pieces of marble spaced along Ted's dusty shelves. Divinely inspired? Only, I was afraid, in the confused imagination of my sick dangerous friend.

"Well, more like a prophecy," Ted explained seriously. "I don't flatter myself into thinking that what I create will *change* anything or anyone. The only hope is that it will prepare us. You see, that's why I couldn't let my work be stopped. I didn't do any of this for *me*, Peg, but for all of us. For, well, humanity.''

"And Ramsey tried to stop you?" I asked, wondering what Ramsey would have thought of Ted's artistic delusions. I just couldn't imagine intelligent skeptical Ramsey taking them seriously for a moment.

"Not directly," Ted replied. "He was too devious for that. And for a long time I actually believed he understood. That he supported me.''

Of course he supported you! I wanted to scream. Supported and protected you. All those years letting you believe you were the voice of one crying in the artistic wilderness. Telling you how great you were, telling all of us.

"And when did he change?" I asked casually, hoping that I wasn't too obviously stalling for time.

"I'm not sure," Ted answered, continuing his obsessional pacing of the carpet. Tall, muscular, sleek, Ted was like a caged animal that couldn't stop moving, pacing, looking for the way out. "But I first noticed it," he continued, "a few weeks after my show. The one at Walden's in October.''

Last October, of course. About the same time Ramsey started demanding kickbacks. Suddenly, too late to do anyone any good, I saw how all the sad little pieces fell into place.

THIRTY-SEVEN

"It was never easy, living with Ramsey." Teddy sighed and shook his head sadly. "It was like I hardly existed unless he was there. Our precious little world—the loft, the place on Fire Island, the trips to Europe and Martinique—they were all Ramsey's doing, Ramsey's show.

"I was a friend to both of you," I pointed out, "and so were a lot of others."

"Were you?" Ted demanded, turning to stare down at me. Once again, the anger and resentment I found in his gaze made me shudder. "Were any of you? I doubt you've ever known who I really was. You only *thought* you knew Ted Manfred, dear heart. But how could you? I am unique. A true artist. The real thing, understand? Not a cheap fame seeker like our dear Theo."

"Leave her out of this," I said. "She never did anything to hurt you. It was her influence, after all, that got you into Greene Street."

"Lies!" Ted cried. "All lies. It's *my* work, *me*—not you or Ramsey or Theo or anyone else—they care about. It's taken me years to finally get here. But I've made it, Peg."

"What happened at Walden's?" I asked lightly. "What really went on? Did Ramsey set that up for you, Ted?"

"If you mean, did old Rams interfere where he didn't belong," Ted retorted, "then *yes*, you're right. You see, Ramsey couldn't stand to let me do things on my own. He was afraid, deathly afraid, of what would happen if I got even a smidgen of independence."

"So then you're saying that it was fear that made Ramsey go behind your back," I demanded, "and underwrite the costs of the Walden show last October? It was fear that forced him to buy—how many pieces were sold, Ted?—three, four?"

"It was not like that!" Ted cried. "Not at all! If you'll j-j-just shut up for a moment and give me a chance, I'll tell you what happened."

"How about the truth, Teddy?" I suggested gently. "What harm can it do now?"

ABOUT A YEAR AGO, during the long humid summer months, Teddy had grown so despondent of his failing career as a sculptor that he had actually contemplated suicide. Ramsey had supported him—financially and emotionally—for years. And yet, despite continual hard work and unflagging rounds to the major galleries, Teddy remained shut out of the big-time art scene.

"No, it was worse than that," Teddy admitted. "Even our bank branch turned down my work when I submitted it for their annual local artists' exhibition. Can you imagine? I was totally demoralized. Sick at heart. It was right about then that I had my first vision...."

Almost every night Teddy experienced nightmares about a nuclear holocaustlike occurrence. The dreams would end with terrible explosions, followed immediately by visions of white rounded shapes, the basis eventually for his marble series.

"After about the sixth recurrence, I told Ramsey about the dreams. And about a lot else....

"I'd been holding back on him, it's true, and I frankly think he was shocked by my suicidal musings. Ramsey insisted that I take some time off, get out of the city. As you'll remember, I spent most of last August out at the summer place....

"It was a lovely time for us. I don't think we'd ever been closer. He was caring, sympathetic. But the dreams didn't stop. When we returned to the city after Labor Day, I started right in on trying to reconstruct those shapes I'd been dreaming of...and Ramsey started in on a project of his own...."

Ramsey had been horrified by Teddy's talk of spiritual omens and holocausts, though he tried to remain sympathetic and supportive. After consulting a psychiatrist friend, Ramsey became convinced that what Teddy was experiencing—far from otherworldly visions—was a very worldly nervous breakdown. All Teddy needed, Ramsey decided, was a show at an important art gallery—and a little attention to boost his flagging self-image.

"All my chatter about being a prophet and having a mission used to drive old Rams right up the wall," Teddy went on, "no matter how hard he tried to hide it. So he came up with this clever little scheme. God, if only he'd had a modicum of faith in me! It never would have happened."

"So, it's true," I interjected. "Ramsey actually *paid* Walden to exhibit your work."

Ted abruptly stopped pacing and turned slowly to stare down at me, his gaze as cold and opaque as a blind cat's. He was right, I thought, I never really had known him. And I was glad of the fact. The self-hatred that had forced him to hide his personal demons from all of us had also driven him to lie and murder. Like so many before him, he had turned his own suicidal tendencies outward. From the beginning, he had simply wanted to kill himself. The glazed look told me one thing: he was still intent on destruction.

"Of course, at the time I knew nothing about it," Ted explained sarcastically. "I was so delighted! So absolutely thrilled that I didn't even question Walden's unexpected call, his at best cursory examination of my work and the incredible speed at which the exhibit was arranged."

"In, what was it, a month?" I asked.

"Yes, we got back from Fire Island after Labor Day. And the show went up October 1. I was so busy through September, I hardly had time to *sleep*, let alone dream."

"No more visions."

"Not then. In that sense, Ramsey's ploy worked, I suppose. But at what a cruel cost, Peg! Think of my dignity, my self-respect!"

"Wasn't that what Ramsey was thinking about?" I asked. "Surely you must realize he did all this because he loved you, Ted."

"But what's the point of love if there isn't any faith?" Teddy demanded. "Isn't that one of the first tenets of Christianity? It doesn't matter how much he cared, how much he wanted to help—the point is, he didn't *believe* in me. He…he sold me out, Peg, as surely as Judas sold Jesus."

"Oh, come on now, Ted," I retorted, forgetting myself momentarily, "your analogy is ridiculously garbled. Ramsey didn't gain anything from your exhibit, in fact, you know as well as I do that he lost."

"You mean the kickbacks?" Teddy asked, his expression brightening. "So you really have put it all together, haven't you, dear heart?"

"It's pretty obvious, Ted," I replied sadly. "Ramsey started to demand kickbacks last October. Same month as your show. He didn't do it for thrills. He did it because he needed the money. To pay off Walden. To pay for the pieces of your work that he bought."

"Right you are, bright little Peggy. Oh, Ramsey made quite a decent salary but, well, with me to support and our life-style to maintain, he just never got into the habit of saving. And he couldn't very well do anything obvious—like take out a second mortgage on the loft—without me knowing. He needed something hush-hush, on the side, something untraceable. Cash, for instance."

"And about the same time this need arose," I thought aloud, "Ricardo mentioned the kickback problem he was having. It must have seemed the perfect solution."

"Hmm, yes. Sad, isn't it?" Teddy mused. "It was such a mistake all round. Dear old Rams, you know, he really didn't have a deceiving bone in his body. It began to eat away at him— almost from the beginning. He got so cranky and suspicious. I knew something was wrong. I assumed, of course, that it had something to do with me."

"Why?" I asked. "What would you have done to upset him?"

Ted ran long pale fingers through his thinning hair. His usually pallid complexion was splotched with color—cheeks flushed red, his lips damp with excitement. It seemed ironic that Ted's angelic features—his limpid eyes, that slightly upturned cherubic nose—never looked sweeter or more innocent.

"My show at Walden's—as far as I knew at the time—had been a stunning success," Ted explained. "And its effect on me was everything Ramsey had hoped. I felt marvelous! Confident, talented and—for the first time in years, Peg—desirable to somebody other than Ramsey."

"You . . . you were unfaithful?"

"Oh, silly Peg!" Teddy let out a snuffled laugh. "You make it sound as though Ramsey and I were an old married couple . . . and I was suddenly having it on with the milkman."

"I thought of you as married, in a way," I conceded. And I knew that Ramsey did, too. What an ugly shock it must have been for him to realize that the plan that had seemed to succeed so well had actually backfired.

"Peg, dear heart, you must remember that Ramsey was almost a whole decade older than me," Teddy went on airily. "I was all he wanted. I was his be-all and end-all. My God, he was perfectly content coming home from the office every night, eating one of my little dinners and settling down with a book in front of the fire. Every night, Peg! That was Nirvana to him. He'd had his wild days. He was through with all that."

"But you weren't," I observed.

"I'd never really played around before," Ted replied, "never experienced any of that crazy nightlife. I mean, Ramsey and I lived right in the middle of all this excitement—the music, the shows, these amazing people—but we never went to any of the clubs. We were like two old maids sitting at home with our knitting."

"I take it you started to drop a stitch or two."

"Yes," Teddy replied with proud defiance. "I started to get out, make the scene. It was wonderful, liberating! Nobody knew me as Ramsey Farnsworth's quiet little artist friend. I was *me*—a successful sculptor, a man with talent, values. People sought me out, Peg, for the first time in my life. I was known. I was envied. I had my choice of partners."

"And Ramsey, I take it, remained at home. In the dark, so to speak?"

"Oh, he knew something was up. He kept his silence, though, probably hoping that I was just going through some kind of phase. That it would pass. Ramsey, you know, despite his ironic facade, was really quite an optimist."

No, I objected silently. Ramsey, for all his irony, really loved you, Ted. And he knew that to confront you, to put limitations on your life, could very well mean losing you. He preferred to live with the pain of what you were doing than to live without you altogether. No wonder Ramsey had been so preoccupied and distant during his last months, I thought. He had created a monster with his kickback scheme, and he was being forced to live with the guilt and heartache of what he had done.

"It all turned around quite suddenly," Ted continued. "Perhaps, if I'd had some kind of warning, it would have been different. Instead, Ramsey came home from work one night just as I was leaving. He demanded to know where I was going."

"Just out," Teddy had replied easily, slinging his new stone-washed jean jacket over his shoulder. He'd become quite concerned about his appearance, giddily spending the money he'd earned from his show on any piece of clothing that took his fancy.

"I gathered that," Ramsey replied wearily. He looked exhausted, flabby and used, his double chin chafing uncomfortably at his shirt collar. "Where are you going? Specifically. And with whom?"

"Come on, Rams, I'm in a hurry," Ted had retorted, trying to push past him. "It really doesn't matter now, does it?"

"Yes, it does matter, Ted," Ramsey said solemnly. "To me, at least. I'm fed up with your sneaking around, with your half lies and partial truths. I'd rather have the facts, please. I'd like to know where we stand."

Teddy had glanced at Ramsey disdainfully, taking in his creased unhappy expression. In recent weeks he'd experienced incredible heights of physical pleasure—a new sexual freedom that made Ramsey's lovemaking seem childishly tame in comparison. What had Ramsey ever offered him besides creature comforts and psychological security? Needs he'd surely outgrown by now.

"If you really want to know..." Teddy had asked, and when Ramsey had nodded his head sadly, he said, "I'm off to the River Room on Twelfth Avenue to have dinner with some friends."

"Friends or friend, Ted?" Ramsey had demanded. "And is dinner all you're really after? Somehow I doubt it."

"Well, it's about time you did, then!" Teddy had replied scornfully. "I've stopped making like your fair-haired boy for some time now. I've been wondering when you were going to wake up to the fact."

"That's all it was, then?" Ramsey had demanded. "Make-believe? Fifteen years of playacting? I'm sorry, I can't believe that, Ted. We've been happy—"

"And I've been suffocating!" Teddy cried, tossing down his jacket. "Not the whole time, that's true. But lately, Ramsey, I feel like I've been in prison, living here with you. I . . . I didn't want to hurt you, that's why I haven't said anything. But really, Rams, isn't it obvious? I . . . I've simply outgrown you."

"I see," Ramsey murmured, "and how long exactly, Ted, have you felt this way? I think I have a right to know."

"Since the Walden exhibit, if you want the truth," Ted had answered boldly. "It took me that long to realize I could stand on my own—without you, without anyone. It took me that long to see how you've been strangling me with your support and concern. I have to be independent, Ramsey. I have to get out from under your weight. And now, at last, I know I can."

Ramsey had waited until that moment to tell Ted the truth about the Walden exhibit. How it was financed. Who actually purchased the pieces that were sold.

"Lies!" Teddy had screamed. "Lies, lies, lies!"

"Go look in my safe, Ted, if you don't believe me," Ramsey had replied calmly. "I've been keeping the marble piece I bought there until I found a better place to hide it."

"THE MURDER WEAPON," I said. "The first of your marble series."

"That's right," Teddy replied. "I guess I went a little crazy after I found it in the safe. I came back into the kitchen and, well, it was so simple really, Peg. I sort of threw it at Ramsey's head. He just crumpled up. That's all."

"But the knife wounds?" I demanded. "Why all that, Ted? Such a gruesome finale."

"Necessary, I'm afraid," Ted answered. "The actual act of killing him was so very simple. It was only later that things got so terribly complicated. In any case, for an alibi I went out and met some friends for dinner."

The east-facing side window in my living room looks out onto the fire escape. The window itself is narrow and rarely opened, so I was surprised to see the curtain billowing gently at its base. I glanced sideways as Teddy talked, trying to figure out how it had come open. And then I saw Cursio's long pale face through the slit of open curtain. He put a finger to his lips, though he didn't need to warn me. I looked away again almost immediately, took a deep breath and asked, "Where did you go, Ted?"

"Oh, to the River Room," he answered simply. "Just as I had told Ramsey. I had a fillet of sole. A bit dry, as I recall. I wouldn't recommend it."

THIRTY-EIGHT

"Okay, that takes care of Ramsey," I concluded brightly, trying to keep Ted's attention focused on me. Inch by inch, Cursio was easing up the window. "But what about Tomi? I don't understand that at all."

"Ah, dear greedy Mr. Tabor!" Ted snorted with disgust. "It's people like him, Peg—successful, commercial, totally exploitative—who are sucking dry the cultural integrity of this country. You know, he actually thought himself an artist! Can you believe that?"

"Is that why you killed him?" I asked faintly.

"Heavens, no!" Ted laughed. "Though, come to think of it, it would have been a much more courageous reason. No, I'm afraid my motive was one of the oldest in the book—fear."

Tomi, it seems, had been hard hit by Ramsey's kickback demands. He was trying to pay off the costs of his new studio, and Ramsey's ten percent off the top was eating away dangerously at his profit margin. When Ramsey decided to up the ante to fifteen percent in order to pay off some of his debt to Walden, Tomi had been devastated.

The night before the Fanpan shoot, Tomi made a surprise visit to the loft, hoping to convince Ramsey—friend to friend—to reconsider his kickback demands. He found the door open, Ramsey dead, and Ted's sculpture nearby. He took it.

"He was no dummy," Ted went on bitterly. "He figured out what had happened. He had me where he wanted me. When I got back to the loft that night and saw the piece missing, God, I didn't know what to think! Why would someone steal it? It seemed crazy. I thought maybe I was going crazy. That I'd dreamed the whole thing. Except, of course, there was Ramsey. Dead. All I knew was that I had to somehow disguise the way he'd been killed. Well, what else could I have done, Peg?"

"So you made it look like a stabbing. You . . . cut him up."

"You can't possibly understand what it was like," Ted insisted, for the first time showing some agitation. His forehead glistened with sweat, and I could see him nervously fingering something in his pocket. The knife.

"It wasn't Rams on that floor, believe me. It was just this big dead *thing*. But, oh, it was horrible, horrible. All that blood! The mess."

"And Tomi?" I asked. In my peripheral vision I saw the curtain billowing wildly. I heard rain splattering against my hardwood floor. Knowing that I had to keep Ted's concentration on me, I went on disparagingly, "What happened with him? Somehow you managed to overcome your aversion to gore. Remember, I was the one who discovered him, Teddy. It wasn't a particularly tidy sight."

"Ah, yes, I know," Ted answered dreamily, "but Tomi was so much easier than poor Rams. You see, Peg, he deserved it.... The bastard waited until it seemed clear that the police didn't suspect me, then he called. To tell me he'd recently picked up a very interesting sculpture of mine. He informed me that he only wanted what was his due. And so the blackmail started. A thousand a month, in cash, delivered to his loft, in person."

"And you made a delivery last night. Only, it wasn't the one Tomi was expecting."

"He was a pig. Greed can make people so ugly, Peg. I brought him the money. A good part of the rent I got for the Fire Island place. I'm just making ends meet, you see, until the Greene Street show. And what do you think Tomi wanted?"

"More," I guessed, suddenly visualizing the scene in Tomi's darkroom.

"Precisely," Ted muttered, "just the way Ramsey had wanted more from him. But I didn't have any more, Peg. I knew it was useless...and that he'd be dangerous if he didn't get what he wanted. So, I simply promised him I'd add another five hundred to the kitty next month, went out and found a knife that was lying around in one of his stock scenes, and came back and drove it straight into his greedy little heart."

"You sound like you...almost enjoyed it, Ted."

"No, I actually didn't take any pleasure in it," Ted answered thoughtfully. "But it didn't take much courage, either. I kept thinking of that poem, you know the one by Dylan Thomas? The one that ends, 'After the first death there is no other.' I kept thinking that—"

"Freeze!" Cursio yelled as he burst through the open window into the room. His revolver was aimed at Teddy's chest. If the wind had not taken that very moment to gust, whipping the curtain around Cursio's arms and momentarily swaddling the gun... well, perhaps everything would have turned out differently. But it's so often the freak accident in life—the misstep on the stairs, the slip in the bathtub—that sends us hurtling into the unstoppable darkness. While Cursio struggled free of the curtain, Teddy pulled me from the couch and crushed me to him. He pressed a cool finger of steel against my throat.

"Ted, don't be a fool," Cursio snapped when he saw what had happened. "You can't get away with this. Cops are swarming the building. We've staked out the entire block. It's no good." Cursio's eyes flashed into mine—a furious blackness that I didn't realize until later was fear.

"I don't want to hurt her," Ted announced, his voice strangely normal and even. "But, believe me, I will have to if you don't do exactly as I say." I could feel his heart galloping at my back. His shirtfront was soaked with sweat, its stale smell filling my nostrils. But he gave no outward signs of nervousness.

His very composure terrified me, but I managed to sputter, "Cursio's right, Ted—you can't possibly hope to get away. Be reasonable... and you won't be hurt."

"Shut the hell up," Ted cried, sliding the knife around and up to my jugular, "or *you* are going to get a whole lot more than hurt, dear heart. I'm serious. I really mean this," Ted went on, flashing the knife under my chin. "I am going to cut Peg's throat unless I get out of here—and away—without any trouble."

"Okay, Ted—" Cursio shrugged "—okay. Nobody wants any more trouble. It's your show. You just tell me how you want to proceed. I can call my men from here and tell them what we're doing."

"All right," Ted replied, tightening his grip around my waist. "Peg and I are going to go up to the roof. I want a police helicopter waiting. I want us to be flown to Kennedy airport. I... I'll give instructions from there. But just remember I'm going to have this knife at Peg's throat every single step of the way."

"I understand," Cursio answered, solemnly meeting Ted's gaze. "Now, listen, I'm going to walk over there to the desk and telephone down to my men. I'll tell them what's going on. What the plan is."

"Okay, no funny business," Ted added as Cursio started across the room. It seemed a lifetime ago that Dan and I had made love. Odd that at a time like this it all came back so vividly. The unexpected silky tautness of his skin. The warm saltiness of his kisses. He had been so gentle, so undemanding. His almost unbearable tenderness had triggered in me the passionate response I'd never been able to give Spencer.

I watched Cursio dial, the phone crooked between shoulder and chin, his eyes never leaving Teddy's. Why didn't he look at me, I wondered? A glance, a half smile—God, I needed something to keep my courage up. But he was all cop now: cold, hard, focused on his job. I didn't know until much later the hopelessness he was feeling.

"Yeah, that's right," he told Tom. "They're going up to the roof. Get a copter ready. That's right, damn it, you heard me. I mean now. And get some searchlights in position so the pilot can see where to land. And listen, Tom, this guy is terribly serious. He's got a knife to her throat. We're going to play this the way he wants to. I want everyone on alert. What? Tell them to go—tell them to lay the hell off for the time being." He slammed down the phone, swearing under his breath.

"What was the last bit?" Ted demanded. "Lay off what?"

"Goddamned press," Cursio muttered, turning back to face us. "*People* magazine caught wind of our little party, somehow. They want to interview you, can you believe this? They're offering half a million dollars for an exclusive."

"You're lying," Teddy retorted, tightening his grip. "This is some kind of setup. A trick."

"Whatever you say," Cursio replied, shaking his head. "I personally don't consider this the optimum moment to give your life's story to the press. The helicopter should be here within—" Cursio glanced at his worn Timex "—ten minutes. Why don't you let the lady sit down, huh?"

"Like hell you say," Teddy replied sarcastically. "She's staying right here with me. Now tell me more about this magazine thing."

"What's there to tell?" Cursio answered, coming back around behind the couch. "Apparently they want your side of the story. The inside dope from the killer's point of view. Nice wholesome family reading material, don't you think?"

"Shut up!" Ted snapped. "What would you know about suffering, about sacrifice, about an artist's life? We are—I have been—driven to the edge of despair because this country hasn't the slightest idea what true creativity is. In France they name

boulevards and buildings after their artists! In the United
States, we're the weirdos, the crazies, the scum—''

"Hey, if you want sympathy, tell it to *People*," Cursio interjected. "I'm fresh out."

"Okay, get 'em up on the roof right now," Teddy commanded, backing toward the window.

I stumbled at the sudden movement, and the knife nicked my
earlobe. Blood spurted down my shirtfront. Cursio took a step
toward us.

"It's nothing," I said. "I'm okay. Do as he says."

"I'll talk to them while we wait for the helicopter," Teddy
went on, edging backward to the window. Rain had soaked the
floor and curtains. "I want to see you dialing as we climb out
of here."

Cursio went silently back to the phone and picked up the receiver. The last thing I heard before Teddy pulled me out over
the slippery windowsill was Cursio saying, "Okay, send the
People guys up. The man wants to chat."

At first I thought it was snowing. The night swirled with tiny,
wet, brilliantly white dots. A blizzard of warm soft flakes. And
as in a sudden snowfall, my familiar street was transformed—
a fairyland of filtered light and muffled sound. And then I
looked down and saw the tubs of searchlights. The conelike
rays that turned the summer rain into white gold dust. And I
saw, too, the barricades at Broadway, the swirling red lights, the
tangle of vans and cars and men. All trained on Ted's and my
ascent of the fire escape.

"I'll tell them, all right," Teddy muttered angrily to himself
as he pushed me ahead of him up the creaking iron stairs. "I'll
give them a story like they've never heard before. Man, they
want the inside stuff, they're going to get it. The whole seething rotten mess. Maybe then they'll wake up to the truth, right?
Maybe then they'll see the writing on the wall."

"Ted, you're hurting me," I cried out at one point, when he
twisted my wrist unexpectedly. And though his grip loosened,
he didn't seem to hear me.

"This is it," he mumbled. "It's all been leading up to this. I
know it now. I can feel it. This is my moment. It's been chosen. It's been ordained...." When we reached the top of the fire
escape, Ted climbed over the railing first, then pulled me up
behind him. We stood at the edge, looking down at the brightly

lighted sea below, a dizzying mirage of people and cars—all warped and running together in the rain.

"Mr. Manfred?" a deep male voice called from the darkness of the roof.

"What?" Teddy whirled around, hugging me to him. "Who is that? Who's there?"

"Malcolm Redding, *People* magazine, sir. I understand we haven't much time, so can we get right down to business?"

I recognized the voice then. It was Tom. Ted's first instincts had been right. This was a setup. I didn't know whether to be relieved or even more alarmed. Ted hated to be lied to. The knife, now slick with rain, lay against my neck.

"Proceed with your questions," Ted cried. "But take one fucking step toward us, and this girl is dead."

"I'm well aware of the conditions of this interview, sir," Tom went on calmly. "Now, if we can continue.... Could you give us, please, a little background on yourself?"

And that was all Ted needed. For ten minutes he rambled, lectured and chastised. His voice grew harsh with emotion, his grip around me even tighter. A lot of what he said, I'd heard before. A lot more—especially his harking on about the artist's rightful place as a leader of society—was new even to me.

"This country is sick!" Teddy stormed, his voice strained to a near whisper. "It's on its last legs spiritually. The moment is coming when the whole world will be submerged in its own blackness, its own filth. I'm here to tell you that—"

Without any buildup, the noise of a helicopter thundered across the rooftop. Oddly, it sounded to me as though it came not from above, but from where Tom was standing.

"I'm sorry, sir, but I've just been told we have to end," Tom cried out over the noise. "We'd like to very quickly take a few photos, if you don't mind. Now, if you'll just stand still for a second, we'll..."

"No!" Teddy cried too late as the flashes exploded in front of us.

I went blind, stumbling out of his loosened grip. Arms reached out for me, gathered me in. Someone was saying my name over and over again. Cursio held me to him as the world exploded—lights flashing, sirens wailing, people screaming. It was only one person screaming. Teddy.

Poor Ted. Oh, Ted. Crying out as he fell backward over the edge of the rooftop into the shining sea that had parted for him at last.

THIRTY-NINE

NATTIE ZELLERMAN HAD been representing Theo for nearly thirty years. He took her on shortly after my father died and long before she had earned any kind of international reputation. Something in those early, wildly symbolic canvases must have told him that this was the wave of the artistic future. He had jumped on and had been riding in Theo's turbulent wake ever since.

Though Nat and Theo had little in common besides the millions they made together each year, theirs remained one of the few enduring relationships in the ever-shifting art gallery scene. Nat was canny enough to know when to leave Theo to her own devices. He also knew when it was time to step in, take the helm, play the starmaker. Theo Goodenough's annual exhibit at Zellerman Gallery was such an occasion for Nat, and he played it to the nines. The one held two weeks before Christmas was certainly no exception.

"Can this be little Peggy? No!" Nattie met me at the door with the same words he'd been greeting me with since I was nine years old. "Not my little Peggy.... Where are the pigtails?"

"Sorry I'm late, Nattie," I apologized, kissing his cheek just slightly north of the beeswaxed mini-Dali-style mustachio. I tried to glance over his shoulder into the huge gallery beyond to see which of the guests I'd invited had arrived, but the room was as packed as the uptown IRT at evening rush hour.

"Late? Come on now, Peg, you wouldn't be a Goodenough unless you were late. Your mother and Elizabeth Taylor, I've always said, are two of the most waited-for women in the world."

"I take it she hasn't arrived," I responded dryly.

"Of course not," Nattie replied, suddenly plumping up his five-foot-four tuxedoed frame as a woman swathed in white mink swept by. "A Getty," he whispered as she made her way into the melee.

"Anyone I know here?" I asked, trying to catch a familiar face in the jumble of tuxes and cigarette holders and glittering necklines.

"Everyone who *is* anyone is here," Nattie replied rather stiffly. "You should know by now that I never invite riffraff to a show of Theo's. Only the crème de la crème."

"Of course, Nat," I answered soothingly, moving forward into the fray and adding to myself, "It's just that sometimes I find it hard to tell the difference." Though this crowd was easy enough to identify. The room literally smelled of money: Patou perfume, the musky aroma of Blackglama, the romantic autumnal odor of Gauloise cigarettes. Cultured knowing voices counterpointed the gentle tinkle of champagne flutes being offered on silver trays.

"Come on, Pappy, I feel like a stuffed walrus in this getup. Let's get the heck out of here." The breathy nasal voice was as discordant in this crowd as a banjo in Mahler's Tenth. I quickly worked my way toward it.

"Victor, J.J.!" I cried, holding out my arms. "I'm so happy you could make it." A purple cummerbund wrapped around his bulging midriff, the bow tie comically dwarfed by his oxlike neck and shoulders, J.J. looked pretty much the way he felt. Victor, on the other hand, seemed perfectly at ease in his formal attire.

"Wouldn't have missed it for the world, darlin'," Victor replied heartily, kissing my cheek. I breathed in his distinctive perfume of expensive bourbon and cigars and felt tears of gratitude sting along my carefully made-up eyelids.

In the difficult, demanding months that had followed Teddy's death, this man had been one of my staunchest supporters. Despite all my efforts, the real story behind Ramsey's and Tomi's murders had come out with a vengeance. A piece describing Ramsey's kickback scheme—and a shocking number of similar scams like it within the advertising community—made the front page of the *Times*. I had been hounded day and night by reporters—including, ironically enough, one from *People* magazine. My notoriety did not, needless to say, endear me to the powers that be at P&Q. In fact, about two weeks after Teddy's sad little funeral, Phillip Ebert quietly informed me that it would be best for one and all if I folded up my tent and stole away.

"She goes, we follow," Victor had informed Phillip as soon as he heard the news. "Which is a goddarned pity, as I just recommended you folks to my good friend T-bone Tompkins, who's lookin' for a new agency for his little enterprise." Well, even the most uninformed consumer has heard of the nation-wide chain of T-bone Steak Houses, and it didn't take Phillip long to see the error of his ways.

"I really appreciate your both being here," I went on, turning my smile from Victor to J.J., who blushed deeply under my gaze.

"Uh . . . listen, I think I'm gonna go get me another drink of this bubbly," J.J. announced, holding up his glass. In his jumbo-size grip, the flute looked as skinny and breakable as an icicle.

"I'm afraid my boy's still got quite a thing for you," Victor said, watching J.J. muscle his way through the crowd.

"Victor, I've never done anything to encourage him," I replied earnestly. "Believe me. I've tried to be honest with him—he just misunderstood." We were both thinking of J.J.'s dis-appearance the night of our ill-fated lunch at Windows on the World. He had ended up in the detox unit at Bellevue after starting a drunken brawl in a seedy after-hours club in the Bronx. No one, including J.J., could figure out how he had managed to drift so far uptown.

"Now you don't have to tell me that, sweetheart," Victor assured me, flicking a fat gold lighter at the tip of a fresh ci-gar. He puffed thoughtfully for a moment or two and added, "He doesn't mean any harm, you know, Peggy. And under-neath that darn temper of his, he's really quite a good boy. I know everybody thinks he's a liability for me, a burden."

"I used to think that myself," I admitted. "But recently—at the Lutèce shoot last month, for instance—J.J. made some good points. Remember how we had the table arranged so that you could hardly read the Fanpan name on the take-out box? If it weren't for J.J., my God, we would have spent ten thou-sand dollars without even getting a decent package shot."

"I know," Victor answered, nodding. "I was proud of him. He may not have the fastest draw in the world, but it's straight. The boy needs a good deal of civilizing, I know. After Mary Jo died—goodness, it's been over ten years now—I just plumb did away with the niceties. That wasn't good for the boy, I see that now. Still, with the right woman's touch, I think he could be shaped up."

"I'm sorry, Victor," I replied lamely, "but I'm afraid that J.J. and I just wouldn't—"

"Good God, woman, I wasn't meaning you!" Victor's warm belly laugh pealed across the room. "No, no.... I was thinking of that little gal you got working for you. Ruth, I think her name is. Didn't you know? J.J.'s taken her out last few times we've been in town. They seem to get on."

Ruthie! Of course! How could I have been so dense? It wasn't a new facial that had suddenly cleared her complexion and injected her skin with a silky glow. And it wasn't finding, at long last, the right diet that was trimming the saddlebags off her thighs. It was J.J. It was love.

"Well, if it isn't my favorite client," Phillip Ebert greeted us with forced bonhomie, "and my prized creative director." As usual, Mark Rollings was in tow. P&Q was now in the final stages of the T-bone Steak House pitch, and everyone—including, no doubt, the man himself—knew how important Victor's endorsement of us could be.

"Victor, how thoughtful of you to come tonight." Mark leered openly at Victor and added in intimate knowing tones, "After all, this can't be one of your usual hangouts."

"My boy, I've been collecting Goodenough since I made my first million back in 1964." Mark was not the only one to stare at Victor, openmouthed with shock.

"You never told me," I cried.

"Why should I?" Victor responded. "It was clear to me, at least when we met, that you didn't relish the idea of being thought of as Theo Goodenough's little gal. So I kept it to myself. But since you invited us all here tonight, Peg, I assumed you've gone from being ashamed of who you are...to being proud of who your Mommy is."

He was right, of course. Ever since she and Cal flew down for Ted's funeral—and stayed with me during the dark week that followed—Theo and I had become friends.

"It's a pity," Theo had told me the day she and Cal we're scheduled to fly back up to Maine, "that it so often takes a death to make us appreciate what we have in life."

"You mean, to appreciate each other, right?" I countered, smiling into her clear ironic gaze. "I've hardly been a model daughter, I'm afraid."

"Well, thank God for that, darling," Theo had responded, hugging me to her. "I wouldn't have know what the hell to do with someone who followed me around asking how to do flower arrangements. And it wasn't you I was criticizing, anyway. It was me."

"You don't have anything to apologize for, Theo," I assured her. "We haven't exactly had a normal life together, but at least it hasn't been boring, right?"

"Ah, darling, you're getting more like me every day," Theo had said with a laugh, leaving me unknowingly with the greatest compliment she could have given.

"Speaking of the devil," Victor announced, gesturing with his cigar to the elevator from which Theo, starkly beautiful in a sleeveless black Krizia chiffon number, emerged with Cal on her arm. So much attention was focused on the guest of honor and her escort that hardly anyone—except me, of course—noticed the odd mismatched couple who arrived directly behind them.

Millie must have devoted a good part of the day to her appearance and, unfortunately, it showed. Her eyebrows had been plucked off and then heavily reapplied in two slightly uneven arcs. She'd brushed her hair up inside a towering red-patterned turban, which sat with dangerous laxity on top of her head. Her dress, a shade of red that clashed with the headgear, was a few sizes too large for her delicate frame. It buckled around her ankles, catching at the spiky white sling-back high heels—the kind high school girls wear to proms. Poor Millie, I thought, her toes must be freezing! And yet, from the way she carried herself and the majestic smile she lavished upon an obviously aghast Nat Zellerman, one would have thought she was Queen Elizabeth sweeping across her throne room.

My newfound prince was her escort. Detective Dante Cursio, bending down to hear her piping comments, smiled at me as he led Millie through the crowd. Knowing I'd be stuck late at the office and concerned about Millie finding a taxi in the Christmas season rush hour, Cursio had volunteered to bring her. She wore a corsage of pale white orchids—which even at this distance I knew to be a gothic floral horror—that I supposed he had brought for her. *He* was dressed in a rumpled black tuxedo jacket, borrowed no doubt from the undercover department, and a pair of regular dark blue wash-and-wear slacks.

"I was just telling the detective how lovely you look, dear," Millie announced. "Positively stunning. I was telling him that I don't know how you work a full productive day the way you do, and come home every night looking fresh as a daisy!"

"Thank you, Millie," I replied, smiling over at Cursio. In her own charming way, Millie had been relentlessly campaigning for a romance between the two of us ever since Teddy's death. The idea must have come to her the night of the tragedy, when he carried me down from the roof in his arms. It amused us both that Millie—who prided herself on her powers of foresight—couldn't see that her promotional efforts were entirely unnecessary.

"You do look lovely," Cursio said, his dark gaze taking in the curving length of my wildly patterned blue silk Kenzo. Though his eyes told me the truth: I looked sexy. I'd changed in my new office—Spencer's old quarters with the built-in dressing room—piling my unruly hair up on my head with a half-moon diamond clip. More diamonds—little-used gifts from Theo—dangled from my earlobes. I smiled back at him. I had dressed the way I always did these days...to be undressed by him.

"Thank you, Detective," I replied. "You don't look so bad yourself." Anyone with a modicum of sexual radar would be able to pick up the hot-and-heavy signals that were flashing between the two of us. Victor looked from Cursio to me, then back to Cursio again, with a pleased smile.

"As I was saying to the detective," Millie went on, "it's not every woman in this city who has a position of responsibility like yours. Then add to that—"

"Right, Millie," I said, cutting her off and reaching for two glasses of champagne from a passing tray. "Now why don't you try a sip of this? Detective?" Cursio's fingers brushed mine as I handed him the glass, sending a pleasant shiver through my already charged system.

"Thanks," Cursio replied, sipping from the glass and letting his eyes stray to my cleavage.

"What's the commissioner's feeling about the Guilden case?" Mark asked Cursio, referring to news that had been making local headlines: Tracy Guilden, Martin's wife, had been arrested over the weekend for erratic driving. Three ounces of cocaine were discovered in her green leather Maude Frizon bag. Subsequent discoveries by the press, however, were even more interesting: Tracy and Cecilia, Louis's wife, had both been in and out of drug treatment centers during the past two years. A CBS/*Times* poll had indicated that Jacob Guilden's chances for a successful mayoral run were just about nil.

"Ecstatic would be too much of an understatement," Cursio responded, smiling. His eyes strayed back to mine.

"Peg, darling!" Theo threw an arm around my shoulders. "Sorry to break up your little clique, but how else do I get to say hello to my daughter?"

"I'm sorry," I replied, kissing her on the cheek. "I thought you were taken up with Nattie's millionaire row."

"Oh, what bores!" Theo cried. "I left Cal to deal with them. Now, come on, darling, introduce me to your friends."

So I did. One by one, Theo shook hands with Victor, J.J., Mark, Phillip and Millie.

"And this, Theo, is Detective Cursio. Dante Cursio. He's the one I told you about, you know, who was involved in Ramsey's investigation."

"Of course," Theo replied warmly, taking his hand. "I've heard a lot about you. A detective! How marvelous. You know," she added, looking him over with a practiced, appreciative eye, "I'm so pleased that Peggy's starting to run around with some *interesting* people. She's been desperate for a little color in her life, don't you think?"